I0731481

A BLOSSOM IN THE ASHES

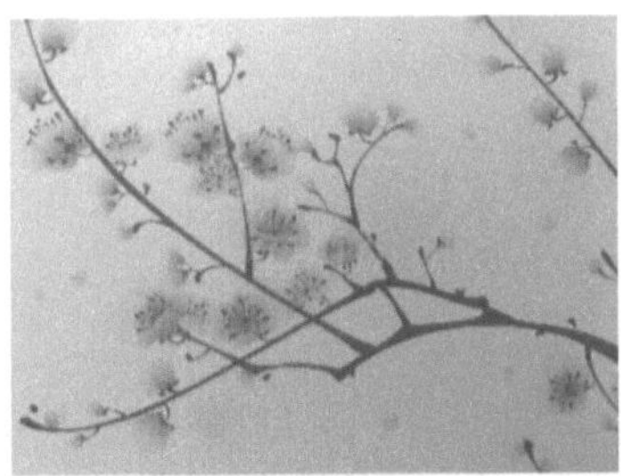

A BLOSSOM IN THE ASHES

BY

RON SINGERTON

www.Penmorepress.com

A Blossom In The Ashes by Ron Singerton
Copyright © 2020 Ron Singerton

All rights reserved. No part of this book may be used or reproduced by any means without the written permission of the publisher except in the case of brief quotation embodied in critical articles and reviews.

ISBN-13: 978-1-946409-92-8(Paperback)
ISBN 13: 978-1-946409-93-5 (E-book)

BISAC Subject Headings:
FIC014000FICTION / Historical
FIC032000FICTION / War & Military
FIC051000FICTION / Cultural Heritage

Editors: Sean Smith, Chris Wozney
Technical editor: Marc Liebman

Cover Concept by Ron Singerton
Cover by Christine Horner

Address all correspondence to:

Michael James
Penmore Press LLC
920 N Javelina Pl
Tucson AZ 85748

In Appreciation

I wish to extend my deepest gratitude to my editors, Sean Smith, Chris Wozney, and Marc Liebman, for unstinting attention to detail and accuracy, as well as their adroit suggestions that were of inestimable value. My thanks also to Michael James, my publisher, for his encouragement and insight in the development of this novel. Thanks to Christine Horner for her cover design, a thoughtful work of art.

And my most sincere gratitude to my wife Darla for her questions, comments and remarkable willingness to listen and evaluate the writing and rewriting of each page. A sign of true love. In addition, I wish to thank her for coming to my aid every time my laptop attempted to implode. Without her uncomplaining assistance, this book would never have seen the light of day.

Review by Marc Leibman:

This is a riveting novel that is a new twist on family relationships during World War II. Two brothers fall in love with the same woman: Tad, a Nisei who is a U.S. Naval Aviator, and Koizumi, a pilot in the Imperial Japanese Navy. Their Russian-born father, Alexei, who served in the Tsar's Navy before he emigrated to the United States, goes back to Leningrad in 1940 to see his dying father and is forced to fight the Germans. The result is a rip-roaring story that spans the most devasting war of the 20th Century. Singleton's characters are interesting, the story is engrossing and fast-paced. It's a must read for those who like this genre.

— Marc Liebman is the author of award winning novels Forgotten *and* Inner Look, *as well as* Big Mother 40, *a top 50 war novel, etc.*

Chapter 1
California
May, 1928

At an elevation of nine thousand feet, Tad peered over the fuselage and caught a glimpse of the Jenny, three thousand feet below. Its pilot, Jack Vestergaard, slipped between one cloud and another, no doubt weighing his options. None of them were good. If Jack had won the toss it would have been him, not Tad, flying the 1918 Packard-Le Pere multi-purpose biplane, with its four-hundred and twenty-five horsepower Liberty V-12 engine, built in Detroit for the Allies. Had the Great War not ended when it had, the biplane would surely have seen service on the Western Front.

With ninety horsepower and a top speed of seventy-five miles an hour, the Curtiss Jn-4D Jenny was a dependable and highly maneuverable aircraft that had served as a trainer for thousands of American fighter pilots. But it was no match against the Packard, so Jack bided his time, waiting for his roommate to make his move—and, he hoped, a mistake.

Both aircraft sped past the boulder-strewn hills of Temecula, some fifty miles north of San Diego. Tad knew that his buddy would try to lure him into a dogfight in which the Jenny's turning ability would enable Jack to get on the Packard's tail. Tad grinned. Too bad for Jack; that was a tactic Jack's passenger, Babs Gilmore, would hardly appreciate. Tad's own passenger was made of sterner mettle.

Tad shoved the throttle forward and turned 180 degrees so the morning sun was behind him. Spotting the Jenny through a fortuitous break in the clouds, he rolled the airplane and pushed the stick forward so the airplane was descending in a steep, diving spiral. The canvas and wood craft was capable of one hundred and thirty-six miles per hour on level flight, and could reach a ceiling of twenty-thousand feet. In a dive, it could attain speeds over two-hundred miles per hour. Amid the roar of the engine and wind tearing past the cockpit, Tad dove on the Jenny.

Jack spotted the "enemy" plummeting at him with the speed and talons of an eagle. With Gabs on board, a gut-wrenching Immelmann was out of the question. Jack tried to evade, but it was far too late.

Passing forty feet above the slower-moving craft, Tad put his fists together as though he were firing the plane's Marlin machine guns, long since removed. Over the whir of the prop Tad laughed, then shouted, "Tat-tat-tat-tat-tat!" mimicking the sound of the machine guns that would have spit thirty-caliber bullets and torn the Jenny apart.

Jack dove, leveling off one thousand feet above the ground, and watched Tad's plane pull up alongside his. With a shake of his head and palms held up in despair, Jack looked over at Tad with an expression of utter exasperation. "Next time!" he mouthed, then grinned as they dove in tandem to tree-top height. People below stopped, glanced upward, and waved.

Except for bedding Babs, there was nothing, thought Jack, better than a mock dogfight in an empty sky.

Tad teasingly put his hand to his brow in the gesture of an Indian on the hunt, and, gleeful at another "kill", grinned and pointed toward Long Beach. Then he glanced to Liz-Hamilton Smythe, his passenger in the rear seat. It was only the second time he had taken the knock-out blonde aloft. She had shown real spunk, he thought. It was one thing to fly in a bucket of wood and canvas for a fifteen-minute level flight, quite another to engage in high g maneuvers that could cause a strut or wing spar to break and the end come in seconds.

But Liz was a girl who loved adventure, and, thought Tad, she loved him. It had been a whirlwind romance, he having fallen for her when he first saw her with the song girls at the season's big game, UCLA against Stanford. Spritely and effervescent, she was dazzling, and he'd had to have her.

Twenty-two, tall, with a mop of golden hair and an affable personality, Tad was pleased that his boyish good looks turned the heads of more than a few girls. Being a university senior with the promise of an engineering degree and a commission as a naval aviator usually assured an easy conquest. But Liz was special, and Tad had turned away from every potential conquest since seeing her.

The biplanes skimmed past scattered barns and houses as they approached the flying field at Long Beach, where the city had built new hangers for the Army and Navy. Years before, planes had taken off from the hard sand of the beach when the tide was low. But that was always risky, and more than one craft had flipped tail over nose. Modernized, the facility and its spectators had inspired the now famous aviatrix, Amelia Earhart.

The plane's wheels touched down, and the aviators taxied to the civilian hangar. As the props came to a halt, Jack and Tad helped their girls onto to the tarmac.

"Oh, that was *ab-so-lute-ly* hip to the jive! But I still have the heebie-jeebies; give me a moment," said Babs, a forthright, modern woman who loved nothing more than shocking anybody over twenty-nine. She fluffed her short, curly hair.

"It was the cat's pajamas," Liz drawled, "and I can't wait to do it again."

Putting their arms around their girls, Jack and Tad led them to Tad's 1921 Roadster, parked near the flight line. Liz hopped in the front passenger seat, and Jack and Babs climbed into the rumble seat with its pillows and spare blanket.

"That Jenny is just too damn slow," said Jack, as Tad drove toward Highway One, which bordered the beach.

"It doesn't matter. In six months we'll both be flying navy fighters off a flat-top like *Saratoga* or *Lexington*. The new Boeing F2B is going to *Saratoga,* and it does over one hundred and fifty miles per hour. So don't get in a fuss about the Jenny," said Tad.

Only slightly mollified, Jack said, "Babs and I are going to spend a few days at the bungalow on the beach. So, Hot Shot, let us off here. Then call me and tell how it all goes this afternoon."

"It will be clear flying," said Tad.

"Sure, sure," said Jack as he and Babs climbed out of the rumble seat. "But if not, I have a full bottle of hair of the dog."

It could not be a better day, thought Tad. Lots of afternoon sunshine, a great time in the air, and a beautiful girl beside him; he'd leave the booze to Jack and Babs. He glanced over at Liz, at her heart-shaped face and dazzling eyes, and took a deep breath. She turned the engagement ring so that the light shone on the little diamond, then leaned over and kissed him. He had given her the ring the night before when he'd proposed, and she hadn't hesitated a second.

Sitting on the beach as the sun dipped below the horizon, they'd talked about the career he was about to embark upon, and how, as a married officer, he might get off-base housing. About how fun it would be to attend the officers' galas with senior staff, and how as a navy flyer he might someday become a squadron leader and rise to the rank of commander.

"Marrying you makes me the luckiest guy in the world," he'd said, his arm around her waist pulling her close. They'd watched sailboats bob over the waters of the Pacific.

"I think we're both lucky," said Liz. "I only wish I had a chance to meet your parents, but our schedules have been so hectic. Promise me, once we break the news to my folks, you will take me directly to yours. I'm sure they'll be as thrilled as mine."

"It's a promise," said Tad. With the setting of the sun a chill pervaded the air, and they'd gone inside the cosy bungalow owned by Jack's parents. A few sandwiches and a bottle of wine later, they were in bed. The night slid by under a quarter moon. They spent that blissful night holding each other close, whispering words of heartfelt love. Their passions built until everything else in the world was forgotten. Tad hoped and prayed that it would be like that forever. It wasn't until three in the morning that they'd finally fallen asleep in a tangle of arms and legs and sheets.

Remembering the previous night, Tad smiled, his eyes full of sunlight and his hands on the wheel. Unlike the cars that Henry Ford said could come in any color as long as it was black, the HCS Roadster was bright yellow with a black canvas top. With the top down, Tad listened to the hum of the fifty-horsepower engine and admired the round metal hood ornament. It had been a gift from his father when he'd entered UCLA. Tad winked at Liz as they sped down the two-lane road toward her parents' elegant Victorian in South Pasadena. Just in time he slammed on the brakes as a traffic light went from green to red. A motorcycle cop on the corner, arms folded, merely shook his head as Tad flashed him a grin.

He knew the area well, having taken girlfriends along route 66, down Colorado Boulevard and past the famous Rialto Theater, purported to be haunted. He had squired young ladies to the Wrigley Gardens built by the chewing gum magnate, and over the ornate span of the Colorado Street bridge, also known as "suicide bridge", over the Arroyo Seco. On lazy afternoons he had ventured on dirt roads into the San Gabriel Mountains where he and whichever girl he was with could enjoy the unfettered view of bucolic Los Angeles below.

Liz kissed him, and he wondered if there were things he should have told her. For a moment, what Jack had said nagged him, but he was certain that all would be well.

At five o'clock Tad was wheeling the roadster up the driveway of Liz's parents' estate. Liz beamed at him as she scrambled out of the car and ran up the steps of the three-story mansion. Overhead, the flat Mansard roof, bay windows, and quaint French turrets glowed richly in the afternoon light.

"Mama!" she called breathlessly, as they burst into the sunroom where her mother was playing Debussy on an upright Steinway piano. Coiffured and elegant, wearing a necklace of over one hundred pearls, Gladys Leighton Smythe looked up. Liz blurted, "We did it! We're handcuffed!"

"Handcuffed?" said Mrs. Smythe, perplexed by the slang.

"Oh, Mother!" Liz said with exasperation. "Engaged! Tad and I are getting married. Look, see my ring! Isn't it just spiffing?"

"Oh, my goodness," her mother replied, rising and giving both a tight hug. She gazed at her daughter with soft eyes and a questioning look. "That is stunning, well, wonderful news, and I'm sure your father will be pleased, but it has all happened so quickly. Of course, Tad is a true prize, and I think the world of him."

"And he's already been promised a commission in the United States Navy. He's going to fly fighters, just like Lee."

Looking up at Tad, Gladys said, "I'm always thrilled to see my son in those Navy whites with the wings pinned to his jacket. My, my, two pilots in the same family. You just have to meet him, Tad. He's returning from San Diego and should be here any moment."

"I'm looking forward to meeting him," said Tad. "There are many questions I want to ask him about the Navy."

"He's a real egg, always making jokes," said Liz, "but you can talk with him later! Come on, Tad, Dad's in his upstairs study. And Mom, you must come, too. This will be so wonderful!" She squeezed Tad's hand and said, "He might be a bit cranky, just ignore it. The board turned down his funding request for the Shakespeare library, but he's very persistent and always gets what he wants. So just be horribly respectful. I'm sure he likes you very much. Isn't that right, Mother?"

"He told me that he thinks Tad is a most interesting young man. Yes, I'm quite sure the Professor thinks the world of him."

Despite the reassurance of Liz and Gladys, Tad had a sense of uncertainty, a lingering memory of the first and only time his fiancée had introduced him to the esteemed and venerable sage of Elizabethan literature, Professor Smythe.

Looking much like the late President Wilson, tall, erudite, condescending, with academic aloofness, the patrician had regarded Tad with cool detachment.

Today the professor emeritus wore a bow tie and grey vest with a pocket watch and solid gold chain. Doctor Conroy Reginald Smythe appeared irritated, but rose to his feet when Liz burst in, followed by Tad and Mrs. Smythe. He removed his monocle and carefully placed it in his vest pocket before giving his daughter a look of exasperation, as if his sanctuary had been invaded by the demented hordes of Genghis Khan.

"Daddy, look! Tad and I are engaged!" she effused, throwing her arms around him. "You're going to have a wonderful son-in-law. I am so excited, I can hardly breathe! Isn't this the most fabulous ring? Tad gave it to me last night. Oh, Daddy," she said, rising on her tip toes, "I just had to tell you and Mom first. Tad's parents don't even know yet."

"Yes, Professor," said Tad, "Liz insisted we come here right off. Your daughter is a most wonderful young woman and I am truly honored, sir." He extended his hand. But there was no handshake. Doctor Smythe glanced at it, his hand behind his back, and slowly shook his head.

"That's enough, young man," said Smythe, as Liz stepped back from her father's cold response.

"Daddy?" said Liz, a frown forming on her once radiant face. "We are so happy, we just wanted to...."

The professor slowly removed his monocle from his pocket and meticulously wiped it with a handkerchief before leveling his gaze on Tad. He seemed to appraise him as one would a mongrel at the local pound. Turning to his wife, he said, "Gladys, as a professor emeritus and member of the Board of Regents I have certain privileges. One is the ability to investigate the background of any student at the university. Documents, admission files, the like. I had a suspicion that something was amiss with this young man. And you know," he said, looking back at Tad with cool appraisal, "I always follow my hunches."

"Yes, dear, of course," said Gladys deferentially. "And you are never, never wrong."

The professor ignored his wife's obsequiousness. "Not surprisingly, I found inconsistencies, indeed, aberrations, in Mr. Kuchenkov's application to the university." Peering with raised eyebrows, he continued. "Yes, there are certain inconsistencies... or should I say, outright prevarications?"

"I did not lie, Professor, I—"

"Please." Doctor Conroy Reginald Smythe held up a silencing hand. Looking at his daughter with a tight smile he said, "I have a friend, an old colleague from when I was on the faculty in the Commonwealth of Virginia. He was appointed to direct the immigration proceedings at Ellis Island. I asked him to kindly find some old records for me, and he obliged. In fact," said Smythe, opening a desk drawer, "I have copies of them right here."

He aimed a cold smile at Tad, flipped open a thin manila folder, picked up an official looking sheet, and, like a detective solving a troubling case said, "Your father, Alexei Kochenkov, fought for the Czar, a not entirely commendable activity; and your grandmother, Olga, when entering this country, stated that she is of the Jewish faith. That, sir, makes you a Jew. A goddamned Jew!"

Tad stiffened, his eyes burrowing into the professor, who seemed quite pleased with his pronouncement, as if his golf ball had just made a hole in one.

Liz stared at Tad, her mouth open. Her head began to shake slowly. "You never told me," she said quite slowly. With sudden fury she said, "Why didn't you *tell* me? I had no idea! I mean, you don't look—"

"But there is more," said the professor, overriding his daughter's outburst. "Would you care to tell us about your mother? The one you implied was of some exotic Polynesian extraction."

Tad sucked in his breath and, knowing that it was over, said, "My mother, now an American citizen and a nurse for the Department of the Navy, came from Japan. So yes, my dear Liz, I am half Japanese. My full first name is Tadichi. The Japanese culture is an ancient and honorable one. I'm sorry it so greatly troubles your father."

"A Jap *and* a Jew," she blurted, her eyes wide with disbelief. Then, in a hushed voice and shaking with rage, she turned to her father and said, "Oh, Daddy, Daddy, I had no idea. I cannot, dare not.... Oh, no."

"Of course not, my dear. It's hardly your fault. He is very cunning, I should say devious, wanting to marry into money. He simply deceived you. If I had investigated earlier, I might have been able to have him thrown out of the university. Unfortunately, it is now too late. But it is not too late to throw him out of my house!"

Taking the ring from her finger, Liz threw it at Tad. It rebounded against this chest, fell to the floor, rolled, and stopped at her feet. He glanced at it, turned, left the sunroom and stormed down the stairs. As he slammed the door behind him, he saw a young naval officer come up the driveway. The man looked at him curiously and gave a slight nod, but Tad stared straight ahead. Lee-Beauregard Smythe turned and stared as Tad started his Roadster, then with a shrug entered his parents' house.

The car sped toward the beach and through more than one red light. Seething at the insults, bitter at his own unwillingness to acknowledge and divulge his heritage, Tad tore blindly down Highway One. Devastated by the loss of

Liz, appalled by her reaction, he raged at his own stupidity. He had thought she might be surprised, perhaps perplexed by his reluctance to divulge his true background, but if she truly loved him....

He shuddered and wondered how, in America, the contempt could run so deep. His father had told him about the Black Hundreds in Russia, the pogroms, the unbelievably intense hatred of Jews as well as Japanese, but this was America, another land, another world.

He knew that he would never see Liz again, and there was a terrible hollow place within him. He had loved her, he told himself, remembering her curled up beside him, giving herself to him....

Two hours later, he pulled up at the bungalow, where Jack and Babs rocked back and forth in a rickety swing. Tad got out of the car and just shook his head. He caught the "hair of the dog" as the bottle sailed toward him. Turning away, he walked down to the beach, sat on a rock and stared out to sea.

Chapter 2
Los Angeles, California
March, 1940

Alexei Kuchenkov frowned as he read the letter for the second time, wondering what words were so egregious that they had to be blacked out by the Soviet censor. "What do you think, Kimi-san?" he asked his wife. She finished pouring his cup of *ocha*, the green Japanese tea he favored, before answering.

"I'm surprised the letter got here at all. The article about Russia in the *Times* makes me think that nothing can get through that doesn't praise Joseph Stalin. The place is a dictatorship, with the NKVD arresting people at whim. And your father wants you to visit him in Leningrad? I know that you haven't seen him in decades, but Alexei-san, it's far too dangerous. His rank in the Party won't protect you."

"My mother wrote the letter, and she's there. They haven't bothered her, and she's been an American citizen for years."

Kimi-san looked at her husband with the magnetic green eyes that had mesmerized him when, all those years ago in Tokyo, he'd been hurrying around a corner with his head in a book and literally plowed into her. The collision had sent her ikebana vase hurtling through the air and Kimi-san flailing in the muddy street. So long ago, thought Alexei, looking at the slender woman whose image had kept him alive, even when his Russian cruiser was being blown apart by a Japanese torpedo-destroyer.

"My father has had a second stroke and probably won't last another month. He wants to see me before he dies. How can I say no? I haven't seen him since the Count died, and that was two years after the war."

"Even then, the Tsar's secret police were watching and you barely made it out," said Kimi-san, pinning on her nurse's cap in preparation for heading to the hospital. "I know you want to see him, and I would encourage you to do so if there was not so such turmoil. I know I can't stop you if you think you really have to go. But please give it serious thought. I fear the world is coming apart."

She had her hand on the door when she said, "Tad's train will be coming into Union Station tomorrow afternoon. He phoned yesterday, and I told him you will be there. He's anxious to see us before he reports to the Navy."

"You're not coming?" asked Alexei.

"I told him we'll both see him in San Diego before he ships out. I'm teaching a trauma class tomorrow and there's no one to take my place. Give him my love. By the way, Jack is with him. You won't be too hard on him, will you?"

"Jack? Of course not, but I might say everything in Russian."

"I didn't think he speaks Russian."

"He doesn't. What he knows is how to crack up airplanes."

"Alexei-san, that was years ago," Kimi said with exasperation.

"It was still my plane. But I promise to appear forgiving; in fact, I won't even mention it."

Kimi gave him a baleful look, sighed, then walked down the steps and got into the Ford.

Alexei again studied the letter. It had taken three weeks to arrive. It would take him weeks to get to Stockholm, a neutral port, then on by the Swedish overnight ferry to Leningrad. What if The Admiral were dead by the time he arrived? Alexei absently turned on the radio. The news from Europe was not good.

* * *

"So, Jack Vestergaard, how many of Mr. Roosevelt's planes did you crack up last week?" Alexei demanded, when Tad and Jack had alighted from the train. Throwing his arms around Tad, he whispered, "I'm deplorable; I told your mother I would be nice to Jack. Of course, one must be respectful of U.S. Navy lieutenants." Embracing Jack in a bear-hug that the younger man seemed to find embarrassing, Alexei said, "So, how many, Jack?"

"Ah, Comrade Kochenkov! Only one, and that is the same number as my good buddy Tad. But mine was an old plane. The one Tad put into the ground was a brand newF4F."

"I heard about that, and I already forgave my son," said Alexei, beaming at both of them.

"It was *not* a new F4F," protested Tad. And I did *not* crack it up! Just a hard landing when the landing gear didn't lock down. It was a damn fine landing at that."

"*Da, da*, all is good, yes? Too bad you two don't have time for dinner at the house. I would cook piroshkies just the way you like them."

"Thanks, but orders are orders, Pop. They want us in San Diego right away," said Tad. "Things are rather unsettled now. Europe and all."

"And the Pacific," added Jack, his eyes following an especially attractive young woman as she walked by.

"Yes," said Alexei. He was quiet for a moment, then said to Tad, "I have to talk with you. But not here."

"Sounds personal," said Jack. He brushed a speck of dust from his naval jacket. "I'll wait in the bar. Maybe I'll meet some girl. I'll find you one too, Tad. They all love pilots."

"Sure," said Tad, "Go get them; you have about nine minutes." Then he and Alexei walked to a deserted spot in the cavernous station.

"What is happening?" asked Tad, seeing the tightening on his father's face.

"I'll be leaving the country for a few months. Your grandfather won't live much longer and I have to see him."

"You're talking about going to *Russia*?"

"He wants to see me. It has been a very long time."

"But Pop, Hitler and Stalin have already divided up Poland. It's too damn dangerous. I know that seeing the admiral is important, but—"

"Your mother said the same thing, but it is something I have to do. When I get back Kimi-san and I will join you in Hawaii. That's where you're being sent, yes?"

"Yes. Jack and I have orders for Pearl. I think our carrier is there now. But really, I hate to see you go to Russia. It's a vile place: executions, arrests and kidnappings. And you being an aeronautical engineer! The NKVD might take a special interest in you. It's a miracle your father survived this long. Why didn't he go to France years ago?"

"I am aware of all that. After all, I grew up there. My father's situation was very unusual. Much as Lenin would have liked to execute another Czarist admiral, even Bolsheviks needed trains to run, and they needed him alive more than they wanted him dead. And, odd as it may sound, he always loved 'Mother Russia' no matter how stupidly the rulers behaved. I will try to cable your grandmother in Leningrad. Maybe it will be delivered. I want her to get out of there as soon as possible, but I doubt she will leave as long as your grandfather is alive."

"It's strange, Grandmother putting herself in such danger. They've lived apart for years. I never did hear the whole story," said Tad.

"It's rather complicated," said Alexei.

"Hey, Tad," called Jack from the entrance to the bar, waving as a nurse slipped him a folded piece of paper, "the train's about to leave without us, and it's a hell of a long walk."

Alexei gave his son a hug and, with a grin, said, "Don't fly with Jack. He crashes planes."

Tad laughed and said, "*Nyet, nyet*, Pop. He's almost as good as I am. Got to go. Give my love to Mom." The two young men made a dash for the train.

Through the open window, the pilots waved farewell to Alexei as the *San Diegan* began its journey to the port teeming with civilian and navy ships.

* * *

"Heard from Babs?" Tad asked, as the train left Los Angeles behind and raced down the tracks on its coastal route.

"Only twice since the divorce, and that was three years ago. It was great while it lasted, at least the first five or six years. But I was just an ensign then and there's no money in that. And Babs needs money; always had to be the 'it' girl, if you remember that silliness."

"Do you miss her?" asked Tad, his eyes straying to the newspaper lying on the seat.

Jack shrugged and said, "It was pleasant to wake up with a hot woman beside me. I will admit I was pretty despondent for a while. But I won't crack up any more planes."

"That will please the Navy."

"Besides," continued Jack with his devilish smile, "there will be a bevy of nurses in Oahu."

"Malarky. You won't have as much time as you think. And if you get behind the eight ball with the old man you'll be handling a truck instead of a fighter."

"Hardly. By the way, you ever her from Liz?"

"No," Tad said shortly. "But I did run into her brother at Portsmouth once. He wasn't friendly."

"Lots of things aren't friendly now. Like this," said Jack, picking up the paper.

"What's it say?" asked Tad.

"It's about Japan. Says the Japs have established a puppet regime in Nanking led by a fellow named Wang Jingwei. They've been fighting in China since '37 and lost a lot of people. I doubt that they will say, 'So sorry for the rape of Nanking, nothing personal, just a minor snafu. We're all going home, have a nice day.'"

A raucous stream of marine non-coms hurried down the aisle, the smoke from their Chesterfield cigarettes clouding the air. One seriously inebriated sergeant turned to Jack, gave a sloppy salute and said, "Sir, don't worry. The Marines will keep you safe."

"Sure you will. You do have our phone number, don't you?" Jack returned the salute in the same half-assed manner. The sergeant grinned, raised his glass, and hurried after his lurching buddies.

"I hope they sober up before meeting some sergeant major," said Tad.

"They'd better. Want some more bad news?" asked Jack.

"Can't wait."

"This is about Europe," said Jack, momentarily distracted, giving his best smile to a pretty blonde entering the car.

"Just read it, will you?" said Tad.

"Yes, sir. Let's see: 'Finland beaten by Soviets after heroic one hundred and five day conflict; required to give up considerable land to Moscow.'"

"That's it?" said Tad, looking at beachgoers as the train ran along the Pacific tracks.

"Not enough? Well, this column says that the Nazis bombed a British ship at Scapa Flow, and Britain and France agree that neither will make a separate peace with Germany."

Jack folded the paper and laid it on an empty seat. "What do you think?" he said, as he followed Tad's gaze.

"I was just thinking about my brother."

"When did you last see him?"

"Not since '31 when his ship stopped here. He got a few hours leave and we went to a tea house in Balboa. We were both in uniform. Later we walked down to the beach. We got some pretty strange stares."

"He was a pilot then, too?"

"You got it. Japanese Imperial Navy. He was assigned to the *Hosho*, first ship designed as a carrier from keel to flight deck. Even our *Saratoga* started out as a battle cruiser. But I haven't heard from him since Japan invaded China. He might be flying combat missions, or dead for all I know."

"Damn strange that he flies for Japan and you for the United States," said Jack.

"Damn strange indeed," Tad said, looking out the window, remembering....

Blood streamed from the boy's nose, but he refused to stop punching the kid beneath him. "You damn Jap!" the boy screamed before a second tooth cracked under Tadichi's fist.

Even before school had let out, everyone except the teachers had known a fight was brewing. Now two dozen boys and not a few girls encircled the two combatants as fists flew.

Though Tadichi appeared no more Japanese than any of the other boys, it was a small town and they all knew his mother came from "the land of the rising sun", and some of his classmates hated him for it.

Being half Japanese was not an easy thing in California, where envy of Japanese and Chinese advancement had turned to anti-Asian racism and exclusion acts.

He'd learned to speak Japanese from his mother when he was little. She would prune the garden, arranging the stones and raking the sand as if it was in Tokyo's Hibiya Park, and tell him about the culture and history of her native land. She often used the term "my homeland," to which Tadichi would say, "Mama-san, this is your land."

She would smile and say, "I love this country, but sometimes my heart is far away." Once she said, "Japan has a beautiful culture. You should be proud of being part Japanese."

Tadichi had nodded, and after a moment had asked, "Koizumi-san lives in Japan. Will I ever see him?"

"Someday we will visit Japan. And maybe someday your uncle Itomo-san will bring him here. He says that your brother is getting better, but not yet ready to travel. He is learning how to write in English. Maybe you two can correspond. He would like that."

Koizumi was Tadichi's younger brother. Moving to California had been a hard decision for Alexei and Kimi; it has been a wonderful opportunity, but little Koizumi had been ill and frail. Itomo had urged his sister to leave the boy with him, so that he and his wife—they had no children— could care for him.

Tadichi missed his brother, and wondered how different their lives had become. Did his brother get beaten up for being half Russian? Did Uncle Itomo have to protect him?

When Tadichi was nine, after he had endured a particularly bad beating, his father had found him on a backyard bench, despondently wiping away tears.

"You have to fight back," said Alexei, sitting down beside him. "I had to learn too, a long time ago."

Tadichi shook his head and said, "I can't fight, and they will beat me up. They always do."

"I can talk to the school principal and have those boys disciplined, but I don't think that will stop them. If you wish, I can teach you how to fight. School will be out for the summer and you will be ready if they try again next year." He reached into a pocket and proffered a white handkerchief to his son.

"Who taught you how to fight?" the boy asked, daubing his still bleeding nose.

"Itomo-san, when I was in Japan."

"Uncle Itomo-san?" said Tadichi, glancing up.

"The same. I was a young saber fencer traveling with the Russian consulate. Itomo-san was a few years older than I, and already an officer in the Japanese Navy. He wanted to learn how to fence, and in exchange for lessons he offered to teach me karate. And that's what we did."

"Did you ever have to use... karate?" Tadichi asked with growing interest, pausing on the unfamiliar word.

"Yes, but that was later, when I was a student at the Naval Academy in St. Petersburg. I was attacked by some upperclassmen. It was called 'hazing' and they were only supposed to get in a few punches. But it turned ugly."

"And you beat them up. I mean, by using karate."

"Hmm, I'll just say they never tried it again."

Tadichi was pensive for a moment, then said, "When can I begin? I want to learn karate."

Tadichi had said nothing to the four bullies as they taunted and surrounded him. Clearly they expected it to be like the previous year with the "Jap kid". There was a sense of glee among them as the biggest boy rolled up his sleeves and charged, fists cocked. But Tadichi stepped to the side, blocked the punch, then, fist down as taught, slammed his assailant with a straight arm blow, catching him behind the ear. The boy clutched his head, and Tadichi's heel drove into the attacker's stomach. Three more fast punches and the boy was curled up in a ball, whimpering and calling for help. But no help came. Mouths agape, the other three boys, and the audience, were slinking away.

After the fourth fight, in which two assailants suffered broken noses, they decided to leave him alone. He had developed a terrible temper, it was said, and the principal dressed him down more than once. But he carried himself straighter and would avenge any slight. He made no friends but was pleased when kids no longer pushed their way in front of him in the lunch line. His eyes took on a look of defiance that very few cared to cross.

"I am an American, as American as you," he screamed at one boy before slamming him into the ground. When Tadichi came home that day with a rare shiner, he walked up to his parents and said, "I am an American, not Japanese. My name is Tad and I never want to be called anything else."

The family eventually moved, and years later, when he entered UCLA, only Jack and a few of his mother's friends knew of his Japanese heritage. And that was just fine with him.

Chapter 3
Honolulu, Hawaii
April, 1941

"Son, allow me to introduce you to Doctor Eli Thompson, my boss and the chief surgeon," said Kimi.

Dr. Thompson shook Tad's hand and said, "Your mother praises you to high heaven. She thinks you're the best fighter pilot the Navy has."

"An exaggeration," said Tad. They were standing in the emergency room of the Aiea Heights Naval Hospital on Oahu, where his mother worked. "I just try not to sink any carriers when I'm landing."

The doctor laughed and said, "Well, your mother is the best trauma nurse I have. I'm glad she came over from the mainland; the way things are going we will probably need every nurse we can get." He smiled at Kimi, then at Tad and said, "So how long might you be in Oahu?"

"Not long. My squadron is on *Yorktown,* and the carrier leaves for Bermuda in about three weeks. Fleet operations."

"Well, you and your mother are invited to my house for dinner tomorrow night. My sister is putting on a big feed for the staff and there will be lots of pretty nurses, Lieutenant."

Tad grinned and said, "If we come I'd like to bring my friend Jack. He's also on *Yorktown* and he majored at UCLA in pretty nurses. I just minored in them."

Again the doctor laughed, then said, "I hope to see all three of you there."

* * *

"Doctor Thompson really thinks a lot of you," said Tad, as he drove his mother to her house three miles beyond the hospital.

"He's an excellent surgeon and a very nice man. And he's been very solicitous since Alexei's been gone, knowing how worried I am. But..."

"But what?" said Tad, noting a hint of concern.

"He's been single and quite lonely since his wife left him, and he has become a bit personal in his interest in me. He's made me his assistant and I accompany him and other doctors on his daily tour of the wards," said Kimi. She looked out the window as they passed the harbor with its warships anchored or tied to their berths.

"He hasn't said anything that could be considered unprofessional, but his manner suggests that if anything happened to Alexei, he would be interested in a different kind of relationship." She shook her head slightly. "I'm nearly fifty-six now, and it seems quite strange that any man, besides your father, would be interested in me."

Seeing his mother's nervousness, Tad said, "But he hasn't asked you out or anything, has he?"

"Oh no, he wouldn't do that."

They drove past little houses as the car climbed uphill.

"We haven't been alone together outside the hospital, and I do nothing to encourage him," she continued. "But I let slip that your father expects to remain in Leningrad a little longer since his father's relapse."

"What did doctor Thompson say about that?"

"Only that he would be someone to speak to if things did not turn out well...."

Her voice drifted off. Moments later the car pulled onto the dirt driveway, flanked by a stand of palm trees and had a view of the harbor.

Tad decided to say nothing more about the doctor's obvious affection for his mother.

There was little crime in the neighborhood, so the door was unlocked. Kimi opened the door and saw that the mailman had slipped a letter through the mail slot. Tad picked it up and gave it to her, then went into the kitchen for a cold beer. Kimi sat in her chair by the window and studied the envelope.

"Who's it from?" asked Tad, popping off the cap.

"From your father."

Kimi opened the letter and was surprised to see that it hadn't been censored. She read it hastily, becoming increasingly alarmed, then gave the letter to Tad. He quickly skimmed it and whistled, saying, "Someone with a diplomatic pouch had to have gotten this out. Pop would have been in real danger if anyone had seen this."

"Maybe he has met somebody in the American consulate. There are no Russian stamps on the envelope. Perhaps Alexei-san and your grandparents can find sanctuary if things get really bad."

Tad shook his head. "My grandfather will be watched by the NKVD, and he will not be allowed near the consulate, even if he is well enough to get there."

Tad reread the letter. It appeared as if it had been written in haste.

My dearest Kimi-san,

I hope this letter gets to you. Do not try to write to me through regular mail because it will be read by the NKVD. I've been told that only official mail can be sent to Leningrad. I will try to have one more letter sent to you before I leave.

My father is very grateful that I have come to visit him, but he now encourages me to return to the United States. Our reunion has been illuminating and heartfelt, but there is nothing more I can do for him. Therefore, I will be leaving Russia on June twenty-fourth by way of Sweden. I think my mother will be leaving as well.

The doctors here have been quite attentive and have tried to make the old Admiral as comfortable as possible. My mother and I visit him every day, and he retains all his mental faculties. And he is a font of information on the real-world situation, though I don't know from whom he gets it, and he refuses to say. Pravda and the other newspapers print nothing but propaganda. He does have a few visitors, other admirals and people from the general staff who survived the purges.

There is still fear that the military staff may fall victim to the secret police, even though the purges have supposedly ended. Perhaps what keeps the remaining Old Guard safe is their irreplaceable experience. It is widely believed that the Soviet Union will not be safe from German invasion much longer, despite the non-aggression pact with Hitler. Stalin has scrupulously upheld his side of the bargain, even allowing the German Air Force to train in the Soviet Union so that Germany will not be in violation of the Versailles Treaty. But the Soviet military is preparing for war, amassing ams and training soldiers. There is now a four-hundred-mile distance between Russian and German forces due to the recent Soviet absorption of the Baltic states. My father said very cynically, "They are now the buffer zone; they will be buffeted first."

However, it appears that Stalin will do absolutely nothing overt that might aggravate Germany, meaning that military commanders have not been allowed (on pain of imprisonment) to establish defensive zones to protect Leningrad or the interior. No talk of war is allowed, and everything between Hitler and Stalin is spoken of in the rosiest of terms.

I miss you terribly, but I expect to be with you in Hawaii sometime in early August. Give my love to Tad, and say hello to Jack for me. Remind Tad not to fly with him!

With all my love,
Alexei

Tad folded the letter and handed it back to his mother. "The twenty-fourth, that's only a few days from now. And he says that he'll be here in Hawaii in August. Who knows, I might get leave and be here when he arrives," he said reassuringly.

His mother nodded. "That would be wonderful. A nice reunion." She was pensive for a moment, then said, "But something bothers me, Tad. I can't put my finger on it, but I have this funny feeling." Then she sighed and said, "I will go to Dr. Thompson's party, but only if you come with me."

"Your escort?" said Tad with a smile.

"Exactly," said Kimi. "And bring Jack along, or else he'll become maudlin. You know how he gets."

Tad was about to leave when his mother said, "Oh, I almost forgot. Silly me, considering that I got her letter a month ago. My dear old ikebana sensei, Mrs. Hiroku Imoto, will be visiting Oahu next week. And she will be bringing her apprentice, Sayuri Saito. I think she's about twenty-six. There is a picture of them in the envelope. I'll get it. Don't go yet."

His mind still on the letter from Russia, Tad absently took the black and white photo from his mother. He glanced down, then stared. "My God, this girl is beautiful. Some guy is lucky to have her as his wife."

"I didn't say she's married. What gave you that idea?" said Kimi.

"Twenty-six. What Japanese woman isn't married by that age?"

"Well, she's not. And I told Sensei all about you, and I'm sure that she told Sayuri."

Tad laughed and said, "How cute. Well, I'll be a good host and show her around. Anyway, I've got to go. Jack said he met a couple of nurses and, out of the goodness of his heart, he insists on introducing me to one of them. Knowing Jack, it's the one he doesn't want. Lucky me."

Kimi watched her son drive off. She closed her eyes and, with an inward smile, remembered a gangly, bumbling *gaijin* with blond hair, ceaselessly apologizing in formal but stilted Japanese as he tried to assist her up from the mud.

Kimi looked out the window at the swaying palms and recalled the night she and Alexei had come together, loving, as their nations edged ever closer to war. Then they had been forcibly separated. It had been years before they'd met again and married. And for all those years since, they had never been apart. Until now.

She picked up Alexei's letter. She read it once again, imagining him in a land so far away, a barbarian place that had once declared unprovoked war on her people. And now her gentle Alexei was assuring her that he would come home in no time at all.

Kimi shivered despite the warm afternoon. *So long ago*, she mused. Alexei's absence made her feel empty, and so terribly alone. But, she reassured herself, he would be coming back to her soon, and their happiness would go on and on.

* * *

The *Sakura Maru,* an eight-thousand-ton Japanese freighter, sidled up to the international dock. Sensei Hiroku and her apprentice Sayuri walked down the gangplank, followed by Koizumi, dressed in civilian clothes. Kimi practically ran forward, stopping to bow deeply to her elderly sensei, then to her son, and finally to the beautiful young woman beside and a little behind Hiroku. Tad simply stared.

After bowing to Kimi, Sayuri bowed to Tad, who, with some self-consciousness, returned the greeting. He finally stirred and, seeing his brother, laughed and hurried forward, hand extended. Taken aback, Koizumi removed his fedora and, with studied seriousness, bowed. Tad checked himself and briefly did the same, before throwing his arms around the brother he barely remembered.

"I'm glad to see you again," Tad said in Japanese.

Koizumi replied, "I am honored to see you. And your Japanese is perfect."

If Koizumi felt embarrassed by Tad's effusive welcome, he tried not to show it. It was rare in Japan to display such emotion, but, thought Koizumi, this was Hawaii, and he had read about American customs.

"Oh, Koizumi-san, I had no idea that you were coming with Sayuri and Sensei!" exclaimed Kimi, gazing at her son's military bearing and dark, penetrating eyes.

"I apologize for not having informed you, but your brother suggested that I accompany his wife's dear friends. I was happy to do so. After all these years, it is so good to see you and my brother. But where is Father?"

"He will be joining us in August when he returns from Russia. I hope you can remain with us that long," said Kimi.

"I regret that the Japanese Imperial Navy has allowed me only a few weeks leave, in addition to the time for travel. And when I return, the ladies will be expected to return with me," Koizumi said in an apologetic voice.

"Well," said Tad, his eyes again straying to Sayuri, "let's go to Mother's house and celebrate your arrival. I think we all have a lot to talk about."

A porter brought the luggage and placed it in the trunk of the '37 Chevy. With Koizumi in the front beside him and the ladies in the back seat, Tad drove while his mother and her former teacher talked nonstop. Koizumi seemed a bit ill-at-ease as they drove past dozens of American sailors and soldiers on the streets of the city, a city that buzzed with bars, shops, snack stands, and flashing signs.

"Perhaps I should stay here," Koizumi said, pointing to the Comstock Apartments Hotel as they passed the building.

"Lord, no," protested Tad. "You all stay at Mom's house. There is plenty of room. I live in the bachelor officers quarters. Very comfortable; I'm sure you know all about that," he said with a smile. "I can't wait to hear about your life and everything happening in Japan."

Koizumi was silent as a pair of P-40 fighter aircraft flew overhead on their way to Hickman Air Field. He frowned, then said, "I will tell you everything I can, *oniisan*."

Older brother, Tad translated to himself. Yes, here, finally, was his younger brother, his *ototo*. How comfortable and relaxed could he make this young man feel? wondered Tad. Though brothers, they were complete strangers. *How does one make a guest of an adversarial nation feel welcome?* Koizumi was probably more aware of the deteriorating international situation than most politicians, Tad reflected.

And then a strange thought came to him. Their uncle was a Japanese admiral who had allowed Koizumi to travel to Oahu. But for what reason? Surely, he had to have received special permission. There had to be more to it than just being a chaperone for the apprentice of a friend. But that thought was interrupted when he glanced in the rearview mirror and saw Sayuri. She smiled; very quietly Tad turned to Koizumi and said, "She is so beautiful. I'm surprised that you haven't already proposed to her."

Koizumi remained silent for a moment, then stiffly said, "I am a pilot in the Japanese Imperial Navy. Any other interest conflicts with my mission. That is the only answer I can give."

"I find that hard to believe. A girl that pretty can conflict with anything," said Tad, nudging his brother. Then he thought, *And what exactly is that mission?*

* * *

Over the next few days, Tad spent as much time as possible at his mother's house. His interest in Sayuri grew each time he saw her, and often he managed to escort her to the back yard, where they would talk for hours. One day he arrived to find a slender young man speaking to Sayuri in fluent Japanese.

"Well, look what the cat dragged in. And here you are, already talking up my girlfriend!" Tad said in English, slapping Jeremy Shinigawa on the back.

Jeremy laughed and said, "Your girlfriend? Hell, she's too damn pretty for you. I just got into Honolulu last night and called your mom. She invited me over, very nice of her."

Tad, smiling, glanced at Sayuri, who had only caught part of the conversation. She wasn't sure if she should be amused or concerned. The undercurrent of rivalry beneath the easy banter of the two friends was perplexing. It was obvious to her that Tad, though pleased to see Jeremy, was not pleased to see him engaging her with his considerable charm.

"I'm actually on my way to Japan," Jeremy said. "I just got accepted to UCLA for a Masters. I'm studying the Tokugawa period with an emphasis on the social and economic influence of the samurai."

"Sounds like a fascinating topic," said Tad. "So, how long are you staying in Hawaii?"

"Not long. UCLA has hooked me up with Tokyo University and I'll be the guest of a professor who was one of my instructors, Professor Shimura. Maybe you remember him; he taught Asian history. Now he's back in Japan."

"Nope, after my time there. But being an American, even a Japanese-American who speaks fluent Japanese, might be a bit worrisome for you in Tokyo right now."

"I'm not doing anything political; I'm just a student. The professor carries a lot of weight. He's well known in the academic community, and he requested me, so I don't think the authorities will bother me."

"I hope you're right. Well, I'll let you chat with Sayuri, but don't get any wild ideas."

"Hell, no. At least, not under your mother's roof. Now once we're both in Japan...."

"Don't even think of it. Anyway, we'll talk later. Koizumi and I are going for a walk. Come on by before you leave for Tokyo. I'll keep the beer cold."

After Jeremy left, Tad and Koizumi set out for a bluff overlooking the city where there were benches and gardens and palms. Meanwhile, Sensei, Sayuri and Kimi repaired to her tree-shaded backyard. They sat at a table and watched a pair of chickens pecking for grubs.

"My sort of pets," said Kimi. "They're ubiquitous to the islands. They make a mess, but they eat pests, and they lay eggs." With a grin she added, "And every once in a while we enjoy a chicken salad."

Hiroku laughed, then said, "I'm so pleased you took the time to drive us around this lovely island. In some ways it reminds me of Kyushu. I recognize some of the same flowers. And yet it's so different. I mean the people, the informality and openness. It's very different in Japan. Especially now."

"It took me many years to accustom myself to American ways," said Kimi. "Here in Hawaii things are even more relaxed than on the mainland. Hawaii has its own culture. There are many Japanese living here, yet they are as Hawaiian as anybody else. I like it here, and Tad comes by often. His ship is based here."

"Tad," said Sensei. "You don't call him Tadichi?"

"No, he has not wanted to be called anything but Tad since he was a child."

"I see," said Hiroku, not wishing to pry further. Conspiratorially she leaned forward and said, "You know, Kimi-san, our Sayuri thinks that he is quite handsome."

Amazed by this bluntness and slightly embarrassed, Sayuri's eyes widened and she put her hand to her mouth.

"Sensei," she blurted, "we have only been here a few days and you are already making such rash statements. I think he's a fine man, but...."

"You see, Kimi-san?" said Sensei. "Have we a budding romance here?"

Kimi merely smiled and said, "Well, I'm sure my son would love her to stay here for a long time." Gazing at Sayuri she said, "Excuse me for being so nosy, but how is it that such a beautiful young lady is not married? Surely any man would give his soul to have you.”

Sayuri blushed, then in a very soft voice said, “Kimi-san, you are too kind. I am twenty-six, and I no longer feel beautiful. To answer your question, I was engaged to a pilot, a close friend of Koizumi, but he died in a training accident, and, well, I have not wanted to catch another man since.”

Catch a man, the Japanese phrase, thought Kimi-san. “I am saddened by your loss,” she said. “It must have been a terrible thing. But surely you do not intend to remain single for the rest of your life. Time passes, and it is good for a woman to have a mate.”

“It is something that I will think about,” said Sayuri.

“And I will be sure that she does,” added Sensei with a twinkle in her eye.

They were silent for a moment, then Kimi-san said, “Sensei, I do not wish to spoil our beautiful day, but you said something that sounds a bit unsettling. You mentioned that this culture is so ‘open.’ What were you implying? And please forgive my impertinence if this sounds impolite.”

“Not impolite at all,” said Sensei, setting down her cup of *ocha*. Then reflexively glancing about, she said, “Kimi-san, I’m sure you know that Japan has been at war with China for almost four years now. It is not the Japan you remember. Everything has changed. There are signs saying ‘Loyalty and Patriotism’ and ‘Work, Work, Honor the nation and its brave soldiers.’ Everyone must be productive. The joy of living in Japan is gone.”

She paused, then said, “In Japan we wear the *mompe* now, colorless peasant clothes. No one wears kimonos, and there are laws against using make-up. Hair-styling is banned. There are real shortages, and long lines for even the most necessary items. Everything goes to the war effort.”

"But Tokyo used to be so cosmopolitan," said Kimi, saddened that the mood of her guests had darkened.

"Theaters and bars are closing, there is a curfew, and women are being asked to go to China to serve the soldiers."

"You mean as prostitutes?" asked Kimi-san, aghast.

"Yes, prostitutes. And I heard that the army has rounded up thousands of Korean and Chinese women for that purpose," replied Sensei.

"But there are other things happening, too. I was working for a women's magazine," chimed in Sayuri. "It was shut down, along with hundreds of other periodicals and newspapers. The authorities said that the magazine was unnecessarily using precious paper. But I think that was only an excuse. Now there is only one source of news, and it comes from the government. I have seen American flags burned, and no longer can we see movies from Hollywood. All films are propaganda, and all war news is only about our victories. But... so many families go to the shrines to pray for their dead sons."

"No one is allowed to talk about it, but we have lost over one hundred and fifty thousand soldiers. And the school children must practice military drills," said Sensei. There is a drum beat for war; parades and crowds are always being organized to see soldiers off to war. And we women must form community organizations to support the war effort. It's called the Imperial Rule Assistance Association, and no one refuses membership."

"It is all very frightening," said Sayuri. "In school we didn't learn much about the United States, except that it supported Russia after Russia attacked our homeland and our navy defeated the Russian navy. Now, we are told, the U.S. uses its military to occupy places like Cuba and the Philippines, encroaching closer and closer to Japan. I hope that nothing terrible happens between our two nations."

"I hope so, too," said Kimi. After a long moment she said, more brightly, "Now, let us talk about more enjoyable things."

The afternoon conversation did become lighter, but beneath it lingered a chilling, dismal fear. Kimi wished that she had not asked Sensei about life in Japan. It might have been possible to avoid the subject for the entire time of her guests' visit. But sooner or later, she thought, it would have come up. Of course, they would not talk any more about it. To broach the subject again would not be polite, and everything in Japan, the Japan she recalled, hinged on politeness.

That night she prayed that there would be no war. War, she recalled, was never polite.

Chapter 4
Honolulu, Hawaii
April, 1941

The park above Aiea Heights Drive looked over the city and the harbor below. Koizumi, in civilian clothes, sat beside Tad, who wore his dress whites. They were silent for a few minutes, watching the wakes of ships as they sailed on the gently rolling swells. A flight of pelicans flew over the water, one following behind the other in perfect formation.

"Wouldn't it have been great if we'd grown up together as real brothers," said Tad.

"And just where would we have done that?" asked Koizumi, wishing that he was wearing his lieutenant's uniform.

"California," said Tad, watching a battleship steaming into the port. He brushed away a pesky fly.

"You don't look Japanese, yet you felt compelled to change your name, Tadichi-san. I do look Japanese, so how would I have been treated in the United States?"

Tad shifted slightly, uncomfortable, remembering the schoolyard battles of his childhood.

"And you could not have grown up in Tokyo, with a Russian father, even if you are half-Japanese. In fact, that would have made your situation worse in the eyes of many. Half-breeds, and their mothers, are not well regarded. Certainly, you would not have been flying for the Imperial Japanese Navy. No, dear brother, we both had to grow up in our own worlds. But maybe sometime in the future we could spend more time together. I would like that."

"So, would I," said Tad, wondering how long in the future that might be. Then he said, "I'm surprised that you didn't stay at Tokyo University. Mother said you were attending classes there."

"Our uncle, Admiral Itomo, was subsidizing my tuition, and I felt bad about him doing so. Besides, I wanted to fly, and Japan needs pilots. Itomo-san got me into Etajima, and I volunteered for flight training."

"Did you begin flight training right away?"

Koizumi gave Tad a wry grin and said, "If only it were so simple. Our training officers were sadistic and we were beaten for the smallest infraction. I don't want to remember how many times I was smacked with a board. If one was punished, all suffered the same. And no one dared make a sound. Sitting down afterwards was painful. But I finally got through it and was accepted for flight training."

"Was that as brutal?" asked Tad.

"We were no longer beaten, but committing the slightest infraction could get you thrown out. We feared the disgrace of expulsion more than anything. We are a very select group; there are not many pilots."

The fly that had bothered Tad was joined by three more. Suddenly, in a blur of movement, Koizumi's hands shot forward and he snatched each one out of the air.

Tad was astonished. His brother simply said, "That was one of our few off-duty pleasures. Everybody caught flies. It's all about speed, reflexes and vision. For instance," Koizumi said, looking into the stark blue sky, "see that star up there, the one to the left of Venus."

"Koizumi-san, this is daytime. You can't see stars," said Tad with a lopsided grin.

"You can if you look hard enough. I can see them, and so can you if you concentrate. It's a way we spot enemy aircraft before their pilots see us."

"Well," Tad said somewhat ruefully, "in the U.S. flight schools we don't catch flies, or search for stars during daytime. But I enjoyed flight training. Sure, many did drop out, and a few crashed. But getting in wasn't too difficult, especially if one had a college education."

"In Japan, over a thousand apply every year but only a hundred or so are accepted. Maybe twenty or thirty graduate. A man can be dismissed even on the last day for an infraction," said Koizumi, looking toward the fleet at the docks below.

"What sort of infraction?" asked Tad.

"I had a good friend who went through flight school with me. He was elated to make it to the last day of instruction. Graduation was scheduled for the next morning; but on that last day he took a fighter and did an aileron roll right over the flying field. In the captain's office he was emphatically told that he had shown poor judgement. I was standing outside and I could hear the captain shout that it was the type of stupidity that would endanger our pilots in combat. On the spot, my friend's name was stricken from the roster.

"Twenty minutes later he returned to the captain's office and kowtowed like a peasant, head on the floor, begging to be reinstated. The captain refused, and my friend drew a knife and committed seppuku right there. I and two others cleaned up the blood. His name was Shima Ohta. He was the pilot Sayuri was expecting to marry. She thinks his plane crashed in a training mission. No one has ever told her what really happened." Koizumi looked into Tad's eyes and added, "And I trust no one ever will."

Silence enveloped them until Koizumi said, "I was sent to southern China when the trouble began there. We call it the Sino-Japanese Incident. On my third sortie, I shot down my first enemy plane, a Soviet-made bomber. There were a lot of foreign planes, and foreign pilots, fighting for the Chinese; I don't know if the pilot was a Soviet Air Force officer or Chinese."

"What were you flying?" asked Tad.

"The Mitsubishi Type 96, very slow."

"Open cockpit, fixed landing gear?"

"Yes. We didn't have the Zero yet. That's the best fighter plane in the world. Very fast, a joy to fly." A brief smile lit up his stern face. "There's nothing it can't outrun. One pilot in my squadron shot down a P-40."

"With an American pilot?" said Tad, suddenly alarmed.

"Yes. It was war. Our people identified him, and your government was allowed to recover the body. I honestly don't know why he was flying for the Communists. But I'll tell you this, Tadichi-san, your P-40 is a good, sturdy plane but no match for the Zero. It's too slow and has a poor rate of climb. I can fly circles around it."

Tad felt a chill in the air, and though he reserved comment, he wondered how many American pilots would die if they had to face Japan's pilots in their superior fighters. Far too many Americans refused to believe that the Japanese could fly at all.

Deciding to change the subject, Tad said, "I have never met anyone like Sayuri. She is like sunshine, radiant but subtle, understated, if you know what I mean. Besides being exceptionally beautiful, she has a certain elegance, ephemeral, almost spiritual."

"I'm impressed that you understand that. Most men don't. In Japan, we use the word *shibumi* to describe people like her. She is capable of accepting the transience and imperfection of life while approaching perfection herself. I know that sounds convoluted, but she is unique. And it doesn't take the tortuous training of a Japanese fighter pilot to see that you are, what do you call it, 'head over heels' for her."

A unabashed grin formed on Tad's face. "Well, Brother, you've got me in your sights. I suspect you like her as well. You're not going to shoot me down, are you?"

"I once read about Icarus who flew too close to the sun. If you fly too close, your plane will disintegrate. I would not fly too close to the sun, Tadichi-san."

Tad heard the warning in his brother's voice. He wondered if it referred to more than Sayuri. He realized that he didn't want anything to come between him and the brother he was rediscovering.

* * *

Tad slowed the car to take a curve and came to a stop beside a grove of coconut palms.

"Where are we, Tad-san?" asked Sayuri. At first, she had wondered if it would be improper for her to be escorted around Oahu by Tad unchaperoned, but neither Sensei nor Kimi had objected. One afternoon, they had strolled along the beach at Waikiki and watched surfers with long boards riding enormous waves. Sayuri had run laughing from the surf that splashed about her ankles. And she enjoyed Tad's company. He was unlike any of the proper, serious young men she knew.

"It's called the Moanalua Gardens. It's very peaceful here. I think you'll like it. There's a koi pond, and a *torii*. It's a bit of Japan here in Oahu for the Nisei when they get homesick."

40

Tad exited the car and held the passenger side door open for her, extending a hand to help her rise, which she did gracefully, in one fluid movement. Tad was enchanted.

Though Koizumi had suggested that she wear western clothing while in Hawaii, Sayuri had chosen to wear her green kimono, one that she had brought for the trip to Oahu. As she looked around, she realized that it made her conspicuous. She looked down, suddenly shy.

Sensing her embarrassment, Tad said, "I think you look beautiful."

"Will I offend anyone?" she asked him.

"Of course not!" Tad reassured her. "This is America, not Japan, and nobody can tell you what you must wear, or who you can or cannot be with." He was relieved when she looked up again.

Side by side, they strolled through gardens, stopping when they came to the koi pond. They stood on the curved red bridge spanning the water and watched the spotted fish slip beneath overlapping lily pads, occasionally finding an insect that alighted on the pond. Sayuri breathed a sigh of happiness. How odd, she thought, that she should have to come here to feel as if she had come home. This place, here, now, felt like the Japan of her childhood. Tad put his hand on hers. Only in private would such a gesture have been acceptable in Japan, but now Tokyo seemed very far away.

Sayuri said, "Even though the clothing styles have changed and more women are employed now, I do not think relations between men and women have changed much in Japan since your mother lived there. Women are expected to be very deferential and married by the time they are eighteen. The Emperor is encouraging married women to have many children."

Tad considered this. "Is Japan is underpopulated, or is there some other reason?"

"I think he wants us to have many children, especially male children for the military. But I'm not ready to marry. I was working for a fashion magazine before the government closed it down. Now I help Sensei in her ikebana shop."

"And you have not accepted proposals from all the men who want to marry you?" said Tad, only half-jokingly.

"I do not have any boyfriends in Japan," she said, shaking her head in a way that made him want to hold her very close.

"And what about in Hawaii?" he said more seriously.

"Maybe," Sayuri said shyly. "Maybe I do. Perhaps just one."

* * *

"She's still getting ready, Tad," said his mother when he came into the house. Having wangled a leave, he had called earlier to invite Sayuri to lunch at a very special place.

"That's fine, we have plenty of time." Looking about, he asked, "So where is Koizumi? I was hoping to speak with him."

"He went out about an hour ago. Did you know that he is a very good artist? He showed me one of his drawings; I think it's a Japanese battleship. It was very good."

"Really? I would like to see it. Maybe he can teach me something; my artwork was never that good. May I see it?"

"No, he took the sketch book with him. He bought it a few days ago. But he should be back for dinner. You can ask him about it then." Kimi smiled at her elder son. She was glad that both her sons were such fine young men, and quietly relieved that they were getting along so well.

Lunch was at Lau Yee Chai, said to be the first Chinese restaurant on the island. Sayuri was amazed by the quantity of food set before her. A few people, perhaps from the mainland, glanced in their direction, but the locals paid them scant attention.

"Hawaiians call themselves 'the golden people'. They are a mixture of Polynesians, Portuguese, Anglo, Chinese, Japanese, people from the Philippines, and anyone else who got washed ashore," said Tad, seeing Sayuri glance nervously about. "It's hard to escape the sun, so almost everyone gets a tan. And everyone here, regardless of where they come from or their ancestry, considers themselves Hawaiian. The original inhabitants, the true Hawaiians, got here a few thousand years ago. They call anyone who is not truly native a *haole*, but it's not an offensive term. These islands are far more welcoming of different races than most other places on earth."

"Sensei told me how your father and mother met, and the difficulties they faced being from different countries."

"It was a very dangerous time. The tensions between Russia and Japan were escalating. And it was eight years from the time they met until they were married, with a war in between," said Tad. But war was the last thing he wanted to talk about. He reached across the table and held her hands. Taking a deep breath, he said, "I wish to say that I am extremely fond of you; I think you know that. And I am so happy that you are here and enjoy being with me. I have never met anyone like you. And I want to be with you and I want you to be with me."

"I would love that, Tad-san. And I pray that someday we can be together. Together for ever. But I have to return to Japan, and you are in your country's navy. I think that the best thing we can do is enjoy the time we have together. But yes, I wish to be with you."

Tad fished in his pocket for a piece of paper and said, "Who knows, someday I might travel to Japan, and I would want nothing more than to be with you again. Will you give me an address so I can find you?"

"Shall I write it in *Konji*?"

"Of course; I can read Japanese."

She deftly wrote the characters and handed him the paper. "I would love it if you could visit me. I live with Sensei above her ikebana shop. It is very pretty, with many flowers and beautiful vases. You will find the shop on *Yuri* street."

"*Yuri*, Lily street. That seems appropriate."

Sayuri smiled and said, "There is a cherry blossom tree beside the shop; a present from your mother, many years ago. Sensei uses sprigs of cherry blossoms for the ikebana projects her students make. It is a beautiful tree."

"I can imagine a cherry blossom in your hair," said Tad, thinking all he wanted to do was kiss this beautiful girl.

* * *

Koizumi looked surprised, if not downright dismayed, by Sayuri's appearance that evening when she came out of her room. She wore a long black evening gown and just a hint of lipstick. Tad, in a double-breasted navy-blue suit, stared at her until his mother said, with an amused smile, "Have you been turned into stone?"

"Actually, I think I'm about to melt," he said. Then to Koizumi he said wryly, "Don't look so happy for me, Brother. If you find yourself a cute Hawaiian girl you can join the party."

Koizumi was scowling as they left.

On the patio of the Moana Hotel, tiki torches sent glowing sparks into the night sky, and dancers swayed to a soothing Bing Crosby melody. The song, "Only Forever," fit perfectly, thought Tad as he brushed Sayuri's cheek with a kiss. He felt her move closer, and Bing Crosby's voice erased the rest of the world.

> *"How long would it take me to be near you if you beckoned?*
> *"Off hand, I would figure less than a second."*

They seemed to meld into one, and Tad was hardly surprised when she said, "I have never done this before or ever asked before, but can we go somewhere to be alone?"

The narrow road bordered by palms was dark but for a quarter moon. Tad drove slowly along the twisting road eight miles beyond the city. Except for the chirp of insects and the rustling of leaves in the night breeze, all was quiet.

"This cottage belongs to a friend of mine. He won't mind if we use it," said Tad as he led Sayuri from the car. They slipped inside. The simple dwelling had no electricity, but there was a lantern. He struck a match from the box beside the lantern, touched the bright flame to the wick, and blew out the match. The lantern issued a soft glow.

She only came up to his shoulder and he felt her trembling as she held onto him. Her face pressed into his chest, and without looking up she said, "Am I being too, too...." She could not think of the word.

"No, you are with me. That is all that matters. You said that we should make the best of the time we have together. I don't know what the future is, but I do know that I love you more than anything else. And I want you so very, very much."

She answered with a kiss. Moonlight danced between low clouds as a pattering rain tapped on the metal roof. He breathed in the scent of her long hair, not noticing or caring how their clothes fell away. So delicate, he thought, as he held her and became part of her. Gently, slowly, their kiss became a deeper exploration and sharing. Tad swept her into his arms and carried her over to the bed. Soft moans and words of love answered his attentions, and down Sayuri's cheeks flowed tears from a decade of despair and loneliness.

Afterward, as he gently traced his fingers over her breasts and through her hair, he said, "Do you think it possible for you to stay here, in Hawaii? My mother will let you stay with her."

Sayuri said nothing for a long moment. "I don't think it is up to me. If it were, I would stay, to be with you."

She was quiet again, then said, "I had no idea that I would meet you, that I would fall in love with you, when I was ordered to accompany your brother and Sensei here."

"Ordered?"

"Yes. As things are right now, hardly any Japanese are allowed to travel here. The government regulates all who desire to leave Japan, even on vacation. I cannot be certain and I have no way of really knowing, but I suspect that Koizumi-san was told to come to Hawaii for a special purpose. Our visit made a convenient excuse, since a chaperone would be required. At the end of our visit the government expects us to return. If we did not...."

"So, my dear brother is here as a spy?" Tad said thoughtfully.

"I do not know if he is a spy in the formal sense or just getting an impression of what life on the island is like."

"But if the visit is about espionage, why would they send a a pilot instead of a trained spy?" asked Tad.

"I can only guess that it is because he is not known to American intelligence, and visiting his mother makes perfect sense. But he is very highly regarded by his uncle, who is an admiral. And from what Sensei told me, Itomo-san is high up in Japanese intelligence."

"That puts the puzzle together," said Tad, deep in contemplation. Frowning, he said, "Do you think that his attention to you is an act? A way of disguising his real motive?"

"I know that he respects me and does not want to see me harmed."

"And he doesn't want me to be with you, that much is clear. I suspect he is jealous of us being together."

"The only thing your brother loves is flying." Then she said, "No, that is not true. Koizumi does like me."

"But does he love you?" asked Tad.

"He is very reserved and has not said as much. But perhaps he does. Sensei thinks that he would be a good husband for me. He has been visiting her at the ikebana shop, and I know it is an excuse to see me."

"And do you have feelings for him?"

"I don't love him, but I do respect him. He was very solicitous and consoling after my intended died."

"So, when you're all back in Japan, I imagine that he will eventually propose to you, if for no other reason than to eliminate competition," said Tad.

"I'm afraid so." Sayuri sighed and curled a lock of Tad's blond hair through her fingers. "It's hard to imagine that you two are actually brothers. He thinks of himself as a samurai. A warrior in the most traditional sense. I think he really enjoys war. You seem so different from him," she said.

"I guess we are different. I'm not pleased about going to war, but I do like to fly. We are both pilots and share that exhilaration. I've had my share of fights when I was young, but I'm not looking forward to killing other pilots, seeing them burn up in their cockpits. In truth, Koizumi is a stranger to me. We are brothers, but we are worlds apart, and I'm beginning to be afraid that he will be my enemy before he becomes my friend. And if he wants to marry you he may never be my friend."

"I will not marry him if I can help it. I want you, only you," she said, her arms pulling him tight.

But the words "if I can help it" sent a chill into his heart.

It was three in the morning when Tad walked Sayuri to the door of his mother's house. They kissed and held each other for a brief moment before she opened the door and stepped inside and Tad turned away. A single lamp glowed in the living room. Koizumi rose from a chair.

"I have been waiting for you. You are very late," said Koizumi in a tense and accusatory voice.

"I was with your brother and was perfectly safe. I appreciate your concern, but there was nothing to worry about," she said with quiet composure.

"You are a Japanese woman and I believe that you have been behaving in a very un-Japanese way. It is not proper for you to be consorting with a foreigner, a possible enemy of your country."

"Consorting? A foreigner? An *enemy*?" said Sayuri, suddenly angered. "I am not 'consorting,' I am in love with this 'possible enemy,' who happens to be your brother. And Japanese or not, you have no right to condemn me."

"But I do! There are things I know about, things I dare not tell you. There is no future for you and this man. We will be..." he paused, and in a barely audible voice said, "enemies. Terrible, terrible enemies."

"You don't know that!" said Sayuri.

The voices had awoken Kimi. Alarmed, she now entered the living room. "What is going on? What time is it?" she asked, looking from Sayuri to Koizumi.

"Too late for her to be coming home," said Koizumi coldly.

"You were with Tad?" asked Kimi in a hopeful voice.

"Yes, and we had a wonderful time. I'm afraid Koizumi-san has never experienced love and knows not what joy it truly is."

"Koizumi-san," said Kimi, kneeling down, "You know and I know that Sayuri-san and your brother care very much for each other. Like you, Tad is a fine man, a noble man. I am pleased that you wish Sayuri the very best, and I know that you believe that she should marry a Japanese man. But it is impossible to argue with love. Let's allow things to take their course. You and I have no influence over fate, and perhaps it was fate that brought Sayuri-san here to be with your elder brother."

For a moment Koizumi was silent. He would not disturb the sanctity of his mother's home, and those last words had struck deep. Not only must a samurai accept fate, an elder brother is owed deference and respect. Nodding slowly, he said, "*Okasan*, I have been too critical, but truthfully I don't know whether to be happy for Sayuri and my brother or terribly sad. She must return to Japan with me, and whether she ever sees Tadichi-san again is, as you say, up to fate."

* * *

A deep, long blast sounded from the ship bound for Japan, as porters carried the last of the luggage up the gangplank. Waiting impatiently, Koizumi stood with his mother while Tad held Sayuri's hands and said, "We will be together. I promise you. No matter what, we will find each other again."

He brushed a tear from her eye, and she said, "I think fate will tolerate nothing less. We will write to each other, and perhaps you will come to Japan. That will make me very happy."

"I will find you and I will marry you. But it may not be for a while."

Koizumi heard the remark and stiffened. Tad turned and extended his hand, but his brother, standing militarily stiff, gave a short bow. Tad considered the coolness and bowed in turn. Then, upon recognizing his rebuke, Koizumi extended his hand and shook that of his brother.

"I wish you well," said Tad. "I hope we can meet again during better times."

"That is also my wish," said Koizumi. Then he bowed to his mother. She put her arms around him and said, "I love you. Be safe; come back to us."

"I shall do all I can to see you again," he said, in an attempt to undo the unpleasantness of the night before.

Tad and Kimi watched Sensei, Koizumi and Sayuri ascend the gangplank and disappear into the ship. Moments later, they appeared on deck and waved. There was another blast of the horn, lines were cast off, and tugs moved the small liner into the channel. Twenty minutes later the ship was a small speck, and then it was gone over the horizon.

"And you too will be leaving soon," said Tad's mother, as he drove them back to her house.

"Tomorrow, I'm afraid."

"I hope you will see her again. She is a lovely young woman. But I am worried for her, for Sensei and Koizumi-san. And I'm worried for you," said Kimi.

"There is still hope," said Tad. "I don't think either Japan or the U.S. really wants war. I just hope that whatever happens we all live through it."

His mother was silent, remembering a past war, and pondering what she knew and guessed.

* * *

On the twentieth of April, *Yorktown* left Pearl Harbor for the Caribbean. Tad stood at the fantail and waved farewell to his mother as the ship, her flight deck laden with aircraft, slowly pulled away from the dock. Beyond the harbor they were joined by destroyers. A signal lamp flashed between the carrier and the closest escort, and then the ships, small toys upon a great sea, moved out until they could no longer be seen from shore.

Kimi drove back to her home and opened a kitchen cupboard. From behind a stack of plates she extracted a single sheet of drawing paper. A map in precise detail sketched the location of barracks, fuel depots, airfields, radar emplacements and the location of ships. She closed the cabinet door and slowly walked to the window that looked toward the harbor. Briefly she considered giving the map to the authorities. But then, she thought, there would be complications, questions asked that might even affect Tad and his status in the Navy. Only problems would result.

She would never tell anyone, she decided, how she had found Koizumi's drawing tablet the night before and looked through it, how she had carefully removed the sketch. Passing his room that morning, she had seen his alarm at the missing page. But he had said nothing, not wishing to accuse anyone or cause an unseemly incident prior to departing.

She looked again at the *Konji* and *hirikana* characters in the margin, all denoting specifics valuable to intelligence agencies. She breathed deeply, sighed, and moved into the kitchen. There she turned on the stove's gas burner. The paper caught fire, and moments later she waved away the last lingering smoke.

Sitting in her garden she wondered what would become of Koizumi-san, her second son, now surely the enemy of her first son. She shivered in the cool air of evening and wiped away a tear.

A BLOSSOM IN THE ASHES

* * *

April gave way to May, and May to June, and Kimi still had not received a letter from Alexei. Doctor Thompson, solicitous as always, said comforting words when he saw her worried and downcast.

"He wrote that he would be back in August, and that's not too far away. We shall have a celebration when he returns," said the doctor.

There was a fine sea breeze on the quiet morning of June twenty-second. Kimi purposefully walked into the waiting room of the hospital. Seeing the receptionist, she said, 'Hello, Sandra. Has Doctor Thompson arrived? He wanted me to see his new patient."

"He's in his office. Some others are there too. I think they're listening to the radio."

A feeling of trepidation coursed through Kimi and she hurried down the hall. Almost the entire staff were huddled in the office, and several were standing outside the open door. As she drew near, Kimi could hear the announcer's voice, but she could not make out the words. When the broadcast ended, Doctor Thompson said, "Okay, we'll see how the German invasion of the Soviet Union plays out. There's nothing we can do about it. It doesn't involve the United States. We have new patients coming in today, folks. So let's go to work."

He spied Kimi standing by the door. Seeing her puzzlement, he motioned for her to enter as the rest of the staff flowed around her, heading out to their rounds.

"Germany has just invaded the Soviet Union. There seems to be some degree of chaos in Russia. There's not much more we know yet."

"Alexei," whispered Kimi, on hand stealing to her heart. "He was supposed to leave in two days. Can he still get out?"

"I don't know," Doctor Thompson said somberly. "Perhaps. Let's hope." Then he wrapped his arms about Kimi and held her as she cried.

Chapter 5
Tokyo, Japan
April, 1941

A light rain was falling. Sayuri removed the wooden *getas* from her feet and and put the damp clogs by the door of the ikebana shop. Sensei Hiroku was helping a tall, blonde woman with a flower arrangement. Seeing Sayuri, the woman bowed. Sayuri bowed slightly deeper, acknowledging the superior status of a diplomat's wife.

"You remember Ingrid Svenson, don't you, my dear?" said Sensei.

"The wife of the Swedish ambassador, yes. You have created a lovely and perfectly balanced floral display," said Sayuri in English.

"You are too kind. I am just a novice, but Sensei is teaching me, and I am eternally grateful. She has even given me a sprig of blossoms from the cherry tree. Such a lovely tree. And she has told me of how I might be of help to you. I hope you do not mind that Sensei has explained your situation, and I really do wish to help. Young love is so romantic, but dangerous in these times. Of course, I must get my husband's approval, and that is not a guaranteed thing. If he does agree, we must be very discreet, and not a word said to anybody."

Sayuri looked to Sensei and said, "I am not entirely sure of what Ingrid-san is suggesting, and I don't want to put her in any danger."

"I will work on my floral arrangement. Why don't you talk to Sensei," said the ambassador's wife.

"Please forgive me if I was indiscreet," said Sensei. "I know that you want to correspond with Tad-ishi without your letters being intercepted. Ingrid-san suggested that your letters be taken out of Japan by diplomatic pouch when her husband's mail goes to Sweden. Diplomatic mail cannot be read by Japanese authorities."

"I don't wish to put Ingrid-san or her husband in any danger," said Sayuri. "They could be expelled or worse if my letters were ever discovered."

Sensei pondered a long moment, then said, "I understand how you feel for Tadishi-san, but you are right to be concerned. You may have to consider other options if the world situation worsens. And Koizumi-san came by early this morning looking for you. I'm sure he intends to propose. Forgive me for saying this, Sayuri-san, but he is a very good catch."

"Sensei, I have no desire to marry Koizumi-san. I know he is a patriot and a good man, but I feel only pain at the thought of being with him. Please understand that."

Sensei looked away for a moment. Then, turning back to the girl, she said, "Perhaps I made a mistake. Maybe I should not have spoken to Ingrid-san."

"It was brave of you to speak to her on my behalf, Sensei. I appreciate it very much, and I want so badly to write to Tad-san. I think about him day and night. I just wish that I could be with him, no matter where he is."

She stopped, looked away, then said, "I would die for him, Sensei. I really would."

Sensei put her arms around Sayuri and in a very soft voice said, "But he is so far away, and I fear that there will be war. A very long and bitter war. Love is romantic, I know; I too loved a man once who was denied me. But Sayuri-san, Koizumi loves you, and he is here. It would be good for you to marry. Koizumi-san can care for you. I am sorry to say it, but Tadishi-san cannot." When Sayuri did not reply, she continued.

"These are difficult times. We women can't always do as we wish, and you will need a man to help you live. I have a premonition that things will get very bad before they get better. So, consider Koizumi. But if you insist on loving Tad-san, I wish you well."

"Yes, it is a dream, Sensei, but I will live my dream. So, please give me a few moments, and I will write that letter. I am more indebted to you than I can ever say or hope to repay."

* * *

Jeremy Shinagawa was paying a visit. He knelt on the tatami mat across from Sensei Hiroku and Sayuri. "Is Kumi-san coming today?" he asked Sensei.

"She should be here soon, unless her patriotic duties have detained her. Perhaps I should caution her about you, Jeremy-san. You Americans are so fast with women."

"Caution her? I am the epitome of a gentleman. I have exquisite manners and only the loftiest intentions toward her," he said with a sheepish grin.

"But unlike Japanese men, you have no sense of subtlety. I am amazed that she wastes her time with you. I should tell her to find a nice pedicab driver instead. He doesn't even have to know how to read or write. Yes that's exactly what I will tell her," Hiroku said with mock seriousness.

"Sensei, I don't think that is subtle at all! I am absolutely mortified. I must beg her forgiveness if I can think of any grievous errors I have committed."

Sayuri covered her face and stifled a giggle.

"Here she is now," said Sensei, as Kumi Hayashi took off her *getas* and walked delicately across the small room. "Kumi-san, I was just telling Sayuri-san about how well-mannered is our scholar, Jeremy-san, who has returned from Kyushu. He will make an excellent history professor. If I were younger and a student, I would surely take one of his classes." Sensei smiled beatifically, leaving Sayuri in near hysterics.

Jeremy rose and bowed to Kumi, saying, "Sensei Hiroku is far too kind. I am but a poor student doing insignificant research. But I am grateful for her kindness; she is so charming and complimentary. I do have tickets to a kabuki play tomorrow night. Would you care to accompany me? Sensei and Sayuri-san may attend too. I did buy four tickets."

"I would love to, but I volunteered to make bandages with the other ladies of our council. Perhaps some other time," Kumi said, with a slight bow.

"Well," said Jeremy, plainly disappointed, "I must be leaving. I told Professor Shimura that I would give him a detailed report of my findings, not that they are terribly significant. But he is very attentive and I am honored, considering how revered he is at the university."

Later that day, Sayuri and Kumi strolled past the shops of the High City, only to be dismayed by the lack of the finery that would have been available only two years before. Disappointed, they took a tram to Ueno park, where the leaves of cherry trees were darkening to summer green.

"So, you do like Jeremy-san," said Sayuri as they found a bench in the nearly deserted park.

"He's very sweet, and I think he is funny. But my parents would never permit me to marry him. After all, he is an American, even though he looks and speaks Japanese." Kumi sighed and added, "It's too bad that he will have to go back to America."

"Did he say when he is leaving?"

"At the end of the semester. But he said that he may come back if he can obtain permission." Kumi's voice trailed off. Changing the subject, she said, "Have you always lived with Sensei?"

"I thought you knew," said Sayuri.

Kumi shook her head. "I don't mean to pry."

"We are distant relatives, and my mother was a friend of hers. My parents had a nice little house with a blue tile roof. I was a child when the Tokyo earthquake struck. When the ground began to shake, we all went outside. At first I was excited, and I ran across an empty field. My parents, standing beside the house, called me to come back. But I grew terrified, the ground was shaking so hard, and I simply crouched down and covered my head...." her voice trailed off, quavering. "When I finally turned around, the house... had collapsed. My parents were killed by falling tiles, half-buried. Sensei came to the house two days later and found me sitting beside their bodies. So many people were killed.... It took the *eta*, the village people, a long time to deal with the dead."

"So, Sensei found you and took you in?" said Kumi softly.

"Yes, and I've lived with her ever since. I have been extremely fortunate. Do you know that Tad-san's mother, Kimi-san, also attended Sensei's ikebana classes?"

"Wa! How extraordinary!"

Sayuri smiled. "His father actually ran into Kimi-san as she was leaving the shop. He bowled her right over. Kimi-san told me that at first she was shocked by this tall *gaijin* who stood over her, babbling apologies. Later she thought it was very funny. Years later, after they were married, they moved to America."

"The only thing I know about America is what I see in the movies. But I don't think any of us will be seeing American movies any time soon," remarked Kumi. Looking into the distance, she said, "I received a letter from my cousin yesterday. Some of it was blacked out by the censors, but he's a pilot with the Kido Butai, on an aircraft carrier at sea. I have no idea when he will be back. My family is anxious about him."

"I think it's far too early to worry, Kumi-san. We are not at war with the Americans. But I will pray for him at the shrine tomorrow," said Sayuri, hoping to calm her friend's deepest fears.

Tokyo
October, 1941

"I just got in; I hope I haven't made you late," Koizumi said to his uncle.

"The meeting has just started. You flew in from Kagoshima?" said Admiral Karamatsu. He stood beside the entrance to naval headquarters. At a nod from the admiral, the armed guards allowed Koizumi to enter.

"Yes, Kyushu Island is a perfect place for training; mountainous, with a city beside the shore. We were testing the new torpedo with the attached wooden fins."

"And were the fins successful?" asked Karamatsu, as they walked down the hall.

"Even better than expected. They were tested under many conditions." Koizumi fell silent, then said, "Uncle, I will tell of my intelligence gathering as you ordered, but I would rather not mention the presence of my brother. It would throw a shadow over my credibility. I do not want them to think I have... divided loyalties."

"Did you communicate anything to him that would jeopardize the mission?"

"No, sir, absolutely not."

"Then his presence is inconsequential. We both know where our fealty lies. Be brief, be succinct, and answer all questions," said Karamatsu. The stopped. An armed soldier saluted and opened the door to the war room.

Combined Fleet Admiral Isoroku Yamamoto, Captain Kanji Ogawa, the officer in charge of Naval Intelligence, Admiral Osami Nagano, and five other high ranking officers looked up from their most recent reports as Admiral Itomo Karamatsu entered the room. They eyed the young officer who followed him.

The admiral bowed to the assembled officers and said, "Please excuse my interruption, but I wish to introduce pilot Lieutenant Karamatsu of the Imperial Japanese Navy."

Koizumi immediately bowed, hands stiffly at his side, then stood at attention.

"You are aware," continued Admiral Karamatsu, "that I, working with Captain Ogawa, sent my nephew here to the island of Oahu some months ago. Naval intelligence communicates with our Embassy there, and we are in contact with a German agent on the island."

The assembled officers gave Admiral Karamatsu their complete attention. As a young destroyer captain, he had participated in the naval battle at Port Arthur that crippled the Russian fleet during the Russo-Japanese war. At the conclusive battle at Tsushima, he had helped sink a Russian cruiser and then rescued an enemy officer who had nearly drowned: a noble act of a true samurai.

"I suggest that we listen to his observations, since he was in direct communication with our informant on the island."

All eyes turned to the pilot, and Admiral Karamatsu took a seat. Standing at attention, Koizumi stared straight ahead. In the silence, he felt very much alone.

"Stand at ease, Lieutenant," said Admiral Yamamoto. "Give us your observations and tell how you were able to obtain them."

"Yes, sir," said Koizumi, bowing. His training asserted itself; he was accustomed to showing respect to superior officers—they just had never been quite so superior before. "Using the cover of a family reunion, since my esteemed uncle's sister lives on Oahu, I was able to travel about freely. Security is extremely lax, and I behaved like the other ethnic Japanese. There are about one hundred and sixty thousand on the island."

"That's a very large number," said Captain Kanji Ogawa thoughtfully. "Are they loyal to Japan?"

"Regretfully, sir, they appear to be loyal to the United States."

"But they might reconsider and collaborate with us if, say, Japanese troops were in the vicinity," pressed the Captain.

"Sir, I fear not. I had the opportunity to sound out many of them in an oblique way, and they consider themselves Hawaiian-American."

"Continue with your observations," said Yamamoto, a one-time Harvard student who was well aware of Nisei loyalty to the United States.

"Yes, sir. I rented a car and drove about the island and observed Pearl Harbor and its defenses. I noticed that fleet operations take place during weekdays and often on Saturdays, but nearly all crews are ashore on Sunday when the majority of the fleet is dockside. Oil storage tanks are not well defended, nor are the airfields. There is a mobile radar installation at a place called Kahuku Point, but it is not always operating and Americans do not put much trust in that technology. On the whole, personnel on the island are relaxed and there is little anxiety about war or an attack. Much of this I was able to observe myself. My questions and observations were answered and confirmed by our agent, who met with me as pre-arranged at a time and place of the Captain's choosing." Koizumi bowed respectfully in the direction of Captain Kanji Ogawa. This was the moment he would have offered up his sketchbook for examination, but the important, detailed drawing had been removed—by whom?—and the other drawings of ships, planes, and the port conveyed no more information that these officers already knew from other sources. He had failed in his most important assignment, and could barely hope that anything in his report was of significance.

He had told his uncle that his attempts to get about the island privately and sketch defenses had been thwarted by the presence of crowds and the excess of family feeling his mother had lavished on him. He had also very carefully trimmed away the ragged edge of the torn page before showing the sketch book to the admiral.

"What you said about Sundays is very interesting," said Mioru Genda, First Air Fleet Commander. "What about fighter air cover? Is that grounded on Sundays?"

"There are hardly any flights on Sunday, Commander, especially in the morning. Most of the military is either at church or sleeping off Saturday night's beer. On Sunday, nothing happens until well past noon."

Commander Genda looked at Admiral Yamamoto and said, "That information was not provided in earlier intelligence. I believe it should be catalogued for future reference." Turning to Koizumi, he said, "I applaud your valuable observation. You have served us and the Emperor well."

"Indeed," said Admiral Yamamoto. "Sometimes it only takes a single fragment of intelligence to change the course of history. Perhaps you have given us that fragment, Lieutenant Karamatsu."

"I believe he has, but now he will wait in the outer office," said Admiral Karamatsu.

Koizumi bowed deeply, pivoted smartly, left the war room.

"He is an astute young man," commented Yamamoto.

"Thank you, Admiral. He has already flown in the China war and has several kills to his credit. I trust that he will prove himself in the future."

Yamamoto looked thoughtful.

Fleet Admiral Osami Nagano spoke up. "I think it's time to begin final preparations. Perhaps it should have been done earlier, but Prime Minister Konoe argued for more negotiations and concessions from the Americans, and that delayed our planning."

"There are difficulties," pointed out Air Commander Genza. "We had to take the airfields in Indochina; the bases were critical. Unfortunately, the Americans froze our assets in retaliation and established an oil embargo. Eighty per cent of our oil came from the United States, which means that our oil reserves for the Navy will be seriously depleted in the near future."

"We did ask the Dutch East Indies for three million barrels, but they only offered to sell us a third of that," said Nagano.

"The Americans also terminated shipments of scrap metal and copper, even though we offered to make peace with China and modify the Tripartite Pact with Germany."

"But Tojo rejected that idea," said Admiral Yamamoto.

"So we must get oil from the Dutch islands and Brunei, and tin and rubber from Malaya. We want the resources of the Philippines, but that is an American protectorate, and that means war," said Nagano.

"They are aware of that," said Admiral Yamamoto. "The Americans expect a strike, but I am confident they have no idea where, how, or when." The admiral glanced at a report he had prepared, then said, "I sent an intelligence section to Italy after Operation Judgment. That attack utilized British torpedo bombers which crippled half the Italian Navy. That very successful attack gave us the idea of how to proceed in regard to America. We expect to carry out a crippling blow to their Pacific fleet."

"In 1904 the Americans praised the same kind of attack we launched on the Russian navy at Port Arthur. Admiral Togo crippled the Russian fleet when it was anchored and asleep. The American press said it was masterful, a virtual repeat of what Admiral Nelson did at Copenhagen during the Napoleonic war. I wonder if the Americans will think our attack so praiseworthy this time," said Genza.

"You are right in requiring a decisive battle with the Americans," said Fleet Admiral Nagano. "Hit them hard enough, put their fleet on the bottom, and they will sue for peace. There is a very strong anti-war movement in the United States. The Americans remember how costly their efforts were in their European war twenty years ago. It will be preferable to agree to a peace with the concessions we demand. Besides, a war against us will bring Germany and Italy in on our side. The Tripartite pact requires it."

Admiral Isoroku Yamamoto sat silent for a long moment, then said, "Admiral, I only hope that you are correct in your assumption of American reluctance to fight. Originally, I expressed dismay about going to war against the United

States, but now, considering the critical situation facing Japan, I am committed to it."

He gathered his thoughts; then, looking at the somber faces, he said, "As you all know, I lived in the United States and went to Harvard University and the Naval War College. I became friends with many Americans. They treated me well, according to their customs. They possess little of our reserve; they are all smiles and often engage in a superficial chumminess. Some would say that they are shallow or flippant, and terribly soft, safe behind their ocean barriers. But I know that appearance conceals a hardened steel core."

There was stillness in the war room when the Admiral, in a cold, cryptic voice said, "I have expressed it before and I will say it again. America is a sleeping giant and I tremble at waking it. Americans have a terrible resolve. Eighty years ago, they fought a civil war in which over six hundred thousand soldiers died because neither side would give up. Therefore, it is my firm belief that we must absolutely destroy their ability to make war in one swift move. Any war with them must last no more than six months. After that, I promise nothing, and I fear the worst."

Itomo Karamatsu rejoined his nephew once the meeting concluded. When Koizumi glanced at him, the Admiral merely said, "You and your squadrons must hit all the targets and do so thoroughly. You must show no mercy. The fleet will fly the 'Z' flag, the same one Admiral Togo flew at Tsushima. This attack must be Japan's finest hour."

"I will do everything in my power, and so will my squadron," said Koizumi. "We will absolutely destroy their fleet."

He thought of his brother, and his seeming indifference to life's exigencies. But then there was Tad's occasional cold, killing stare, the one of a fighter pilot.

Koizumi did not sleep well that night.

Chapter 6
Tokyo, Japan
November, 1941

Jeremy Shinagawa fairly raced from the university to Professor Shimura's house. Bursting in, he bowed to his mentor and said, "Professor, I have discovered an amazing thing! Samurai Nigato of the Tokugawa did *not* commit seppuku, as was believed. No, after his sister was beheaded by the Tokugawa, he switched sides and was killed when riding alone a week later. To save face, the shogun of the Tokugawa covered up the murder. And since he wrote the history, nobody ever knew the truth."

Professor Shimura nodded and said, "Very interesting." He sneezed three times and wiped his nose with a well-used handkerchief.

Jeremy waited for him to say something more, since they usually spent an hour over tea discussing the what ifs and misconceptions of history. But now the professor sat at his desk, his eyes not focused on anything.

"Doctor Shimura, are you okay?" asked Jeremy. The professor was always the model of hospitality and civility, offering his guests *ocha*, the green tea of his childhood. Now, instead, he sat silently, staring into a distance Jeremy could not see.

Finally, without looking up, the professor spoke. "I really don't know an easy way to tell you this. You are my finest student; I think you know that. And I value the historical work you have accomplished while at the university. But something has happened and things have changed. Changed terribly."

Jeremy waited. The house was silent. "I need not remind you, Jeremy-san, that although you look Japanese and speak Japanese, you are an American, a citizen of the United States. And though our countries are not yet at war the government has put certain restrictions on aliens, especially those whose interests do not coincide with Japan."

Taking a deep breath, the Professor said, "I had a visit this morning from the Kempeitai. They wanted to know the names and locations of every non-Japanese in my department and throughout the entire university. They are aware of the fact that you reside in my house. They informed me that there is now a prohibition against aliens, particularly Americans, residing on the campus or in the homes of instructors. There will be an expulsion of all such students in the coming days. I must obey the order. I regret it deeply but I have little choice. It was made quite clear to me that not reporting students would be considered a high crime for which I could be imprisoned."

"I understand," said Jeremy, visibly shaken. "I... I appreciate the honor I have enjoyed of being a guest in your house. I will cherish the memory of your hospitality for many years to come."

Silence permeated the room.

"Professor, what do you suggest I do?"

"I wish I could tell you. The Kempeitai asked where I thought you might go, might flee to. I told them that as far as

I know, you have no place to take sanctuary. I suggest that you go to the American embassy, and go there quickly. I understand that a number of Americans are doing the same."

"Then I will hurry. I don't wish to put you in any danger," said Jeremy. "I will pack and be gone in twenty minutes. Again, I value everything you have done for me."

He bowed deeply, and the professor did the same.

Suitcase in hand, Jeremy exited the house, put on his shoes and began to walk. He stopped at a corner where five Japanese soldiers were waiting to cross. He suddenly felt out of place, conspicuous with his suitcase, unwelcome, an enemy; an alien.

Two of the soldiers turned to him and gave him a curious look. Instantly Jeremy bowed. The soldiers nodded curtly, then purposefully crossed the street. Jeremy stood rooted to the spot. He looked up and down the street, the realization coming to him that he truly was a *gaijin*, an 'outside person.' The bustling Tokyo crowd belonged here; they were part of the fabric of the culture and supported the Emperor and his government in everything required of them. And he did not.

How quickly things had changed. Only days ago, *hours* ago, he had been a dedicated graduate student, given respect and assistance in his research. He had been a guest speaker in front of Professor Shimura's classes where undergrads listened intently to his discussion of samurai tactics of a bygone age. In this period of heightened militarism, the ethos of the samurai was, for many Japanese, something to emulate. But it had become progressively harder for him to glorify the Tokugawa samurai while Japanese soldiers were bayoneting Chinese civilians. He had answered students' questions with politic care, knowing that the "Co-Prosperity Sphere" was touted as a boon for all Asia.

On occasion, he would be asked about life in the United States, for he'd made it known that, though his parents were from Japan, he had been born and raised in California. Inevitably, the question of Japanese-American relations arose. He tried to be as diplomatic as possible; he knew that plainclothes members of the Kempeitai attended classes to determine if anything subversive was being taught.

The chill of the November night descended upon him as he purchased a bag of hot chestnuts from a street vendor. He mulled the idea of going to the American embassy, but the place was so formal it intimidated him. What would he say? Would the embassy even be open this time of night?

A trio of Japanese men passed by, discussing Japan's triumphs in China and speculating about where their military would advance next. That's when it sank in: it was time to leave Japan. He was no longer a researcher. He was, as far as the authorities were concerned, an enemy alien. He would go to the embassy in the morning, first thing.

He spent the night at a ryokan and avoided conversation with the *obasan's* daughter, who, hearing his American dialect, was curious about life in California. Laying on his futon, he pondered his future in American academia. Would his studies of fifteenth-century Japan be considered viable in his work toward his master's degree? In the present political climate, would they be accepted toward a doctorate? But in light of the professor's warning, such thoughts seemed no more consequential than dead leaves that tumbled in the winter wind. He was too wound up to sleep; it was near dawn when his eyes finally closed.

* * *

"Jeremy-san!" Sayuri exclaimed, when he entered the ikebana shop. "We heard of the new rulings. Foreign students at the universities are trying to find passage to America. What are you going to do?"

70

"I'm going home. I just wanted to stop by and tell you, Kumi-san and Sensei. I have to get word to my folks; perhaps the embassy can send a telegram. I'm going there after I leave here."

"Sensei is out shopping with Kumi-san, but I will tell them you were here. Be careful. Take the tram; the crowding may make you inconspicuous. I wish you well, Jeremy, I really do. Maybe someday you can return to Japan. I would love to see you again."

"You and Sensei have been kind to me. We had some good times. If I ever run into Tad, I will tell him you are well."

"And tell him, truly I think of him every day."

A cold rain had begun to fall. Jeremy pulled his fedora low over his head and raised the collar of his coat. The first two trams were filled and rolled past, their occupants gratified that they either had a seat or, clinging desperately to a strap, were at least out of the rain. A disconsolate crowd gathered, umbrellas dripping water. Store lights reflected in the street, and a lone rickshaw, an archaic reminder of the past, sped past.

A half-filled tram finally screeched to a stop and two dozen people began to push their way in. Jeremy was about to board when something blunt and hard pushed into his back. Stiffening, he turned his head and heard a voice say, "You will not board the tram. You will come with us. Do not make a fuss."

Jeremy soon found himself sitting between two burly men in the back seat of an underpowered Toyota that drove off through the rain and the dark. The car windows were up, muffling the sounds of the streets. "Am I under arrest?" he asked cautiously.

"You will be, if you do not cooperate," said one of the men.

"Are you Kempeitai?" asked Jeremy, wondering just how much trouble he was in.

"No, not Kempeitai. Imperial Japanese Army."

"Army? Why would the Army want anything to do with me?" Jeremy asked, stunned.

Neither of the men replied, and Jeremy lapsed into silence. They drove through the emptying streets as the downpour increased. Twenty minutes later, they arrived at a gate with a sentry box. The driver showed his identification and was waved through. The car rolled up to a heavy brick building guarded by more sentries. A soldier opened the car door, and Jeremy, without his suitcase, was marched into a stark room, empty except for two chairs, a table, a flag, and posters extolling Japanese armor as soldiers routed a Chinese garrison.

One soldier pointed to a chair and Jeremy sat. From across the hall he could hear teletype machines clacking and orders being issued. The waiting was interminable. Why was he here? What interest would he possibly be to the Japanese army, unless, perhaps, they wanted an historian? But then, would they not have contacted the Professor and gone through academic channels? No, he thought, this is hardly a courtesy call. Anxious, he drummed his fingers on the table; then, conscious of it, he stopped and folded his hands. There was nothing yet to worry about, he told himself. He had done nothing wrong, and if it was a matter of mistaken identity he would surely be released. But the back of his mind was keenly regretting that he had not gone directly to the American Embassy.

"Stand!" commanded a sergeant as he entered the room. He was followed by an officer. Jeremy stood and bowed deferentially. The lieutenant sat at the table across from him.

When Jeremy began to sit, the sergeant slapped him hard across the face. "Stand! You do not sit until told to."

Face stinging, Jeremy stared straight ahead. Dread coupled with contempt assaulted him. He was aware of stories of military discipline in the Japanese army. The constant beatings, the degradation and bestiality were intended to hammer soldiers into total obedience. But he had only met officers, and they were reserved, correct, and unfailingly courteous. This was something else, something unexpected. This was treatment for the lowliest of recruits.

The lieutenant placed a folder on the table, scanned it, sat back and stared at Jeremy. "When are your parents returning to Japan?" he demanded.

"Sir, I am not aware of their desire to return to Japan. And since I am no longer a student at Tokyo University, I will be sailing for California as soon as possible."

"I don't think so," said the lieutenant. "You are only going where I send you."

The officer leaned forward on his desk and crooking his finger, indicated that Jeremy should come closer. In a conspiratorial manner the lieutenant said, "I am a military man, and I am aware of the strain America is putting upon Japan. Make no mistake, there will be war. Now about your parents; exactly where do they live?"

"In California, sir."

"Yes, California. I was there once and saw fertile land farmed by Japanese people like your parents. When war comes, your parents will be enemies of the United States. Do you actually think that they will be allowed to keep that land? Coveted land? I think not. They will be imprisoned, or shot, or maybe put on ships, and sent where? To a desert? Maybe some island in the Caribbean if they are lucky. But I do know this, the world they know is over. You should not be naïve."

Jeremy thought for a moment, then, attempting to make the best of a horribly deteriorating situation said, "Is the Japanese military intending to employ me for some academic purpose? Perhaps to write the history of military units and their accomplishments?"

The lieutenant snorted and his hand slapping the folder, sending papers across the floor. "Do you think this is an interview? *Baka!*"

It had been many years since anyone had called him stupid. "Where do you think you are? *Who* do you think you are? I will tell you. You are in a prison, and you are a traitor!"

"Sir, respectfully, I am an American citizen and you have no right to detain me."

The punch sent him sprawling. "You never speak that way to an officer of the Imperial Japanese Army," screamed the sergeant, grabbing Jeremy's shirt and throwing him against the wall.

The room spun and his head felt like it had been slammed onto an anvil. Dizzily, he looked up. All was a blur. The sergeant stood over him, bandy-legged in flaring jodhpurs and leggings.

"Put him in the chair," the lieutenant said casually, as he lit a *Kinshi* cigarette and blew smoke rings toward the ceiling.

Jeremy put his hand to his face and attempted to focus. Swaying in the chair, he sensed the presence of the sergeant, who seemed all too ready to hit him again.

"You see," said the lieutenant with quiet demeanor, "the Imperial Japanese Army as well as the government regard those of Japanese heritage as Japanese. It does not matter where one resides or how long the family is away from the land of the Rising Sun." Abruptly turning toward the flag, he said, "That is your flag. You and your parents and all 'Nisei' can pretend to be American or anything else you wish, but you are Japanese, and now you are going to serve your true country."

It began to sink in. *I am a prisoner*, thought Jeremy. *They are not going to let me go.* Perhaps he could bargain if he spoke very respectfully.

He nodded his head as if in agreement, then, after glancing at the glowering sergeant, said through swollen lips, "Sir, you consider me Japanese, and yet I am no longer allowed to continue my research at the university. How is it that I am Japanese enough to serve the Emperor in the military, but not Japanese enough to continue my studies? Excellency, I am a scholar. If I am to serve Japan, please allow me to use my special skills for the enlightened teaching of Japanese history."

"I think that is a splendid idea," said the lieutenant with an appreciative smile. "Has your research included any archaeological work, perhaps what they call a 'dig' at some ancient site?"

"In fact, sir, I have worked on digs, with pick and shovel in many cases. Arduous work," Jeremy added, with a lopsided grin, the swelling slurring his words.

"I am glad to hear that you can use a shovel. So very few academics ever see truly physical work, and I deplore a disdain for hard labor. So, that particular skill will be very useful, since you will be assigned to a work battalion. Yes, we will value your service. In the Pacific. You will be digging defensive positions, mostly on coral atolls. Who knows, perhaps you will even find something of archaeological value, such as cannibal bones. Or maybe an unexploded mine."

Then, with a snap of his fingers, he said, "Sergeant, the internment compound."

* * *

The rank odor of hundreds of men, the noxious smell of diesel oil, and the throbbing of the tramp steamer's antique engine filled the hold. The previous night's rain dripped from the top deck's rotted seams and, pregnant with rust, plopped into buckets of rain water or onto the huddled forms that lay beside them.

Only during meal times were the two hundred and seventy-four men allowed to leave the lower decks of the *Kawasaki Maru*. A dozen armed guards were stationed amidships as the prisoners lined up for a bowl of salty fish and rice. Upon receiving a ladleful, they were ordered back into the cramped hold.

"What is your name?" Jeremy asked a slender, ascetic man with pocked skin and a scraggly beard.

"Aoki Rituo, from Nagoya. What about you? I can't place your pronunciation."

"Call me Yoshi. Yoshi Shinigawa."

"That's not your real name?"

"It's what I want people to call me," said Jeremy. "I lived in America when I was very young, so some of my words sound a little funny."

"I see. Where we are going it's best that you not stand out. I know about that."

"Where are we going?"

"You don't know? I guess you wouldn't; I found out because I overheard one of the guards talking about where they are taking the women. You know, for the soldiers to hump. I think the women are in the forward hold where the guards are billeted. There are about eight or nine of them, Korean and Chinese, who were abducted by the army. And there may be a few Japanese prostitutes for the officers. Special stuff, since they speak Japanese and are more receptive, if you know what I mean. They mentioned a place called Nggela Islands."

"I never heard of it. Why there?"

"You've seen the construction equipment on deck, right? I suspect that we're going to do a lot of work. That's what we are, slave labor. I did the same in a coal mine after I was arrested. If it's anything like that, most of us won't live three months."

* * *

A short, thick officer stood stood on the quay, holding his sheathed sword at his side. His narrow gaze flitted over the men as they stumbled down the gangplank and assembled on the weathered dock. Standing at attention behind him was a captain couching a swagger stick, and thirty troops with bayonets fixed to their rifles.

Looking about, Jeremy saw that the *Kawasaki Maru* was the only ship in sight. Beyond the dock were a jumble of tents and barracks for soldiers. A dense, steaming jungle crawled over a mountain of volcanic rock that tumbled within an eighth of a mile of the shore.

"Attention! You will stand at attention!" shouted the captain. When the men assumed a semblance of order, the major spoke.

"I am Major Hatori Abe," he said. "You are part of an advance labor battalion that will prepare fortifications on this island. It is critical that you do your work well, with as much fervor and dedication as the soldiers of the Imperial Japanese Army who will eventually garrison this island. Your work day will begin at sun up and will end with sunset. You will be given twenty minutes of rest every three hours. Failure to rise to my expectations will result in the cancellation of that respite."

He nodded once, vigorously, as if to convince himself of his magnanimous generosity. Satisfied that the unshaven and malnourished men were in full compliance, he continued. "Each of you will report to my adjutant, Captain Igaki, and state your name and your crime against the Emperor. Once done, you will be assigned a specific task. Everybody's work will be inspected each day. Failure to complete your assignment will be met with the most severe punishment."

Following the major's oration, Captain Igaki handed his superior officer a thin folder. The major skimmed it and in a strident voice said, "Which of you is Jeremy Shinagawa?"

There was silence in the motley ranks.

"I repeat, who is Jeremy Shinagawa? If this traitor to the Emperor does not come forward, each of you will be beaten thirty times."

Jeremy glanced at Aoki, then stepped forward and stood before the major. The captain tapped his stick against his leggings, then in one lightning move slammed it into Jeremy's face. "That," he screamed, "is for disobeying a command. No one disobeys a command! This man will be given special discipline for his disloyalty."

Jeremy swayed, the wallop so stunning that he neither heard nor saw the second blow. He staggered back and was only held up by two men behind him. The entire world spun as he put a hand to his head. It came away sticky and covered with blood, and he sank to his knees.

The captain barked an order and the rows of men, seeing the result of disobedience, limped away from the dock as quickly as they could.

The *Kawasaki Maru* slipped its lines at dusk. Several of its crew stood by the port railing and stared down at the inert figure kneeling on the dock. They said nothing, and as the old steamer pulled away, they repaired to their quarters or to work details. Jeremy hadn't moved for two hours, and no soldier came to investigate the condition of the man all now knew was an American.

Except for a sliver of moon, it was dark when Jeremy crawled to the edge of the dock and lowered his legs over the rough planking. Somnolent wavelets lapped rhythmically against the pilings, and moonlight reflected off the sea. The black, oily water seemed so peaceful, so alluring. The slap, slap of the waves was hypnotic, and Jeremy thought how easy it would be to slip into them. He would not attempt to swim, not even a stroke. The current might pull him a few dozen yards, but that would be of no consequence. And how long would it really take to enter that next, sublime world?

It was so tempting. He stared into the water and imagined that the reflections were winking eyes and the soft sea sounds were whispering to him: "Come in, come in, the water is warm and it welcomes you. You have nothing to fear; your spirit will join others who vanished into the sea."

He inched forward, peering into the blackness. A silvery fish came to the surface. Its fathomless eyes peered at him and a bubble arose from its tiny mouth. Then it sped away, and Jeremy wondered if, as a spirit, he could swim with it to some mysterious place where nothing would ever harm him again.

He moved closer to the edge. His weight was pulling him forward when an arm grabbed his and gently pulled him back.

"It's not a good way to die," said Aoki, kneeling beside him.

"But it will end the pain for ever," mumbled Jeremy.

"My friend, my *tomodachi*, nothing is for ever. Not even this hell."

Fishing in a soiled sack, Aoki pulled out a rice cracker and said, "I know you are hungry; eat this."

Jeremy appraised the tiny cracker, then reached for it. "I don't want to go on this way, being beaten at somebody's whim. See," he said, pointing to the sea, "I can just go out there and this will be over. No more pain. It's so simple, so peaceful, so... final."

"I met a soldier who's here. I went to school with him in Nagoya and he remembered me. He was the one who gave me rice crackers. And see," Aoki said, producing a flask, "Saki too. Drink this; it will make you feel better."

Accepting the cracker and the saki was a commitment; after all, he was consuming precious nourishment that might never be available again. Acceptance of it would be a travesty if, moments later, he committed himself to the sea. But this virtual stranger had risked punishment by coming to his aid. That in itself was heroic and deserved fidelity.

Jeremy closed his eyes and sighed deeply. His head throbbed as Aoki helped him rise.

"There is room in my tent. We are only six. The others know that I came out here for you. They are waiting and we should not waste time. There will surely be guards patrolling the dock. Tomorrow might not be so bad, since the officers have already made a spectacle of you."

Yes, Jeremy thought, if they really need workers they might not beat me again, since workers must have some strength. But if they do, well, the sea is never very far away.

Chapter 7
The Pacific
November, 1941

The *Kido Butai*, the Japanese Navy's carrier flotilla, sailed from Japan to the rendezvous site at Hitokappu Bay in the Kuril Islands. The entire fleet came together, consisting of six aircraft carriers, battleships, cruisers, destroyers, and auxiliary vessels. To Koizumi and other pilots on board the new carrier *Shokaku*, the fleet seemed invincible.

The ship's crew and pilots were unaware of the great debate that had taken place between Admiral Yamamoto and the highest placed officers of the Imperial Japanese Navy. It was the admiral's view that, in order for the attack to be successful and result in America suing for peace, a total of six of Japan's carriers must be deployed. He believed that central to America's offensive capabilities was the battleship, of which the U.S. Navy had eight berthed in Pearl Harbor: seven at Ford Island and one in dry dock. However, Commander Genda of Japan's naval air fleet insisted that the American carriers must be the priority target. Only when Yamamoto and Genda put their combined ideas and prestige on the line did the general staff agree to the attack. It was, however, a severe disappointment to Commander Genda that his desire to have the Imperial Japanese army invade Hawaii was denounced as too risky and too costly.

Despite this rebuke, plans for the attack went ahead, on the assumption that at least three American carriers would be at Pearl Harbor. Their destruction would most assuredly cripple any American counter-attack and thereby allow Japanese forces a free hand in the conquest of Malaya, Singapore, and the Dutch islands.

The first cryptic message came on December 2nd from a communications center on Hokkaido, the most northern island of Japan. "Climb Mount Niitaka" was received by Vice Admiral Nagumo aboard his flagship, the carrier *Akagi,* authorizing the attack on Pearl Harbor. The fleet, under radio silence, sailed through waters not frequented by naval or commercial vessels on a course to a position northwest of the Hawaiian Islands, knowing that American search planes ignored that region and patrolled to the south and west of Pearl Harbor.

At dawn, pilots began to assemble for a sparse breakfast of red beans with rice, tai, and red snapper. Talk was quiet and sparing. Koizumi was somber, wondering whether this day would be his last. He wore the white *hachimaki* headband emblazoned with the red Rising Sun emblem and a slender white loincloth, the *mawashi.* Cleanliness and purity were central to the Samurai spirit. He vowed to press the attack, as had the Samurai of old.

In devout supplication, he prayed before the Shinto shrine beside the ready room. Would fate and the gods accord him good luck and good hunting, he wondered? Would they allow him to return to Kimi-san with honors, so that she would embrace him as a patriot and warrior, one whom she dared not refuse?

He breathed deeply and bowed again before the altar. A sudden and strange thought came to him. Would he engage his brother Tadichi, if his carrier was at Pearl Harbor? And if so, should he pray for his soul? But now others were waiting their turn at the shrine and it was time to go.

Fifteen minutes later, the pilots assembled for one last time. Small cups of saki were distributed. An officer wished them success, and in a ritual practiced for hundreds of years the liquor was downed, and the great event was set in motion.

Koizumi and dozens of other exuberant pilots scrambled from the ready room to their aircraft positioned for launch on the flight deck. Already, over fifty of the one hundred and thirty-five Zero fighters assigned to the attack were in the air. They would be cover for one hundred seventy-one Nakajima N5N torpedo bombers and the one hundred eight "Val" dive bombers. Never before in naval history had such an armada been assembled.

Sitting in his cockpit, his adrenalin building, he heard the roar of dozens of engines, saw the excitement of deck crews who wildly waved their caps and shouted "*Banzai!*" as each plane lifted off the deck. Aircraft circled, formed into echelon and climbed to altitude in the balmy sky. Koizumi, squadron leader, saw Konji Shemato, his wingman and closest friend, wave as he brought his Zero to within ten yards of Koizumi's wingtip.

The aircraft maintained radio silence as they followed the beam of a Hawaiian radio station's electric guitars directly toward Oahu. Koizumi noted that, without the station's music, the flight plan would have been several degrees off. He wondered how many of the American carriers would be in port, and how effective their air cover would be. It was legend in Japan that a squadron of fighters had shot down ninety-nine Chinese aircraft with but a loss of two of their own to ground fire. Now elation coursed through him as flight after flight of aircraft closed on their target. The verdant mountains of Oahu came into view, and the planes dipped and twisted as they stayed low to avoid radar.

The honor of leading the first of the two waves of planes had been awarded to commander Mitsuo Fuchida. Now he flashed to all pilots, *"To, To, To,"* the signal to attack. Minutes later, when he detected no American opposition, Fuchida's second radio signal went out, *"To ra, To ra, To ra!"* Excitement gripped the pilots upon hearing the code words, "Tiger, Tiger, Tiger!"

Koizumi glanced at his watch. It was seven forty-three in the morning. His fighters were assigned four major targets, including the thirty-three long-range Catalina flying boats, Wheeler Field north of Pearl Harbor, and Hickam Field with its aircraft parked wing tip to wing tip. But the most significant targets were the aircraft carriers and battleship row at Ford Island. He remembered how relaxed the bases had been on Sundays, and wondered how Japan's declaration of War had been received. Would the Americans assume that Japan would leave Hawaii alone out of respect for the Nisei population? Would they assume the announcement was mere oratory, posturing on the part of a small and insignificant island nation? Or would they assume that, even if the declaration of war was serious, that Japan would move slowly, taking weeks or even months to mount an offensive against small targets like Malaya? Americans thought that fights had to be a prolonged struggle; they did not understand the Samurai philosophy of striving for unattainable perfection: the conflict decided by a single stroke of the sword. This attack was that single stroke.

What none of them knew was that clerical errors in the Japanese war office, and slowness in decoding the final pages from the message had resulted in a fatal delay: the official declaration of war had not yet been transmitted. They were, by accident and against their own code of honor, mounting what would look to the world like an unprovoked act of war, a "sneak attack."

And it was Sunday. A few alert airmen reported sightings of bogies, but these warnings were for the most part disregarded by superior officers, intent upon their routines of leisure. And so....

Within minutes of Fuchida's final message, the U.S. Army's aircraft at Wheeler Field were in flames. Hurtling down, Koizumi leveled off and fired rapid bursts into parked aircraft. One after another erupted into flame. Other Zeros bombed hangers. Sailors, soldiers and civilians were strafed, while hundreds, panic-stricken, ran for cover, like terrified sheep. Burt he also saw personnel, in complete disregard of their own safety, push undamaged aircraft away from those that were already engulfed in flame. *They are men of honor,* he could not help thinking.

Defying bombs and machine guns, soldiers and sailors began firing at the attacking planes, and one man, apparently a marksman, actually fired into cockpits, downing aircraft.

Roiling black smoke from scores of gasoline and oil fires blackened the sky, making it hard for pilots to see, and aircraft dove over targets already hit. Having laid waste to dozens of parked aircraft, Koizumi and his wingman pulled up. Not far away, an American P-40 and an obsolete P-36 pursued and downed several Zeros.

"Should we give chase?" Shemato radioed Koizumi. To see a famed Zero being chased by the Americans was repellant, but Koizumi said, "No, we must protect the torpedo bombers attacking Ford Island."

Climbing back to five thousand feet, Koizumi could see rows of huge oil tanks, of which only a few were camouflaged. No Japanese planes appeared over them. These, thought Koizumi, must surely be on the target list. *It is the oil they refused to sell to us,* he realized. He wondered if the general staff had assigned other squadrons to vector on the submarine pens and the subs themselves; he saw no fighters or bombers over those targets of opportunity.

Hours of ship recognition exercises had familiarized Japanese pilots with the American ships. Koizumi, flying low over the harbor, spotted the *Arizona*, already pouring smoke from a bombed turret. Then an N5N *Kanyo* from the carrier *Kaga* dropped a seventeen-hundred-pound armor-piercing bomb between its two forward turrets, and the ensuing explosion, rising thousands of feet, sent a shock wave across the sky that rocked his Zero. In the maelstrom of evading enemy fire, blasting parked aircraft and raking ships, time blurred into eternity.

He decided that there was one thing he had to do before low fuel levels forced him to return to the carrier.

Sending his wingman off to attack shipping again, he skimmed past the Naval hospital and its nearby houses. He slowed, peered down, and came around again, then pulled the stick back, rose, and flew toward the open sea. A few figures ventured out and watched the Zero disappear.

The assault continued, taking a toll of infrastructure, ships, cars, trucks and citizens. Thirty minutes after the *Arizona* blew up, the *Pennsylvania* was heavily bombed. The battleship *Oklahoma* capsize while hundreds of men crawled down her exposed hull, slipping and falling into the sea. Dozens of boats were plying the burning waters, pulling in men covered with oil, while other boats lay wallowing, their crews dead or dying.

The second wave of carrier planes arrived to find the defenders much more prepared. Anti-aircraft guns on every warship still afloat were blazing as the torpedo bombers came in low. Over a dozen were shot out of the air, crashing into land or sea. Still, one dive bomber roared down and a moment later the destroyer *Shaw* was blown apart, her magazines exploding with an enormous concussion.

The U.S.S. *Nevada* took damage and ran toward shallow water at Hospital Point. If she sank in the channel, her bulk would block the egress of other ships for weeks to come. But no other bombers attacked her, and she ran aground beyond the channel.

Now it was nearly ten in the morning, the hour when the attack was to end. Still the sky was peppered with deadly bursts as Japanese planes dodged ack-ack and each other in dives against American ships. Some pilots scanned the sea far beyond Pearl Harbor. What they were looking for was nowhere to be seen. Had Nagumo not sent the third wave?

* * *

On board the carriers *Akagi, Kaga* and *Soryu,* tension mounted as planes lowered their landing gears, caught the arresting wires and came to an abrupt stop. Pilots were met with cheers as they emerged victorious from their planes. The same elation occurred on the *Hiryu, Shokaku,* and the huge *Zuikaku,* but there were somber looks as officers checked off each plane recovered. Twenty-nine had not come back. Still, it was considered a small price compared to the crippling of an entire fleet.

Nagumo had decided not to press the attack any further. Steaming at high speed, the Japanese fleet sailed for home and safe waters. Jubilation reigned aboard the carriers, battleships, and cruisers as word spread. Every pilot was considered a hero. In carrier ready rooms and officer quarters, pilots talked excitedly about the massive explosions following their bomb hits, the devastation of their torpedoes and the terror incurred as parked aircraft were shredded into scrap metal.

Surely no American interference would delay the acquisition of the Dutch East Indies, what the Japanese high command referred to as the "southern resource region." Giddy with success, mechanics and damage control personnel labored lovingly over aircraft, repairing fuselage and wings struck by anti-aircraft rounds, while pilots were feted below decks.

Though some might have had reservations, most believed that news of an American capitulation and suit for peace would be immediately forthcoming. After all, it was reasoned, what occurred at Pearl Harbor was analogous to the great battle of Tsushima in 1905 against the navy of Tsar Nicholas II. Hadn't Admiral Nagumo on his flagship flown the same battle flag Admiral Togo had flown when he sank thirty of Russia's forty-two war ships?

After defeating China in 1894, Japan had expected to acquire Port Arthur in Manchuria, a most valuable possession. But that outcome had been denied by the European powers. Furious at foreign intervention, Japan had invested in state-of-the art battleships constructed in British yards, resulting in Japanese domination of the seas in the northern Pacific. No one had to remind the pilots and crews that it was the decisive victory at the Straits of Tsushima in waters off Korea that began the astounding rise and prestige of the Imperial Japanese Navy.

"We in Japan saw what was happening in the world," Itomo Karamatsu had told his nephew. "In 1898, the United States defeated Spain and took control of Cuba, took the Philippines, Guam, and many islands in the Pacific. Britain and other European nations put a yardstick over the map of Africa and divided nearly every inch of it among themselves. France took Indochina and enslaved thousands in work camps. In Peking itself, under British rule, there were signs that said, 'Dogs and Chinese stay off the grass.' Can you imagine! The last straw was when Russia built the Trans-Siberian Railway to bring troops to Manchukuo and Siberia. We looked about and asked ourselves, Will we too be a colony of the West, or even worse, of Russia?

"And now the West condemns us for doing exactly what they have done. The Dutch still rule over their dominions, the British still have Singapore, the French claim Vietnam, and the Americans have Hawaii, which they seized, deposing the rightful queen in 1893. Who are they to criticize us?"

It was a powerful, convincing argument.

"Remember," his uncle had continued, "it was an American general who convinced the Emperor to expand into Korea following the Russo-Japanese War. But how quickly nations forget understandings and agreements when it no longer serves their purpose.

"Hypocrisy," said Admiral Karamatsu, "is in the small print of a victorious nation's calling card."

* * *

"I'm going up to the flight deck," Koizumi said on the evening of December 7th, tiring of the accolades pilots showered upon each other.

"I'll go with you," said Konji Shemato.

They stood at the aft end of the flight deck and looked at the phosphorescent wake of the carrier.

"What's the matter?" asked Shemato. "You look like you swallowed a frog. It was a great victory; you should be pleased. I only wish that I had destroyed as many enemy aircraft as you did. Your shooting was remarkable."

"It's not particularly difficult to destroy parked airplanes," replied Koizumi.

"Perhaps not, but the Americans won't be flying them ever again," stated his wingman with satisfaction.

Koizumi lit a cigarette and watched the smoke dissipate in the night's cool air. "There was miscalculation."

"Miscalculation? What do you mean? Our attack was perfection!"

"You really think so? I saw dive bombers strike the airfields before hitting the ships at Ford Island. That mistake alerted shipboard gun crews. Our formations came apart, and we never practiced an attack with the sun in our eyes as it was at Pearl Harbor. Our training, our difficult, brutal training, was insufficient," said Koizumi bitterly.

"We spent ten months preparing for the attack," said Shemato. "Our training was intense and many men were lost, planes crashing into one another in night training in all kinds of weather."

"It tell you, all that was wasted effort! Commander Fuchida's own bomb missed. And he is keenly disappointed that the carriers were out to sea. The only reason he signed on was to kill the American carriers, and they weren't in the harbor. What we hit were battleships, and we may be facing five or six carriers if the Americans don't surrender."

"But still, we destroyed their hangers, their planes, and probably their morale," Shemato protested.

"They can rebuild hangars and build more planes. Did you see any of our planes attack the oil tanks, or the submarine pens?"

"I can't say that I did."

"Loss of that oil would have been a serious blow, and what about the subs? I haven't heard of any of those being sunk. That's something for us to worry about."

Shemato pulled his flight jacket close, then said, "Tomodachi, I think these are thoughts you should keep to yourself. There are men on this ship who would think them unpatriotic, treasonable. You are accusing very high officers of incompetence. If anyone ever asks me, I will say that I never heard you say these words."

"I understand," said Koizumi. "I will never repeat them to anyone. You need not worry."

It was getting late, and the two men descended to the lower deck.

He reflected for a moment on the statements he had made to the general staff at the Admiralty. Was he culpable for what he considered a very flawed mission? Would any of the men who made the final decisions admit ineptitude? In light of the enormous destruction visited on the Americans, there would be no mention of failure. Instead, there would be great rejoicing and high expectations.

"But even monkeys fall out of trees," his uncle used to say, an old Japanese proverb. And then he would add, "How well they survive depends on how hard they hit the ground and how far they fall."

That night Koizumi pulled a blanket over his head, and as pilots whispered about honor and homecomings, he wondered how far they might have fallen that day. And how quickly the burned Americans might rise from the ashes.

Chapter 8
Pearl Harbor
December, 1941

Inky black smoke still stained the air from a dozen ships, broken like children's toys following a horrible tantrum. Rescue details had clambered up the slick hulls of capsized ships, hammering on steel plates and listening for the desperate response of trapped men still inside as air pockets filled with carbon monoxide. The search was hampered by oil fires on the brackish water of Pearl Harbor.

On the capsized battleship USS *Oklahoma*, crews with acetylene torches worked day and night to cut holes into the armored hull so that survivors could be pulled from the wreckage. Barges ferried repair parties and equipment to ships still seaworthy.

Other launches prowled the water looking for the bodies of dead sailors and Marines. Lifted from the sea, blackened by oil, they were carefully brought aboard. Still other craft transferred the wounded to hospitals and trauma centers filled with hundreds of wounded or dying men.

Dr. Eli Thompson drove slowly on the two-lane road leading away from the hospital. It had been an excruciatingly long day and neither he nor Kimi-san had the energy to say much at all. Checkpoints had been erected and they were stopped numerous times. They showed their credentials to wary guards, many of whom were of Chinese or Japanese descent.

Cresting a rise, in the dim glow of hooded lamps Commander Thompson could see soldiers and Marines digging trenches and installing artillery in anticipation of the expected invasion. A blackout had been decreed, and cars were driven with only their fog lights. Autos without them had black cloth taped over headlights. In defensive positions, troops with bayonetted rifles stood guard. Tension and anxiety gripped the island.

"Do you think Hawaii will be invaded?" Kimi-san finally asked.

"They must know how vulnerable we are. Certainly the fleet, or what's left of it, will be heavily out-gunned. And we have damn few aircraft left. If they want to, they can take Oahu with fifteen or twenty thousand men."

"We have so many wounded," she said softly. "What will happen to them?"

"We'll evacuate all we can, put them on undamaged ships for the big island or Kauai and hope that they aren't attacked on the way. But to be perfectly honest, a lot of them won't make it.

"The Japs—excuse me, I'm just pissed. The Japanese seem to be attacking everywhere all at once. Singapore, Malaya, maybe even India and French Indochina. They might even invade Australia and New Zealand. Kimi, we were asleep at the wheel. And now we have one hell of a mess."

They were stopped at another checkpoint, and a Marine only glanced at Dr. Thompson's ID but made a close scrutiny of Kimi.

"Japanese or Chinese?" Asked the marine.

"That's not of concern to you, Corporal," said Thompson. "She's with me, and she's a nurse. Who knows, she might be the one stitching *you* up in a week or so."

The marine said nothing, winced at the rebuke, and grudgingly saluted the commander.

"You were very rough with him," said Kimi-san. "He's on edge, like everybody else. You really can't blame him."

"I've seen that kind of racism before, and I won't tolerate it. Anybody giving you that crap will be doing latrine detail until the cows come home."

"What time is that?" asked Kimi-san.

"Hell if I know. I've never been around cows. But pretty late, I think."

She rolled her eyes, then turning serious said, "Most of the wounded I treated were very appreciative, but some gave me questioning looks, even fearful ones. I told them that we are all Americans, even if some of us look different. Some nodded in agreement, but others...."

"You'd think they'd see you for what you are, a nurse saving their lives," said Dr. Thompson.

Shuttered shops and blacked-out windows gave an eerie and unnatural feeling to the streets as other vehicles, including military trucks, passed at glacial speeds. Thompson eventually broke the silence by saying, "Considering the current situation, Kimi, you are welcome to stay at my place. I have an extra room, and since we should be at the hospital early, it would save time if I didn't have to pick you up at your house. With all these checkpoints, I'll have to start an hour early."

The offer, Kimi thought, was reasonable. Nothing mattered more than aiding the wounded, and time was precious. They had spent the previous night at the hospital, taking only brief naps between cases. But one night at Dr. Thompson's house might lead to more, and though Dr.

Thompson had been entirely correct and professional at the hospital, evenings in his house away from curious eyes might lead to something else, something that under anxious and fearful circumstances, with a very handsome man, might involve intimacy she dared not contemplate.

"Thank you for your consideration, Doctor Thompson, but I have to be in my own home. I hope you understand."

"Of course, but I did ask you to call me Eli when we're away from work. It will make me feel much more human, if you can imagine that."

He turned and gave her a brief smile, and she felt his need for a sense of humanity in the midst of so much loss, suspicion and grief.

They pulled to the curb and the car's fog lights reflected off the mailbox standing at the edge of the lawn. The metal flag was up, indicating mail delivered.

"I can't believe that the postman came today," said Dr. Thompson.

"Oh, it was up before. I was about to fetch it when the attack began, and then reading mail was the last thing I was thinking about."

He turned off the engine and opened the car door for her. She thanked him, went to the mailbox, and extracted two advertisements, a card inviting her to a nurse's reception, and a letter from someone whose name was a smeared scrawl.

Escorting her to her door, the doctor said, "Well, I'll pick you up early tomorrow. But the offer is still open, anytime you wish. Now get a good night's sleep. It's going to be a busy day."

"Yes, Eli. I will do just that," she said dutifully. She watched as his car slowly drove away. She went inside, drew the drapes, and settled into her chair. In the dim light, she peered at the handwriting on the mysterious letter, smudged and rumpled as if it had been handled by many people. There were numerous stamps on the envelope, some from as far away as England. With growing trepidation, she pulled out handwritten pages on flimsy paper.

It had been a long, excruciating day, but she was suddenly wide awake. She scrutinized the letter, then held it to her face. With a long plaintive sob she cried, "No, no, not my dearest Alexei."

The tear-stained letter slipped from her fingers.

Dear Mrs. Kuchenkov,

I am a reporter for The Times *(of London), until recently assigned to Moscow. If you remember, I had the privilege of befriending you and Alexei many decades ago. It was I who formally introduced Alexei to your father during the reception at our British Embassy in Tokyo. I recall how Alexei reacted when saw you in the company of your father, mother and brother Itomo. Did he ever tell you how astonished he was to see you there? He told me once it was as if Heaven had heard his prayer and granted his heart's desire. Then, when you met again in England, during the state visits for the coronation of King Edward VII, I gave Alexei the key to a flat which, I was told, served as your refuge when the Cheka pursued him. They are now the NKVD. Alas, they have only gotten worse under Comrade Stalin.*

I fear that I digress, but memories of long ago... Now to the point.

Last week, I ran across Alexei at the Moscow train station, where he was helping unload art treasures from the Hermitage. He told me that he had been rounded up with thousands of others and taken to the Luga Line, a defensive perimeter intended to fend off the Nazis. But the line disintegrated, and he got back to Leningrad only to find that his mother and father had been killed in the German bombing of that city. There was much panic in Leningrad, and people were needed to save precious art. He joined other volunteers and accompanied the art works to a safer place. In all the confusion at the station, he managed to get away to meet me several blocks from the Lubyanka prison, not far from the Kremlin. An inauspicious place, but the best we could manage under the circumstances. A far cry from an Embassy reception, eh?

After a rushed conversation we parted. I was reluctant to write to you (Alexei told me that you are at Pearl Harbor, Hawaii) but he asked me to do so, even though what I have to say may be less than comforting.

We parted ways, and I saw how, as he passed the prison, a number of men apprehended him and hustled him away. I tried in vain to learn what became of him afterwards. So many men are taken, either to the front or the GULAG. These are desperate times in Russia. I am still trying my best to determine his location. As he is an American citizen, he might be treated better than most. I will attempt to contact the American embassy here, and I will write again as soon as I learn anything definitive.

Again, I apologize profoundly for this bleak news, but truly, "the world has turned upside down," as Cornwallis said at Yorktown long before our time. I do hope for the best. You may write to me now that I am back in London.

A BLOSSOM IN THE ASHES

The very last moment I saw Alexei he shouted to me, "Tell Kimi-san I love her."

I think that is the message that you should carry with you. I do hope that we can all be together in the not too distant future.

> *Your friend eternally,*
> *William-Stuart Jones*

She turned off the lamp light, opened the drapes and stared into the blackness of the night. Where was he? she wondered, as tears slid down her face. They had read accounts of atrocities perpetrated by "Uncle Joe" Stalin and his feared henchmen, the secret police. Even the most loyal Bolsheviks, as they were once called, were being executed in droves for mere suspicion of disloyalty. Ah, had she not pleaded with Alexei not to go? Even Tad, now somewhere at sea, had warned him of the danger, but to no avail; and now this.

Intermittent fires burned in the harbor. An ambulance passed, then a convoy of military trucks. A troop of marines followed, their column silent but wary.

The black ink of the letter, smeared by her tears, lay on the table beside her chair. She felt alone, so terribly alone. Her mind drifted to the time with Alexei in William-Stuart Jones' flat above the Rising Sun tavern. It was the first time they had held one another, the first time they had given to each other all they were. Despite everything, she could not help but smile as she sank into the oblivion of the dark, late hours of night.

* * *

A pungent sea breeze, tainted by the smell of burning fuel, permeated the air when Dr. Thompson pulled up to the curb. He noticed that no lights were on in Kimi-san's house and wondered if she had not yet awoken. But she was always punctual. Had it not been for some overzealous military guard posts, he would have arrived a half hour earlier.

He walked up the porch steps, knocked on the door and waited. Ten seconds later, impatient, he knocked again. He did not see the woman who followed him up the steps, but he felt a delicate touch on his arm. He turned and saw a diminutive woman of Portuguese heritage looking at him with tearful eyes.

"They took her away an hour ago. It was still dark when they came, a whole squad of them in a big truck."

"Who came?" asked Thompson, a hard look on his face.

"The army. They already had a dozen, maybe two dozen women in the truck. They just barged in, they would not even listen to her. I came out and tried to tell them the good work she does at the hospital, but they paid me no heed. I was praying that you would come by. I know that you pick her up in the morning. I am terribly worried."

"Do you know where they took her?" asked Thompson.

"I heard that they're going to a Honolulu detention center. That's what a man told me, a neighbor of mine. I think a lot of Japanese have been taken there by now."

Dr. Thompson tore past one check point after another, holding his ID card out the window. Shouts and threats from guards pursued him, but most could see the decal on the window indicating his rank. He was relieved that no shots punctuated their orders to halt. At long last, he reached his destination.

Hundreds of worried and disoriented people, mostly of Asian heritage, but a sprinkling of Germans and Italians, were crowded into the building. As trucks rolled up, armed guards herded bewildered men, women and children toward a hastily reinforced compound.

"I want to see the person in charge of this facility," Dr. Thompson demanded of a harried sergeant seated behind a desk cluttered with lists of detainees.

A corporal approached and said, "Commander, he's awfully busy right now. If you wish to wait sir, I will—"

Pushing his way through an anxious crowd, many with documents indicating respectability and loyalty, Thompson found a door guarded by two marines.

"Sir, I can't let you in there unless you have special credentials," said a private.

"I damn well do, son. I have a forty-five caliber pistol in my car and I'm the chief surgeon at the Naval hospital." He held up an identification badge and stormed through the door.

When another guard held up his hand, Commander Thompson waved him away and strode to a desk, behind which were seated two men in suits and two military officers. Tall and imposing, Thompson said, "Excuse me," to a tearful elderly woman, gently moving her aside. A marine captain looked up from a list of detainees and, seeing the doctor's uniform beneath an open surgical coat said, "Sir, I'm not sure what you want, but there is a protocol in place."

"My protocol, mister, is to locate a woman named Kimi Kochenkov who I understand has been forcibly brought here. I want to know where she is and I want her immediately released. She—"

"She is on a list," said a man in a suit. "We are the Federal Bureau of Investigation." The agent indicated himself and his partner. Holding up a sheet of paper, he continued, "This is a custodial detention list compiled by the Bureau. We are charged to investigate the loyalty of everyone on it, and we have jurisdiction over the military in this regard. In addition, Governor Poindexter has declared martial law. So I would say, Doctor Thompson, that you are out of order."

Leaning over the table, Thompson stared into the man's eyes and said in just above a whisper, "You tell me where my trauma nurse is, or I'll be using a scalpel on you in a very inventive way. So, I repeat," he shouted, "where the fuck is she?"

"Sand Island, Commander," said the army major beside the F.B.I. agent. "That's where they are all being taken. She was in front of my desk about two hours ago. She showed me her ID and I was in favor of sending her home, but the Bureau agents overruled me." He glared at the agents, who bridled. "I will put a call in and tell them to have a boat ready for you."

It had been called "Quarantine Island" in the nineteenth century when boatloads of immigrants were held there until it was determined that they were free of diseases. Virtually overnight, a five-acre detention camp had been established with barbed wire and guard towers.

After producing his credentials, Dr. Thompson was waved through a gate guarded by soldiers with fixed bayonets. He drove past rows of tents, their sides rolled a foot off the ground. A large section had been established for men, a separate section was set aside for women. Several latrines, a mess hall, and a small building were the only other features the desolate space. Peach-fuzzed high school and college students from the Hawaii Territorial Guard imperiously patrolled the interior of the camp, giving orders to worried people, some of whom had, until a day before, been their teachers and professors.

A long line of Asians snaked down to a basement where they were searched for weapons or any contraband, including pencils, pens or paper. One uniformed youngster had been assigned the duty of roll call; before him stood a long line of prisoners, obediently answering when their name was called. Kimi was near the head of the line when Dr. Thompson descended the stairs and passed those waiting in line.

"I'm the head surgeon at the naval hospital, and this lady is my most important trauma nurse," he informed a Navy lieutenant. "Unless you want more sailors to die because you delayed her release, I suggest that you strike her name from that list. And I mean right now, mister."

The cramped room was stifling, and the lieutenant glanced at the line of people who stretched out the door. With no more than an acquiescent nod, he scratched a line through Kimi's name and said, "Sir, under the circumstances and with concern for the wounded, nurse Kochenkov is free to go. There will be no further investigation. I will release her, but she is your responsibility. You will be required to sign a release statement."

Following the signing, Thompson and Kimi made their way to the gate of the compound. A copy of the release form was shown, and they walked to the dock where the boat was tied.

"Thank you," she said, when they got into the doctor's car forty minutes later. "I had no way of calling you or anybody else. They treated me like an enemy agent and no one would listen to me. If you hadn't come along...."

"That's over now, but these raids are not over, and they may come to your house again. I would put you up in a hotel, but those are being raided too. So...."

"I don't want you to have to bail me out again. If you are suggesting that I stay at your house, I will accept," said Kimi-san, staring blankly out the front window.

"I think it's best. The roundup should be over in a few days, and then you can return to your home. I will write and sign a statement for you. But now we have work to do. Are you up to it?"

"Yes, I am."

She shuddered, sensing that a pall of fear and suspicion had descended upon the once peaceful island. And then she wondered what might happen in Dr. Thompson's house. Wasn't she exchanging one danger for another?

Chapter 9
Tokyo
March, 1942

A cold rain was pelting down. Koizumi removed his shoes and entered Sensei's ikebana shop. His sudden appearance startled Sayuri, who was handing a letter to Mrs. Svenson. Quickly, the Swedish woman slipped the letter into her pocket, but not before Koizumi noticed. Suspicious, he glanced at all three women, then bowed and said, "Excuse me, I hope my entrance didn't cause alarm."

"None at all, Koizumi-san," answered Sayuri, bowing deeply. "The women's community council will be giving a celebration of our great victory, and we have been exchanging notes with the international community." Her voice was a bit strained. "Of course, we hope that they will all attend, since it will be a splendid event. Perhaps you might attend. It takes place in four days."

"I regret that I cannot remain."

There was a long moment of silence before Sensei said, "We listened intently to every report on the radio about the attack on Pearl Harbor and all our victories since. We are pleased to see you in good health."

"I was wounded by an American bomber, so I was in the hospital briefly. But the American planes are inadequate, obsolete, and we shoot them down easily.

"Yes," said Sensei, "I'm sure that the Emperor and his staff are planning celebrations as well as future operations."

Koizumi nodded slowly and said, "We are all hoping the same, but the Americans have not yet surrendered. Eventually, after continuous defeats, they will realize that they have lost the war."

Another silence followed before Sensei asked, "Will you be receiving a medal for valor?"

"No, Sensei, the only medals are posthumous. The Navy does not hand out medals for simply doing one's duty. On occasion, promotions are given. When I achieve many more kills I may be promoted."

Shifting his gaze to Sayuri he said, "A promotion means more money, and after the war I will be able to buy a house. It could be comfortable for us." When Sayuri failed to respond, Koizumi reached for her hand, but Sayuri pulled away.

"I have to speak with you," said Koizumi. "I want to talk to you in private."

"Koizumi-san, I do not want to hurt your feelings, but we really have nothing to discuss," said Sayuri.

"But we do. You know I want to marry you; if not now, then after the war."

"Please, Koizumi-san," she said, wishing that the conversation was not taking place in front of Sensei. Indeed, she wished that it was not taking place at all. But as Koizumi had laid his soul bare, in front of witnesses, risking loss of face, she said with as much deference as she could, "I apologize for my obstinance and rudeness. I ask for your forgiveness, Koizumi-san, but a fine officer like yourself does not want a wife who is old."

"Then you should at least marry a Japanese sailor or soldier who is fighting for our nation. Not an enemy intent on destroying us!"

"Koizumi-san," she said, taken aback, "Perhaps your brother is your enemy, but he is not mine."

Koizumi starred at her, faced tight, before he said, "If I see him in my gunsights, I promise you I will shoot him down. He will plunge into the sea and be food for things that crawl on the ocean floor. I promise you that!"

Turning to Mrs. Svenson he said, "I demand to see that letter. Yes, the one you tried to hide from me. I know it's intended for the American, and that's espionage. Give it to me!"

She stuffed her hand protectively into the pocket of her apron, but he gripped her wrist.

"I am a Swedish citizen and you have no right, no right at all, to take anything from me," she said, trying to fend him off.

But Koizumi was much stronger and pulled her hand away, grabbing the envelope.

Sayuri dashed forward, snatching the letter out of Koizumi's hand. She ripped it into pieces. Enraged, he slapped her, and she reeled back against the wall.

"I nearly died fighting those savages!" he screamed. "I saw dozens of my comrades go down in flames, and you, you," he sputtered, "write love letters to a man who intends to kill me? This is insane. This is treason and treason is punishable by death!"

Looking wildly at the three women he shouted, "You are all accountable, all guilty. And you will be charged!"

Stone-faced, Koizumi stormed out of the shop.

Not a word was said for several minutes until Mrs. Svenson, still shaken, said, "I will tell you this, but you must not repeat it. As the wife of a consular official I attend functions, many of them hosted by embassies and consulates that are not at war with Japan. The Japanese military sounds very self-assured and promises victory, but I hear the talk at the parties by people who know what's really happening."

She stopped, rubbed her wrist and said, "The Americans are hardly beaten. In fact, they are engaged in the biggest naval build-up the world has ever seen. They are constructing thousands of ships and planes and are training millions of men: soldiers, fliers, marines, sailors. And America has one hundred twenty million people, almost twice the population of Japan, because for centuries they have welcomed refugees from around the world: Russia, Poland, Ireland, even Germany. Young men whose great-grandfathers were slaves have enlisted to fight for their freedom. So this war will go on for a very long time. Japan may enjoy some victories, but in the end...."

Her voice drifted off, leaving Sensei and Sayuri staring at one another.

"And we will lose?" whispered Sensei.

The Swedish woman breathed deeply, and nodded. "Both of you must try to survive. Do what the authorities tell you, but be vigilant. Things in this land will become very distressing. I am sorry to have to tell you this, but I know that you value the truth. Now I must go, and it may not be possible for us to meet again. I wish you well; you have been wonderful friends."

A BLOSSOM IN THE ASHES

Tokyo
April, 1942

Kicking off her *getas*, Sayuri rushed into the ikebana shop and excitedly said, "Sensei, I found apples, a whole dozen of them!"

She came to an abrupt halt and stared about the room, aghast. The tatami mat floor was strewn with fragments of broken vases, torn papers, and wilted flowers, some brushed into little piles. A splintered shelf, formerly the display showpiece of the shop, hung forlornly from the wall. Kumi-san, broom in hand, face streaked with dust and tears, looked up and stared at Sayuri.

"Sensei said that Koizumi's threat was just bluster, but they came while you were away. There were five of them, Kempeitai, and they did this."

"Where is Sensei?" murmured Sayuri, taking in the empty shelves, the torn shoji screens and ripped calligraphy scrolls that hung lopsided on the walls.

"She said that she couldn't stay here any longer, not with her life's work in ruins. She went to Kanagawa Prefecture, where her sister lives. It is south of the city near the Japan Steel Corporation, where her sister works."

"Will she be coming back?" asked Sayuri.

"I do not know. I told her that I would clean up and tell her guests to come back in a week or so. Sensei was very distraught. The police even went upstairs to ransack the entire house."

"I should have been here," Sayuri whispered.

"No! It is best that you weren't. Koizumi was here, but he stayed outside. I know he wanted you to be here so he could show you what he is capable of doing. He was the one who led the Kempeitai here."

"He would not have been so proud of himself if I had been here." Sayuri's voice was uncharacteristically grim. She knelt, picked up a dust pan, and held it as Kumi-san swept in shards of porcelain.

"They found postcards from Hawaii and a blouse made in America. Sensei told them that she had been there before the war, accompanied by Koizumi. When they heard that, they took the cards and left."

"What else did they say?" asked Sayuri, picking up shards of pottery.

"They warned us that any messages sent from here to a foreign embassy would be considered treason and we would all be imprisoned." Kumi-san sighed and added, "Those men, they were horrible. They didn't even take off their boots, and they turned over everything. It was wanton destruction. I think they were looking for letters; Koizumi must have told them that secret messages were hidden here. They seemed disappointed by not finding anything."

"I imagine that Koizumi was even more disappointed," said Sayuri bitterly. "Sensei will never be able replace everything. Some vases were antiques."

"Working and living here is becoming untenable, Sayuri-san. Perhaps we should go to Kanagawa and find jobs in a factory. The steel company must need women to help in the kitchens. We could meet Sensei there and see what she wants to do."

"I'll help you clean up, and then in a few days we'll go. Do you think they work on Saturday?"

"Of course they do. It's wartime. Everybody works on weekends."

As Kimi dumped shards in a trash can, Kumi said, "After the men left, the Swedish woman came by. She told Sensei that her husband forbade her to ever come here again. She said that it was too dangerous, that the neutrality of her husband's legation could be compromised if the Kempeitai found any of your letters. She was very distraught, and very sad. She offered quite a bit of money to help, but Sensei refused to accept it. They were both in tears. But she did leave this," said Kumi, handing Sayuri a very small envelope. "She said it came with the embassy mail via Switzerland, and that you should burn it once you read it."

Sayuri's hands were trembling as she tore open the envelope.

> *Dearest Sayuri-san,*
>
> *I hope you receive this letter and it finds you in good health. I love you with all my heart. Stay safe. I think you should go to the countryside where the air is clean and where people will welcome you. Wait for me if you can. Pray for me, as I pray for you.*
>
> *Love,*
> *Tad-ichi*

Blinking away tears, she read the letter twice more, then handed it to Kumi. Her friend placed it over a candle and lit the wick. A trail of smoke rose, and Sayuri wafted it away as the words turned to cinders.

"He wrote in Japanese," said Kumi. "And you saw how he signed his name. Strange."

"His mother taught him to read and write Japanese," said Sayuri. "I'm sure he wrote it that way in case the letter was intercepted by the Kempeitai. It would just sound like a love letter from any man who longs to see his girlfriend."

Tokyo,
April 18, 1942

A thin haze had settled over the city. An air raid drill had been carried out earlier in the day, but no sirens had sounded. Even though anti-aircraft guns had been installed all around the city, the Emperor had assured citizens that Japan would not be bombed.

There was no reason for the nation's citizens to be particularly concerned about the progress of the war. There been no American invasions of Japanese-held territory, not even in the eastern-most reaches of the Pacific; by all accounts the enemy was reeling from one defeat after another. Nevertheless, barrage balloons floated over Tokyo and surrounding prefectures.

For a few lucky citizens, Saturday was one day they could still enjoy the parks and shopping, even though shortages and rationing greatly limited selections. Japanese films and German films with subtitles played in the few theaters still open; bars slaked the thirst of those who enjoyed a day off.

A message had reached naval intelligence of an American task force was sighted hundreds of miles off the coast of Japan. Search planes were sent up, but no sign of an American force was seen, so the message was designated a false alarm, even though the trawler that had sent the message was not responding to radio signals. Surely the coastal vessels would report any threat, and nothing of the sort had arrived. Just to be sure, the Imperial Navy deployed a string of picket vessels to detect any American presence.

"Is Sensei's sister working today?" asked Sayuri, as she and Kumi-san departed the train station.

"I'm sure she is, but it will be lunch time when we get there. Sensei told me that her sister eats at a restaurant right next to the factory. I think it's owned by the steel company so that workers would not have to go far or be late to work.

Sensei says it's very convenient, and the food is good because the factory is very important to the war effort."

"There's the factory, the big one with the smokestacks and the railroad siding," said Sayuri.

They walked between industrial buildings in a soot-laden part of town inhabited by factory workers, many of whom had come from the countryside to work for the steel corporation and the nearby Showa Electric company.

Some citizens, not familiar with aircraft, waved as planes flew at treetop-level over the coast. The deep, throbbing sound of twin-engine B-25 Billy Mitchell engines caused people to look up as one plane after another roared overhead. Only a few noticed the stars on the wings. The planes ascended to twelve hundred feet, heading for a wide range of targets.

Sayuri and Kumi-san peered up as the strange planes started their bomb runs. Mystified by the sudden commotion, passersby watched in growing alarm as high-explosive and incendiary bombs detonated amid aircraft factories, petrol dumps and warehouses. A number of homes were hit, but most of the low-flying planes were able to strike targets with accuracy. Belatedly, anti-aircraft batteries began to splatter the sky with black splotches. Some of the anti-aircraft fire struck barrage balloons which, trailing their steel cables, came crashing down, adding to the destruction.

"Run!" shouted Kumi, as a ball of fire blew the roof off the steel factory. A second bomb struck an area where lunch was being served. The bombers raced over the city, and even though Japanese Zeros rose to intercept them, the fast-moving B-25s were out of range before they could be engaged. Fire trucks and ambulances began to wail through the city.

Taking shelter beside a wall, the two young women watched as smoke and flame billowed up from the steel corporation and its surrounding buildings. Screams sounded from the rubble, and those not wounded hurried to free bloodied workers from a jumble of jagged beams and broken concrete. Craters pock-marked the road around the building, slowing the fire engines whose sirens adding to the cacophony of terror.

Suddenly desperate, Sayuri lead the way to the factory restaurant. Dust and smoke choked her, and she held her sleeve before her face. She stopped where a partially collapsed roof and an array of toppled stoves covered the bodies of a dozen people.

Feeling ineffectual, she attempted to lift one of the splintered wooden beams. A leg, severed from its body, stuck out; a head, its eyes still staring in disbelief, rolled to her feet. She screamed and, looking upon the face, screamed again when she saw it was Sensei. Kneeling, with tears rolling down her cheeks, she lifted the woman's head, then gently placed it back down and covered it with a shred of tablecloth.

Shuddering, she backed away, sobbing unintelligible words of anguish. Then, overcome with fright and revulsion, she shrieked, "Koizumi, you did this! You made Sensei come here! You are evil and I hate you! I will hate you for ever!"

* * *

At the railway station, people spoke in subdued voices. No one dared acknowledge that the Americans had had the audacity to bomb the land of the Rising Sun. How could a nation whose navy had been devastated be capable of flying bombers all the way to Japan and evade detection? How was it that the vaunted Japanese air force was so indolent that they could do little more than race futilely after enemy planes that vanished into thin air? Not one enemy plane had been shot down, not a single pilot captured to face the fury of Imperial Japan.

Sayuri took no part in these murmured conversations. She was silent, overcome with grief. Sensei, the woman who had raised her after her parents died, who had smiled so warmly, who was the epitome of quiet, impeccable grace, was gone. There was a ragged, hollow place in her heart now, and a cold fear seeped in. Mrs. Svenson had been right. She'd said that vengeful Americans would come. And they had. *What has our nation done?* she wondered.

It was dark when she and Kumi-san returned to the ikebana shop. Sayuri lit the candle, the only light in the room. A wind had risen and it had the sound of a dirge. Kumi made *ocha* and found a handful of rice crackers. They sat together, knees tucked under them, sipping their tea. From time to time Sayuri cried and Kumi-san held her close.

The wind rose to a howl, as if the spirits of the dead screamed in terror. Death had struck from the skies, instantaneous, unimaginable, and irrevocable. It was the end of the end of the world, thought Sayuri, for people who had gone about the ordinary affairs of living only twenty-four hours before.

* * *

Sayuri woke to a soft knock on the door. Stirring, she surmised that one of Sensei's clients had come for an ikebana lesson. For a moment Sayuri was confused, never having slept downstairs. Her tiny bedroom, not four tatamis long, was above the shop. She was about to call Sensei and tell her that a student was waiting when awareness struck like a tsunami. Paralyzed with grief, she watched as Kumi opened the door and let in the last person Sayuri wanted to see.

Koizumi removed his boots and noiselessly knelt before Sayuri. He leaned forward and bowed, his head nearly touching the floor. He stayed like that for a long moment before sitting up. He looked empty of life itself.

In a barely audible voice he said, "I beg you to forgive the unforgivable. I was angry, foolishly angry, and jealous beyond anything you can imagine. But I never wanted this to happen." He stopped, seeking her approval to continue, then said, "Now, perhaps as you do, I feel an emptiness. I cared greatly for Sensei. It was terrible to read of her death—the *Asahi Times* listed the names of the dead and wounded this morning. I, who have been trained to ignore all feelings, felt ashamed. And I hurt you. Now I must bear the unbearable, as you are doing now."

He dropped his eyes to stare down at his hands. Then, looking up, he gazed into her eyes. She said nothing, but stared back at him, her expression one of inconsolable sadness. Was it for him, or Sensei? Or for a world gone horribly mad?

Kumi spoke up. "It is good of you to come here. Perhaps our hearts will mend someday. For now, we must simply do what we can, and what we must."

Koizumi bowed low, then slowly rose to his feet. "I must do what I can to protect our nation. I must do what I can to protect a dream, even if it never comes true."

He turned to Sayuri and said, "I will never intrude upon you again. I say goodbye."

He went to the door, wondering if Sayuri would say anything. She did not.

He closed the door behind him one last time, and walked down the street to rejoin war. Perhaps he would die a samurai's death. That, he thought, was the least he could do.

Chapter 10
The Pacific, off Tulagi, Solomon Islands
May 4, 1942

The realization was borne home that the United States was going to commit its forces in the Pacific, and this convinced the Japanese high command that Japan needed a defensive barrier of islands. One of the earliest efforts by the Imperial Japanese Navy was to capture and fortify Port Moresby in New Guinea. A strong defensive position there would play havoc with Allied efforts to supply Australia, and would also interfere with American fleet actions in areas surrounding the Solomon Islands.

A convoy of Japanese transports, supported by the light carrier *Shoho*, steamed toward New Guinea. Those on board expected to summarily overcome the Australian detachments guarding the region's capital.

The *Shoho* had not originally been intended as an aircraft carrier and its conversion was an ad hoc affair of questionable design, making it slow to bring aircraft up from from hangers to the flight deck. Being smaller than the *Shokaku* or the *Zuikaku*, it was primarily used to convey aircraft from one location to another. When American bombers and torpedo planes located it off the island of Rossel, the ship had only nine first-line fighters for defense.

The initial bombing pass only raised water spouts. Those on deck jeered and shouted insults at the attackers. But then thousand-pound bombs slammed into the vessel, followed by torpedo plane strikes. In flames and taking on water, the *Shoho* was the first Japanese carrier to be sunk by U.S. Navy airplanes in the Battle of the Coral Sea. An American pilot, *Lexington's* Lieutenant Commander Robert E. Dixon, laconically sent back the message, "Scratch one flat top."

Shoho's demise, with the loss of over eight hundred crew, ended Japan's attempt to take Port Moresby.

* * *

The carrier *Lexington* joined *Yorktown* to complete the assemblage of Rear Admiral Frank Fletcher's Task Force 17. Its primary objective was to find and destroy the Japanese carrier force, the same armada that had devastated Pearl Harbor. A large but lightly armed oiler, the *Neosho*, kept the fleet fueled and capable of continuous action.

Throughout May 5th, Americans and Japanese scout planes went aloft in search of each other's fleet, but both navies remained elusive as squalls and heavy cloud rolled over the Coral Sea.

That night, Jack and Tad went to the catwalk and peered out at the distant destroyer screen and the cruiser U.S.S. *Minneapolis* off the stern quarter.

"I'm amazed those B-25s got airborne without landing in the drink," said Jack. "The *Hornet* is even smaller than this ship, and I can barely get my Wildcat off the deck."

A gust of wind sent spray over the exposed catwalk.

"The Doolittle raid was quite a surprise, and not just for the Japanese. One hell of a morale boost for the folks back home," commented Tad.

"One hell of a surprise for Tojo. Can you imagine what they must have been thinking when those bombers hit a dozen cities and flew *right over* the Emperor's palace? It must have scared the bejeezus out of him. But I don't know why they didn't bomb the palace," said Jack.

"Killing the Emperor would infuriate the Japanese and bond them together even more. Kind of like the Blitz over London. A lot of people died, but it gave the Brits one hell of a spine. Unintended consequences."

"Well, unlike the Nazis, I guess the Doolittle boys weren't going after civilians, just military targets and factories," said Jack.

"But a lot of civilians work in military targets," said Tad, hoping that the ikebana shop in which Sayuri lived was far from the bombed factories.

Jack lit a cigarette, inhaled deeply, and said, "That was a carrier raid by army bombers, and I doubt we'll pull that stunt again. And I'll bet even money we get a few black eyes before we do any more raids on Japan."

"Yeah, I imagine you're right," said Tad, his mind miles away.

"Not feeling conflicted, are you?" asked Jack, flicking an ash and watching it spiral toward the sea.

"Against Japan? For what they've been doing against us and all of Asia? Hell, no. I want to beat the crap out of them. I barely remember Japan, and I'm American. My mother used to talk about the serenity and etiquette of her home country, but the Japan we're dealing with has none of that, not the military and not the government. I suppose ordinary people still do, but not the ones going on the offensive. No, Jack, I have no qualms about shooting their planes out of the air."

"Damn right. Flame their asses. I want a string of Mitsubushi flags on the fuselage of my Wildcat."

Tad grinned and said, "Just be sure that some hot shot Nip ace doesn't paint your plane on his."

"Not a chance. By the way, have you ever seen one? A Zero, I mean? The army pilots I spoke to at Pearl said they turn and climb a hell of a lot faster than our older stuff. A P-40 is totally outclassed."

"I'd say the planes matter, but outcomes come down to experience. A trained pilot knows how to get the best out of whatever he's flying. I'm not sure about their tactics. Do they work in pairs like we do, or do they go at it alone? I heard that they don't coordinate very well."

Suddenly Jack laughed and said, "About coordination, I had this idiotic recollection last night. Remember when we were sophomores at UCLA and we got that summer job as camp counselors?"

Tad groaned and rolled his eyes. "That was a nightmare. What made you think of that?"

"Well, it just came to me. You were driving the bus with all those kids and we stopped at the gas station on Highway Sixty-Six among all those cows."

"When you forgot to take the nozzle out of the gas tank. Yeah, how can I forget?" said Tad.

"And you drove off and the whole gas pump went with you, careening across the road for three or four miles. I was driving behind and traffic was tearing off the road to get out of the way. Sparks everywhere, and people were trying to flag you down, but all the kids were waving, not knowing about the pump," said Jack.

"You could have helped me out," said Tad sardonically.

"Hell no! I wasn't going to get anywhere near you. But then the pump took out a fence and about three hundred cows got loose. Remember what the judge said when they hauled us into court?"

"Something else I want to forget. But we sure learned how to ride horses."

"Yep. 'You boys will round up every one of those damn cows or I'll fine your ass three hundred dollars for every one.'"

"Only because it was his ranch and his cows. But that was no worse than the time I let you fly my dad's biplane."

"The time we crashed?"

"The time *you* crashed, with the nose in the dirt and me in the rear seat fifteen feet off the ground. I look around and I see you sitting on a stump explaining to a tree why half the prop was buried in it."

"I thought it was only right to offer an apology. Kind of like my people do before they cut down a tree. You have to apologize."

"You're such a jerk. I don't know why I let you hang around me."

Jack grinned and said, "Because of my wit and innate intelligence." He studied the stars half covered by scudding clouds, then said, "By the way, have you talked to the new guys, the ones who came on board at Pearl?"

"Not really, just said hello to a few on the hanger deck."

"You'll never guess who I saw. Couldn't imagine that he would show up on the *Lex*."

"Who?" asked Tad.

"Your old nemesis. I wouldn't have recognized him, but I saw his name on the flight roster. And he's in our squadron. Can't miss the name, Lee-Beauregard Smythe, with a 'y.' How's that for green tomatoes?"

Tad gave his friend a baleful look, then said, "You've got to be joking."

"Nope. I can't wait to see the love fest. But maybe bygones are bygones. He might just looooove to talk to you about your fun times with his sister. And you can tell him about the 'hair of the dog.' Remember that?"

"There are things I choose to forget, Jack. And that is one of them." There was a hard edge to Tad's voice, and Jack realized he may have gone too far.

Tad changed the subject. "I'm heading to the hanger deck. I want to check my prop and that hook; I might have damaged something when I took that first arresting wire."

"Good idea; miss the wires and your plane becomes a sub. Personally, I don't fancy going down a thousand feet. I've heard it gets very cold down there. I'm getting some coffee; meet you in a bit."

"The Japs can barely get their planes off the ground. Hell, I myself saw three Nips collide at an air show once. The only reason they've had any success in Asia is because they're flying against the Chinks, and they can't fly either." A pilot outside the ready room was "enlightening" a young ensign.

"That's bullshit," said Tad, walking over.

The pilot turned his head and was about to answer when he glanced at Tad's name tag. He leaned against the bulwark and drawled, "My, my, look who we have here. Who the hell let you on this ship?"

"The same Navy that let you on. And what you're telling this ensign is wrong. The Japanese pilots are among the best in the world. You better have eyes in the back of your head and check you six every five seconds."

"Really? I guess you know all about it, you Jap. And a goddamn Jew to boot. What a combination. I think you're in the wrong navy, buster."

Smythe didn't even see the fist that sent him to the deck. Nor did he see the second one that doubled him over. Tad grabbed his throat, stood him up and, with a clang, bashed his head into the bulkhead. Lee-Beauregard swung a wild punch at Tad, but it was way off the mark.

"Enough. Belay that!" bellowed grave-voiced John McGill. "What the hell is this? In my quarters, in three minutes, both of you. And you, mister, wipe that blood off your face. Three minutes or you're both grounded!" He stalked off, his head lowered like a bull's and fists clenched by his sides.

The ensign stared, aghast, as the two pilots, glaring daggers at each other, one of them daubing his profusely bleeding nose, turned to follow.

In short order, they were standing at attention in front of an extremely irate squadron commander.

"You're not goddamn twenty-year old kids," seethed McGill. "You are both senior pilots, and a whole bunch of young ensigns are depending on you. I have every right to put you on report and file this with the carrier air group commander. But he has a bit on his plate right now, and busting both of you back to ensigns is not something I care to burden him with. We're facing a whole Jap carrier task force, in case it slipped your minds. Would it be too much to ask you *gentlemen* to save your enthusiasm for bloodshed for the actual *enemy*?" His voiced dripped sarcasm.

A trickle of blood oozed down Lee-Beauregard's chin. He clenched his teeth and stole a glance at Tad, who stared back. For a brief moment Tad wondered what McGill would say if he knew Tad's heritage. Had he heard Smyth's taunts, or only seen the fight?

"If I ever hear of something like this again, I will have your miscreant asses in a sling, do you both understand?" rasped McGill.

"Aye, sir," replied the two men stiffly.

There was a protracted moment of silence, then the commander said, "Scouts have reported sighting a Jap carrier group, so get ready to go to work. Now get out of my quarters."

The two saluted and left. Tad stopped outside the commander's quarters, crossed his arms and raised his eyebrows as Smythe. Half under his breath he said, "We're not done, mister. Not by a long shot."

"Fine with me. Get in front of my guns and I'll flame your ass. You think I'm kidding?" Smythe snarled. "Don't even worry about pulling the chute. You won't have a chance."

"The feeling's mutual. Stay out of my sights!"

Any further exchange of compliments was prevented by the ship's klaxon going off.

Tad's squadron was assigned to CAP duty, flying cover for the task force, and specifically the "Lady Lex". On the flight deck above, the engines of Grumman F4F-3 Wildcats were roaring to life. Clipboards in hand, pilots loped toward their waiting aircraft.

* * *

Earlier in the morning, an aircraft had landed on board the *Shokaku* with several mail bags. Letters in hand, Koizumi and his friend Taicho, avoiding the noise of returning search planes, retreated to the now quiet ready room.

"A letter from my wife and son," said Taicho, opening the envelope and grinning at the straggling *Konji* characters written by his six-year old son. His wife's letter wished him success and prayed for his safety. The letter ended with, "The thoughts of the entire nation are with you. I send my love and can't wait to see you home safely again."

I must not disappoint her or the nation, thought Taicho, returning the letter to the envelope. Turning to Koizumi he said, "Well, who wrote to you?"

Koizumi held up the envelope and Taicho, snatching it, said, "Oh, from the young beauty you talk about in your sleep. So read it to me. Don't keep me waiting."

"I'm certainly not going to read it to you," said Koizumi pulling the letter out of his friend's hand. He studied the delicate writing on the envelope and hesitated. What could she possibly say to him? He was no longer part of her life, and it was hopeless to think that someday he would hold her in his arms. No, he would never feel her body against his on a cold winter night. But now a letter from her.

He took a deep breath and gently slid a single sheet of rice paper from the envelope.

Hello, flight officer Lieutenant Koizumi Karamatsu.

Not a very auspicious beginning, certainly not one expressing any affection. But he had not expected such. Koizumi read on.

I hope that this letter finds you in good health. Despite the words I said regarding my wish to not see you again, I felt that I should express my hope that you survive the combat you have prepared for all your life. I know that your devotion is to our Emperor, our nation, and all its people. In no way do I fault you for that, for I too love this land.

I have been grieving over the loss of Sensei for many weeks. This house is empty and I do not imagine that I will linger here much longer. I am ashamed that I have also been grieving for my own situation, a selfish thing, considering the sacrifice of so many brave soldiers and sailors in this war.

I realize now that although I cannot forgive your behavior toward Sensei, I understand that it was done out of anguish at not having a woman you love. About that I can do nothing, but I truly hope that you will find a lady who can give you what I cannot.

I pray that you will return to find peace and serenity within your own soul. I think that you are essentially a good man who must find solace in the midst of what must be terribly painful.

May fate favor you,
Sayuri

Koizumi studied the letter, then read it to Taicho. There was a long period of reflection before the pilot said, "She expressed noble sentiments, *tomodachi*. After what you told me of the death of her Sensei, I am surprised that she wrote at all. But as she said, she wishes you no ill will, and that is generous of her."

"She said nothing about me having success in battle," Koizumi pointed out.

"She did say that she hopes you survive and return to find peace and serenity. Do you expect her to say that you should kill your brother, the American pilot, the one you told me about? I say this as a friend: I think it's time to concentrate on what we are expected to do, and it's time to put her and your brother out of your mind," said Taicho solemnly.

"But what if I do kill him? What then?"

"You're asking me if eliminating him would change how Sayuri feels about you?" Taicho gave Koizumi a sad smile and said, "War is war, and it may happen. But we rarely see the face of the man we have just shot down, so even if it does happen, you will most likely never know. If it happens and you *do* know, you must never let her find out that it was you who killed him, because you would kill her too."

"I would never tell her; nor will I reply, nor speak to her again. But I will do my duty," Koizumi said with brittle determination, "no matter what fate requires."

He folded the letter and slipped it into his pocket, vowing to keep it by him forever.

Chapter 11
The Coral Sea
May 7, 1942

"The search planes found an American carrier," Taicho Igumi reported excitedly. "At least one *Saratoga* type and escort vessels, perhaps even cruisers and a battleship. And they may not have seen our scout. It could be a complete surprise." He and Koizumi slapped their hands together, then raced to their fighters.

The drone of engines made it impossible to hear anything else as seventy-eight planes, *kanyo* torpedo bombers, Zeros and dive bombers, began to lift off the decks of the *Shokaku* and the *Zuikaku*. At 0730 the aircraft, cheered on by crewmen shouting "Banzai!" and waving caps in the air, climbed into a clear sky and coalesced into attack formations.

Finally, thought Koizumi, *a chance to destroy the carriers that we missed at Pearl Harbor.* If only they had waited a day, even a week, they could have crippled the American Pacific fleet; now they were facing a vengeful enemy, alert and stalking the Imperial Japanese Navy.

As the flight droned on, he glanced out at the massed squadrons, an armada of invincibility, the best they had, experienced pilots all. What would the Americans think, what fear would these samurai inspire as they plummeted out of the sky like birds of prey upon hapless crews below?

He knew that the targets were at the extreme limits of their fuel and that the attack would have to be quick and decisive. Sink the carriers, destroy any combat air patrol, head home. That was all that mattered. Once accomplished, Japan would be free. The people, *his* people, would sleep safely upon their tatami and futons with not a worry in the world.

He patted the pocket of his flight jacket. The letter, *her* letter, was there. It would be the only keepsake he would ever have from her; and yet, was it not a rejection of his love? Was it not a dismissal masked by a wish that he survive the war and find another woman?

Why, he wondered, had she written at all? What solace did she think her letter might afford him? Was she ashamed of the way she had treated him, or was there something else? Time. He would give her time. How long could her love for an enemy last if she never see him again?

Yes, he reasoned, some years from now, after the war, he would return and find her. He envisioned himself standing proudly before her, hearing her say in her soft, caressing voice, "Koizumi-san, you have come back. Forgive me, forgive me. It has been so long."

Sunlight and the deep blue of the empyrean overhead recalled Koizumi to himself, and he remembered his purpose. A bitterness rose within him. No, there would be nothing like that. Her lover, and most assuredly he *was* her lover, would be killed; and she, his Sayuri, would be a bitter woman, spiteful to any and all who sent Tadichi to the bottom of the sea.

"There they are! I see two ships, turning now," said Taicho, excitement in his voice.

"Dive, dive!" yelled the flight leader. "Fighters, cover the bombers and torpedo planes."

From out of the sun the bombers dove from twelve thousand feet through the azure sky. Suddenly, black bursts peppered the air, and a bomber began to spiral uncontrollably, a wing blown away. The other pilots clenched their teeth, knowing that it could soon be them trapped by the g forces with only seconds to live.

Koizumi lost sight of a *kanyo* torpedo bomber that had cartwheeled into the dark blue sea, but he did see the explosions that wracked the ships. Great plumes of inky smoke and fire erupted on the largest of them. Near misses sent waterspouts high into the air. Following the bombers, the torpedo planes unleashed their javelins, one after the other blowing great holes in their quarry.

A second smaller vessel, most likely a destroyer, was also struck and flames raged along her deck. That there was no air cover, not the slightest sign of CAP, surprised Koizumi. Could the Americans actually be so fast asleep? Was it like Pearl Harbor all over again? How could they possibly be so inept?

Peeling off with Taicho on his starboard wing, Koizumi followed the torpedo planes down, and at three hundred and fifty knots sped over the two stricken ships. Both were flaming wrecks with smoke billowing skyward. Koizumi pulled up, banked, and with a puzzled look, passed over them again.

Amazingly, an anti-aircraft battery on the larger vessel still sent flak skyward, but a Zero soon silenced the forty-millimeter gun. "Why isn't she sinking?" asked Taicho.

Koizumi, with utter fury said, "That's not the problem. The problem is that we hit an empty oiler and a single destroyer. That burning hulk is not a carrier! This is all for naught! A damn oiler, and she won't even sink!"

A BLOSSOM IN THE ASHES

Fifteen minutes later, the aircraft squadrons, minus three brought down by enemy guns, headed back to the *Shokaku* and *Zuikaku*. Their crews, puzzled and tired from the long flight, congregated in the hanger deck as their aircraft were refueled and rearmed. An undertone of disappointment permeated the group. Any satisfaction in crippling American ships did little to soften the fact that their efforts were so terribly misdirected and three valuable aircraft had been shot down. How could the scouts have been so horribly wrong?

"The American ships surely reported that they were under attack," said Taicho as he and Koizumi went to their quarters. "If any of their search planes spotted and followed us, they now know our position. We surprised them this time, but I don't think we can do it again."

The pilots silently walked past somber crewmen. On the bridge the general staff prepared for the next day. Rear Admiral Chuichi Hara still had over one hundred and fifty aircraft and highly trained crews. Yes, he thought, tomorrow must be a much better day.

* * *

There was tense but quiet excitement in the ready room as Lexington's pilots took last-minute notes on the positions of enemy ships. "Our scouts did good stealth work," Jack said in an aside to Tad.

"I'm amazed they got close enough to get this intel without being intercepted," Tad replied. "Amazed, and grateful. Wonder who we have to thank."

"Maybe they're Apache," Jack said with a grin. "Tonto takes to the air."

The *Yorktown* was the first to get its F4F Grumman Wildcats in the air to cover Torpedo 5, which proceeded at one hundred and thirty knots. At 0907 Commander Bill Ault led his squadrons off *Lexington.* Fighters climbed to eighteen thousand feet and headed toward the day's targets: the Japanese carriers.

Tad, following the lead aircraft, glanced over at Jack on his right wing and saw him hold up his talisman, a cheap plastic grass-skirted Hawaiian doll he had won in a shooting gallery at Pearl. Jack swore by it, despite Tad telling him it was the most ridiculous thing to bring to a dogfight. Jack had answered that it reminded him of the best piece of ass he'd had in a long time, and that was worth fighting for.

"I just hope I can find her again," Jack had said. "It was so good I might even marry the girl."

"Right," said Tad. "If you can even remember what she looks like. And she seemed to fancy that Aussie corporal. I think he was the next one in line."

That bit of intelligence did little to dampen Jack's recollection of the less-than-amorous twenty-minute sex fest. Now Jack was grinning, pointing down to Lee-Beauregard's plane, which was wobbling slightly, as if flown by an unsteady hand.

Twenty minutes later there was chatter about enemy aircraft flying on a fast track toward the American carriers. Over the radio came the order, "Don't engage. Repeat: do not engage. Continue on mission. Let the combat air patrol fellows do their job. They're itching for the chance."

Not long after, the entire Japanese strike group of two massive formations passed below on an opposite heading. *We better get this over with damn fast*, thought Tad, *because those planes will probably bust through our own CAP and there will be hell to pay.* It was a hard thing to watch them flying inexorably towards his friends.

"Carriers below! Watch out for Zeros. Torpedo Five is going in!" The order crackled over the radio.

A Blossom in the Ashes

One torpedo plane after another sent its fish toward the *Shokaku*. Her captain, calculating the direction of the aircraft and the incoming torpedoes, adroitly turned the ship, evading one torpedo after another. A fusillade of deck gunfire began shooting down torpedo planes, and curvetting Zeros, their pilots braving their own ship's anti-aircraft fire, flamed others. Enemy fighter pilots caused havoc, striking impetuously at the American formation.

The torpedo planes had failed; it was the SBD Dauntless dive bombers' turn next. Again, Mitsubishi Zeros tore upward to challenge the Americans. Tad spotted a Zero targeting a Dauntless; he shoved the nose around and pulled hard as he rolled in on the zero. Sensing danger, the Zero pilot turned toward Tad, who managed to get off a burst. Smoke then flames bloomed from its fuel tanks, turning the Zero into a lethal orange-red-black flower as it plummeted toward the water.

Tad broke off and turned tightly to clear his tail and spotted a second Zero attacking another SBD just beginning its dive on the *Shokaku*. Tad lined up behind the intruder, but had to immediately pull up as another F4F cut him off, fifty-caliber guns blazing. The Zero banked away, did a loop and dived on its assailant. Turning in a tight, twisting circle, Tad reentered the melee to see the Zero gaining on the slower, less maneuverable Wildcat.

It was Lee-Beauregard. Flashes spewed from the Zero's machine guns, ripping holes into Smyth's wing. Barreling in, Tad saw Beauregard frantically twisting his Wildcat to keep it from being hit. Apparently, he'd forgotten the first rule in fighting a Zero: when attacked, dive away.

"Someone, anyone, get the bastard off my six!" shouted Smythe as the Zero closed the range. He glanced to his left and saw Tad lined up on him, a furious, intent look on his face. He was dead in Tad's sights.

"No!" he screamed as Tad waited for the exact moment.

Concentrating on finishing off the damaged Wildcat, the Zero's pilot didn't notice Tad's F4F until a fusillade of fifty-caliber rounds ripped the Zero's fuselage from one end to the other. The plane flipped over and spiraled into the sea.

"You're all shot up," Tad called out to Smythe over the radio. "Recommend you head back to the *Lex*."

There was no answer from Beauregard, but Tad saw his plane head toward their carrier. Glancing down, Tad saw two more Zeros splash into the ocean. Near misses erupted around the *Shokaku*.

Then five fresh dive bombers sped down, and an enormous explosion erupted on the forward flight deck. Moments later, a second thousand-pound bomb struck the center. The huge carrier turned into an inferno as munitions and fueled aircraft exploded, sending oily black smoke hundreds of feet into the air.

Circling above, Tad could see hundreds of crewmen abandon ship, while more explosions blew aircraft and crew overboard. The air battle broke off as Japanese pilots, seeing the utter destruction of their carrier, flew toward the *Zuikaku* to protect that ship from a possible enemy strike. But that was not to be; the American aircraft were out of bombs and torpedoes.

Somewhat to Tad's surprise, the surviving Americans reached the carriers ahead of the Japanese formation. *I guess our guesses are better than theirs*, he mused. *Either that, or we have better intel*. Either way, he was vastly relieved. Jack, however, was chagrined.

"If we had more planes with bombs and torpedos, we could have gone after the other cruiser while it was so lightly defended," he muttered in an undertone to Tad. "Think about it! If we'd destroyed both carriers, any Zeroes that did survive an attack against the *Lex* and the *York* wouldn't have any carrier to return to! They'd all plop into the drink and drown when they ran dry. Now they're still out there."

"Maybe you should be an admiral," Tad replied. He could see that Jack had a commander's eye for strategy. But as he took in the purposeful movements of men aboard the carrier, the calls, the banter, the familiar smells of fuel and paint, the clang of metal and rumble of the engines, he was glad they'd returned in time to intercept, not overtake, the incoming Japanese squadrons. He might not care for every man aboard, but he couldn't wish a flaming death on his worst enemy.

Crews set about rearming and refueling aircraft, making quick repairs on damaged planes. One petty officer sarcastically thanked a pilot for bringing back an 4F4 that was so shot up his team were counting bullet holes and shaking their heads. "Sooner them than me," Tad heard one of them remark. He hurried after Jack to the ready room for another briefing

A number of pilots were there already, engaged in describing their encounters. Lee-Beauregard Smythe was one of them, and he broke off when he saw Tad enter. All talk stopped; nearly everyone was aware of the animosity between the two men.

Tad, ignoring him, was about to pass when Smythe said, "Hey, hold up." Tad stopped and looked at him, his face devoid of expression.

"I, uh, I just wanted to say thanks," Smythe said. "I thought for a moment I was in your gun sights."

"You were. But I had a juicier target. Try not to cut me off again. Something bad might happen."

"Yeah, well, it was pretty dicey with the Ja... Nips all over the place."

"Sure was," said Tad. "The Nips know how to fly. So don't go telling ensigns otherwise. If they go up there expecting easy targets, they won't survive."

It was a truce, of sorts.

May 8, 1942

A *Kawanishi* scout flying boat was downed by Wildcats shortly after Tad and the strike group returned to *Lexington*. Assuming that the downed plane portended incoming flights, more F4Fs rose off the decks to join the Wildcats circling overhead, and surveillance teams scanned radar scopes. A series of false alarms by scouts from both carriers were belied by empty skies.

Then the radar operators detected two incoming "V" formations that matched the description of the anticipated raid. Seventeen fighters, Tad and Jack among them, took off to intercept enemy torpedo planes and dive bombers, climbing at maximum power to get above the incoming Japanese airplanes. *Yorktown*, seven miles distant, launched its own CAP.

"Do you see your buddy Smythe?" Jack radioed Tad.

"Just fly your damn aircraft," answered Tad. Then, "Bogeys nine o'clock low. It's a mix of bombers and fighters and torpedo planes! Follow me."

Jack dove and fired on a torpedo plane before it launched its fish, causing it to erupt in a massive midair explosion as the torpedo's warhead detonated. "Splashed one!" he crowed, although nothing larger than fragments remained to fall into the water. The explosion rocked his fighter and he heard thunks as his plane was hit by debris. Trusting his sturdy Wildcat to withstand the damage, he lined up another torpedo bomber in his sights. It went down in flames. To the east he could see puffs of black smoke from anti-aircraft bursts and planes circling. Occasionally, one would start to trail smoke.

But nearly seventy Japanese aircraft continued to roar toward the carriers. Formations dissolved as opposing fighters and bombers broke off to engage in duels, explosions bloomed and tracers arced across the sky, and gun crews on the carriers and support ships sent up thousands of rounds of anti-aircraft fire. Flaming Japanese aircraft, their pilots still firing at targets, screamed past American ships and spiraled into the sea.

A parody of a Lufbery Wheel circled below Tad: an American plane followed by a Zero chased by a Wildcat pursued by another Zero, engaged in a deadly game. Tad entered the fray, firing at a Zero that abruptly pulled up and rolled onto its back. As he passed the Japanese fighter, he could see the pilot slumped in the cockpit.

Two Zeros were suddenly on his tail, firing furiously. The rounds were riddling his Wildcat; one struck his landing gear and three pierced the cockpit. He felt sudden pain in his left calf and shoulder, and something grazed his forehead. Wiping blood from his face, he spotted another Zero on the tail of an F4F that had already taken a number of hits and was smoking. The pilot attempted to evade by executing a roll followed by a dive then a side slip, but the Zero pilot stayed on him, firing bust after burst.

Tad gained altitude and fought off a bout of dizziness. As he closed with the Japanese aircraft he realized he had expended nearly all his ammunition. But the Zero was just beneath him. He fired and missed. The briefest of glances skyward showed Tad that Jack and another pilot were effectively distracting the two Zeroes that had shot up his Wildcat. As a pulsing stream of blood ran over one eye, he squeezed the trigger and held it, firing his last rounds. The Zero burst into flame.

Koizumi watched his friend's aircraft spiral downward. There was a splash, a brief moment when a wing appeared to float, then nothing. The Wildcat was now a thousand feet above him, but shot up and flying erratically; the pilot was probably wounded. Koizumi fired into the damaged plane. The American aircraft shuddered and dove toward *Lexington,* and Koizumi followed, intent on finishing off whoever had just killed his one friend. But gunners on a close-in cruiser spotted the red "meatball" on his Zero's wing and banged away with twin forty-caliber mounts. At four hundred feet above the water and with a half-dozen rounds streaking past his cockpit, Koizumi pulled out of the dive and roared over the carrier's screening destroyers.

There was nothing Tad could do to stop the bleeding. The deck was above him, then below, as the damaged aircraft wobbled toward the carrier. Dizzily, Tad tried to focus on the centerline. *Wheels down*, he reminded himself, trying to blink away the blood. An anxious crewman on deck was waving his paddles, ordering him to circle back around. Two fighters were already on deck, one just beginning its forward roll. His radio crackled, "Wave off! Wave off!"

Tad tried to follow the order to circle about and return, but the Wildcat seemed unresponsive; he was fading fast.

"Tower, Wildcat Zero Five, am wounded. Can't go around."

Wheels down, hook down, flaps down... he reminded himself, trying to blink away the blood. The plane hit hard and the landing gear collapsed, causing the plane to skid, missing the first arresting wire. Crewmen scattered out of the way. The tail hook caught the second wire and the airplane slid right and slammed into the superstructure, ripping off a wing. For Tad, everything went black.

A BLOSSOM IN THE ASHES

Men scrambled to pull him from the cockpit as the remaining fuel spilled onto the deck. Once he was on a litter, crewmen pushed the destroyed fighter plane over the side to sink beneath the waters, as another fighter tore off the deck.

* * *

Jack Vestergaard stopped an orderly outside *Lexington's* on board surgery. "The pilot who was just brought in, is he going to make it?" he demanded.

"They're giving him blood and extracting bullets. Time will tell. Sir, I've got to get going, we have more wounded."

"Is he going to be okay?" asked another pilot, veering towards the operating room.

"They won't let you in there," replied Jack, moving towards a ladder.

"But I'm asking, are his wounds fatal?"

"How the hell would I know?" said Jack irritably.

"The bastard saved me again. He damn well better live," said Lee-Beauregard Smythe.

The *Lexington* shuddered as a torpedo hit home. Just as Jack regained his footing and started up the rungs, a second shock reverberated through the carrier, and he heard the announcement, "All damage control and corpsmen forward!"

Coming on deck, Jack and Smythe saw smoke and flame rising up from a hole in the side of the ship. Firemen were already wielding fire hoses while other crew frantically pushed airplanes to safety.

"We can still get in the air," called out Lee-Beauregard as they loped towards two readied Wildcats, cockpits open.

"Better hurry, they're coming again. Let's go!" shouted Jack. As he was waved off the deck, he was wondering if they would have a carrier to return to.

The Japanese formation closed on the American carriers. Eighteen torpedo bombers dropped to one hundred feet above the water to make their runs. Koizumi saw four of them head towards *Yorktown,* while the rest targeted *Lexington.*

A sudden dive from a pouncing Wildcat and one of the torpedo planes burst into flame. Koizumi cursed. Each plane, each pilot was precious. Along with fourteen other Zeros, Koizumi sped toward the American fighters. Debris rained down; there were more than a dozen burning and exploding planes, Zeroes and Wildcats, streaking across the sky or plowing into the ocean below.

Cruisers and destroyers sent thousands of rounds toward the torpedo bombers, which had split into two groups in an attempt to hit *Lexington* on both sides. Two more torpedo planes burst into flame as the American combat patrol dove on attacking aircraft before they could launch their fish. Slow and unable to maneuver, they were easy targets for the Wildcats.

As soon as the Japanese planes had been detected on radar, *Yorktown's* Captain Buckmaster had ordered flank speed. At thirty-two knots, the big carrier sped away from incoming torpedoes. The *Lexington,* Koizumi saw, was not so fortunate. Four Japanese torpedo bombers, evading intense anti-aircraft fire, had launched their weapons at the great ship's port bow. Two torpedoes went too deep and passed below her hull, but first one explosion, then a second, told that the remaining torpedoes had found their mark.

Koizumi tore over the stricken carrier as he pursued a Wildcat. The slower American aircraft attempted to climb, but the Zero's guns ripped into the fuselage. The F4F sputtered, leveled off, then pancaked into the sea. As Koizumi climbed to find his next target, he glimpsed the F4F pilot clambering into a rubber raft as the ocean's current pulled him away from the battle.

Then Japanese dive bombers came out of the sun and plummeted toward *Lexington* from over thirteen thousand feet. One bomb struck an ammunition locker, causing an explosion that immolated an entire gun crew. A second bomb struck the island superstructure. It did little damage, but it set off the ship's siren, which proceeded to blast throughout the remainder of the attack, hindering communications.

Pilots from the *Zuikaku* launched themselves against *Yorktown,* and though many bombs missed, one struck the flight deck, temporarily halting all air operations. Crews worked frantically to extinguish the fire and cover the gaping hole with steel plates. Above her, dogfights at all altitudes raged on.

Flying at ten thousand feet, Jack spotted three Mitsubishi Zeroes escorting a lone Zeke torpedo bomber. He streamed down in a steep hit-and-run pass, aiming for the Zeke, but it was too closely defended. In the short time of his approach and pass his Wildcat took a pounding, but his guns ripped into one Zero. It rolled over and burned like a torch before it splashed into the sea.

The Japanese attack finally expended itself. The remaining Zeroes headed out of range and back to the *Zuikaku.* Except for combat air patrol above the carriers, American aircraft began to land on the slow-moving *Yorktown* and the smoking *Lexington.* Damage control teams on both ships worked feverishly. Badly shot-up planes were taken below. Wounded pilots were hustled to surgery.

Shortly after noon, Jack returned to *Lexington.* He was gratified to see that most of the bomb damage had been cleared away and the flight deck was serviceable. A few minutes later, Lee-Beauregard Smyth's Wildcat touched down. The two pilots were descending toward the ready room when Smythe stopped and said, "I smell fumes, port side."

"Maybe from the gasoline tanks. I think damage control is trying to vent the compartments. The torpedo hits must have holed the pipes."

Hoses snaked along passageways, and damage crews were scrambling up and down ladders, trying to clear out a build-up of fumes near the motor generator compartment. Suddenly, an enormous explosion ripped through *Lexington,* severing communication and killing dozens. Sparks from severed wires had ignited the particulate-laden air. As strike groups returned from their attack on the *Shokaku,* more fires broke out below decks.

In the midst of the confusion, a second and even more violent explosion wracked the *Lexington,* reducing the hangar deck to a mess of twisted steel.

Jack turned to Lee-Beauregard and said, "Tad's in sick bay. I'm going down; I've got to get him out. This ship will be taking on water."

"I'm going with you," said Smythe, and they descended into dark passageways clogged with fallen wires and overhead piping. The muted glow of flashlights illuminated cabins and shone on bulkheads as corpsmen carried litters topside.

Entering the smoke-filled surgery, they saw a doctor directing medical crews for the evacuation. Jack shouted a question above the roar of the fires. "The lieutenant's over there," answered an orderly. Smythe and Vestergaard lifted Tad onto a litter and hustled him to the flight deck alongside dozens of other injured.

Three destroyers were ordered to assist the stricken carrier. A third explosion shot fires aft; fearful of even more explosions, crews began flooding the ship's magazines.

Control of the rudders had ben lost, and *Lexington* was moving in a lazy circle. Finally, Captain Sherman ordered everyone to abandon ship. The wounded, Tad among them, were lowered to a waiting destroyer and transported to sickbay as over twenty-seven hundred men went over the side.

It was quite dark by 1800 hours when a final, massive explosion detonated in the center of the ship. Aircraft were blown off the flight deck and fires, glowing like great beacons, engulfed aircraft still on deck. As stoic sailors and airmen watched from rescue vessels, *Lexington* continued to wallow in the waves until the destroyer *Morris* was ordered to torpedo her. A rumble of explosions could be heard as boilers exploded, and the great carrier slid to the bottom of the Coral Sea.

The slugfest between the pilots of both navies had failed to produce a decisive victory for either fleet; but for now it stopped the Japanese invasion to capture the Australian base at Port Moresby, New Guinea. The Imperial Japanese lost one light carrier, and two of its largest fleet carriers were heavily damaged; *Shokaku* would not see action until March 1943. *Zuikaku's* squadrons had been decimated.

The United States lost *Lexington* and 69 planes. That night, *Yorktown* led Task Force Seventeen on its journey back to Pearl Harbor.

* * *

Dr. Thompson and Kimi rushed down the hallway, crowded with incoming wounded. All available doctors and nurses had been summoned. The most serious cases had been transported by ambulances; the walking wounded had ridden over from the harbor in Navy buses.

"Did you have a chance to see him?" panted Kimi as they made way for a gurney with an IV attached.

"Just for a second. I came to get you right away. Doctor Whitefield, the new surgeon, is with him."

Operating room curtains concealed the bed. Doctor Whitefield looked up from his clipboard when Thompson and Kimi parted the curtains and entered the small space. Standing by the narrow bed, Kimi stared into her son's drawn face. His eyes were closed and bandages swathed his head.

"Coma," said Whitefield. "The doctor on the ship said he suffered two broken ribs, a broken ankle, a bullet wound in his left calf, and a grazed forehead. Apparently, he went into a coma after crashing on the deck. He hasn't woken up since, and that was four days ago. Not a good sign. I wish I could give you more heartening information, but I'm afraid I can't."

Kimi lightly touched Tad's cheek, took a deep breath and closed her eyes. "I have seen so many come through here," she finally said. "And everyone was special. But my own son...." She broke off and a tear ran down her cheek.

Dr. Thompson put his hand on her shoulder and said, "He could come out of the coma any time. If he does... *when* he does, he will mend. He's strong, and none of the wounds are mortal."

Kimi nodded and said, "I would like to stay with him for a while. Then I'll join you in surgery, if that's okay."

"Take your time," said Dr. Whitefield. "I'll leave him in your hands for now, but I'll look in on him later." He took himself off, to tend to the next patient.

Thompson stood with Kimi by Tad's bed and said, "I know how distressful this is, and you don't have to deal with it alone."

Kimi looked up at him. "Tad is my son. I won't burden you with his fate."

"Not a burden. Later, come and talk to me if you wish." He was about to leave when he stopped and said, "Kimi-san, you don't have to spend tonight alone."

* * *

She moved through the rest of the day robotically, looking in on Tad whenever she could. He looked peaceful, she thought, but every once in a while he would moan or shake when a spasm shot through him. Holding his hand, she'd say, "It's going to be okay. Just wake up. That's all you have to do. Just wake up."

In medical journals she had read that people in a coma might yet hear voices and sounds around them, that their involuntary movements might be the reliving the desperate moments just prior to the injury. Soothing words, familiar voices, she thought, might resonate, might get through. So Kimi spoke to him in a gentle tone, saw the flicker of an eyelid, heard his breathing relax.

Her shift over, she stayed by her son for several hours, then drove home. She sat in her chair beside the window and looked out upon the dark city. The immediate fear of invasion had passed, but stringent blackout regulations prevailed. On occasion a truck or car would pass, creeping along with its lights off. A flight of fighters took off from Hickam Field, their engines droning until they were far out to sea. Then all was quiet once more.

The phone rang. It would be him. She let it ring four times before picking it up. She let him talk for several minutes, then said, "Yes, I will be there. Soon, yes. I don't want to be alone tonight. But just tonight."

He had made soup, a salad and a chicken dinner. "One of my best hens," Thompson said with a grin.

"You are a wonderful surgeon, but somehow I can't see you plucking feathers," said Kimi.

"Just like pulling stitches. The main difference is, my patients live."

"I wasn't surprised that you called. If it was your son, I would have called you. You made dinner; you must have anticipated I would come."

He shrugged. "I was hoping you would."

Over dinner he asked, "Have you heard anything more about Alexei? Any letters, anything from the American embassy in Moscow?"

She shook her head slowly. "Nothing. It's been over a year since I received the letter from the English journalist. He hasn't written since. We all hear the same news about Russia and the Nazis. Moscow was spared, but the Germans are still there. I don't even know if my husband is still alive. The Soviets won't say anything about their losses, but we've heard that they are estimated to be in the millions. No, Eli, I pray for him every night, but I have nothing. I just feel... empty."

They talked into the night, she half reclining in an easy chair, he across from her. He made no attempt to hold her, though he badly wanted to do so. His eyes held hers when she looked at him, her own eyes dark with melancholy and despair.

Once, when she wept, he rose and handed her a tissue, then said, "It is a terrible war, and the world will never be the same. I try not to think of the future, and it's difficult to contemplate the present. I know that this doesn't make things any easier, but I think of you every day and night, Kimi-san. You know that I love you. I love you very much, and there's nothing in the world I can do about it. And believe it or not, I pray for Alexei too. And now I also pray for Tad."

"You are a dear man, Eli. If things were different..." She let the sentence slip away and after a while said, "I would like to go to sleep. I will see you in the morning."

He nodded, showed her the spare bedroom and went into his own.

An hour later, there was a tap on his door, and it opened. Moonlight shone through a curtain; he rose on one elbow and he saw that she wore but a thin slip. Approaching the bed she said, "Hold me, Eli. I just need to be held, it has been so long."

Later she wrapped her legs about him as he smothered her in kisses. As he brought her to a searing climax she whimpered and called out, "Alexei, oh, Alexei, please, please, please."

Tears flooded down her cheeks, and she drowned in her desire for love, lust, and compassion in a world gone mad.

Doctor Thompson left his house very early the next morning. Kimi thought she felt him kiss her gently on the forehead; then she heard the front door close and his car start up, but she did not rise until much later. Memories of the night moved glacially through her mind, a fog of guilt, despair and remorse, but there was something else too. She had shared a moment that gave intense pleasure to another human being, a caring, unselfish man whom she greatly admired. He was not her Alexei, no one would ever be that, and she would never repeat the night again. But the emptiness was not quite so vast as before.

He was not there when she arrived at the hospital. Doctor Whitefield met her in the hallway and said, "Dr. Thompson left a note for you on his desk. I saw him leave in a staff car an hour ago."

"Did he say where he was going, or when he will be back?" Kimi asked, puzzlement visible on her face.

"No, but he said something about orders coming through."

"Kimi-san" was the only word on the envelope. She extracted the one-page letter and peered at the barely legible scrawl, the same that she had seen on so many reports.

My dearest love,

I do not wish you to keep this letter, for it will only cause distress if Alexei returns to you, as I sincerely hope he will. Some weeks ago, I applied for duty in the Pacific, for I suspect that surgeons will be greatly needed there. My orders came through this morning. I will have already shipped out by the time you read this.

Last night you were the ultimate gift to a man who loves you more than you can ever imagine. But your pleas were for the arms and the soul of another man, one whose absence I can never fill.

I leave with the most tender feelings for you. I will relive last night, perhaps selfishly, for the rest of my life, never expecting to have the joy of holding you again. But I will dream, and I will see your face until the end of my days. Be well, and pray for us all,
With all my love,
Eli

She sat on a bench in the shade of the building, the letter returned to the envelope. She would not keep it, he was right about that. The emptiness that had subsided returned in full force. Doctor Thompson had mentioned nothing to her about an assignment in the Pacific. But with the exception of accidents, either with aircraft on ships, life at the naval hospital had nearly returned to pre-war conditions, and the doctor's skills would surely be needed where the war edged closer to the enemy. He would, she mused, want to practice medicine where he was truly needed.

But still, had his action been based in part on his unquenchable love for her, one that could never be consummated night after night? Had he resolved to leave a painful and hopeless situation behind?

It had been obvious, even in the first early days, that he loved her. He'd tried to keep it secret, but everyone knew. Unspoken but understood glances had been telegraphed among the staff. And they knew how correctly he always acted around her, and how she had responded in the same professional way. All the nurses and most doctors knew that Alexei was somewhere in Russia, if he was alive at all. But as time went on and they heard nothing more, she sensed that many of the staff thought that after a suitable time, a union would be made between herself and the doctor.

There had been nights, terribly conflicted nights, when she had asked herself if she loved Eli, for they had developed a true bond. They had spent so much time together, sometimes laughing or just sitting in silent contemplation. There were the times—too many of them—of shared commiseration for the final moments of a young soldier or sailor. She respected him, enjoyed his company, and was always impressed by his strong, honest demeanor. But, she had told herself, that was different from love. And until told otherwise, she was a married woman and in love with a man very far away.

"I will miss you, Eli Thompson," she murmured. "Yes, I will miss you, but now we both have work to do, and perhaps I will see you again. Until then, Godspeed."

She wished that she could have told him that in person, but upon reflection, she knew that he would smile and say, "You don't have to explain. We are adults, and there are things we can have and things that we can't. And that's all there is to it."

Her reverie was broken by an orderly running down the path towards her and calling out, "He's awake! Just woke up a few minutes ago! Doctor Whitefield sent me to get you." Swiftly, Kimi-san rose and followed, her heart in her throat.

Two doctors and a nurse stood beside Tad's bed, checking his pulse. He was sitting up, the bandage on his forehead had been removed, and a thermometer protruded from his mouth. He gave his mother a lopsided grin when the nurse removed it.

Kimi kissed his cheek and said, "Thank God! We were all so worried. But Doctor Whitefield says that you should make a full recovery."

Tad nodded, closed his eyes for a moment, then said, "Have you seen Jack? Is he okay?"

"He came by yesterday. He comes by nearly every day, now that the carrier is in port."

"The *Lex?*"

There was silence for a moment, then Whitefield said, "She had to be sunk after the battle. Most of the men got off. The captain made sure of that by personally searching every place he could access after the explosions. But a lot has happened since then, some of it good. I'm sure Vestergaard will tell you all about it when he comes by. There's another pilot who tags along with him. A Lee-Beauregard Smythe. He says that you two are old buddies. Says how you saved his life. Jack says that Smythe even helped get you off the *Lex* before it went down."

"Is that so?" said Tad. "If you see him before I do, tell him no flowers."

There was a commotion in the hallway and an orderly was heard saying, "You can't go in there! Only doctors and nurses are allowed."

"The hell we can't, mister!"

The curtain was pulled back, and Jack and Lee-Beauregard ambled in.

"Why the hell are you still in bed?" demanded Jack. "You're wanted in the ready room and the ship leaves in three days." Turning to a nurse he said, "Ma'am, you got a wheelchair? This man's got to fly."

"Don't be ridiculous! This man will be recovering for months. Now off with you, and stop disturbing our patients." The nurse made shooing gestures and glared at them. "Pilots!" she muttered. "Think they run the world!"

As they were ushered from the room, Tad called after them, "So Lee is my new buddy? Now I *know* we're going to lose the war."

Chapter 12
Oahu, Hawaii
August, 1942

Early-morning light streaked into the ward. Tad stirred, opened his eyes, and blinked several times. A muted groan came from an army officer four beds away; his arm had been amputated three days earlier. *I loathe hospitals*, Tad thought, but at least he was in one piece. He was getting restless, but according to the doctor he would be a "guest" of the hospital for weeks to come. He closed his eyes again.

"Is that all you do, sleep? Gonna rest on that Silver Star you earned while we're out saving the world? You do know there's a war, don't you?"

At the sound of Jack Vestergaard's drawl, Tad's eyes flew open. Jack was leaning against the open doorway, Lee beside him, looking down the hallway to make sure no nurse was advancing to evict them.

"I think I heard about that. You two idiots in it?"

"Ye-ep. With all your happy sleep I'm guessing you're behind on the news. Now if you have a few minutes, we can fill you in." Both pilots entered the room.

"Oh, I'd love to hear all about it, but I have a polo match in twenty. Of course I have time, you sap! Where the hell can

I go? I'll be here for three more months, if not longer. So stop grinning and tell me."

"We beat the tar out of them," said Smythe. "We sank the bastards, the ones that hit Pearl."

Tad propped himself up and said, "I heard snatches of conversation but not the whole story. Care to fill me in?"

"Only the highlights. Can't have your slothful self pretending you were there just to get some starry-eyed doll to fall into your arms, when we deserve the rewards!" Jack said, grinning.

Tad wanted to throw a pillow at his friend, but revenge would have to wait until he didn't risk tearing his wounds open.

"So here's what happened," Jack went on, more seriously. "Nimitz, Fletcher and Spruance took Task Force Sixteen and Seventeen to a spot called Point Luck, off Midway Island."

"It was supposed to be Halsey's command," Lee interjected, "but he got beached for—get this!—*dermatitis* and had to hand over the fleet. Can you beat it? Dermatitis! He finally gets the command assignment he's been pushing for, and he loses it on account of a lousy case of pimples. And he wasn't saying why, either, I can tell you. I got the story from a nurse who... never mind. Anyway, we were on the *Enterprise*. The *Yorktown* and *Hornet* sailed out as well."

"Last I heard, *Yorktown* was near sinking," said Tad, wincing from the pain in his mending ribs.

"She's a tough old lady," said Smythe. "Got back to Pearl and every repair gang went to work. She was back out in seventy-two hours. Not perfect, of course, but serviceable."

"So why Midway? That's just an atoll with a tiny airstrip," asked Tad.

"I have no idea," replied Jack, "but the brass must have thought it was important. We do have a sub base on Midway, and an airfield. Admiral Nagumo's carriers bombed the hell out of the place and shot up the aircraft we had there. Meanwhile, out at sea our scouts found them before they found us. Nagumo had four carriers, the *Hiryu, Akagi, Kaga* and *Soryu,* along with battleships, cruisers and a dozen destroyers, but the big-gun ships were supporting the invasion force and not guarding the carriers." Jack shook his head at the folly of commanders.

"No admiral wants to present one big, fat, appetizing target to the enemy," chided Smythe. "If they could sink our carriers there would be damn little to stop an invasion of Australia, or any place else. They were looking for us, because if they could sink our carriers they could rule the Pacific. I think they suddenly felt vulnerable. Maybe it was the Doolittle raid, even though it didn't do much damage."

"Except to their sense of invincibility," said Tad.

"Yeah, that must have been a shock to Tojo. Anyway, once we knew where their carriers were, Spruance orders an attack. But it wasn't coordinated, and it started out as a real snafu. Every one of our torpedo planes from *Hornet* were shot down, and the torpedoes that did hit were defective. Only one man survived," said Jack grimly.

"But the Zeros were off nailing the Devastators and not protecting the carriers or watching for another strike. That was the amazing thing," said Smythe. "Because three squadrons of our dive bombers from *Enterprise* and *Yorktown* were able to target the *Soryu, Kaga* and *Akagi,* the big fleet carriers! And that was where luck was with us. They must have been rearming aircraft and refueling them. There were bombs all over the deck. We came down on them like banshees, and our bombs detonated their bombs. They blew themselves up."

"And you two were in on it?" asked Tad.

"No, we were flying cover for our carriers, but we got the scuttlebutt from the guys flying the SBDs. The *Kaga* became a fireball. The *Soryu* and the *Akagi* turned into floating infernos. The pilots said it was one hell of a sight, all three ships on fire, explosions everywhere," said Jack.

"You said that there were four Japanese carriers. What about the other one?" asked Tad.

"Oh, we got her too. That was the *Hiryu*. We got her later that afternoon, but their dive bombers and torpedo planes came after us. Unfortunately, three bombs hit *Yorktown* and put out her boilers. They got the Old Lady started again, but there was a second attack and two torpedoes got her. She was abandoned and went down. Most of the crew go off, though," said Smythe.

"And we shot down a whole lot of Nip dive bombers. The survivors had a bad surprise waiting for them when they returned. With the carriers gone there was nothing for them to land on except water," said Jack, making way for nurse Crocker, who eyed him sternly but did not otherwise object to his presence.

"Even with *Yorktown* sunk, it was still one hell of a victory," he continued. "We even sank a heavy cruiser. Now the Nips only have one or two big carriers left, and we're getting a whole new type of carrier, the *Essex* class. Damn big, and lots of them. You should have been there, Tad, it was quite a show."

"Yeah, I should have been." Tad stirred restlessly.

"Well this war is far from over, and once you get out of here you'll be back in the air. The Marines have gone into Guadalcanal and have a hell of a fight on their hands. We'll need every fighter pilot we've got, so you get better damn soon," said Smythe.

Tad gave him a long look, then said, "So now you're my new buddy?"

"Sure 'nuff. Lieutenant Lee-Beauregard Smythe, son of the old South. What do you say, Mr. Tad?" grinned Smythe, holding out his hand. "As I said, you saved my ass twice. That makes you a genuine fucking hero."

"Personally, I think it was a lot more fun before, but if you insist, sure. And thanks for getting me off the ship." Tad gripped the proffered hand and shook it firmly once.

"Now, Lieutenant, turn over, I have something nice for you," said nurse Crocker.

Tad groaned and Jack said, "Oh, that's a big needle. You'll like that, Tad. Only one, Nurse?"

"For now," she grinned. "But we do have a whole lot more, and I like to give shots. And he is just sooooo sweet."

It was two days later when Kimi came in with an orderly and a wheelchair. "The doctor said that you need fresh air, so we're going to take you outside for a while," she explained.

"Fantastic," said Tad, scooting out of bed and easing himself into the chair. "Do you have any idea of when they will release me?"

"Not as soon as you would like," she replied with a smile.

"I just want to fly. I'm not doing any good here."

"I know, but for now you're grounded. I'll wheel you into our little garden, so you can admire the flowers."

"Sure, I can use the change of scenery." Tad fell silent until they were away from the halls of the hospital and under trees, then asked the question that had been bothering him. "I was wondering, have you heard from Dad?"

"Not for a very long time. I pray that he is still alive," his mother said slowly, sadly. They sat quietly, watching the ubiquitous chickens that ran free on the islands. After some minutes, she stood up to return to the ward.

A few minutes later, an orderly found Tad and said, "Sir, I have today's paper. Care to read it?"

"Sure, sailor. I haven't seen a newspaper in a long time. With the war going on it just feels too damn peaceful being stuck here."

"Yes, sir, I'd give my left arm to be in it about now. Give me a tin can or light cruiser and I'd be happy as a clam."

"Not a carrier?"

"Hell no! Those fly boys scare the crap out of me. No, sir! Destroyers are fast and can get in close. Outrun a carrier any day."

"Be careful what you wish for, sailor. Tin cans are fast, but they have a real downside."

"What's that, sir?"

"They sink."

"Have a nice day, sir," said the orderly, laughing and shaking his head on the way to the ward.

Tad unfolded the *Honolulu Star-Bulletin*, skimmed the first-page articles, then focused on the lead story. "U.S. Marines continue drive into Guadalcanal," read the headline. The article provided an upbeat analysis of the landings on Tulagi and Florida in the southern Solomon Islands, where U.S. marines defeated fierce Japanese resistance.

Admiral Ernest King pushed for a full-scale invasion of Guadalcanal, a very strategic island. It has been reported that the first major offensive launched by U.S. forces against Japan is moving steadily ahead on Guadalcanal led by Major General Alexander Vandegrift despite fanatical resistance by Japanese forces. Although the initial landings were unopposed, Japanese forces moved into the jungle and the enemy high command appears determined to commit large numbers of troops to regain the island. The island's airfield is strategically located for future operations against Japanese installations and has already been put into operation with the addition of Wildcat fighters and Dauntless bombers.

Tad glanced skyward as a B-17 flew low over the beach, then returned to the paper.

Abandoned Japanese trucks and dozers have been put to good use by the Marines in the construction of the airfield even though intense heat and humidity has made work extremely laborious.

A Japanese bayonet charge led by Colonel Ichiki was met and nearly annihilated by intense Marine counter fire and the Colonel committed suicide. However, the Japanese have been reinforcing their positions by night use of fast destroyers Americans call 'Rat Runs.' Thus new offenses by Japanese are expected, but U.S. reinforcements are reportedly on the way.

Another article announced that Nisei volunteers were joining the newly formed 442 Army Infantry Regiment, and Hawaiian men of Japanese descent were being trained for combat in Europe. Further down the page were reports of Jews in Poland being murdered by the Gestapo, and German saboteurs executed in Washington, D.C. Another article stated that Marshal Zhukov had been appointed to lead resistance at Stalingrad, where soldiers and civilians were defending the city against the Nazi advance.

The final story Tad read was about the Soviets' defense of besieged Leningrad that had been going on since the beginning of the Nazi invasion of Russia.

Already, hundreds of thousands of the city's inhabitants have died from starvation as well as

German shell fire. Attempts by Soviets to bring food to the city have had limited success. With the Germans moving toward Moscow, there is little hope of soon lifting the siege.

Folding the paper, Tad wondered what had become of his father. Was he in Leningrad, or Moscow, conscripted to join in the fight? Was he even still alive? Russia was an ally, but not a particularly comfortable one. There were odd rumors of civilians rounded up and transported to Siberian prison camps by the NKVD, where they were worked to death in war-related industries, or dragooned into suicidal "penal battalions" and ordered to the front.

Tad closed his eyes. That there was no news of his father lay heavy upon him. Kimi's letters to the U.S. embassy in Moscow had been answered tersely: millions were in dire circumstances, her husband could not be located.

"Lieutenant," said an orderly, waking Tad from a light slumber, "There are some people who would like to speak with you. They are in the office, sir. I'll wheel you in if you don't mind."

"Fine. Who are they?"

"Not sure, sir. They look important, and they don't look happy."

"Well, neither am I."

Tad sat in the wheelchair, looking up at men dressed in three-piece suits such as no one on Hawaii ordinarily wore. Holding out an official-looking badge, the tallest of the three said, "I'm agent Johann Repper and this is agent Giovanni Sciprio. We're both from the Bureau. And this," he said, as if indicating an unnecessary appendage, "is Mr. Griffin representing the Office of the Military Governor. We have some questions we want to ask you, Lieutenant."

"What business does the F.B.I. have with me? Do I look like a spy?"

"Not a spy; a person of interest," said Sciprio, a short, slender man who spoke softly and looked too small for his fedora. "You have been under surveillance for some time. Specifically, since you began a relationship with a Japanese lady named Sayuri Saito. There is also a matter of a Japanese Imperial Navy pilot, one Koizumi Karamatsu."

"That's right, I saw them both before the war. I haven't seen either since."

"True, but you have written to Miss Saito since the war began. Communicating with an enemy national during time of war, especially for one in your position, can be a serious offense. As a carrier pilot you are know sensitive, top secret information."

"Information on ship movements, military capabilities and weaknesses. All of which are of vital interest to the enemy war effort," added Johann Repper.

Tad cocked his head but said nothing. He was finding it was profoundly ironic that a German American and an Italian American were accusing a Japanese American of espionage for a foreign power, and was debating whether or not to point this out.

A long moment elapsed before Griffin said, "We are not accusing you directly. We understand that you fought bravely at Coral Sea and, it appears, are still recovering from wounds."

"Yes, it *appears* so." Tad allowed himself that much.

Ignoring Griffin, Agent Repper said, "Lieutenant, we intercepted a letter you wrote in April to Miss Saito. I have a copy of it with me. The Bureau ascertained that the original reached the Swedish embassy in Tokyo, where very likely it was read by the Japanese secret police before it was delivered to Miss Saito."

The agent slipped an envelope from his jacket pocket and slowly waved it back and forth. Tad showed no emotion but said, "Secretary of War Henry Stimson said that gentlemen don't read each other's mail. I guess the Bureau operates by different rules."

"Rules of war, Lieutenant. I think you understand that."

"Uh huh. Well, I'm still a bit groggy, so maybe you can read it to me," said Tad, motioning away the envelope.

"I'll be happy to," said Repper, and did so.

"Dearest Sayuri-san, I hope you receive this letter and it finds you in good health. I dream of you day and night. I love you with all my heart. Stay safe. I think you should go to the countryside where the air is clean and where people will welcome you. Wait for me if you can. Pray for me, as I pray for you. Love, Tad-ichi'."

He scowled over the paper at the man in the wheelchair.

"Tadichi," said Sciprio. "Not a very American name, is it?"

"My name is Tad, and it's just as American as Johann or Giovanni. German and Italian? Correct me if I'm wrong, but I think we're at war with those folks, them being Nazis and all. Perhaps you still have relatives there? My mother, the head trauma nurse here, was born in Japan. 'Ichi' in Japanese just means first son."

"I see," said Repper, not at all pleased by the reference to his relatives.

"And my love letter? Espionage, right?" said Tad, baiting the agent.

"It could have hidden meanings. Countryside, clean air and the like. But no, I don't think it's espionage or treasonous."

"Then what's this about? You're really not making my day, Agent Johann Repper. But if it will make you feel better, I won't be sending any more letters to be opened and read by snoopy people in the Bureau."

A tense moment passed before Sciprio said, "Oh no, Lieutenant. You don't understand. We want you to send letters."

Tad frowned and leaning forward said, "You *want* me to write to her?"

"Exactly. We surmise we can get your letters to her through the Italian Embassy. We have connections. We ask you to communicate with Sayuri. We think that she may be able to provide us vital information. Living conditions, morale, perhaps things regarding their military. You see, we really don't have agents there. Far too dangerous now for a westerner, or even a Nisei."

Something in his voice made Tad certain the Bureau had learned this the hard way.

Tad stared at the man, then said, "But not too dangerous for a lady I happen to love. A woman who will be shot when the Kempeitai learn of her spying. And they will. No, I will not put her life in jeopardy, mister. I know she loves me, or at least she did before the war, but that doesn't mean that she's disloyal to her country. I think you gentlemen are out of line."

The door to the office opened and Tad's mother came in, followed by Vice Admiral Spruance. "Who's out of line?" demanded Spruance. He was wearing his dress whites and cap with "scrambled egg" on the brim and looked every inch the admiral.

Tad made a reflexive effort to rise, but Spruance said, "Oh, no you don't, mister. Just sit back down. Now, who's out of line?"

"No one, sir," said Repper. "We just had some questions to ask the lieutenant."

"And a request on the part of the F.B.I.," added Sciprio.

"Really? The F.B.I.? Are you in some sort of trouble, Lieutenant?"

"No, sir."

"Well," the admiral said, eyeing the visitors and their suits, "this looks like an interrogation to me. And I don't like one of my best pilots being interrogated." Turning to Tad, Spruance said, "What's this about, anyway?"

"I had a girlfriend, sir, a Japanese lady I met before the war. These men want me to correspond with her and make her a spy. I can't do that, sir. It would put her in great danger and, well, in spite of the war, I still care for her deeply."

"I see. Well, mail delivery to Japan is a bit sketchy right now. And I think the whole concept is bizarre, unless she has indicated that she *wants* to be a spy. Has she?"

"No, sir."

Facing the three men, in his quiet, thoughtful manner Spruance said, "So, I suggest an alternative concept."

"And what would that be, Admiral?" Repper sounded cautiously hopeful.

You see that door?"

"Yes, sir."

"Well, it's made so people can come in and go out. And you had better get the hell out of this office. Now."

"But we were conducting—" began Repper.

"Now!"

With studied animosity, Sciprio said, "Very well, but you will be hearing from J. Edgar."

"Right. Have him send the message in a bottle. We'll be fighting somewhere in the Solomons. Out!"

A smile came to the admiral's lips after the three departed, the two angry agents and the apologetic-looking Griffin. The door closed a bit too hard behind them. "If I could, I'd put every one of those fancy pants on the beach at Guadalcanal," he remarked. "Right in front."

"Admiral," said Kimi, "we have enough wounded men coming back from there as it is. We don't need more."

"Who said anything about bringing them back?"

Then Spruance gave a shy smile and said, "But I came here to spend time with my pilots. I'm promoting you, son, and I need you airborne as soon as you can fly. We're moving on, and we need experienced men."

Tad spied a crutch lying against the wall and said, "Admiral, if you can give me a hand and that crutch, I'll see what I can do."

"Tad," said Kimi, "The doctor said—"

Spruance snatched the crutch and helped Tad to his feet.

Shakily, Tad stood, braced himself, then took a few steps.

"Damn fine, Commander. Now let's take a walk into the sun."

Chapter 13
Tokyo, Japan
April, 1943

"The rations are in!" shouted the runner of the neighborhood association. He ran up the block, narrowly avoiding Sayuri and Kumi as they walked to the Meiji Gaien Stadium for the air defense practice.

"Do you think anything decent will be left when we get back?" asked Kumi.

"Maybe rice and lentils. Did you hear? Some of the school children were fed cooked sparrows. The birds were eating the rice crops, so farmers were told to capture them."

"That's hardly a delicacy," said Kumi.

"It is if you're hungry," replied Sayuri.

They joined the ranks of hundreds of women assembled in long rows for the fire drill, all of them wearing *mompe* pantaloons and heavy head coverings to protect them from cinders. Dutifully, they waited for practice to begin.

A military officer spoke through a megaphone to remind the women of the importance of combined effort in extinguishing conflagrations from American bombers. Chanting a cadence, the women passed one bucket after another to put out small fires ignited for the drill.

"Do you think the Americans are coming?" asked Kumi afterwards, as they walked home. "I mean, maybe all the bombers have been shot down. My cousin, Takagi, said that he destroyed two of them near Guadalcanal."

"I don't know," replied Sayuri. Her hands were raw from handling the wire bucket handles. "But I do not think the government would waste our time. I'm sure that they would prefer to have us work in the factories or fields if putting out fires were not so important."

"You know," said Kumi, "if the fire is not near the river, or if the hoses are destroyed, we will be helpless to put out a really big fire."

"Maybe that's why some children and their mothers have gone to the countryside," said Sayuri.

"But people going to the countryside are not very popular with people who have to share their homes and their food," remarked Kumi.

"Perhaps, but it also means more people to do the farming, so maybe some of them will be welcomed. Even if they are not treated politely, it's better than sleeping in a cold factory and eating rice and wheat flower *nukapan* cakes," replied Sayuri.

"I had to eat that at the factory. They're horribly bitter."

Sayuri suggested that they walk through Ueno Park, a shortcut on the way to the ikebana shop where they still lived. The park was the oldest one in Tokyo, and until 1941 it had been a place of elegant gardens, fountains and sculptures. But now everything made of metal, including railings, decorative iron work and bells, had been removed and melted down. Weeds grew where not a blade of errant grass would have been tolerated previously. Throughout the capital, a state of disrepair and neglect cast a pall over the landscape.

They passed a building that sported a banner proclaiming that it was the women's "Imperial Rule Assistance Association." Beneath that banner was another stating that "Good mothers comfort injured soldiers and bereaved families. Do your patriotic part."

"I heard that the assistance association in the Tsukishima district is asking unmarried men and women to enroll at the medical clinics," said Kumi.

"To give blood?" asked Sayuri.

"No, to put their names on lists saying that they are available for marriage. The district captains promise that those who marry get homes and the women will not have to work. Maybe we should consider it," said Kumi.

"Marry just so you don't have to work?" said Sayuri, disapprovingly. "Soon everybody will have to work, no matter what they promise. And there you are with a husband you hardly know, much less care for. No, I'm not interested in marrying any of those men."

"But there are other men. You know, Sayuri-san," Kimi said conspiratorially, "my cousin Takagi-san likes you, and he is very handsome. He's in the same squadron as Koizumi-san."

"Don't mention Koizumi-san, and what do you mean your cousin likes me?"

"What do you think? He told me that he wants to marry. Maybe not right now; perhaps when the war is over. But he would like to speak to you about it. It would be good for both of you."

"He is a nice man. And yes, he is quite handsome, but you know who is in my heart."

"You are my very best friend, Sayuri-san, so I feel that I must tell you the truth. Please forgive me for saying this, but the one in your heart is unattainable, and you are not getting any younger. Dreams are one thing. But I fear that you are harboring a nightmare and it will end very badly."

The two remained silent for the rest of the way. They stopped once when the street was blocked by several thousand former students, all in uniform and carrying rifles, marching past and chanting a war song that ended with the words, "Naturally we don't expect to return."

* * *

Sergeant Takagi and Lieutenant Commander Koizumi walked across the airfield to inspect the new Mitsubishi Zeros.

"Congratulations on your new assignment," Takagi said.

"Don't congratulate me," replied Koizumi. "I didn't ask for it and don't want it. What I want is to fly those fighters."

"It's no small matter to be the aide of Admiral Karamatsu. He could have picked anyone, but he chose you."

"He is my uncle, and I could hardly refuse. Now I shuttle him and his staff around in a cranky transport while my squadron is flying off carriers and shooting down American planes. I would trade places with any of them."

"Koizumi-san, your uncle doesn't trust his life to some kid who can barely land a plane. You are an ace, one who advised the general staff before Pearl Harbor. You have been accorded a great honor and should be grateful," said Takagi, striding resolutely toward the flight line.

The aircraft looked sleek and powerful, and Takagi ran his hand lovingly along the wing. "It was once the best fighter in the sky," he said with admiration.

"Yes, and not so long ago. It's still a fine plane, and with an experienced pilot there's no much that can outfight it."

"The lack of experienced pilots is the problem. You remember what a horrible time we had in flight school? How many potentially good pilots were washed out for minor infractions? Now we need those men, but many are already dead. That was a strategic error."

Takagi stared into a gloomy sky, then said, "How the hell did they find Yamamoto's plane?"

"I don't know," replied Koizumi. "Maybe there were spies who saw him get on board and informed the Americans when his plane took off. Or maybe they were just lucky and picked up a Japanese plane on radar and shot it down."

"One of our scout planes counted sixteen of the twin engine devils, the P-38 fighters that shot him down. Why would they put sixteen planes up in such a desolate location? And from what I heard, the flight was highly secret. Yamamoto was the best officer we had." Takagi lit a cigarette. "First Guadalcanal, now we have practically lost New Guinea."

"You are just full of good news, aren't you?" said Koizumi. "Tell me something I don't know."

Takagi laughed and said, "Fine. What if I told you that I need your consent? Not necessarily permission, but perhaps your approval."

"What nonsense game are you playing? What approval? Do you want to fly solo and sink an American carrier? Sure, you have my approval. Just give me all your money before you go. I will arrange a nice send off, lots of saki and rice cakes."

"I want to marry Sayuri Saito," Takagi said flatly. "I request your consent and a formal introduction."

Koizumi stared at his friend and said nothing for a very long moment. "You don't need my consent and I will not introduce you."

"Then you do still want her. I'm sorry to have made a fool of myself. Please accept my apologies."

"What I want is of no consequence. I don't care if you marry her. Do as you wish, but I told her that I would never bother her or see her again. How can I suddenly appear and say my *tomodachi* Takagi-san has just decided that he wants to marry you since I can't? Do you think she'll jump up and down with boundless elation? A bit of reality is in order, Flight Sergeant. There is nothing more to say."

Scrupulously avoiding Koizumi, Takagi spent the next four days on the flight line training very green pilots in fighter tactics and observing their takeoffs and landings on a strip determined to be the length of a small carrier. Each of the students was excited about fighting for the Emperor, but Takagi knew how few would survive against veteran American pilots.

After numerous wave-offs by "deck crews" crisscrossing their signal paddles, the neophytes would pull up and circle around for another attempt at snatching the wires strung across the simulated carrier deck. After one student failed on the fourth pass, he was instructed to land on a parallel field of much greater length.

Disgusted, Takagi turned away. Not for the first time, he regretted the waste of pilots dismissed from his own training days. *What the navy wouldn't give now for a pilot like Shima Ohta,* he was thinking bitterly, when he saw Koizumi walking toward him. Coming to attention, Takagi bowed. With cool and exacting courtesy he said, "Good morning, Squadron Leader Itomo Karamatsu."

A slight bow in return, then Koizumi made a dismissive wave and said, "Screw the formality, Takagi."

Takagi gave him a questioning look and said, "Are there new orders for me?"

"No, but I would like to speak with you about the request you made."

"You needn't concern yourself about that," Takagi said stiffly. "I'm shipping out in five days. Besides, my sister told me that Sayuri-san isn't interested in marriage. So don't waste your time."

"Walk with me," said Koizumi. Silently they crossed the flight line and sat on a bench beside a hangar. Takagi stared ahead, a petulant, exasperated expression on his usually jovial face.

"I apologize for my arrogance," began Koizumi. "You have every right to speak with her. And I will not be breaking my vow by formally introducing you, since I am not asking anything for myself. Once I make the introduction I will remove myself so as not to be a complication. What you say to her and what she replies is between the two of you. And I don't care if you tell me what she says or not. It's not my affair. I do wish you success. However, there are matters you are not aware of, and it's not my place to tell you. That is up to her, and they may be unsurmountable."

"Unsurmountable?"

"As I said, that's for her to explain."

"I asked you before and I'll ask again, because as much as I care for her I will not torture my best friend. Do you still love her?"

Koizumi leaned back and stared at the sky. "Do you remember when, in training, we were taught to see the stars in daylight? Sometimes I thought I saw them; we all claimed to. But usually it was ephemeral, something we badly wanted to see, but at best it was fleeting, or not there at all. Love can be just as ephemeral, and if it isn't reciprocated it evaporates and you never know if it was truly real at all. I loved her, but she was unattainable. So I put that dream in a box and the box at the back of a drawer. And I don't open it ever again. That should answer your question."

At dusk a leaden sky lay over Tokyo and a cold rain splattered on their umbrellas as Koizumi and Takagi approached the ikebana shop. At the doorway they removed their shoes and entered. Koizumi noticed the shop was nearly devoid of flowers.

"Dear cousin, and honored Koizumi-san," said Kumi, bowing to the uniformed men. They kowtowed in turn, and she saw how uneasy Koizumi appeared.

"Is Sayuri-san here?" asked Koizumi, his eyes taking in the sparse furnishings, secondhand items purchased from families evacuating to the mountains and countryside. All the delicate, original pieces had been destroyed by the Kempeitai.

"I will get her. She is upstairs, but she is not feeling well. I think it's the strain of factory work and the fire defense. We are all exhausted."

"Yes, I understand. I've heard that the conditions are affecting a lot of men and women. I've heard of absenteeism and illness at the factories. Please tell her that we won't be long, and that I appreciate her willingness to see me," said Takagi.

The wait seemed interminable to Koizumi. He gave a fleeting smile to Takagi to reassure him, but he could not wait to flee from this place. The very air felt oppressive.

Wearing her formless *mompe*, Sayuri followed Kumi down the stairs and stood before the two men. The only sound was the patter of rain. After a moment, Sayuri bowed and Takagi and Koizumi followed suit.

"We regret disturbing you," said Koizumi, looking at Sayuri. She appeared drawn and distant. "Had we known of your illness we would not have come. We apologize for the inconvenience."

Sayuri nodded and said, "You have not inconvenienced me, and I'm sorry to appear in this condition." She indicated the unflattering clothes. Then her eyes caught those of

Koizumi and held them for a long moment. "It is good to see you again. I am pleased that you are well."

"Thank you," replied Koizumi, thinking that there was so much he wanted to say, yet so little he dared say. Another moment passed and he looked up and said, "I want you to know that I did not come here to ask anything for myself." He stood straight and forthrightly said, "I wish to formally introduce my esteemed friend, navy pilot, Takagi Hayashi."

Turning to Takagi, he said, "And I wish to introduce you to miss Sayuri Saito, a lady of talent and grace. I can attest to this since I have known her most of my life."

Having said this, he curtly bowed. "Now that I have fulfilled my comrade's request, I will give you privacy and wait outside."

"Wait, Koizumi-san," said Sayuri. "It is raining and I do not wish for you to be standing out in the cold."

Lips tightly pressed, he took up a position in the furthest corner of the room and turned his gaze to the rain-spattered window and the darkening street beyond. A vase of cherry blossoms from the tree in the garden offered the only color in the darkened shop.

Again Takagi bowed to Sayuri. He was surprised and disappointed that his cousin did not go to her room upstairs. He had been hoping that he would have time alone with Sayuri.

"I asked my *tomodachi* Koizumi-san to formally introduce me to you, since all others who might have done so are on station across our empire. He has been most gracious in doing so and does not oppose what I wish to say."

Takagi glanced back to Koizumi, then paused, while Sayuri waited, knowing what was about to be asked of her.

"I have been lonely for too long and…" He stopped, then, changing course, began again. "I do not deserve to have a woman of your beauty and graciousness, for I am but a low-ranking soldier."

Again he halted, searching her eyes for any sign of encouragement. "But I ask you consider me as a suitable husband who will care for you."

When Sayuri said nothing, Takagi haltingly said, "Would you consider me worthy of being your husband?"

Sayuri bowed very low, and when she straightened Takagi saw her eyes had filled with tears. He waited. The rain pattered on the roof and the wind caused a twig to tap against the window.

"Takagi-san, from what your cousin says I know you to be a good and honorable man. But I would be leading you astray if I offered a commitment, either now or in the future. And that would be terribly wrong for both of us."

Takagi nodded and said, "I appreciate your candor. Perhaps it was foolish of me to think that I might have a chance."

He gazed at her face, which had become serene. Suddenly she reminded him of a ghost, like the one in a *Noh* play his grandparents had taken him to see in childhood—the ghost of a woman who loved beyond life itself. Carefully he asked his next question. "I would like to ask if there is somebody else in your heart? I mean, if there is not, then perhaps in time things between us might change."

Kumi lit a kerosene lamp and it cast shadows upon the bare walls. She folded her hands and bowed her head. It was terrible that Sayuri had lost Shima Ohta, but she had refused Koizumi, and she was refusing Takagi, both honorable men, heroic warriors of the Empire. Why were men so blind? There were young, unmarried women at the factory who prayed for an honorable husband to whom they would be devoted. And here were two men, young, handsome, courageous, refusing to see anyone but the one woman who would say no. It was profoundly exasperating.

Worse, she could not help longing for a home, for a family, for children of her own. She knew Koizumi's faults, and in the secret part of her heart she still had not forgiven him for what happened to Sensei Hiroku; even so, she thought he would be a husband a woman could be proud of. So, for that matter, would Takagi.

Sayuri hesitated, then said, "There is a man whom I hold dear in my heart. I have not seen or heard from him in several years. And yet, I cannot cast him aside as long as I think he might still be alive."

"Is he in the military, a soldier or sailor?" questioned Takagi respectfully, for it was an honorable thing to retain one's love and devotion for a warrior of the Emperor, even if dead or badly wounded.

Sayuri's eyes flitted from Takagi to Koizumi, who lingered in the shadows, wishing the conversation had never taken this course.

Sayuri lowered her head, then looked once again into Takagi's eyes. "Yes, he is in the military, the... navy," she said after a pause.

"I see. Would he be a pilot?" he persisted.

"Yes, he is a pilot."

When she failed to add anything more, Takagi turned to Koizumi and warily said, "Is there something else? Something Sayuri-san wishes to keep to herself? But perhaps something I should know?"

"The man Sayuri-san loves is my brother," said Koizumi.

"I didn't know you have a brother," replied Takagi. "I have known you a long time, and you never mentioned a brother. He must be an exceptional fellow to have won Sayuri-san's heart. I would like to meet him, a fellow pilot."

"That's quite impossible, except perhaps in the air if he's still alive," said Koizumi tersely.

Takagi frowned, a chill creeping in.

"My esteemed brother is an American, a fighter pilot in the American Navy. Yes, *tomodachi*, our lovely Sayuri-san is in love with an enemy of the Empire of Japan. This is why I did not want to introduce you to her."

A deadening silence pervaded the room. Takagi stared uncomprehendingly at Sayuri. "An *American* fighter pilot?" he said, taking a step back. "How could you? This is beyond unseemly. It is treasonous!"

"I met him in Hawaii before the war, before Japan and America were enemy countries, when our families were closest friends," said Sayuri in words barely audible. "We do not choose who we fall in love with. I do not know if he is still alive; perhaps he was killed at the start of the war. But I cannot give unswerving love to anyone else as long as there is hope."

"Hope for an American pilot who will send us flaming into the sea?" demanded Takagi angrily.

"My hope and prayer is that all of you will live long and happy lives." Then, bursting into tears she said, "I don't want anybody else to die! Yes, I love Tadichi-san and nothing in the world will change that. I am sorry, I truly am. Condemn me if you wish. Perhaps I will never know joy or see him again. I feel pain each day. Perhaps fate will damn me, but I cannot forsake my love any more than I can end this horrible war!"

Deflated, wraithlike, she seemed to shrink away, and like a closing curtain on stage, she drifted toward the stairs. Turning to Takagi, she said, "I'm sorry; I am so sorry."

The two men walked in silence down the dark street. In the distance they heard a watchman scold a woman whose kitchen lamp light was not completely concealed by heavy drapes.

"I should have told you," said Koizumi. "It would have saved embarrassment and pain."

"Perhaps," agreed Takagi, "But I insisted, and you were honorable in acceding to my desires. I am disappointed, but in a strange way I feel sorry for Sayuri Saito. She seems to be worshiping a dead idol. She'll never be happy. No other man will bring her joy. And if anyone ever learns of whom she truly loves, she could be in grave peril. I will not tell, and neither will you, but I wonder where her allegiance really lies."

"You are asking if she might be a traitor? A saboteur? No," said Koizumi. "She is just a sad, hopeless child whose life will be discarded and forgotten. Like so many others. She is a ghost."

"And our lives, Koizumi-san? Will we be discarded and forgotten?"

"That's up to fate, *tomodachi*, and it does not always serve us well. But we can meet it with resolve."

Chapter 14
South China Sea
July, 1943

How ironic, thought Jeremy Shinagawa, that he was once again on the same filthy tramp steamer, the *Kawasaki Maru*, that had delivered him and hundreds of other slave workers to Nggela Island. Intense heat, near starvation, beatings and excruciating toil had depleted the force, reducing the survivors to emaciated wraiths. When the Japanese high command determined that the Americans were about to invade Guadalcanal and the surrounding islands, including Nggela, they decided to remove the workers and guards to a location closer to the home islands. Therefore, on the night of August 5th, one hundred forty-three workers, along with guards and a handful of women, were hustled onto the transport beside the island's dilapidated dock.

"Have you heard where are they taking us?" Jeremy asked Aoki Rituo. He was glad his friend had survived, and knew he himself never would have without him.

"I got word second-hand. Someone overheard Major Abe telling Captain Igaki. that we were sailing to an island named Ishigaki-jima. He said that it's going to be a very long voyage."

"I don't know where that is; do you?"

"Yes, my mother took me there years ago. It's in the Yaeyama Islands, an archipelago about four hundred and twenty kilometers from Okinawa. It has a big mountain called Omoto-dake and lots of coral reefs. The sea is clear, and it's tropical. There are many other islands nearby. A group of native people took us to one island by canoe. We explored some caves and it was very exciting. Of course, that was before the war. I expect things have changed."

"What do you think they'll have us do there?"

"I don't know. Gold was once mined there. My mother bought a little gold charm, but I don't think we'll be mining gold. Whatever it is, it won't be pleasant."

With the death of so many workers there was more room in the hold of the *Kawasaki Maru,* but the treatment was no better than during the previous voyage. Sweltering below decks, each man was given only one cup of water a day; and, if fortunate, a bowl of rice in the morning. The main difference was that the guards had become familiar. Prisoners now knew which ones were slightly more humane, what village or city they came from, and how to placate them to avoid a beating. And instead of being chained in the fetid hull for the entire duration, small groups were allowed on deck for twenty or thirty minutes at a time.

Lookouts were posted on the bridge and the stern to spot for aircraft or a submarine's periscope, but there were only calm swells and the incessant chugging of the engine.

At midday, with the temperature at one hundred-fifteen degrees below decks, the grate securing their cell was opened. Jeremy, Aoki and a half-dozen others were allowed onto the top deck. A guard, his rifle slung over his shoulder, directed them to a sealed hatch just forward of the bridge. A gentle breeze welcomed them, a glorious respite from the dank, foul air below.

Jeremy lay back on the weathered deck and, closing his eyes, imagined a sun-drenched California beach upon which pretty girls frolicked in the surf and biplanes pulling long advertisements buzzed overhead. If he tried hard enough, he could almost smell hot dogs being cooked while his little brothers built sand castles and ran up and down the beach. He imagined an airfield five miles inland and the drum of engines, perhaps an army scout or an army bomber on a takeoff and landing exercise. Indeed, the sound in his mind was almost audible. He opened his eyes and blinked in the blinding light of the afternoon sun. Sitting up, he saw Aoki stir beside him and raise himself on an elbow. Jeremy looked about, but the other men, grateful merely to be on deck, had barely moved. Glancing toward the bridge he saw a sailor raise his binoculars, then stiffen.

Suddenly the man was shouting into a speaker phone and pointing to an object high above. Within seconds, four guards rushed to a heavy machine gun at the ship's bow and tore off the tarpaulin. Only then did the other prisoners begin to stir.

Two black dots came out of the sun, very high; two more came in below them, mere feet above the water. The machine gun spat bullets, first at one, then at the other of the lower, closer planes. One began to trail smoke, wobbled, and skimmed the waves before slowing to a rocking halt.

Jeremy watched as the pilot threw back the canopy and dragged a life raft out of the sinking plane. A rear gunner also extricated himself and joined the pilot. It was evident, however, that this man had been shot. Without the assistance of the pilot he would never have gotten into the orange raft.

A BLOSSOM IN THE ASHES

But there was little time to consider their fate. The wingman of the downed plane had closed the range, and Jeremy saw bright spits of fire rip into indolent waves before others tore into the bridge of the *Kawasaki Maru*. Windows shattered and chunks of metal were ripped from the low superstructure. A scream reached Jeremy's ears, and he saw the lookout man spin into the sea, his torso a bloody mass of shredded flesh. More shouts and wails came from inside the bridge, and the ship began to veer from its course.

"Run!" shouted Jeremy. He and Aoki launched themselves toward the bow as the ship's machine gun swiveled after the departing aircraft.

From high above, the two aircraft began their dive. As they plummeted, implausibly fast, each discharged a black object that descended independently, growing larger as it closed the distance. One bomb struck the ship's stack, blowing it overboard along with deck housing and a dozen crew. A shrill whistle erupted from a severed steam pipe and a great pall of smoke rose and trailed aft. A second bomb plunged into the sea and exploded only yards from the port beam. A geyser of water laced with steel fragments rose high above the deck.

The planes wheeled, curving upward and away, and vanished from sight.

The ship heeled to port and shuddered. Remaining crew members tugged fire hoses, most of which immediately sprang leaks. There had never been any practice drill, Jeremy realized; what else aboard the ship didn't work? Was there even a first aid kit? There was a torrent of commands, and prisoners were rushed on deck to fight the fires and gather the wounded.

As smoke roiled up from below decks, the *Kawasaki Maru* appeared to be balanced between righting herself and heeling over to end her hapless existence.

With the desperate aid of the prisoners, the fires were gradually extinguished, and but for the moans and cries of the wounded, silence reigned. All searched the sky for another attack, one that would surely send the ancient ship to the bottom. But none came. Perhaps, thought Jeremy, the old tub was not worth another bomb, or at least not worth the possible loss of another plane. They were only prisoners, after all.

The engines had died and the ship drifted ever closer to the Americans in their canvas raft. Only the pilot, with a single paddle, was able to row, and with the weight of two men he made scant progress. He gazed up at the wounded ship as it drifted abeam, a look of dread on his face.

One of the guards tossed a knotted line to him. With trepidation, he climbed up the listing hull. Once he was on board, the guard who had thrown the rope clubbed him with the butt of a rifle. The wounded man in the raft was shot. Four more rounds punctured the raft, and soon it and the rear gunner slid beneath the waves.

Under the shouted directions of the surviving crew, guards and prisoners labored to plug the ship's gaping hole, and manned pumps chugged away to offset the intake of seawater. Slowly the ship righted itself, and several engineers working together were able to repair the engines. At barely five knots, the blackened and mangled hulk resumed its voyage to Ishigaki Island.

Twenty-three men were dead and fifteen were wounded, including Major Abe. The American pilot, still unconscious, was taken below and tossed in with the surviving laborers. A number of them, saddened by the loss of friends, talked of killing the pilot, but Jeremy spoke up. "They want to interrogate him; that's why they didn't shoot him. You will be in trouble if you kill him without permission."

Grudgingly, the workers left the unconscious man alone, knowing that whatever befell him would be quite unpleasant.

Eerie sounds rose from the bowels of the wounded vessel as darkness fell over the sea. Jeremy and Aoki settled against a bulkhead and watched the wounded American. A single bare lightbulb swung on its cord above the cell; under its dim and wavering light, fifty-one men snored and tossed on a rising sea.

Hours passed. Eventually, the man stirred, moaned, and attempted to rise.

"No, stay still," said Jeremy, waking from a fitful sleep. "Pretend to be unconscious. If they see you are awake, they will torture you."

The man, a great bruise from the gun butt on his forehead, strained to see who could possibly be whispering to him in English. The gloom and the uniformity of squalor all around him defeated his efforts. Lying back against the cold metal, he said in a low voice, "Who are you?"

"Jeremy, and this is my friend Aoki. I'm American, or I was. Now I'm a slave laborer. Who are you?"

"Where is my tail gunner?" the man demanded, ignoring the question.

"He was shot. Went down with the raft. I'm sorry. Who are you?"

"Lieutenant J.G. Steven Whitcomb. Do you have any water?"

"A little." Pulling forward a rusty pot, Jeremy filled the only cup one third full. "We're rationed. This is all any of us have most of the day."

"Thanks," grunted Whitcomb, who drank thirstily, then closed his eyes. "My tail gunner, Jameson, was only a kid. Just married too. Fucking shame."

"So is this whole war. I'm sorry about the kid, but I'm glad you didn't sink us."

"It doesn't matter. Some sub will put a fish into it sooner or later."

They lapsed into a silence for many minutes before Whitcomb said, "So how in the hell did *you* wind up here? It doesn't look like you volunteered."

"I didn't volunteer. I was a graduate student in Tokyo before the war. I was picked up by the secret police and put into a work battalion. All of us, even the women in the officers' quarters, were building fortifications. We'll be doing the same pretty soon on another island—if we're not sunk first."

"You said that there are women aboard?"

Jeremy nodded. "They're called 'comfort women' by the Japanese. Sex slaves, mostly Chinese, but a fair number from Manila and any other place they invaded. The ones handed over to the enlisted troops get raped seven, eight times a day. Maybe more, I don't know. More than a few have committed suicide. But the ones on board are reserved for the officers."

A groan of rasping steel made them stiffen. When the sound of tortured metal subsided, Jeremy said, "So you joined the navy to fly fighters?"

"Yeah. It was an impulse thing, not that I regret it. Not until now."

"You got talked into it by your buddies?" asked Jeremy, looking toward the open hatch above where an intense conversation in rapidly spoken Japanese was underway.

"Talked into it? Not exactly. It's a short story, but I can make it longer if you wish."

"Concise and to the point, my teachers always told me."

"Sure. I was a medical student, had one more exam to take before the med board would allow me to intern at the hospital." Whitcomb sighed and reflected for a moment. "I had a girlfriend, and she knew that I would pass the exam; I did too. She invited me to her place for dinner and a few drinks. We went to bed, had a sweet time. The exam was for early in the morning and I was already worried about being late. Got outside and it had snowed. Boston, you know. Had to get clear off the car, which refused to start. When it did, the road was a mess. So I got there after the exam was over. And they wouldn't let me take it, then or any other time. I was accused of being immature and irresponsible, and they smelled liquor on my breath. So all those years of study went up in smoke."

"But... for all intents and purposes, you are a doctor."

"I don't want a damn thing to do with medicine. That afternoon I marched myself to the navy recruiter. I said I wanted to pilot Wildcats and blow Zeros out of the sky. I showed him my degree, he looked me over and said, 'Sign here.' The rest is history."

A command was issued from the deck above; a sergeant and three guards scrambled down the ladder. Whitcomb lay his head back and feigned sleep, but the sergeant knelt down and slapped him hard. The lieutenant grunted and sat up.

"Baka! Baka!" shouted the sergeant.

Whitcomb didn't know that he had just been called "stupid" but no translation was needed. Two guards grabbed his arms and shoved him to the gangway, then up the ladder.

"You too," said the sergeant, pointing at Jeremy. "You do not talk to him without my permission. But you will tell me what he says."

In what remained of the enlisted men's quarters, Jeremy saw that the American had been made to sit on a chair. His hands were tied behind his back; his feet were tied together. Guards with guns stood on either side of him. Captain Igaki glared at the prisoner and, pointing to a corpse on the floor, blurted, "This is what you did! You killed him! But now you will tell me everything I want to know. No refusal, no stupid answers. No name, rank and serial number, or I throw you overboard." Turning to Jeremy, he ordered, "Tell him."

"He wants you to tell him stuff. Says that he will throw you overboard if you don't."

"Tell him to fuck off. Tell him that I am Junior grade lieutenant Steven Whitcomb, serial number 87762—"

"Stop! I know English numbers," interrupted Igaki, motioning to a corporal, who punched Whitcomb in the face so hard he fell to the floor.

"Your ship. What is the name of your ship?" growled the captain, as the lieutenant was hauled up and dumped back onto the chair.

Through the blood running down his face and swollen lips, he spat out a tooth and mumbled, "Lieutenant J.G. Steven Whitcomb, serial number 87762443—"

The door burst open and a sailor hurried in, came to attention before Igaki and said, "Major Abe is bleeding to death and his arm is nearly off. He asks that you cut it off, and if you can't you must help him to carry out seppuku."

"I am not a doctor. You know that. Have the corpsman attend to it."

"He's dead, sir. Major Abe insists that you do it."

Igaki stood motionless, then said, "Tell him that I will help him in the ritual death."

"Ca- Captain Igaki," stammered Jeremy, coming to attention and bowing deeply. "This American was in medical school before he became a pilot. He is actually a doctor."

"What the hell are you telling him?" blurted Whitcomb.

"The thing that's going to save your life."

"A doctor?" said Igaki, leaning toward the American with a dubious stare. Then with intense hatred he said, "Why isn't he attending to wounded soldiers instead of flying aircraft?"

"Excellency, he was late for an exam and wasn't allowed to graduate. Out of anger he joined the navy."

"He was late, or he failed the exam?"

"Late, sir."

Igaki again leaned toward Whitcomb and said, "You will save the major's life. If he dies, you die." Jeremy translated.

"No shit," said the lieutenant. "That's one fucking incentive."

On a stretcher, Major Abe was carried in and laid upon a table. Bright red blood pulsed from the gaping wound near the elbow. Whitcomb looked at the arm while his own blood dripped onto the major. Captain Igaki motioned to a guard and said, "Get him a cloth for his nose. And a bucket of water and soap. He must wash his hands."

Whitcomb turned to Jeremy and said, "Give me your belt, that rope holding up your pants. He needs a tourniquet."

As Whitcomb tied the rope around the major's upper arm, he glanced at Igaki and said to Jeremy, "You tell him that this son of a bitch has a fifteen percent chance of making it. Period. Now tell him that I need antiseptics, a saw, needle, thread and clean bandages. And something to reduce the pain because this is going to hurt. Chloroform, ether, anything."

"Maybe he needs a blood transfusion," said Jeremy.

"I don't know his blood type. And even if I had a matching blood type there's no way to sanitarily transfer blood."

Soon the tourniquet was secured and the dead corpsman's medical tools were laid on the table alongside a bottle of rice wine.

"No antiseptic?" said Whitcomb.

"The wine," replied Jeremy.

Whitcomb snorted and said, "My grandpappy's moonshine or some Jack Daniels would put him out of his misery, but not saki. And they better get him something to chomp down on or he will break his teeth."

"You're wasting time!" shouted Igaki. Binoculars hung from a cord around the major's neck. Whitcomb was about to remove them when Abe shook his head. Deciding not to contest it, Whitcomb pointed to Abe's arms and bandy legs and said, "Tell the guards to hold the bastard down." Jeremy translated this, with emendations. Upon the captain's command, four men held the major down. His eyes widened and his legs began to shake as Whitcomb wiped down the shattered arm.

"I've never seen an amputation," said Jeremy. "Do you just cut off the arm and bandage it?"

"Basically. You get rid of damaged tissue, check pulse, temperature, leave as much healthy tissue as possible. Then you seal off nerves and blood vessels and file down any jagged pieces of bone, and hope he doesn't die from shock. it's called a trans-humeral amputation. I have to prevent hemorrhage and pull the surviving skin over the bone and sew it up. Normally he would be in recovery for two weeks or so. But these conditions are no better than the Civil War when my grandpappy had his leg cut off. Amazing that he lived. Most did not."

When the saw tore through the skin and touched the bone, Major Abe writhed in pain and bit down on a wooden spoon so hard it broke into pieces.

"Get that out of his mouth and get a bigger stick!" Whitcomb commanded, forgetting for a moment everything but the patient. He looked at the four men and said, "Jeremy, tell them to hold him down. Hold him down hard!"

Major Abe's eyes protruded as the fine-toothed saw bit into the bone. He thrashed about, requiring the grim-faced sailors to intensify their hold and lean down on him. Captain Igaki grimaced as blood dripped from the severed arm.

A guard, staring at the major, inadvertently prodded Whitcomb with his bayoneted rifle.

"Tell that son-of-a bitch to get that bayonet away from me or I'll make sure this guy dies in agony!"

Jeremy said a half-dozen polite words to Igaki, and at the officer's quick gesture, the guard retreated.

Fifteen minutes later, with the bone filed and the stitches complete, Whitcomb laid the instruments down, washed his hands and turned again to Jeremy. "Tell the captain that I have done everything I can under less than desirable conditions. Without antiseptics there is a good chance of infection, and I do mean gangrene."

As Jeremy translated, Whitcomb grabbed the bottle of saki, took a swig, then thumped the bottle on the table beside his patient. Igaki gave him an astonished look, then grunted that he understood.

The captain inspected the amputation and listened to the major's ragged breathing. "Sir, is there anything I can do for you?" he asked.

Abe shook his head, rose on one elbow and stared at the bandaged stump. Then he fell back on the litter and said, "Give the doctor full rations. He and the translator can sleep on deck. I must have the bandages changed daily, and the stump must be checked for infection."

"The major is an honorable and generous officer," Igaki said as he led Whitcomb and Jeremy to a sheltered place at the bow. "He is allowing both of you to sleep here rather than below decks. You should be grateful and show deference for his generosity."

"Of course," said Jeremy, not wishing to jeopardize the much better conditions. "Sir, would it be possible for me to speak to my friend, Aoki, for a brief moment?"

"Yes, but only once. Then you are to remain on deck. If you disobey me I will order you below for the rest of the voyage."

"What is happening?" asked Aoki, when Jeremy brought him a bowl of rice.

"The American pilot is really a doctor. He successfully amputated Major Abe's arm. Now the lieutenant and I are allowed to sleep on deck. But I cannot visit you any more until we dock."

"Some of the men down here are not doing well. The heat. But it's a little quieter now."

"One of the boilers can't be restarted, that's why it's quieter, but it also means we're going slow. We'll probably be at sea for at least two more weeks. Try to hold out. Perhaps Major Abe will treat us all better now that he has been saved," said Jeremy.

"I don't know why a man who has lost an arm will be any more pleasant. I don't think we will ever see home again, Jeremy. But I wish you the best."

"We just have to survive," said Jeremy. "You helped me when I was sure I would die, when I wanted to. I will do what I can to help you."

"Yes, survive. And no matter what, you have been a good friend."

* * *

Each morning for the next nine days Whitcomb attended to Major Abe at 0900 sharp. Soiled bandages were removed and new ones were tied on the stump. The lieutenant, with Captain Igaki in attendance, inspected the sutures and applied the rice wine where there appeared the slightest sign of inflammation.

Turning to Jeremy, Whitcomb said, "Tell the major that there is no serious infection and that he should enjoy a full recovery. But the bandages must be changed for the next three weeks. That should keep out flies and dirt, of which I think we'll see a lot."

Major Abe was silent while Jeremy translated. Then in perfect English he said, "Lieutenant, you are my nation's enemy. In battle I would have had you killed. I know that you operated on me under duress, and I appreciate your attentiveness. But if you ever call me a 'bastard' again I will have you shot. Now leave. I have duties to attend to."

"Oh shit," said Jeremy after they left the major. "I had no idea that he spoke English."

"Well, now we know, and we better be careful around him. For all we know, he wanted us on deck to listen in on our conversations. Too bad for him we only talked about home and girlfriends. So, what's the bastard like when he's not getting an arm amputated?"

Jeremy shook his head. "He will assert his authority when we get to the island. He's pretty tough, and I doubt that he wants to be sent back to Tokyo. He certainly won't show any kindness to us when anyone else is around to see, so don't expect any. But I wonder if he'll retain you as his doctor."

"Hell no, he won't. Can you imagine an American lieutenant treating a Japanese major surrounded by Japanese medics and doctors? Not a chance, Jeremy."

Late that afternoon, sea birds cried and swooped overheard, and the ocean color changed from dark blue to aqua. Soon after, the lookout sighted land and shouted.

The sun was dipping below the horizon as the *Kawasaki Maru* chugged unevenly toward Ishigaki's port three miles distant. Whitcomb and Jeremy, standing at the port bow railing, studied the island. From the remains of the bridge Captain Igaki and Major Abe scanned the port, and seamen prepared lines for docking. A three-quarter moon rose over the sea, its soft light playing upon indolent waves that gently rocked the ship.

In the dimness Whitcomb touched Jeremy's arm and pointed to an approaching freighter. It was traveling so fast that the prow made a bow wave, unusual for a ten-thousand-ton vessel, considering the need to conserve precious fuel.

"She's in a big hurry," remarked Whitcomb.

"Loaded, too. All those crates and logs piled up aft. Strange cargo," said Jeremy.

"Maybe teak. Some general may want a fancy desk back in Tokyo. But if she doesn't keep a distance she may capsize this tub."

"Hardly," said Jeremy. "It will take more than a bow wave to do that."

A phosphorescent streak three meters down sped past the bow of the *Kawasaki Maru*.

"Jesus!" blurted Whitcomb. Another torpedo passed beneath the ship just as the huge freighter came abreast of the *Kawasaki*. Three seconds later the freighter exploded as both torpedoes found their mark. A blinding flash was followed by multiple detonations, either from stored munitions or fuel catching fire. Stacked logs sailed upward, along with flailing, shrieking sailors, crates, steel bulkheads and deck housing. Fires raged from ruptured fuel tanks and the conflagration spread quickly over the surrounding sea. The grinding sound of tearing metal and the wails of burning crewmen merged with the groan of a great vessel plunging toward the bottom.

Jeremy stared aghast at the smoking whirlpool where the ship had been, but Whitcomb scanned the horizon for any sign of incoming torpedoes. It seemed likely that, as the only other freighter on the water, they'd be the next target. Nudging Jeremey he hissed, and said, "Another one! Starboard bow. Shallow. Get down and hold on!"

The torpedo struck the *Kawasaki Maru* just behind the ship's stack. An explosion rent the vessel in half, and the severed stern rolled over while the bow rose toward the night sky. Pitched backward, men who'd survived the blast were flung into the roiling sea, among them the two Americans.

Jeremy, rising to the surface, saw Captain Igaki and Major Abe thrashing about, choking on sea water and the diesel oil coating its surface. He turned in a circle, treading water, hoping to see his fellow prisoners, but the darkness and the waves made it impossible to see far. He felt a tugging, sucking motion under the waves and began to swim as furiously as he could away from the pull, not daring to look back at what he knew he would see: the ship's bow sinking into the dark water.

A current carried Jeremy and Whitcomb away from the disaster. A detonation rumbled from deep below as a boiler exploded, and plumes of oil roiled from the depths. Sparks ignited the oil slick, and a sheet of flame illuminated the night as they struggled to reach a half floating container.

Whitcomb heard a strangled plea. Turning about, he saw a bobbing head covered in oil and the stump of an arm waving inches above the waves. Whitcomb shouted, "Jeremy, swim to the nearest log. I'll get back to you." He swam back, grabbing Abe by his shirt collar. Then, paddling with one arm, he towed the drowning major toward the logs. Jeremy had draped himself over one and was holding onto another that still had a bit of rope attached. Straddling this one and aided by Jeremy, Whitcomb slid the rope under Major Abe's arms so that his upper torso remained above water.

The current carried them past Ishigaki Island, and Whitcomb feared that it would sweep them out to sea. As the island lights dimmed behind them, the logs swept toward a large atoll a mile further on. A small lagoon appeared, then sand, and the sound of the surf of an incoming tide that nudged them towards the land.

Jeremy and Whitcomb staggered ashore with the barely conscious Abe supported between them. They trudged across the short beach and into dense foliage. Abe coughed up seawater and collapsed, unconscious, beneath a thicket of low palms.

"Leave him, we've got to talk," said Whitcomb.

He and Jeremy pushed into the tangled underbrush, stopped, and listened for any sound. Only insects broke the silence. Finally Jeremy said, "This place may not be inhabited."

"And I doubt that anybody from Ishigaki saw us get here. I think their attention was on rescuing survivors and retrieving any of those floating crates. The last thing we want is for them to know we're here," said Whitcomb, swatting at a mosquito.

"Did you see Igaki?" asked Jeremy.

"He might have gotten picked up. I saw a boat and some people with flashlights. But I really don't give a damn about him."

"If he did survive, he could be trouble," Jeremy said. "We can venture inland in the morning, see if anybody is here. But what do we do with Abe?"

"We take him with us. We can't allow him to get to Ishigaki. He'd tell them that we're here, and we'd be hunted and taken prisoner. By the way," Whitcomb said, "I took the pistol from his holster when we got him onto the beach. He had twenty rounds in his ammo pouch, and I got that too."

"So now he is our prisoner," said Jeremy.

"That's right, and that's the way it's going to stay."

Chapter 15
Iriomote Island
August, 1943

Humidity and a dank smell of dense vegetation wrapped the three men like a smothering, unwashed blanket. The air was alive with gnats and mosquitos, and their salt- and oil-stained clothes clung to them as they moved off the beach and found respite beneath a copse of palms.

Major Abe leaned back against a tree, glanced at his binoculars that now hung around Whitcomb's neck, then noticed his pistol secured on the lieutenant's belt. Whitcomb looked into Abe's eyes but said nothing. The major looked away. There was nothing to be said; the tide of war had turned.

"You didn't have to come back for me, Lieutenant. Under the circumstances it would have been justified if you had left me to drown."

"I could have done that. But maybe I put too much effort into your amputation, or maybe I wasn't thinking at all. You were drowning, and I was only a few yards away. I might have to kill you yet, but letting you drown, no. So there you have it, pal."

"Pal? I don't know that word."

"It's American slang," piped in Jeremy. "It means friend."

"But don't take it too seriously," added Whitcomb.

Abe nodded and made a vain attempt to smile. "Like *tomodachi* but behind a kabuki mask," he remarked wryly.

Looking seaward, they could see two Japanese warships dumping depth charges which sent up columns of water. The dull thump of the explosions reached their ears.

"They're hunting the sub," said Whitcomb, "but he'll have made tracks. Probably running deep and quiet."

"The depth charges aren't helping any survivors," said Jeremy.

"By this time, there are no more survivors."

A searchlight from a closer vessel swept over the beach and Abe was about to stand when Whitcomb said, "Don't you dare. Just because I saved you twice doesn't mean I won't break your neck. And yeah, I know how to do that, too. Jujitsu, as a matter of fact."

"Impressive," said Abe cynically. "So, Lieutenant Jujitsu, what will you do with me?"

"That's still a puzzlement, but I can't let you go. We all stick together like a bunch of gleeful campers. For the rest of the war."

Abe snorted and said, "What's the American word? Bullshit. Yes, that's it. Bullshit. There's a mountain on Ishigaki called Omoto-dake. It's five hundred and thirty meters high and from there the Japanese scouts can see everything for miles around, including this island. It's unlikely there is a base here, so any fire tells them that that survivors landed here. They will come. And one more thing: there is an airfield on Ishigaki, and pilots will be looking for anything suspicious. So perhaps it would be best for you to surrender and throw yourselves upon the mercy of a high-ranking officer."

"Not a chance," said Whitcomb. "Your rank is worth spit if a colonel wants our heads on a pole. Nope, we head inland with first light. And we're keeping your legs hobbled. You haven't given your parole, and I'm not sure I'd trust you if you offered it. Can't have you running off and alerting the enemy now, can we?"

Jeremy, despite their miserable situation, rubbed his lips. He wondered if the major appreciated the reversal of fortune.

It rained that night, and again their clothes became soaked, but at least the sweat and ocean salt washed away. Jeremy and Whitcomb stirred with the dawn, while Major Abe lay disconsolate beside the tree. Then they all moved a hundred yards further into the jungle and came upon a field of untended sugarcane. A plane droned in the distance, and as it drew closer Whitcomb covered Abe with a palm frond, then he and Jeremy did the same. The aircraft glinted in the sun, the red "meatball" on the wings clearly visible.

Abe slid the frond off his face and glanced upward. Then, turning his head, he stared at the pistol leveled at his eyes. The trigger was cocked and Whitcomb said, "I told you last night, I won't hesitate. The rules of the Geneva Convention are not very legible right here. Do you understand?"

"I understand," said Abe. "But the Convention allows a prisoner to escape."

"Funny how you recall these details when they apply to you, not when they apply to others. Now, let's go up that hill like family and see what we can see. When it's dark, we might come back for some of that sugar cane, but we'll just have to stay hungry while that plane is buzzing the island."

* * *

Captain Igaki stood at attention before Colonel Odomitsu and said, "Sir, have your men found Major Abe?"

The colonel shook his head. "No, and you said that his arm was amputated. A man would have a hard time swimming with only one arm. Many men drowned last night, and the sub that sank our ships got away."

"Sir, the sub might still be in the area," said Igaki stiffly. He held himself upright, refusing to favor his burned and bandaged leg.

"We will be vigilant."

"And we lost the workers, the men in the hold."

"We will bring in other workers, Captain. And two of the women were saved. We had nine here for the officers and men. Two committed suicide and one escaped some months ago. She was quite pretty and spoke three languages. I let my sergeant have her, since he has been very effective. Now I will take one of the new ones, and give the other to you."

Agaki said, "I would welcome that."

The colonel nodded and asked, "Is your leg any better?

"It is healing and I can walk. What are my orders?"

"You are to supervise the construction of defensive works as you've done before. In a few days, I will send divers down to the ships and see if there is anything we can salvage. Many crates with valuable equipment were on the deck of the freighter."

"I saw many of them floating away. Perhaps some of them beached on nearby islands."

"Yes, that is possible. So, you will take a patrol and locate them. A retrieval detail will follow. Now rest, and I will send one of the comfort women to you."

* * *

A rock struck Jeremy in the chest. A second one hit Major Abe, and a third sped past lieutenant Whitcomb. It was followed by a spear impaling itself in a rotting palm. Jeremy rubbed his chest and reassured himself that the none of his ribs were broken. He looked about, hoping to see the assailant, but whoever had thrown the rocks was nowhere to be seen. Whitcomb helped Abe to his feet and pulled the spear from the tree.

"I thought no one lived here. Apparently somebody does, and isn't favoring guests."

"At least they didn't shoot," said Jeremy.

"Maybe he doesn't have a gun, or doesn't care to make noise. But we better find out who has taken offense to us," replied Whitcomb.

The overgrown trail led past a mangrove forest and sandstone outcrops. A scream erupted from deep in the foliage. Jeremy glanced up in time to see the flash of a light-colored shape leap from a tree branch and disappear back into the thicket.

"What was that?" asked Abe, wishing that he had his sidearm.

"An animal, some sort of cat," said Jeremy.

"A cat doesn't throw rocks or spears," said Whitcomb.

They pushed through dense jungle and came upon a narrow trail. A little further along they reached a small clearing. Whitcomb stopped suddenly and pointed upward.

"A mountain!" exclaimed Jeremy.

"From the summit we can see everything," said Whitcomb. "That's where we have to get."

"I'm not feeling well and I won't be able to climb up there," said Abe. "You should leave me somewhere. And I think my stump is infected. If I have gangrene, I'll be dead in a week or two."

"It looks like there's a cave just up there, by that ledge," said Whitcomb. "You can make it that far, and I'll look at your arm. I'm not leaving you here to signal your friends."

They began to climb and another spear whirred past Abe's head. "Up there!" shouted Whitcomb, and he ran forward. A slender, dark-haired woman dashed behind a palm, then emerged with a rock, which she promptly threw. Whitcomb twisted and the rock passed harmlessly by.

"Stop! No more!" he shouted. The woman, who Jeremy could now see was wearing torn trousers and a man's loose military shirt, stopped and stared at Whitcomb. Then, in accented English, she said, "Who are you, and who are those Japs?"

"I'm Lieutenant Steven Whitcomb, U.S. Navy." Pointing down the slope he said, "That man is Jeremy Shinagawa, an American."

"But the other one wears a Japanese uniform. He's no American," said the woman suspiciously.

"No, he's not. He's a Japanese major and he's my prisoner. We are survivors of a ship torpedoed by an American sub. Now, who the hell are you and what are you doing here?"

The woman said nothing, sizing up the three men. "If that man, the major, comes near me, I will kill him. Understand? I'll kill him."

Without another word she turned and headed up the trail to the barely visible cave. Whitcomb turned to Jeremy and said, "Let's follow her."

When they reached the narrow entrance of the cave, they saw it extended back, intersecting with other branches. An interwoven thicket concealed a cache of sharpened sticks just behind the opening. On rough ledges were laid a few pots, a pan, and bits of clothing. There were also several piles of coal, and a pit had been dug thirty feet from the entrance, so that smoke would not rise from the cave's mouth. A warm, dim light emanated from the pit.

The woman silently sat near the embers, while the three men stood near the entrance, their eyes adjusting to the dimness. "May we come in?" asked Whitcomb.

"If you behave," was the wary reply.

The three men sat on an opposite ledge but said nothing, while the woman skewered a decapitated pit viper on a blackened stick and held it over the coals.

"What's your name?" Jeremy asked, wondering how she'd killed the snake.

She didn't look up but said, "This snake is called *habu*; it is venomous and can kill you. You must always watch for them. But they taste good when cooked." She remained intent upon her cooking, then said, "I'm surprised that you weren't stung by the jellyfish when you came through the surf. They're also poisonous. Never touch them."

Again she concentrated on the snake before looking at Jeremy and saying, "My name is Maria Aguinaldo. I am from Pasay City in the Philippines, and for a while I was with the *Hukbalahap*, the guerrilla resistance. But then I was captured and made to service the Japanese."

Whitcomb glanced over at Jeremy, who looked sick.

"I was taken to Ishigaki Island to please those monsters," she said, with a vicious glare at Abe. "During the day I washed their clothes. At night I was raped. Every night. One night I snuck away with another girl. We stole a boat and paddled here. But she died."

Major Abe said stiffly, "Many women, including Japanese, volunteered to comfort our soldiers."

If Maria was surprised to hear him speak English she did not acknowledge it. Instead she said, "I haven't seen any volunteers. Philippine women were taken at gunpoint. Do you know what happened when any of us got pregnant? The babies were murdered at birth for being half-breeds. That happened to me the first year. Afterwards I was hurt inside by more men, and now I can't have children even if I want them."

Bitterness hung in the air. Jeremy, hoping to reduce the tension, said, "Where does the coal come from? I thought this island is volcanic or sandstone."

"Most of it is, but there are coal deposits that were worked by the Ryukyu and Okinawa Mining Companies before the war. The natives who originally lived here called it 'burning stone.' The Japanese brought in people to work the mines. Of course, the workers weren't told about the malaria, which killed most of them. Then those that survived were conscripted into the army. There is still a lot of coal lying around."

"But coal is filthy," said Whitcomb. "Why don't you use wood? It's everywhere."

The wood is always wet. It rains every day. So I use coal. No one can see the fire I make in this cave, and the mosquitos don't like the smoke."

"May we stay in this cave?" Whitcomb asked.

"I don't want men in my cave. But there is another one higher up. From there you can see the shore down below. It would be better for all of us for you to stay there. I like my privacy," she said, inspecting the cooked snake.

"Very well," said Whitcomb. "We go there."

The men were at the entrance of the cave when Jeremy said, "It would be good to be friends, Maria. If you ever need help you can call on us."

She nodded, then said, "I worked for General MacArthur. I was a secretary in Manila before the war. He said that he will return. Do you think he will?"

"I'd put my money on it," said Whitcomb. "It might not be soon, but he'll be back."

They ascended to a cave three hundred feet higher, found a pile of coal already there beside another pit, and started a fire. In the final light of day, while Major Abe brooded,

Jeremy and Whitcomb walked to the entrance and looked toward the beach a mile away. An object caught his eye and Whitcomb raised the binoculars.

"One of those crates from the freighter is wedged into some rocks. It must have been brought in by high tide."

"Maybe we should go down and get it," said Jeremy.

"In the morning. It will be dark soon, and we don't want to run into any of those snakes. And I don't think the crate is going anywhere."

Back in the cave they rummaged through things left behind by previous occupants. A few picks and shovels, old Japanese newspapers, and an iron skillet lay scattered on the floor. Making a torch from littered sugar cane stalks, Jeremy and Whitcomb explored two chambers that ran off the main cave and returned to their fire a few minutes later.

They listened to night sounds in the semi-darkness. Presently, Abe asked, "Do you think the Americans will take Guadalcanal?"

"Yes, and every other island the Japanese occupy. We know it will be costly, but it will happen," said Whitcomb. "We have a much larger population and more resources than Japan. And we haven't forgotten Pearl Harbor. That was a big mistake, pal. It's inevitable, like a tsunami from deep below the sea. Unstoppable and relentless."

Abe considered this, then said, "Perhaps that is so. But in Japan every man, woman and child has been trained and is willing to sacrifice their lives to defend the homeland and the Emperor. What happens when the Americans invade Japan? How many marines is America willing to lose to guns and spears? How many children will they have to kill before it's too much to bear? Tell me, Lieutenant, what will become of American resolve when your public sees films of hundreds of thousands of dead babies, women, and children? Take all the islands you can, but you will not take the land of the Rising Sun."

All was quiet. Abe added, "The names of missing Japanese soldiers and prisoners are erased from the town rolls. That person ceases to exist. You saved my life, Lieutenant, but as far as the Japanese government is concerned, I am already dead. Whatever happens to me is of no consequence. It doesn't matter whether I live or die."

Jeremy spoke up. "I don't think you want to die, Major, and I don't think you want to commit seppuku. Real samurai, ancient ones, rarely committed suicide. Your army distorted history and fed propaganda to the uninformed, the vulnerable. It's a travesty, and as a result hundreds of thousands are going to die needlessly before all this is over. As an officer, you, just like Tojo, are to blame for encouraging fanaticism. All those deaths you say we will cause, the deaths of your people, you made that inevitable."

Silence filled the cave, and for a half hour nobody spoke. Then Jeremy, tired of the mutual hostility, said, "Major, where did you go to school, I mean university?"

Abe wondered if he should condescend to answer the question, then, reflecting that an exchange of information might be to his advantage, replied, "Tokyo University, of course."

"I was there, as a graduate student in ancient history. Japanese military history. I studied under the supervision of Professor Takeo Shimura. In fact, I was his house guest until the war."

"Sneezing Shimura?" Major Abe asked, suddenly curious.

"The same."

"How interesting! Yes, I was also his student for military history. I was always terrified of catching cold around him, though I suspect it was allergies. What was your era of research?" Abe asked, as if he had just been introduced to an academic colleague.

"The Tokugawa, and a murder that had a great effect upon the dynasty. Then, because of the Kempeitai, I could no longer attend the university or stay in his house. I left my work with the professor, but I have no idea of what became it."

"And you were conscripted after that," said Abe matter-of-factly.

"According to the military, I am a Japanese national. They got that wrong."

A damp chill seeped into the cave and the three men huddled around the fire in a mutual need for warmth. They shared a pineapple and smoked fish Maria brought and left outside the cave. Jeremy thanked her profusely before joining the others. After their hunger was assuaged, fatigue took over. The cave walls seemed to close in, adding to a sense of isolation to the unknown.

"Is this not bizarre?" Abe said, as Whitcomb stirred the coals.

"How's that?" asked Jeremy.

"I, a major in the Imperial Japanese Army, reminiscing with an American student in a cave while an American lieutenant who has saved my life looks on with my pistol in his belt."

"Something to tell your grandchildren about," said Whitcomb, licking the taste of fish from his fingers.

Abe snickered. "Grandchildren? What makes you think that I will live that long? That any of us will live that long?"

Then with sudden rage he shouted, "It's over! It's all over!" With that he rose and hobbled to the far end of the cave.

"Maybe he's right," said Whitcomb. "But there will be hell to pay first."

Chapter 16
Iriomote Island
August, 1943

Next morning, glum and dispirited, Major Abe followed Jeremy and Lieutenant Whitcomb down the trail to Maria's cave, where they found her sitting outside, preparing a fishing line.

"Where are you going?" she inquired, giving the men a quizzical look.

"You can't see it from here, but from our cave I saw a container wedged into some rocks just beyond an inlet," said Whitcomb. "We're taking the trail down. I want to see if there's anything of value in it before I destroy it. I don't want a Japanese patrol to find it."

"You can't get there using this trail if it's in the inlet I think you're talking about. There's a cliff that blocks the way. The inlet's hard to find, but I know of a trail leading there."

"Will you guide us to the beach?" asked Jeremy.

"Yes, if you share whatever you find in the crate."

"Deal," said Whitcomb, and the men waited for Maria to stow away her line.

"Maybe there's some medical supplies or tools in the crate," said Jeremy.

"Or a machine gun," said Whitcomb, taking up a pickaxe from the entrance of the cave and starting down the path. Then he stopped, turned, and waited.

Maria emerged, carrying a lengthy spear with a fire-sharpened point.

"That looks like the ones you threw at us. I'm glad you missed," said Whitcomb.

"I wasn't trying to kill you. If I was, you would be dead. I've killed wildcats and even snakes, and never go outside without one," she said with a determined look.

"Fine," replied Whitcomb, "It's good to have another armed person."

Maria didn't reply but ahead of them down the trail, her long black hair waving in the morning breeze.

Under his breath Whitcomb said, "I get the feeling that a certain young lady isn't into making nice. A real snafu we got ourselves into."

"What's a snafu?" asked Jeremy, glancing back and nearly falling over a slippery log.

"A military term. 'Situation normal: all fucked up.'"

Jeremy grinned, then started to follow Maria as she moved along the path. Pretty, he mused, even in the ragamuffin clothes she must have scrounged from abandoned dwellings. In an evening gown she would be a knockout. But that image belonged to a very different world.

Whitcomb, seeing Abe's listlessness, said, "I'll check on your stump when we get back. We can boil some water and wash the bandages."

The major merely nodded. He started after Jeremy, and leaned on a walking stick he had fashioned that morning. Behind him, Whitcomb kept an eye peeled for any aircraft that might stray over the island.

They arrived at the beach to find an expanse of yellow sand and ocean-tossed boulders to one side and a towering cliff on the other, blocking sight of the shore beyond. The day was blustery; a squall was in the offing.

"We won't have much time before we're drenched," said Whitcomb, surveying the horizon.

Jeremy, Whitcomb and Maria negotiated their way between boulders, then looked for a place to crack open the fifteen-foot-long wooden crate.

"Look, it's broken open on this side," said Maria, who had rounded the boulder.

"I can go along the beach and see if there are any two-by-fours that floated in. If so, we can use them to pry the crate further open," said Jeremy.

"Nope, I think we better stick together. Let's get what we can and come back later," said Whitcomb.

A three-foot-long rectangular box, its lid torn away, had fallen out of the crate, along with a length of cloth. Reaching inside the crate, Whitcomb dislodged a box of ammunition and a half-dozen hand grenades, which promptly rolled out. Whitcomb grabbed two and pushed the others back in. He spied Abe peering at the grenades and gave him a sharp look.

Even with Whitcomb swinging the pickaxe, it was difficult to crack open the large crate despite the damaged end. Jeremy and Maria pulled at the loosening boards, while Abe stood to the side and watched.

"You could help," Whitcomb finally said, exasperated with the major's recalcitrance.

"I'd rather not," Abe replied, turning away.

Very well, thought Whitcomb with sudden bitterness. He stared at Abe, then thought, *Fine if he chooses to be cocky and impudent. He's really my enemy and I'm not required to aid him. Let his stump fester, then see how indifferent he is.*

They toiled over the container while Abe stared at the sea. Then, quite suddenly, he trotted a dozen yards down the beach, as fast as the rope around his legs allowed. Whitcomb, focused on the crate, failed to notice until Jeremy said, "Lieutenant, we have visitors!"

A twenty-foot craft ferrying five men had rounded the cliff. One man stood, pointing to the beached crate. Other men held rifles, which they aimed as the motor craft sped toward the inlet.

"Get back!" yelled Whitcomb, and dove towards the cover of the jungle as the boat ran up on the beach. Jeremy and Maria followed, but Abe ran toward the boat. Captain Igaki was the first ashore, followed by a sergeant and three soldiers. Abe reached them, and the captain saluted.

From where they hunkered behind rocks, the three saw the Japanese advance toward the crate, weapons in hand. Whitcomb drew his pistol and motioned for Jeremy and Maria to stay down.

"They'll come after us first," he whispered. "They'll deal with the crate later."

"They surely know where we are," said Jeremy. "Maybe we should make a break for it."

Whitcomb peeked above the rocks and saw the major, unfettered, advancing with the other five. Pulling a grenade from his pocket, he slammed it on the rock, activating the timer, and threw it. The explosion ripped apart two of the soldiers, but now the rest knew their position. Igaki, the sergeant, and the surviving private charged toward them.

"Him!" hissed Maria, pointing at the sergeant. "He's the bastard who raped me!"

The enraged Filipina sprang from the rocks and charged. Jeremy and Whitcomb emerged and dashed forward. Igaki, seeing Whitcomb with pistol in hand, fired, his round striking the lieutenant and spinning him into the sand.

Next the sergeant raised his rifle and aimed it at Maria, but her spear was already in flight. Impaled, stunned, the sergeant stared down at the shaft and, dropping his rifle, vainly tried to yank it from his stomach. On his knees, he was still struggling when he looked up to see Maria holding a heavy stone. She slammed it down on his face, and he fell to the sand.

Dashing past Maria, the major sprang for the pistol, still clutched in Whitcomb's hand. The lieutenant rose to his knees and, as Abe reached for the weapon, whipped it across the major's forehead. Abe fell onto Whitcomb and the two tussled, rolling over the other. Igaki ran towards them; seeing the American on top of the major, he raised his gun and took aim, his eyes dark with hate. Whitcomb, in a desperate move, rolled once again as Igaki fired his pistol, and the bullet struck Abe in the back.

The major screamed and fell face forward. Whitcomb rose to his knees and, through blurred vision, fired at the infuriated man rushing toward him. Igaki crumpled, pulling the rifle trigger one last, desperate time. The round went wide, and no more shots came.

With fixed bayonet, the surviving private was already charging toward Whitcomb, oblivious to Jeremy, who found the pickaxe. As the soldier pulled back the rifle, preparing to skewer Whitcomb, Jeremy swung the sharp end of the tool into the man's stomach and wrenched him back. The private gasped, dropped his weapon and fell face-first into the ground, clutching the mess that had been his abdomen.

Whitcomb held his hand over the bullet hole in his shoulder and, wincing, said, "Jeremy, there's a length of cloth that fell out of the crate. If you get it you can staunch the bleeding."

Moments later, Jeremy, wrapping the wound, said, "I think the round went clean through. There's an entry and exit wound."

"Maybe I won't bleed to death, but you'll have to cauterize it. Get that man's bayonet. I'll show you what to do with it."

"We'll get you back to the cave, and I'll boil and sterilize the bandage. At least the bleeding has slowed."

"Is he dead?" said Whitcomb, nodding toward Major Abe.

"Very," replied Jeremy.

"Yeah, I think I hit him at least once, but I couldn't be sure. Now you better see about Maria."

Maria sat on the sand, not far from the sergeant whose eyes, still open, stared directly at her. The sight of the spear protruding from the sergeant's stomach riveted her attention. She trembled, raised her hands to her face and wept.

"It's over, it's all over," said Jeremy, wanting to put his hand on her shoulder but not daring to touch her. She looked as coiled as a viper, as feral as a wildcat. "The lieutenant has been wounded; we have to help him back to the cave. It's time to go."

"I want to stay here and see the pain on his face. I've waited and prayed for this day. Each time he forced himself on me I thought of how I would kill him. Now I've impaled him as he impaled me," she said, pointing to the sergeant, whose mouth was frozen in a silent scream. "I did it, I finally killed him. Each time he raped me he said, 'I know what you are thinking, but it will never happen. Just accept your fate.'"

She suddenly stood, pulled the spear from the corpse and thrust it into his body, wailing, "I killed you! I killed you!"

She dropped the spear, sank to her knees and gave a great sigh.

"Yes," said Jeremy, "He deserved it. But please, help us now."

She looked at him blankly. Kneeling beside her, Jeremy said, "I killed a man who raped my sister. No one ever knew I did it. I left home very quickly, even before the investigation began. I never told my sister, and she has no idea who killed him. But I don't think she will ever be the same. I can only guess how you must feel. Come, I'll push his body into the sea, but then you must come with us."

"I will help you and the lieutenant. I think you are good men," she replied, standing shakily.

Jeremy took the corpse by the feet and dragged it into the surf. A strong current swept his body beyond the beach and out to sea.

"He has blood on him and there are sharks," said Maria, not needing to say anything more.

Whitcomb struggled to his feet.

"Can you walk?" Jeremy asked.

"Yeah, but you better see if you can find any medications in that box."

"I can do that, but what about the other bodies?"

"Perhaps you better get rid of them. They'll send out a search party."

"Then we better not go back to the cave," said Jeremy. "It's too easy to find. Maybe we should take the boat and find another island."

"There's no time. Japanese search planes will be all over the place, and if they find us at sea we're dead."

"There is a better hiding place, a cave, on the other end of this island. It's behind a waterfall," said Maria, wiping blood from the lieutenant's wound. "The falls are called *Pinaisara-no-taki*. It's through the jungle about four hours from here."

"It will take a lot longer," said Jeremy. "The lieutenant will have to rest on the way. I'll stay here and get rid of the bodies." Turning to Maria, he said, "Leave stone markers and take Whitcomb to the waterfall. I'll follow and scatter the stones."

"No, I'll help you, then we will go together. Alone, you will never find it before dark. And dark here is very dangerous."

As swiftly as they could, they dragged the bodies and parts of bodies to the sea. While Jeremy rooted in the crate until he found a box of medical supplies, Maria stopped to strip one of the bodies.

"Why did you do that?" Jeremy asked her, watching her gather the soldier's belongings.

"I think we should keep a uniform. You look Japanese; who knows, you might need it sometime. I have my spear, but you should take the rifle and bayonet."

"I don't care to wear a Japanese uniform, and I don't know anything about shooting that rifle."

"Maybe you should learn," she said.

When they returned, Whitcomb said, "One more thing, Jeremy. Get a grenade from the crate and push the boat into surf. Then toss in the grenade."

"How do I set off a grenade? Pull a pin?"

"Japanese grenades don't have a pin. They slam it against their helmet or hit it against a rock. Do it, and throw it. Do you have a good arm?"

"Yeah, I was a pitcher back home."

"No strike outs. Put it right over the plate, and be sure to duck."

They passed several abandoned shacks but had no time or energy to see what might have been left in them.

It was nearly dark when they made the final ascent, sliding behind the falls and into the cave. Sweat-drenched and exhausted, they dropped everything and sank to the floor.

Jeremy looked at Whitcomb and said, "I'm amazed that you made it here."

"Decapitation by samurai sword is a real motivator."

"True enough. So how are you?" asked Jeremy.

Whitcomb smirked and said, "How do you think I am with a big fucking hole in me? Check that box before it gets totally dark and see if there's antiseptic or anything for pain."

Rising to his knees, Jeremy opened the lid and extracted a compass, a first aid kit, quinine tablets, flares, bandages and a Lucky Strike cigarette lighter.

"Strange that an American lighter would be in the box," said Jeremy. "I'll look around for something to burn for a fire. Then I'll clean up your wound."

"You better check on Maria. I think all the killing has gotten to her," said Whitcomb.

Kneeling beside her, Jeremy touched her forehead and said, "You have a fever. Did you ever have malaria?"

"Before. I took quinine until the Japanese came. The fever went away but it comes back. It's what killed my friend, the lady who escaped with me."

"I'll make sure it doesn't kill you."

"You will help me?"

"Of course. You have to get better. I don't know how to cook."

Shivering, she only had energy to shake her head. "Men are worthless," she said, wrapping her arms about herself.

"I was hoping you'd laugh. I'll start a fire and get you the quinine. Then you get a good night's sleep."

"You know," said a freshly bandaged Whitcomb, leaning against the cave wall, "only the Japanese have quinine now. The U.S. had to come up with a substitute, Atabrine. It was a pretty frantic thing, because so many of our people on Bataan and Corregidor got malaria. That had a lot to do with our defeat. Even when the troops were very sick they wouldn't be sent to sick bay unless they had a one-hundred-and-three-degree fever."

"So why do the Japanese have quinine and not us?" asked Jeremy, slumping down beside Whitcomb.

"They took Java from the Dutch. Quinine was made in the Netherlands and shipped there. Cutting us off from the supply nearly near did us in."

"But we must have had supplies in the U.S.," Jeremy protested.

"Some, sure, but not enough for a war and hundreds of thousands of sick men."

The fire warmed the air and they looked toward the waterfall illuminated by moonlight. "This cave is okay for right now, but we have to find someplace else," said Whitcomb. "The dampness won't do Maria any good. Perhaps tomorrow you might consider looking around. I should be okay in a day or two if there's no infection."

"I'll start early in the morning and see if there's anything of use in the abandoned huts," said Jeremy.

The sound of the plummeting water was comforting and they listened to it for some minutes before Jeremy said, "Why do you think Abe did what he did? I mean, you saved his life twice."

"You mean, why did he attack me and try to get the grenade? I think it's obvious. He was a Japanese officer who suddenly had a chance to kill Americans, and he was about to be rescued by his second-in-command. No other thought would have entered his mind. The fact that I saved him was of no consequence."

"Did it bother you to have to kill him?"

"Did it bother you to kill the private?" retorted the lieutenant.

"No, but I didn't know him."

"I should have tied him to a tree. Then even if his men had rescued him, he'd have lost so much face he would have had to kill himself." Whitcomb sighed.

It took well over an hour for Jeremy to pick his way along the overgrown trail and through a mangrove swamp to reach the first of the abandoned houses. He worried that somewhere along the way he made a wrong turn; nothing looked as it had the day before. Then out of a thicket of low palms he saw the remains of a low dwelling.

Its door was held on by a single hinge. There was no glass in the two windows, only torn mesh screens covered the openings. The door, when he pushed it open, hung at an angle, and Jeremy peered inside the ten-by-twenty-foot room.

At one time a family might have lived here. He hesitated, then entered the house. A few rusted pans, picks and shovels, a machete and several canteens lay about the floor, through which weeds had grown knee-high. Jeremy stood the rifle against the wall and rummaged in what remained of a chest of drawers. Utensils, canvas sacks, a few photos in a tin box, and a small mirror, things left behind, perhaps in haste, he thought. He knew that the former inhabitants would not be coming back, but taking their belongings still felt like theft.

He gathered up all he could carry and sat on the dilapidated steps. It occurred to him that the three of them might yet survive. Of course there would be hardships, but anything was better than slave labor on an island that might be invaded and heavily shelled. At least here there were no overlords with bayoneted rifles, nor the constant fear of being beaten or shot.

And then there was Maria.

Wearily, he rose, stuffed all he could into canvas sacks, picked up the machete and shovel and, slinging the rifle, retraced his steps. At one point he stopped and listened, thinking that he heard men's voices. Kneeling in dense foliage he strained to listen, but the sounds had drifted away. Only the drone of insects broke the quietude.

Nevertheless, he should be stealthy, he told himself. He would have to learn how to move through the mangroves, swamps and jungle so as to leave no tracks, no broken branches, nothing to indicate the presence of a human. He would have to assume that there was danger everywhere, and that a noise or the flash of metal could result in disaster. He remembered reading about the *Rio de Muerte* in the Amazon; Theodore Roosevelt's expedition traveled that deathly river in 1910 and never saw or heard the natives who watched their every move. Only when the party's dogs returned pierced by five-foot long arrows did they know how close they had come to death. That's how he would be, he told himself as he inched his way back to the waterfall and the cave that lay hidden behind its spray.

On the final approach Jeremy felt good about having found it, having survived his first solitary sojourn. He looked forward to bantering with Whitcomb and seeing Maria again. He had promised that he would help her, and she had seemed appreciative. Yes, it would be okay. The war won't last for ever, and life was full of possibilities.

It was quiet. Far too quiet. There were boot prints in the damp soil in front of the waterfall. He stopped and peered at the print of a shoe, the heel small. He merged into a shadowed crevice beside the entrance and listened. There was no sound. Despite the humid air he felt cold. After some minutes he stepped inside, the rifle's bolt pushed forward and down, a round in the chamber.

Resisting the urge to call out their names, Jeremy inched forward, hoping to see them, perhaps in hiding near the rear of the cave. But nothing stirred. Then he saw Whitcomb, shot multiple times, and bayonetted. Shell casings littered the cave floor. Beside him were two dead Japanese soldiers, their limbs askew, their expressions barely registering that their world had ended.

Maria was gone. She had said that the cave would be a safe place. Or had she said a relatively safe place? But someone had known of it, and their tracks to the cave would not have been hard to follow. How many soldiers had come, he wondered. How many were left, and where would they have taken her?

Sweat ran down his face. Fear, dejection, and a sense of isolation overwhelmed him. He knelt and looked upon the holed corpse of Whitcomb, wondering what his last moments had been like. The pistol was gone, but the knife lay by his side. The blade was unbloodied; the invasion had been fast and over within a minute or two.

Shakily, Jeremy stood. He left Whitcomb where he lay, but took his dog tags and cigarette lighter and stuffed them in his pocket. He had no time for a burial. He looked upon the dead officer and anger welled up. They murdered his friends and they would kill him too. But killing could go both ways, and he had done it before.

It was time to find Maria. It was time to spread terror and it was time to kill.

Chapter 17
Iriomote Island
August, 1943

With foliage affixed to the Japanese helmet on his head, Jeremy lay concealed in the heavy brush. He traveled light with only the pistol, a machete, binoculars, canteen and first aid supplies. The Japanese helmet had been a last-minute decision.

There were only four of them, a rather small number sent to investigate the disappearance of an officer and his men. But perhaps there were others who had come ashore at nearby inlets. A pair of A6M Zeros skimmed over the island and one wagged its wings as it sped past the three soldiers guarding their prisoner on the beach.

Jeremy did not know how long they would remain before a boat picked them up. He pondered how he might lure them away from Maria, whose hands were bound behind her back. She lay on the beach just above the high tide mark, her knees pulled to her chest.

He peered through Major Abe's binoculars and saw one of the soldiers rip her ragged shirt, revealing a breast. The man laughed and motioned to his friend, who squatted beside him and rolled a nipple between his fingers. He was laughing when the third soldier nudged them both hard. They leapt to their feet and came to attention as the fourth soldier, a sergeant, approached.

It had been two days since the murder of Whitcomb and the kidnapping of Maria. At night he'd heard the soldiers' shouts and the woman's cries. Three of the men's voices had been raucous; a fourth belonged to a youth who was mocked and beaten for not taking part. His sobs were followed by more insults and the sound of thrashing. The deep-voiced sergeant inflicting the punishment seemed sadistic. From the sound of the boy's voice, he was maybe fifteen years old. As Jeremy contemplated the killings to come, he considered the youth's potential hatred for his assailants.

Jeremy inched closer to the tree line behind the beach and saw one of the privates leave the group, saying that he had to urinate. He was chided for not doing it right there in front of the woman. He laughed and, unbuttoning his trousers, said that he would be doing her in short order.

The soldier ambled up the trail, his pants open. Holding his rifle in one hand, he searched for a good place to pee, apparently wanting a degree of privacy. He was startled when her heard a voice in Japanese say, "Help me, please help me. I am Corporal Orihama, a survivor. I can't walk; you must help me."

Propping the weapon against a tree and hitching up his open pants, the soldier moved toward the strained voice hidden in the brush. A Japanese helmet came into view, then an Asian face. Not until it was too late did he see the machete that sliced open his chest. He stared at Jeremy in disbelief, and died open-mouthed without a sound. A moment later his body had been dragged deeper into the brush.

Three more, thought Jeremy. But to leave the underbrush and confront the others would be folly. It was best to wait.

Minutes dragged by. The deep-voiced noncom shouted out, "Ishigara, how long does it take to piss? Get back here and start a fire before the insects eat us alive."

There was no response, and the sergeant disgustedly ordered one of the privates to fetch him.

With bravado the man called out, "Ishigara, you fool, if your cock wasn't only an inch long you wouldn't be ashamed to pee in front of the woman. Get down here! Sergeant Kakuri doesn't care if you're done pissing or not!"

There was no reply, and the soldier became alarmed. The island was abandoned, but there were poisonous snakes and jungle cat predators. Warily, he gripped his rifle with both hands and advanced cautiously.

"Where the hell are you, Irashimi?"

There was worry in the man's voice. As Jeremy saw the soldier approach, he called out with feigned disgust, "I'm all tangled up in here, I need help."

"I don't see you, Irashimi. I don't think you're tangled up and I don't like playing games. Where the hell are you?"

"Behind you."

As the soldier turned, the machete sliced. With a look of horror the soldier reached up to his nearly severed neck. Sucking for breath that could not reach his brain, he sank to his knees and crumpled forward, blood pouring from the wound. A spasm convulsed his body, his limbs thrashed, then all was still. Jeremy sat down, a sudden trembling in his arms. He had been lucky. Surely the sergeant would not send another man alone. He shivered. The soldiers were trained in hand-to-hand fighting, and he had never been in a fight in his entire life. It did not bode well. He looked down at the corpse and, with one heavy swipe, severed the arm just above the elbow. He advanced to the edge of the tree line, laid the arm beside him and covered it with brush.

Sergeant Kakuri stood over Maria and was sneering at the youth, "Have you ever had a woman before, Hanabe? I imagine not. Maybe I will let you look at her little treasure. Come here, take off her pants and see what a woman really looks like. It was too dark for you to see anything last night. Take off your pants and show me how you do her."

Hesitating and backing away, Hanabe said, "Sergeant, I obey all your orders but she does not excite me. Not the way she looks now. I would fail and—"

"Fail? Of course you would fail! You're a child. A fucking embarrassment! I should execute you for insubordination. You are not a soldier! A soldier obeys orders!"

Livid, Kakuri glared at the youth, his hand reaching for his pistol. Then, exasperated, he said, "Go find them! I want them here now. Fail this and I will shoot you for sure. Run, child, run!"

Ashamed and humiliated, the youth tore pell-mell into the jungle as the sergeant fired a shot, kicking up sand only a yard behind his boots.

An arm suddenly encircled his neck, pressing against his windpipe. Hanabe attempted to scream, but Jeremy pulled him down and hissed, "Not a sound, or you die."

Slowly the arm pulled away and the youth, terrified, slowly turned his head. The first thing he saw was a bayonet at his throat. His body quaked as Jeremy's eyes bore into him. A quick snatch and his rifle was in the hand of this *omi*, this demon, then he was propelled past a thicket of palms.

"The sergeant will kill you," Jeremy hissed, pushing the youth down beside a fallen log. "If not today then tomorrow or the next day. You know that, don't you, Hanabe?" The youth stared at his captor.

"You know that, don't you?" Jeremy repeated, the bayonet only inches from Hanabe's chest.

This time the soldier said, "*Hai. Hai.* He will murder me. But how do you know my name, and who are—"

"We'll talk later. Sergeant Kakuri is committing war crimes, and he is going to die today," said Jeremy just above a whisper. "For all the beatings, you want him dead, don't you?"

The boy, still quaking, gave a slight nod and in a barely audible voice said, "How? I am afraid."

"Follow my instructions. You bring him here and he will never hurt you again. But betray me and you will die. Understand?"

The youth swallowed hard, then said, "You have my rifle. I can't tell him I lost it. I must have it back or he will be suspicious."

Jeremy handed the weapon to Hanabe; then, picking up the severed arm, he thrust it toward him. Instantly Hanabe backed away. He stared at the bloody limb and was about to protest when Jeremy clutched his shirt and said, "Take it! You show this to the sergeant and tell him he must come. Tell him that the soldier was attacked by a big cat and it's still out there. Hold it by the end, so he does not see the cut."

"Big cat," Hanabe repeated, nodding. "Yes, I will tell him. But don't shoot me. Please don't shoot me."

Hanabe was about to go when he said, "You killed them, the other two, didn't you? Are you a soldier, a deserter?"

"No questions. Not now. Bring him here. Hurry, and look very scared."

There was no need to tell him that, thought Jeremy, as the spindly youth fled to the beach holding the arm as far from his body as possible. He began shouting "Sergeant! Sergeant Kakuri!" He waved the limb over his head as he stopped before the noncom, saluted and in a breathless voice said, "Private Naguchi. His arm, sir. I found his body and there were paw prints. I heard a sound like a cat. Will you come, sir? I think Naguchi is still alive."

The sergeant wrenched the limb from Hanabe. The skin, he observed, had been shredded as a cat would have done, but the bone had been cut clean.

"Cat, you say? I don't think so. Maybe you killed him. And maybe you want to trick me, is that it?"

Hanabe bowed deeply, then said, "No, Sergeant, no matter what you think of me, I am a soldier of the Emperor. I do my duty, sir. I request that we help Private Naguchi before he bleeds to death."

"I think he is already dead. Did you see private Irashimi?"

"No, Sergeant. But maybe he needs help too."

Kakuri stared hard into Hanabe's eyes, then holstering his pistol, picked up a bayonet and affixed it to the rifle he grabbed from Hanabe.

"Show me!" said the sergeant, shoving the youth before him. Looking back, he saw Maria prostrate on the sand. *She won't be going anywhere*, he thought. With a hard thrust he prodded the boy with his bayonet, forcing him to leap back. Spurred by the steel prick, Hanabe darted up the trail to where he had last seen Jeremy.

"Into the trees, as fast as you can," said Jeremy as he used the bayonet to sever Maria's bindings. "I will find you. Now hurry."

"Where are you going?" she said, her voice hoarse and raw from screaming.

"I have work to do. I'll find you," he repeated as he slid the bayonet through his belt.

"Should we go back to the cave?" she asked, her voice anxious.

"No, the mountain. Climb the mountain."

"Be careful, please be careful."

Careful, yes, he thought. By now the two soldiers were in the jungle, and he was sprinting across the beach. Earlier he'd had a line of sight on them, an advantage he no longer possessed. Now he would have to confront Kakuri, a man enraged and seething to kill. A cold sweat ran down his back.

Jeremy knew that the terrified young soldier would lead the sergeant to the body and perhaps find the second one. Kakuri would know that it was no cat that killed Naguchi and Irashimi, and he would know that Hanabe was lying. Furious and aware of being duped, he would certainly kill Hanabe then rush to the beach and find Maria gone.

There would be no chance for subterfuge. This murder would have to be fast, and he would be facing a veteran soldier, a man trained in jungle warfare. A sudden dread swept through Jeremy. It was good, he told himself, that he had freed Maria, but had he made a terrible mistake? He should have shot the non-com when he had been the only one guarding Maria. Once that had been accomplished he would have had time to cut Maria's bindings. But it was too late to think about that.

"Baka!" the sergeant hissed when he came upon the bodies. "No cat killed either of them. How did you come up with such a story? You are trying to get me killed, aren't you?" he shouted. He aimed the rifle at Hanabe.

A shout diverted the sergeant's attention. Spinning away from the quaking youth, he saw a strange soldier rushing forward, machete in hand. For a split second Kakuri hesitated, wondering who this soldier was and why he did not recognize him. Then self-reservation kicked in. He easily parried the swing of the machete, then twisted the rifle and thrust at his attacker. Forced back, Jeremy pivoted, flailing at the rifle. The blade slid off the barrel, barely deflecting the deadly thrust, and Jeremy tumbled backward as the rifle discharged. The round grazed his forehead and Jeremy was too dazed to move. With a terrible scream, Kakuri leapt forward, bayonet pointed at Jeremy's chest. Immobilized by fear, he looked into the sergeant's eyes. There was unbridled fury for the loss of his men and the duplicity he now faced. With a vicious jerk he shot the rifle bolt forward; eyes locked with those of the unknown traitor, he aimed the rifle again.

Then all motion stopped, and the man stiffened. As if afraid of what he would see, he slowly stared down at a bayonet thrust through him. Protruding six inches beyond his ribs, a stream of blood ran off the tip. His hand circled it, and he made a rasping, guttural sound. Blood frothed on his lips.

Jeremy leaped back. The sergeant dropped to his knees and, still clasping the bayonet, fell forward.

Private Hanabe stared at the man he had murdered with a fellow soldier's weapon. He quaked uncontrollably, then tore down the pathway, tripping over logs and stones until he reached the incoming tide. Sobbing, he waded into the surf and started swimming out to sea. Tearing after him, Jeremy charged into the water and, grabbing the boy's collar, dragged him up the beach.

Collapsing onto the sand, the boy began to keen with a long, wailing sob.

"He tried to kill you, Hanabe," said Jeremy, kneeling beside the youth and shaking his shoulder. "You fought in self-defense. And you saved me. There is nothing to be ashamed of. There is no need to die; it would gain you no honor and no solace. There would be no contrition in suicide."

The young man shook his head and said, "I murdered a sergeant of the Japanese Imperial Army. I am a traitor. I should commit seppuku. I have a bayonet. Yes," he said, with sudden conviction, "That's what I must do. It's the only honorable thing."

"Bullshit!" said Jeremy, suddenly furious. "You will do no such thing. Nobody in the entire Japanese army cares if you kill yourself. Stop crying. We don't have much time before it's dark and we have a jungle to deal with. Now get up; we have to move."

Blinded by tears and sea water, the youth rose shakily to his feet ands prepared to follow the strange man who had delivered him from one hell into another.

"Will they be coming for us?" asked Hanabe. He and Jeremy sat beneath a canopy of palm fronds.

"Not for a while, though they will be very curious as to why two search parties never returned. But I doubt that they will send a third unless it's in force. After all, there are snakes, and mountain lions. And deadly jellyfish."

"What happens when they find us?" the youth persisted.

"They won't find us. Not this time."

Insects approached the faint glow of the banked fire, then, feeling the heat, sped off to a safer place. The scritch of crickets surrounded them. Jeremy replaced the kerchief over the bloody nick on his forehead.

"You are a well-trained soldier," said Hanabe. "Were you and the lady sent here to watch Japanese activity?"

"Well-trained soldier?" said Jeremy incredulously. "I'm not a soldier at all. I was a graduate student in Japan and am here only because the ship I was on was sunk. And Maria escaped from Ishigaki Island. I am an American. There was another man, a pilot, who was killed by the men you were with."

"Yes, Sergeant Kakuri and Irashimi killed him. I never killed a man until Kakuri. I suggested to Kakuri that we take the officer prisoner, but he said it would be too much trouble and sent me outside the cave to keep watch. Then they found the woman and dragged her out. She tried to fight, but Kakuri hit her hard and she stopped. They raped her that night. I have thought about having a woman, but not like that. They hurt her, and I'm ashamed to say that I did nothing."

"You would have been one against four and they would have killed you," said Jeremy, swatting away a very large ant. Then he said, "I think you're brave, but not cut out for soldering. Were you conscripted into the army?"

"I wanted to be a musician, and I was in high school. My father was very poor and we lived in the mountains. He had seven children and was often drunk. One night he brought over an army recruiting sergeant who needed to fill a quota. The sergeant said that he would give my father part of his bonus if he would send me into the army. I was taken away and had to become a soldier. I was told that it was an honor to serve the Emperor. But in training I was beaten continuously. I had heard that such a thing was common, but I didn't think it would continue when we left Japan. But it did."

He said all this without a trace of emotion.

"Cruelty has many masters," said Jeremy. "Americans can be cruel too, especially if you are different or are seen as a threat. But we are not out to conquer the world."

"We are very militaristic," Hanabi continued. "Signs everywhere proclaim the superiority of our Navy and Army. And yet I heard stories about American marines."

"Like what?" asked Jeremy, staring into the fire.

"Like when they use flamethrowers to burn our soldiers out of caves. I heard from a survivor that with teeth and bare hands the Marines ripped out throats of those trying to escape. How could they be so bestial? We were taught that Americans are helpless children."

"I think you were taught wrong, about both of those things," Jeremy said, wondering how accurate the atrocities were. But perhaps it was true, he thought. Seeing friends bayoneted unleashes raging barbarity, sometimes in the best of men. The bloody image of Lieutenant Whitcomb came to mind, and he knew the power of the urge for vengeance.

After a while Hanabe said, "Are you and the lady going back to the cave?"

Jeremy weighed the question, then said, "No, we won't go back there. And neither will you. I told her to climb the mountain. From the summit we will be able to see the beach and anyone coming ashore. I intend to build a dwelling and fortify the perimeter. You can help if you wish."

"Of course, if I am allowed to stay."

"You're allowed."

"But the lady has been raped by Japanese soldiers, and I am a soldier. Or at least I was. She may not want me there. She may want to kill me."

"I don't think so. You did her no harm and she knows that. She'll think you are a good lad."

Hanabe smiled and said, "My mother said that I was naive and unworldly. She said I should become a monk and play the flute. Maybe I will make a flute and play it for you and the lady."

"That would be good," said Jeremy, exhausted, his mind wandering to Maria.

He wondered how far she had gotten before dark. Then he realized that she had nothing with which to start a fire, nor a weapon of any kind. Worry chilled him. Only now did he realize that she should have stayed near the beach, just inside the tree line. She might have been safe there, no matter the outcome.

The jungle sounds all around them slowed, then stopped. Hanabe and Jeremy became alert as if the silence itself were a sound. There was a cry, not unlike one made by a large cat. The sound came again, but in anguish as if the cat were caught in a trap.

Picking up a stick, Jeremy thrust it into the fire until it caught. Handing his pistol to Hanabe, he clutched his rifle and moved to the edge of the clearing. The cry came again, followed by a moan and a stifled sob. "Stay here and don't shoot. That's not a cat," Jeremy hissed.

Holding the burning torch ahead of him he plunged into the undergrowth and shouted, "Maria, where are you? Call out, call out!"

* * *

Jeremy, Maria and Hanabe fashioned walls and a roof covered with layers of palm leaves. From an abandoned house they took shovels and picks and began digging a moat, setting bamboo spikes in the bottom. They covered the ditch with thin branches, soil and leaves, leaving only one pathway that meandered half-hidden a dozen yards from the well-marked trail.

The entire project took three weeks. At night, before stretching out to sleep, Hanabe, who had indeed whittled a flute, would softly play the songs of his village. Jeremy and Maria slept in the main room of the earthen floor house. They tried to remain silent during their lovemaking, and Maria would give the boy a sheepish look in the morning. But Hanabe tugged Jeremy aside and said, "Please tell Maria that in Japan where the walls are only shoji screens, we learn to not listen when pillow talk is made. She should think that, at night, I do not even exist."

No more was seen of Japanese troops, and life high on a mountain became routine. It was hardly an idyllic existence, for there was the fear that another patrol might be sent from Ishigaki. Jeremy was sure that the Japanese command would want an explanation for the disappearance of two well-armed squads. Each morning he and Hanabe would climb to the summit of Mount Komodake. Scanning the sea and beaches with Major Abe's binoculars, they would reassure themselves that they would be safe for one more day.

"I want to find other clothes," Hanabe declared one morning. "I no longer consider myself a soldier and will never return to the Japanese army. I once saw some worker's clothing in a hut beside a mangrove swamp. They would be quite serviceable. I also want to see if any boat or raft is still hidden in the cove. Someday we may want to leave this island."

"And any boat not already damaged would need fuel. What if we run out of that halfway to some island? We'd be an easy target for Japanese aircraft or picket boats. And besides, where would you go anyway?"

"There are other islands; we can see a few from the mountain peak," said Hanabe.

"True, but those may be occupied by Japanese troops, and even if uninhabited, life there may be worse than here."

"But maybe, just maybe there are some islands inhabited by natives," Hanabe said in a boyish voice.

Jeremy sadly shook his head and said, "I'm sorry, but Maria and I will not leave here until the war is over. If you sail to some unknown island, you would not likely make it. Japanese planes regularly fly scouting missions, and if found you will be shot as a deserter. They won't believe that you are simply a survivor of some vague catastrophe."

"So I will spend the rest of my days here," Hanabe said with resignation.

"That's better than the army on Ishigaki, even if they spared your life. You saved mine, and I'm indebted. No war lasts forever. So, come, Hanabe-san, we will find you a new set of clothes and perhaps a hat like the Emperor wears."

"A top hat, yes, that would be fine," laughed Hanabe.

They set out together, spears in hand, and walked carefully along the path, mindful of snakes and other hazards until they reached the hut beside the lagoon.

The noises of the jungle drowned out the sound of approaching aircraft until the roar of two Zeros was almost overhead, at treetop level. Jeremy shouted, "Get in!" and he pushed Hanabe through the doorway. They tumbled to the bare floor as the planes circled around for another look before climbing away.

Their earlier levity vanished. Jeremy watched the aircraft become dots in the afternoon sky. A shudder ran through him and he said, "We will wait here until the shadows are deeper. They may be back."

"For a moment, I almost forgot about the war," said Hanabe.

"Unfortunately, it hasn't forgotten us," Jeremy replied.

Chapter 18
Tokyo, Japan
March, 1944

The afternoon sun did little to warm the city; temperatures hovered just above freezing. Sayuri and Kimi put on heavy coats before they stepped out of the flower shop and began walking toward the train station. Trains to downtown Tokyo were packed. It was said that new food stalls had been opened and Kumi had suggested that they might find something if they went early.

Sayuri never liked traveling by train during busy times, for although Japanese men were extremely correct at work and in public places, the teeming railroad cars made it easy for men, with arms held at their sides, to grope women pressed tightly against them. There was a sense of anonymity and commonness about it that women, diffident and submissive, were expected to tolerate, especially during war.

The train trundled past billboards exhorting citizens to take the "Air Defense Oath of Certain Victory" administered through the neighborhood associations. The ubiquitous organizations were the fount of all local information, patriotic fervor and family assistance. The Oath required all able-bodied citizens to fight fires, dig protective shelters, and cooperate with what was euphemistically referred to as "structure evacuation".

When Kumi asked what the latter term meant, Sayuri pointed to a great swath of bulldozed houses and shops. "Firebreaks," she replied, looking at the demolished buildings stretching a half mile.

"But we haven't been bombed in two years. Why would the government think we would have to do that?" asked Kumi.

"I don't know. The radio announcer says that we are winning the war and it won't last much longer. But maybe the government knows things we don't," said Sayuri.

"But where will all the people go?" asked Kumi in a hushed voice; it was unlawful and dangerous to question the actions of the authorities.

"To live with relatives, perhaps. Maybe in the countryside if not in Tokyo."

Alighting from the train, they walked to the market and got in a line for vegetables.

"Did you listen to the radio this morning?" asked Kumi.

"No, did I miss something? Perhaps American jazz?"

Kumi laughed and said, "Don't be silly. We haven't heard that in years. No, the government announcer, Matsumura Hideoshi, said that it's always darkest before the dawn and that victory is not far off." She sighed and gazed at the populace in their drab and worn clothing. With an air of resignation, she said, "Nothing is much fun anymore, but I guess it could be worse. I feel so badly for the young men who might die in the fighting."

A sullen woman with three missing teeth wrapped turnips in newspaper and placed the bundle in Sayuri's bag. They visited a half dozen other vendors and watched a dozen school boys march down the street carrying their school stove suspended on shoulders by wooden poles. One boy carried a sign proclaiming proudly that the stove was the property of the Tomigaya National School.

"It must be for the scrap metal collection," said Kumi, as the twelve-year old children labored under its weight. Three teachers walked alongside them, encouraging them to continue singing the school song.

"It's not much of a sacrifice," said Sayuri. "Schools haven't had fuel for the stoves in a very long time, and soon it will be summer."

It was only mid-day and they did not have to report for fire drill practice until late in the afternoon. Kumi said, "Let's go to a movie. I haven't seen one in a long time."

Tucked between two closed bars was a small theater with a marquee advertising two films.

"Let's see *Kyushu's Patriotic Doctors*, said Sayuri, handing yen to a young ticket woman inside the lobby.

"I'm sorry," said the attendant, "the film broke in several places and has to be repaired. But *Navy Pilots in Action* is just starting. There are still seats."

"I really don't want to see that. Why don't we just go home," Sayuri said to Kumi.

"We're already here. Let's see it. And it stars Takashi Shimura; he's one of my favorites."

Apprehensively, Sayuri followed Kumi into the theater. Sitting six rows in front of the screen, they watched as martial music accompanied the credits. The black and white film began with the words, "The Japanese Imperial Navy presents this true and compelling account of its heroic ships and pilots in the war against American aggression in the Pacific. All glory to the Emperor!"

The first scenes were of the fleet carrier *Hiryu* steaming full speed toward the viewer, its bow wave splitting before the seven-hundred-and-forty-six-foot behemoth. The camera then panned over its flight deck, upon which were fighters and bombers, pilots manning their planes as deck crews prepared them for take-off.

The captain on the ships bridge issued terse orders that were repeated with rapid obedience as the ship turned into the wind. Turning to the fleet admiral, the captain said, "One of our scout planes has found the enemy fleet. I request permission to launch two squadrons to intercept."

With the admiral's consent more orders were given and the camera focused on pilot Lieutenant Shamura, a white bandana with a red painted sun tied about his forehead, who closed the cockpit of his fighter and returned the salute of the ground crew before his fighter tore down the deck and formed up with his squadron.

"We will gain altitude and take out the patrol covering their biggest carrier first. Stay with me and hold your fire until we begin our attack," said Shamura.

The audience watched with rapt attention as squadrons flew majestically through broken clouds. Intense aviators checked their instruments and acknowledged the presence of wingmen.

"Carrier!" said one of the pilots. The squadron rolled into a steep dive and plunged toward the American ship and its protecting aircraft.

"They're going in!" said an excited viewer, hands clapping as the Japanese fighters dove like birds of prey upon the American planes. From far below, anti-aircraft sent black bursts aloft, one of which clipped a Zero. There was a gasp from the audience as the pilot announced, "I'm losing fuel but will attack the carrier."

"Yes, get the carrier, Corporal Omeda, then head back to the ship. You are doing an honorable thing to attack by yourself. The Emperor will be proud of you!"

Five American Wildcats rose up to challenge the Japanese, and a wild dogfight ensued. One after another the

American planes were torn apart by the Zeros, and theater-goers cheered. Torpedoes were seen in the water streaking toward the American carrier. Then the camera concentrated on an American pilot, fear in his eyes, as he tried to evade lieutenant Takashi Shamura's machine gun bullets.

As the tension increased, the American pilot, his words translated, screamed, "Someone get him off me!"

Sayuri gripped Kumi's hand, her eyes wide as bullets ripped through the cockpit, setting it on fire. "Yes! Yes, flame him!" shouted one patron as the plane corkscrewed through the air, black smoke and fire rampaging behind it.

Again, the camera focused on the pilot, his eyes wide with fright, as fire engulfed him. Ripping off his goggles and headgear, he tried to open the cockpit, but it was too late. Starring into the camera he yelled, "No, no, no!" as his plane disintegrated around him. The audience clapped and cheered, the sound filling the theater.

"Tad!" screamed Sayuri. "It's him, it's Tadishi, oh, Kumi-san, it looks just like him! Tad, Tad," she sobbed.

People stared at her with disbelief. A man in Navy uniform stood and leaned toward her. "What did you say? You know this man, this enemy pilot?"

Others were standing, peering at the woman who now seemed to be babbling.

"No! She doesn't, blurted Kumi. It's the fire, she's traumatized by fire. Her mind isn't right. Her brother died in a fire. He was a navy pilot on board the *Shokaku*. Pay her no attention. I'll take her home!"

Holding her hand over her mouth, Sayuri followed Kumi from the theater as people shook their heads. A few followed them outside but decided against running to the authorities; the two women were already merging into the crowded street.

A trolley topped and they got on. Sayuri, balled up against the window, said nothing. Passengers looked at her sadly, assuming that she had learned of a death or serious injury. Kumi sat stiffly beside her, eyes turned away from other passengers.

"Someone should console her. She looks so frail," an old man said to Kumi.

The ikebana shop was cold when they returned; the coal had run out weeks before. Sayuri, knees drawn up, pulled a futon around her.

Kumi sat across the room, mute. Long minutes passed before she said, "You embarrassed us. No, you defiled us. What were you thinking? I doubt that the American pilot was your Tad. The man was probably a prisoner playing the part he was told to. You are so foolish, Sayuri. So foolish. It's a wonder that we are not jailed by the kempeitai, accused of supporting enemies of Japan."

"I am sorry for embarrassing you, Kumi-san. It's just that he looked so much like him. I couldn't help it. I didn't want to see the movie in the first place. I had this terrible feeling that..."

"That what? Our navy would fail? That the Americans would sink one of our carriers and kill our pilots? *What side are you on?* Have I been so naïve for so long?"

"I don't know what to tell you. I do what I'm told to do, just like everyone else. I don't want Japan to lose the war. I really don't."

"But you don't want us to win if it means the death of an American pilot, *your* American pilot. Is that so, Sayuri? Do you think that this is some sort of romance novel?" cried Kumi, incensed. She stood, shaking.

"It's not a romance novel, Kumi-san. It's horrible. We all know that Pearl Harbor was bombed and Americans were killed. We have been fighting a war and we're told that it has been victorious. I don't think it is. I really don't."

"If we aren't winning it's because of people like Tad! People who are killing our brave soldiers and sailors!"

Sayuri wiped her face and sighed deeply. "The Americans must be very angry with us. Our navy must have killed many of them at Pearl Harbor. I think they are vengeful." She looked at Kumi with blurry eyes and said, "I don't know what to tell you, Kumi-san. I just don't."

"And yet you are still in love with an American pilot who might have been flying one of those planes. I have tried to be your friend, but to tell you the truth, I have come to hate you. Yes, it has taken a long time, but I hate you! I hate you!" said Kumi, her voice tight with anger.

Sayuri bolted upright, her eyes wide. Never had she heard such words from her only friend. She looked blankly at Kumi, then shaking her head, said, "You can't mean that, no, no. Tad-san, he would not want to hurt you or me. He is a kind, loving man. I know this."

"You know nothing, Sayuri! If he's still alive he will follow orders. He would drop bombs on us. They all would, and you know it," said Kumi bitterly. "Don't forget, it was the Americans who killed Sensei, our dearest friend. And you have dreams of consorting with an enemy of Japan. An enemy who kills our brave pilots!"

Her breath came in bursts and she said, "Oh, Sayuri, I tried to ignore your wistful comments. For a while I thought of it like a Shakespearian play, a Romeo and Juliet, like we read in school. But not anymore. I can't and I won't. I will not live in the same house with a woman who prays for our enemy."

Tears rolled down Sayuri's cheeks and she sobbed, "I want you to be my friend, Kumi-san. I have no other friends. I didn't make this war any more than you did. And I don't know what Tad-san is doing. I don't even know if he is still alive."

"You are worshipping a specter, a ghost, and I hope his bones are at the bottom of the sea. I hope that Koizumi, the man you should be married to, shot him down years ago. Your silly, childish dream is over, but our nightmare is ongoing. On hands and knees, you should go to Koizumi and ask for forgiveness. Yes," Kumi declared, her fury raging, "You should prostrate yourself before him and beg him to marry you."

Gathering her coat and a satchel of belongings, she went to the door and slid on her wooden getas.

"Where are you going?" Sayuri said, swiping at her tears.

"Away from here. As long as you have an enemy in your heart you are my enemy. I am sorry, Sayuri. It became obvious today, but I should have seen it a long time ago. I should have seen it when Koizumi and Takagi came here and were humiliated. I felt indescribably sad for them, but I tried to put my feelings aside. No more, Sayuri. I will find someplace else, and maybe some honorable soldier or sailor who needs a wife. *Sayonara*. Maybe I shall pray for you. Or maybe not."

The door closed behind her, and Sayuri sat alone. A cold rain began to fall. Kumi's vehemence had shocked her. The sudden realization that the pliant, agreeable Kumi-san had secretly despised her was unbearable. Sayuri had not suspected the rancor, had not been aware of her friend's dismay. And yet, she should have sensed it. Each time she'd murmured, "I wonder how Tad-san is," or "I do hope to see him again," Kumi had either said nothing or feigned not hearing. But there had been that disapproving look, those pursed lips. The warning signs had all been there.

Sayuri looked out the rain-streaked window, hoping to see Kumi across the street. But she wasn't there. Without her irrepressible chatter the ikebana shop was devoid of life. For a moment Sayuri thought of finding her, saying how thoughtless she had been and how repentant she was. But Kumi would not listen to half-truths.

Half-truths, thought Sayuri. Her friend had said that Tad-san was dead. Did she know that for sure? Had Koizumi said something to her in secret? Had he seen Tad-san actually shot down somewhere in the Pacific? Maybe she should go to Koizumi and ask, she considered. But Koizumi, out of spite or hatred, might say yes, he had sent his brother to the bottom of the sea, whether it was true or not.

What should she do if Tad were truly dead? What should she do if he were not? And did it really matter? What, she suddenly wondered, had she been thinking for the last three years as the war came ever closer to Japan? Could she really see herself falling into his arms when and if he came to Tokyo? When and if the Americans won? What would people say, what would they think of a Japanese woman so terribly in love with an enemy of her country?

And then there came another thought. What if he actually came and took her away, perhaps to America? What would those people think of her, especially those who had lost sons or fathers in this terrible war? She would be shunned, vilified, spat upon, and Tad-san would be helpless to protect her from their wrath.

It was folly, stupidity and treason, just as Kumi said. Perhaps it was time to speak to Koizumi. Not to question whether or not he killed the man she loved, but to make amends. Even marry him, if he would have her. And if Koizumi showed disdain for her contrition, then perhaps she should appeal to Takagi. Maybe he would have her. It was time, past time, to give her country her complete and utter loyalty.

The last tepid dregs of tea were far too bitter. It was all too much, too dreary. The world seemed to close in upon her. She would sleep. Sleep would be a fog of comfort and forgetfulness in which she could close all the portals so no ghosts could come near. Tomorrow she would think of what to do, where to go, and what future awaited her. If there was any future at all.

Chapter 19
Pearl Harbor
Early August, 1944

It was one of the rare days that Kimi was at home instead of the hospital. Work was all she had left, now. Her friend and fellow nurse called to see if she was okay.

"Delores, Jack Vestergaard and Lee-Beauregard Smythe will be here soon," said Kimi, glancing out the living room window. "Oh, I see a car pulling up to the curb. I'll tell you what they have to say, but I doubt that it's good news. You know about the letter I received from the War Department. I feel like crawling into a hole, but I know I'm not alone. And yes, we still have a job to do."

"Well, I wish you the best," Dolores said. "I think there's a hospital ship coming in tonight. All the doctors and most of the staff will be here."

"Please tell Doctor Whitefield that I will be there early. Oh, they've arrived. Have to go. Thanks for your concern, Dolores. Bye."

She swung open the door on the first knock and gave both aviators a hug as they entered the house. Clouds had built up all morning, and the first drops splattered down. Thunder reverberated across the darkening sky.

They removed their caps and stood uneasily. Kimi said to Jack, "I'm glad you called. I just made a pot of coffee, so sit down and relax. I'll be right back."

After she'd moved into the kitchen, Jack glanced at a stack of newspapers on the coffee table and spied the open War Department letter.

We regret to inform you that your son, Lt. Tad Kuchenkov, has been reported missing in action. All efforts will continue to locate him...

Glancing over at Smythe, Jack took a deep breath and whispered, "This isn't going to be easy."

Kimi returned with cups of coffee and sat down across from them. She looked drawn and older than when they had last seen her after the Battle of the Coral Sea, two years ago.

"Oh, forgive me; I forgot the sugar. I saved a bit; I'll get it. My mind is just not working too well. I'm sorry there's no cream. I wish I had some to offer you."

She began to rise when Smythe said, "Oh no, don't bother. We like it just as it is, good and black. And it's a world better than what we get on board ship. That stuff tastes like motor oil and is usually four days old. So this is just great. No additives required, Mrs. Kuchenkov."

"Lee-Beauregard, you call me Kimi. Nothing is formal around here."

Smythe grinned, then, his smile vanishing, he said, "Jack and I had hoped to be here earlier, but operations around Saipan have kept the fleet pretty busy. We wanted to see you and tell you what we know about Tad."

Pointing to the letter, Jack said, "That's pretty cryptic and doesn't give much hope."

"No," said Kimi. "I also received a letter from his commanding officer, which was very complimentary. I had it framed. Still, it said much the same thing, that he was lost at sea after downing several enemy aircraft. I have been waiting for another letter, but nothing's come."

She looked out the window to the gathering storm. Turning back she said, "It is good of you to come, but to be honest, I have little hope."

"The Navy picks ups fliers all the time," said Smythe. "Sometimes they float around in their rafts for days before being hauled aboard a fishing boat. I wouldn't give up hope. Tad's one tough guy."

Kimi nodded, then said, "Can you tell me what happened? I mean, what you remember or saw?"

"If you wish," said Jack. "I can explain the operation."

"I read about it in the paper, but you two were actually there, so I wish to hear it from you."

"Yes," said Jack, nodding his head. "Okay, Smythe and I were attached to Task Force 58 of the Fifth Fleet, and the basic mission, which included fifteen carriers and support ships, was to protect the Marines landing on the Mariana Islands, and Saipan specifically. Lee and I were on *Lexington*. The battle was closer to Guam than the Philippines, but it's being reported as the Battle of the Philippine Sea."

"We'd already punctured the outer island defense ring by taking Tarawa. Admiral Spruance was in charge, but Vice Admiral Mitscher commanded the Fast Carrier Task force," said Smythe. "Apparently, the Japanese wanted to disrupt the invasion of Saipan and hoped to destroy the U.S. fleet in one major battle. They had five fleet carriers, four light carriers, battleships, and a lot of land-based aircraft. Essentially, they threw everything at us. They first attacked our carriers with thirty-five planes from Guam, but we shot them all down. We lost one of our own. When you compare that to what happened two years ago, you have to wonder what sort of training their pilots are getting these days."

"And our planes are better," added Jack. "The admiral sent up all our fighters and bombers, since radar detected another sixty-eight planes coming at us. We shot down twenty-five of them, losing a Hellcat. Those are good planes, faster than the Zeros and as maneuverable, and they can take a lot of punishment. One of their planes did put a bomb on the battleship *South Dakota* and there were casualties, but she stayed on station. Then we detected another hundred aircraft in attack formation. God, they were relentless! We went back up and flamed almost all of those. And that's how it went. We shot down three hundred and fifty enemy planes on the first day and lost thirty of our own."

"Was one of those Tad's?" asked Kimi. Sho was appalled by the extent, the enormity of the losses. *Those poor, poor families. Did they receive letters like mine?*

"No, he was in the thick of it, and we landed back on the *Lex*. We thought that our part in the fight was over, but it had just begun," said Smythe.

"We went after their carriers," Jack continued. "But it was the subs that sank two of theirs, the *Taiho*, their newest and biggest one, and the *Shokaku*. That meant they lost many sailors as well as air crews. Most of their pilots were inexperienced. As one of our guys said, 'It was like a down home turkey shoot.' Then late that afternoon, we learned that the Japanese fleet was about three hundred miles out and still had big carriers. Even though it meant our aircraft might be returning after dark, Mitscher decided to attack. We put up two hundred and fifty fighters and bombers. I wish I could describe it. There's the sound, the vibration, not only of your plane but of dozens of them around you. Your buddies are there, some of them above, some beside, some behind, and we're watching out for each other. For a while, all you can see is the water below and the sky above and all around you, and the formation. Then you see the fleet, and if you remember Pearl, or Coral Sea, that can be a bad moment. And it was bad. We sank one of their carriers and damaged three others, and Tad was in on that, but we lost about twenty planes, mostly to anti-aircraft fire from their escorts. And we were almost out of fuel, and it was already dark." Jack's face worked for a moment, and Kimi wondered what he was remembering.

"What happened next was amazing, considering that enemy subs might have been in the area. We had only the faintest idea of the position of our fleet, and many of us were so low on fuel we were figuring we'd end up in the soup. We found out later the admiral ordered *every ship* to turn on its searchlights. It was like Christmas, and we landed on whatever carrier we could."

"The sad thing was, after surviving the battle, about eighty of our planes did run out of gas," put in Smythe. "Eighty." he sighed, regret in his voice. "Destroyers went out, and about sixty pilots were found. Many went down close together. But others, well...." His voice faded.

"But," said Jack, finally breaking the silence, "not all ships that rescued survivors have been sent here yet, especially if they haven't suffered damage. If they're on patrol or escort duty they would not return just to deliver pilots. In fact, they might not be back for weeks."

Kimi nodded, then stared down at her hands. "I hope this war ends soon. I really do. And I pray that you two and the rest of your friends can return home. But I think it will go on for a very long time. I see those boys, the Marines who are brought into my ward, and I try very hard to keep my composure. They are so young, and hurt so badly."

She sighed, then said, "I am glad you came. I know how hard it was to tell me this, but I thank you. You are always welcome here, and I wish to see both of you again."

The two pilots stood. She hugged them, then escorted them to the front door. A few moments later, their car started up. Kimi stood on the porch and waved as the old Ford disappeared in the gloom of the overcast.

Three hours later, she drove to the hospital and was greeted by Doctor Whitefield.

"The postman came by this morning and dropped a letter off for you," he said, as they walked from one ward to another looking in on patients.

"Do you know who sent it?" she asked.

"Nope, I didn't recognize the name, but it had a lot of foreign stamps, mostly European. It's on my desk. We'll be done with this inspection in a few minutes, then you can read it, unless you want to get it right now."

A letter with foreign stamps, thought Kimi. *Who would send me a letter from Europe?* Then an electric jolt shot through her and she bolted from the ward, shouting, "It's from Alexei! I'll be back in ten."

"Sure," said Whitefield, never having seen her so overjoyed.

It was not from Alexei. She read the name on the envelope, but it was one she had never heard of or seen before. The letter had obviously passed through many hands. She opened it with curiosity and a measure of trepidation. There were four sheets of thin typewritten paper.

She put on her reading glasses, sat at the neatly organized desk and turned on the reading lamp. Taking a deep breath, she peered at the first sheet and began to read.

Hello, Mrs. Kuchenkov,

A BLOSSOM IN THE ASHES

Although I have never had the pleasure of meeting or speaking with you I am a good friend of William Stuart Jones. I am a Portuguese journalist and was in the Soviet Union with Jones until I was wounded while covering Operation Bagration, the Russian offensive against the center of the German line. William asked me to write this letter and mail it to you after I left Murmansk, since all letters to or from Russia are read by NKVD. What he related to me would have meant a firing squad if he or Alexei had attempted to write it while still in the Soviet Union.

Although I personally did not see your husband, I have attempted to faithfully relate exactly what Jones told me. I have endeavored to make no omissions, but some time had passed before I could compose this letter on board ship. I am currently residing in Lisbon and you can write to me if you wish, but I am relating everything I have been told about your husband, Alexei.

I pray for his complete recovery and that he survives the war. He is a very brave soldier. Apparently, the Soviets think so too, for he has received the Order of Bogdan Khmelnitsky 1st Class and the Order of Glory for gallant conduct in this horrible war.

I wish you the very best. May God be with you and your family,
Jose Joaquin de Silivia

The following is what I was asked to write by my friend and fellow correspondent, Mr. William Stuart

Jones, one of the most courageous and resourceful men I have ever known:

> *Dear Mrs. Kuchenkov,*
> *My name is and I wrote to you after I met my old friend, your husband Alexei, after the fall of Leningrad. As you may recall, I am a journalist with the* London Times, *until recently assigned to the Moscow Bureau.*
>
> *I do hope this letter finds you well. I have news that may hearten you, but I extend it with extreme caution due to the continuing Soviet offensive in Eastern Europe, a venture that has cost millions of lives.*
>
> *I saw and spoke to Alexei several days ago.*
>
> *Although twice the age of most Russian soldiers at the front, Alexei has shown enormous valor. He is recovering from a bullet wound he received while performing a very heroic act, one that allowed him to reenter the regular ranks of the Soviet military. His commitment is extraordinary, considering the hatred he must have had for the system he has been forced to defend. And he has experienced horrific events that would have left a less determined man suicidal, including incarceration and service in a penal battalion which sustained enormous casualties. I cannot help but think that, although he loves America and would live no place else, he is at heart still a Russian and would die in defense of his original homeland.*
>
> *The chance encounter with him came at a front-line hospital near the Polish border where Soviet forces had engaged and routed the Nazis. Very few foreign journalists have been given permission to*

visit the Front but a few of us, closely monitored by the secret police, have been allowed to visit regions liberated by the army. Of course, everything we write must be approved before publication. I was able to elude my NKVD minder and speak with Alexei.

Alexei wants you to know why he has not been able to write or return to you during these terrible years. He has been in the thick of it all, and only fate and the thought of you has kept him alive. He sends you his love, thinks of you constantly, and wishes to return to you. It is my fervent hope that he will. He spoke of what had befallen him during the last three years. Much of it was quite harrowing, and I will spare you the details, but in essence the following is what he related to me.

Alexei was caught up in the defense of Leningrad. Upon its fall (following the death of his parents) he got swept up by the NKVD along with hundreds of thousands of others and sent to Moscow. The fact that he had volunteered in the construction of defenses on the Riga Line made little difference to his accusers, who considered him an American spy. His protests and his request to contact the American embassy were ignored, and he was sent to the gulag, the Main Directorate of Corrective Labor Camps. Only the intervention of an NKVD major, a pre-revolution acquaintance, kept him from being executed.

He toiled in a copper mine east of the Urals for a number of months, where the death toll was appalling. The deceased were taken beyond the barbed wire for burial, so many workers attempted to escape by playing dead. To end these desperate attempts, the guards bayoneted each corpse. But as the Nazis drove ever closer to Moscow—the Soviet army had already lost two million men—there came a need for more front-line troops.

An NKVD colonel came into the camp and demanded four hundred men be released to him for military duty in the penal battalions. These units were deemed expendable, made up of real criminals and anyone considered a threat to the regime. Many of the latter were previous military officers (Stalin ordered the execution of most of his officers in 1937) as well as high officials in the Communist Party accused of disloyalty. The men of the penal battalions were referred to as shtrafniks and would be executed by NKVD machine gunners if they retreated in battle.

Although the men were considered a criminal class, they could redeem themselves through heroic action. The bravery Alexei demonstrated came when he and the rest of his unit were exhausted and facing extermination from entrenched German forces backed by heavy tanks with fighter aircraft protection. The event described to me occurred two weeks before I met him. He said that as panzer armor drove toward them, he firmly believed that it was his last day. Out of sheer despair (or the last dregs of furious determination) Alexei sprang from their trench with a handful of grenades and managed to circle a tank, shoot its commander and toss several grenades into the open hatch, killing the crew. No sooner was he back on the ground than an ME 109 began a strafing run. With what must have been maniacal resolve, Alexei picked up a dead soldier's sub-machine gun and began firing in the very path of the aircraft. One bullet from the plane tore through his left arm, but the plane ignited and crashed behind the line of Soviet trenches.

There were many witnesses, including the unit commander. Alexei, sprawled on the ground and bleeding profusely, was picke dup and whisked to an aid station and awarded medals for gallantry. The policy of the army is that any member of a penal battalion that destroys an enemy tank or aircraft has redeemed himself and is freed from captivity.

His arm is still bandaged and he will remain here for another few weeks. He will likely be questioned thoroughly by staff officers before they return him the front. He believes that he will be fighting all the way to Berlin. There is even the prospect that he will be re-commissioned as a lieutenant, the rank he held during the Russo Japanese war.

I seriously doubt that I will be able to meet with him again during the course of the war, as I am returning to Moscow. Perhaps, once victory is achieved, he will be able to approach the American Embassy and through their offices return to the United States. That, at least, is his most fervent desire.

I regretfully must conclude on this uncertain note, but at least you now know that at the time of this narration he is alive and has a chance of remaining so.

Perhaps we will all meet when this war is over. We will have many stories to share, some of them worth remembering! Again, I wish you and Alexei the very best.

Your friend,
William Stuart Jones

Kimi held he letter in her lap. Her Alexei was alive, at least at the time of the writing, which had been weeks before. If only there was a way she could write to him, she thought. Only through a diplomatic pouch could she get a letter to the American Embassy in Moscow, but they would not have the time or staff to locate Alexei, she told herself.

Doctor Whitefield stuck his head into his office. "Was the letter from your husband?" he asked solicitously.

"From a friend of his who saw him in Russia."

"So he is alive. Wonderful! Will he be coming home soon?"

Kimi shook her head. "He has been conscripted into the Soviet Army. I really don't know what will happen to him, but he has been decorated for valor."

Whitefield nodded silently, then said, "You look very tired, and we have a light load. Why don't you go home and get some sleep? I'll get someone to fill in for you tonight."

There was a scurry of activity in the hallway, and Dolores entered the office. "Sorry to interrupt, but a hospital ship and its escorts just arrived from Saipan. The wounded are coming in now."

At once Dr. Whitefield was all business. "I'll be in the operating room as soon as I scrub."

"I'm staying," said Kimi, and she followed him and Dolores past medical personnel preparing to meet the patients.

It was four-thirty in the morning before she left the operating room and drove home. With dawn and the end of blackout, lights were coming on in homes of people for whom the work day was just beginning. In the harbor, dozens of ships were either in dry dock or at anchor. The big hospital ship was moored at the dock, with ambulances, staff cars and a few taxis parked nearby. A half-dozen picket ships patrolled outside the harbor, and Hellcats flew toward the horizon.

Rarely had she felt so tired. As she parked by the curve she saw that the living room light glowed; she could not remember turning it on. Why would she have, she wondered, since it was still light when she had left for work? And there was a Navy jeep parked next door. Her neighbor's son was stationed in Europe with the Army Air Corps. If he had come home he certainly would not drive a Navy jeep.

She picked the letter off the seat and slipped it into her purse. Then she saw the window curtains part, and she stopped.

The door opened and Tad stepped out. Kimi flew into his arms, tears running down her face.

"A tin can finally fished me out of the drink. I swear I was half way to Japan," he said, lifting and spinning her around.

"I was so worried, so terribly worried," she blurted when he finally put her down. "I got a letter from the War Department saying that you were missing in action. I feared the worst."

"There was a time when I was wondering how to make friends with sharks, but I'm back, Mom, at least for a while."

"How long?"

"Scuttlebutt is that my carrier will be in tonight but needs some refitting. Maybe a week or so."

"Then it's back to the war?"

"I'm afraid so. But I have a week's leave, and we'll paint the town red."

She laughed, then said, "There is so much I have to tell you. I just received a letter from an old friend of Alexei's. I think your father is still alive."

"Wonderful! What great news!"

"Yes," said Kimi, as they walked up the steps. *But the letter was old*, a voice in her head warned. Anything might have happened since it was written. Then she brightened. Tad was home; for today and tomorrow she would forget the war.

Chapter 20
Tokyo, Japan
November, 1944

Koizumi and Takagi stepped out of the staff car and entered a narrow tea shop with four tables. A deferential server brought *ocha* in small ceramic cups and placed a teapot on the table. Koizumi warmed his hands over the steaming brew, then said, "I offer you my congratulations, *tomadachi*. You're a lucky man. She is very pretty and will provide you many sons."

Takagi nodded. "I didn't expect it. I was quite astonished when I received her letter."

"You said that you two spoke when your carrier returned. How did it happen?"

"We agreed to meet in this very place and she wore a kimono, even though she got some disapproving stares. She looked quite beautiful, much more so than when we were all together at the ikebana shop, and not at all as I remember her from family gatherings when she was a kid. Our parents were cousins, you see."

"So what did she say?" asked Koizumi, sipping his tea.

"That she was very embarrassed by the way we were treated by Sayuri. And she particularly felt very bad for me."

"But you were asking for the hand of Sayuri."

"Which I was denied. Later, Kumi-san told me that she knew that Sayuri would refuse my proposal and thought that I conducted myself in an honorable way. And she said that she wants a husband, one who is serving the nation. I didn't detect any romantic feelings, but I know that she likes me and that's good enough."

Koizumi nodded and said, "Was Sayuri with her when you two met?"

"No, Kumi-san has moved away. She's caring for orphans at a neighborhood clinic. It's a government facility for children whose parents were killed or badly injured in the bombing. It doesn't pay much, but she can sleep there, and food is provided."

"So she no longer sees Sayuri," said Koizumi, putting it all in context.

"That's right. She said that she could not abide Sayuri having feelings for a man whose country is killing our women and children. It made her feel unclean and ashamed. So she left."

"And Sayuri is alone now."

"I think that is best for all of us," Takagi said pointedly.

* * *

The caretaker's house in Ueno Park was unheated. Frost obscured the windows in the early dawn, and soft, thick snow covered the roads. A coal-burning stove heated a tea pot. Five chipped and stained cups sat on a low table. Wearing a monocle, long coat and fedora, Shunroki Hitanka, an assistant advisor to the war minister, sat across from Prince Norobutzu Yodaki of the Supreme War Council.

Hitanka checked his watch. He was about to say, "They're late," when the door opened and three men entered, bowed, and gravely knelt on worn tatami mats.

"Did anybody see you?" asked Prince Yodaki.

"No, there's no one about. The park is deserted," said Kenji Kado, an unusually tall man with a thin moustache and piercing dark eyes. As the chairman of the Tokyo Business Association and owner of Rising Sun Steel Corporation, he was the wealthiest of the five, but very much junior to Sadeo Yoshizawa of the House of Peers, who accompanied him. The last man to settle into the small room was dour Vice Admiral Yoshimuchi Abe, now in civilian clothes.

The teapot was passed from man to man, and there was a long moment of silence. The wind picked up, and snow spattered the windows.

"There are many who think as we do," said Prince Yodaki, lighting a cigarette, "but it is essential that nothing we say or do be revealed to anybody. Absolute secrecy is required. What we contemplate would be regarded by most as duplicitous, if not treasonable."

"We have little choice, after the failure of Operation Sho," remarked Vice Admiral Abe.

"The extent of that failure was not made public, and I only heard rumors," said Kado. "I presume that the survivors were sworn to secrecy." Turning to the admiral, the industrialist said, "Can you tell us what happened?"

"You know that our defensive sphere has continued to shrink after the loss of Saipan and the Marianas. The Americans, under their General MacArthur, were preparing to attack our forces at Leyte in the Philippines. Success would place them ever closer to Okinawa and Japan proper. It was essential that this invasion be halted. However, the Americans did land on Leyte in mid-October and have been making considerable progress, even with high casualties. Operation Sho was intended to destroy American carriers, leaving their forces on Leyte isolated and vulnerable to air strikes and naval bombardment."

The admiral took a sip of tea, then said somberly, "Operation Sho involved over ninety ships and much of the fighter aircraft we had left. Four of our carriers were to lure the Americans away from the San Bernardino and Surigao Straits under Admiral Ozawa, while Vice Admiral Kurita sailed through the Palawan passage. But these fleets were intercepted by American carrier aircraft, submarines and surface ships. Our task force, seemingly invincible, was shattered at Leyte Gulf. It was a disaster. There is no other way to put it."

"How bad were our losses?" asked Sadeo Yoshizawa, thinking of how the catastrophe would be received by the House of Peers and wondering if the Emperor really knew the extent of it.

"How bad?" replied the vice admiral. "We lost three battleships, four carriers, nine cruisers and eleven destroyers. And irreplaceable crews. Almost all of our aircraft were lost. The fighting effectiveness of our navy has been erased. Much of the Imperial Navy is at the bottom of the sea, and what remains is stranded for lack of fuel oil; our reserves are nearly exhausted, and the Allies are choking off the supply of new oil from our Southern Resource Zone."

"Which means that we no longer have ships or planes to protect Japan," said Prince Norobutsu.

"I'm afraid that is so," replied the admiral.

Following stunned silence, Hitanka said, "What about the *Musashi*? I have a nephew on board, a gunnery officer."

"Yes, a fine young man. I had the pleasure of meeting him when the ship was commissioned. I will check to see if he survived. Some did."

Hitanka nodded and said, "He was proud to be on it. The greatest battleship in the world, certainly, with its eighteen-inch guns, more powerful than any of the American battleships."

"Unfortunately, big guns are of little value against airplanes and submarines," said Kenji Kado, whose steel company had manufactured the ship's massive steel turrets.

"That's true. The *Musashi,* like her sister ship *Yamato,* never had an opportunity to engage the American battleships. The *Musashi* was hit by torpedoes, and these torpedoes did not bounce off harmlessly, as the old ones did. Then a bomb struck the forward magazine and she blew up."

"If only Admiral Yamamoto had not been killed," lamented Shunroki Hitanka. "He was the heart and soul of the Japanese Imperial Navy. I still wonder how he could have been shot down. His mission was completely secret, yet the Americans knew exactly where his plane was. How could that be possible?"

"And they knew that our fleet was heading toward Midway two years ago, and that was also top secret."

"Might there be a spy?" asked Prince Yodaki.

"Perhaps," replied Yoshizawa, "but if so, he is planted very high in the chain of command. I just hope that, if he exists, he knows nothing about this."

"Then we should not waste time. We must consider two possibilities for the future," said Hitanka. "One is that we confront the Americans when they land troops on our home islands and bleed them so badly that their public demands an end to the war. The other is negotiating a settlement to end the conflict as soon as possible."

"Regarding the invasion," said the prince, "we have two and a half million troops in Japan for defense. That includes police forces, women's brigades and reserves. That is a considerable number, and they will fight to the very end."

"The women's brigades are armed with spears and knives," scoffed the admiral. "There was a women's brigade in the Marianas, the Lily Brigade. Very brave, but they were annihilated. The concept is called the 'spirit of three million spears' and the women are to fight like samurai. A romantic notion, but spears are useless against tanks and heavy artillery. To really defend Tokyo and the other cities we would have to bring back the twenty-seven divisions in China."

"Is that even possible?" demanded Prince Yodaki.

"It's doubtful that very many of the divisions would get back to Japan even if the high command was willing to give up China. We simply don't have enough troopships, and American submarines patrol those waters as well as the straits between our four islands," replied the admiral.

"So now Japan is vulnerable. Each of our islands can be invaded from all directions, and without ships, troops on one would not be able to reinforce those on another. Our forces on each island would have to face the onslaught alone."

"To make things worse, if the Allies defeat Germany they could direct hundreds of thousands toward Japan. That might include the Soviets, if they declare war on us. The Americans are tough fighters, but the Russians are savages," said Yoshizawa of the parliament. "There would be millions of them, and I assure you, they would rape every woman," he concluded.

"This is true," said Hitanka slowly. "But soon we may have a new weapon developed by our scientists that may be a great equalizer, even though it will be costly in precious equipment."

"What could that possibly be? asked Prince Norobutsu hopefully.

"It is too soon to speak of it yet," Hitanka replied, "but I will tell you more as progress is made at the University. And there is another innovation that could have a devastating effect upon the American fleet. I am speaking of what Rear Admiral Masafumi Arima has resorted to, and that is the kamikaze, the Divine Wind. It's the same spirit that destroyed the Mongol fleet in the thirteenth century. It involves dedicated pilots who with utter resolve hurl their aircraft against American ships as if they were flying bombs."

"They commit seppuku by sacrificing themselves?" said Kado with unabashed admiration.

"Precisely. Those that have penetrated the American fighters and anti-aircraft screen have had stunning success. A number of ships have been sunk or badly damaged. Thousands of Americans have been killed. It must be absolute terror for the Americans to see these heroes tear into their ships. The pilots wrap the *hashimake* around their foreheads, drink a cup of saki, and to the shouts of "Banzai!" take off on a one-way mission for the Emperor," extolled Hitanka, the assistant secretary to the war minister.

There was a moment of appreciation before the admiral said dryly, "A brave act, a heroic act indeed, but it leaves us with even fewer aircraft. Personally, I would not waste the planes or the pilots. It may give the Americans pause if enough ships are sunk, but unless we can sink dozens of carriers, I have only limited hope of the kamikaze idea."

Prince Noributzu Yodaki's cigarette smoke drifted across the low ceiling as the men contemplated the unthinkable. "So," began Kenji Kado, "there are three questions that come to my mind. The first is, would the Americans and their allies even consider a peace settlement? Their president Roosevelt, along with Churchill, speaks of fighting on until there is unconditional surrender. That is unacceptable."

"I have also heard that most Americans want the Emperor hanged, along with Tojo and the war cabinet," said Yoshizawa. "The thought of the Emperor being eliminated is unthinkable. The people would not stand for it."

"Which brings me to my second thought," said Kado. "In any dealing, the retention of the Emperor, a living deity, must be nonnegotiable. His presence must be retained at all costs."

"And the third?" asked the admiral. "That Japan must continue as a nation, not a disparate group of islands controlled by various Allied powers."

To all of these there was unanimous agreement. The next step, yet unspoken, hung in the smoke-fouled air.

"I think we have to face reality, difficult as it may be," said the parliamentarian, Sadeo Yoshizawa. "And that's why we are here. We all represent various important aspects of the government, military and civilian. We know that the war is nearly lost; continued fighting will result only in more casualties and waste of irreplaceable resources. As it is, we have lost nearly two million soldiers and sailors, and now countless civilians are at risk. The Emperor knows this, and would not oppose a settlement if our conditions are met. This I have heard from high sources. The Emperor does not wish the destruction of Japan. Therefore I believe we can initiate contact with representatives of the enemy. At this point, no one else will."

Yoshizawa, considering the political mind of the House of Peers, said, "We have, through Kanayama, our ambassador to the Vatican, broached the subject of negotiation with the Allies. His contact is Giovanni Montini, the acting Secretary of State for the Holy See. But as of yet the Vatican has not made any commitment to assist us."

"The Vatican may eventually prove instrumental, but it will move slowly and deliberately," said Prince Noributzu. "After all, it has made certain agreements with Nazi Germany. No, the Vatican will not offend Hitler, even though it may wish to help Japan."

"And that's why we must deal directly with the Allies if we are to initiate the peace effort," said Vice Admiral Abe. "There are certain assets at my disposal we can employ. I have not mentioned this to anybody, but through a foreign embassy I have already established contact with an American source. I will not name him, but he has influence with Roosevelt. If we establish consensus, we shall pursue the plan I have conceived. Regardless of the dangers, we are all involved no matter where it takes us. If it fails, we may have to commit seppuku. We will have no choice, and we must consider this. Those intent on continuing the fight will consider us traitors. So, shall we meet again with our final decision?"

"It is my opinion that we make a decision now," said Kenji Kado. "The Kempeitai are everywhere. We can assemble here only once without them knowing. If we all agree to proceed, we should place our trust in the hands of Vice Admiral Abe. The time is now, not later. The fate of Japan hangs in the balance."

There were furrowed brows as the men considered their course of action. At a nod from the Prince, they cast their votes.

One by one, they solemnly filed out and disappeared into the gloom. Once again, the caretaker's house was empty, the teacups back on the rough wooden shelf.

One hundred yards away, kneeling behind snow-covered bushes, a man raised his binoculars and whispered to another, who jotted in his notebook. Only after the last conspirator departed did the two men rise and quickly walk in the opposite direction. They had much to say, but not to each other.

* * *

Sayuri wrapped herself around him, soft caresses, whispered words of endearment and the entwining of their bodies drove her to the rapturous moment of fulfillment she desperately craved. The words, *Tad-ishi, Tad-ishi*, swirled in her mind as she synchronized with his every movement, every touch, in a cocoon of peace and harmony. As in a silvery cloud, they drifted on high, all cares left in valleys of fear miles below.

She even heard the soft giggling of Sensei, who could hear her sighs and would remind her of how a Japanese lady, even in the throes of carnal delight, should restrain pillow talk so as not to titillate or intrude upon others. Then Sensei would smile and say how wonderful it is that Sayuri had found true love.

The blissful cloud began to dissipate and Tad-san was a bit further away, just out of reach. His hands no longer held her; his touch, his face, his presence, blurred and faded away. Sensei's words no longer reached her, as she too became distant. The silver, gleaming cloud which had wrapped them in a womb of warmth and pleasure became a dark, forbidding thing, and the sounds that came to her were not those of Sensei, but rather of distant explosions.

The dream vanished with the blaring of sirens. Drawing the thin blanket closer, she huddled in the narrow trench dug behind the ikebana shop. The advice of the neighborhood association, previously ignored, was now imperative. Virtually every family had a trench or cave-like depression to protect them from flying debris.

Sleet splattered on a tarpaulin that Sayuri had laid across the trench, but water trickled in. Today the bombers were obliterating a district two miles away, and the earth shook. A few anti-aircraft guns threw up desultory fire, but heavy clouds made their quarry invisible. The B-29s flew higher, seeking concrete structures to level with thousand-pound bombs. A flight of American fighters accompanied the bombers, speeding toward any Zero that dared to contest the city's destruction.

Sayuri shivered and, wrapping the blanket about herself, went back into the shop. It would not make any difference, she thought, if an errant bomb were to drop anywhere near. The shop would become her burial mound. Wet and cold, she changed into the only dry *mompe* pantaloons she had left, washed her face and knelt in a corner of the shop.

She gazed at the few remaining vases with their long-dead flowers, and imagined the kimonoed ladies who used to come and seek the advice of Sensei, who, with soft gentility, would suggest the inclusion of a special flower or reed. So long ago, such a world away, thought Sayuri. Would anybody have guessed that it would come to this? She listened to yet another siren as a fire truck pressed through narrow streets to pour a thin stream on an immolated building, or the charred remains of an unfortunate soul.

Alone. So totally alone. Sensei was long dead, and Kumi was gone. And she would never return, thought Sayuri. Why should she? Any one of those American fighters, so insolently ripping through the skies over Tokyo, could be flown by her American lover. But no, it could not be her Tad-san; he was a Navy pilot, and she had heard that they were not escorting the bombers. But that was only rumor, and there were so many of those.

A carrier, she realized, might be only fifty miles off the Japanese coast. It's planes would have much more time over Tokyo than planes based hundreds of miles away. She might ask someone who better understood such things. But who?

Alone. The word came to her again. It was more than a word; it was a state of being, or, in her case, not being. In times of great distress, she thought, people gather empathically. They comfort one another and extend solace. For a while she considered going to the neighborhood meeting hall to commiserate with the unfortunate. But what would she say when asked about her misfortune? She could only speak of Sensei, and she was a fading memory, like the world they had all once lived in.

The cold penetrated her worn and tattered clothing. She held tightly to the teacup, its steam rising and dissipating. She stared at the wall with its faded, ancient woodblock drawings of seventeenth-century women in colorful kimonos. Alongside the drawings was a poem, black hiragana characters drawn with a bamboo brush. A thin layer of ash powdered its surface.

It read,

> *If someone considers the spirit of Shikishima,*
> *the essence of Japan,*
> *it is the cherry blossoms of Yamazakura*
> *that are fragrant in the rising sun.*

Tacked on the wall was a framed black-and-white photo of her and Sensei smiling into the camera in front of the Shirokiya department store in the sophisticated High District beside the Nihombashi bridge, now demolished by American bombs.

Was it time at last to make a decision, she thought? Was it time to put away a silly dream and do what was sensible? She had delayed the next step for so long. Romantic notions were no longer of concern. Survival was. She needed a strong person, an indomitable person to provide food and a bit of support.

Tad-san could not do that. She would have to seek out somebody else. For several minutes she weighed the possibilities, the manner in which she might approach him, and what she would have to say. Would he return her submissive bow with a formal bow? Or would he respond with contempt, or say nothing? That most terrible rebuke would leave her eviscerated. Maybe he would say that it was too late, that she was no longer desired, no longer desirable. Maybe, maybe.

It wasn't with great resolve that she donned her soiled jacket and stepped into the street with its new covering of snow. It should have been pristine whiteness, but finely powdered ash left it a mottled and dismal grey.

The train station was crowded with school children and their mothers, all fleeing to the countryside to pin their hopes on the mercy of peasants, folk having little in common with those of the city.

She cared not about the pushing and touching now. Her mind blanked that out and only tried to compose the right words. She had once read a translation of an article written by Samuel Clemens, the great American author. In it he talked about writing and said, "The difference between a word and the right word is the difference between lightning and a lightning bug."

The thought made her smile, but that evaporated when the right words did not come.

After thirty minutes the train edged into the station where workmen were repairing the roof, a bomb having ripped away blue tiles that lay in heaps.

Her steps toward the guarded gate of the building were slow, the place intimidating. She found herself stopping several times as if pulled by a weight from behind. But she started again and approached a guard. She handed him a slip of paper and was told to wait. He handed it to still another and resumed his post. The soldier entered the building and she took a deep breath and waited. Eternity, she thought, and then the soldier emerged.

A wind buffeted her and cold snow descended. The soldier handed her a note, turned about and reentered the warmth of the building. She read the note, slipped it into her pocket and watched the snow fall upon the ground. With a deep sigh she turned away and began to walk, one mile after the other.

Chapter 21
Tokyo, Japan
Late December, 1944

A twin-engine transport touched down at Okinawa's Yontan military airfield, built only months before. Two plain-clothed men were driven up a winding road to a cave entrance that looks down on Naha city. The cave, consisting of four-hundred-fifty meters of tunnels, had been carved out of solid rock by the Navy Corps of Engineers and was the nerve center of the Kaigungo Navy Headquarters. The cave descended below ground, one section serving as the intelligence office for Rear Admiral Minoru Uta and other officers, both Army and Navy. Koizumi Karamatsu met the two civilians at the entrance and escorted them into the bowels of the complex, where hundreds of sailors worked, diligently preparing for the expected invasion.

Vice Admiral Itomo Karamatsu's office was next to Uta's, and he could read Uta's favorite poem affixed to the wall: "Born as a man, nothing fulfills my life more than to die in the name of the Emperor."

The two men bowed and handed Admiral Karamatsu an envelope containing a single sheet of paper. He read it, made a notation, and thanked the two Kempeitai officers. Again they bowed and were escorted back to the waiting vehicle. Twenty minutes later, they took off for Tokyo.

Itomo Karamatsu stepped out of his office, approached Uta and handed him the note.

"They are here, in Okinawa?" asked the admiral.

"They came in last night. Apparently, Prince Noributzu has been acting strangely and the Kempeitai decided to keep an eye on him. They're not sure what he has in mind, but he's not alone."

"Then we must also be vigilant," said Admiral Uta.

* * *

Sayuri yawned and pulled the blanket more closely around her. It had snowed again during the night, and that would make her day all the harder. She had enrolled in the trench brigade the week before. Now hundreds of men and women were employed in the task of digging protective depressions in urban areas and around factories as the bombing continued.

Another hour of sleep, she thought, before she would trudge off to the neighborhood association's meeting house. She was thankful that she could still sleep in the ikebana shop when so many slept on factory floors after the sixteen-hour workday.

She had put a salve on the blisters that had broken; her hands were sore from the shovel's rough handle. Her back ached too, for the shovel given her was short, requiring her to bend low when digging into the hard soil. Many women, unused to the tedious and difficult work, had taken days off, complaining of bleeding hands. Sayuri could legitimately have done the same, but the *nukapan* meal offered at the congregation site was filling, and remaining in the empty shop was too depressing.

But the cold made it impossible to sleep any longer. She rose and put the teapot on the burner and dressed for the day. She had sewn herself two pairs of heavy socks to keep her feet relatively warm, since the clogs now worn by working women did little to protect feet from the cold. She turned on the radio and heard the announcer cheerily say that new observation posts would give the citizens of Tokyo much more time to take cover should the B-29s come again. This announcement was followed by martial music and stories of heroic soldiers.

Having finished her tea, she slipped on the clogs and opened the door. The steps were coated with six inches of fresh snow; and tiny, glistening flakes continued to fall, giving a fairytale feeling to the shops across the narrow street. Icicles hung from the roofs and slivers of blue tile peeped out from the snow.

Sayuri stepped onto the porch and breathed in the clear air. The street was virtually deserted, save for some elderly women sweeping a sidewalk. Patches of sky appeared, then were covered by swirling wisps. Her eyes adjusted to the brightness of the snow and swept along the street until arrested by a figure sitting on the curb, snow thick on the hat and coat. She stared at the form and wondered if it was someone who had frozen during the night. On more than one occasion it had been reported that homeless persons had failed to find shelter and had expired from hypothermia.

Worried, Sayuri crossed the street, knelt and placed her hand on the person's arm. A woman, her face blue with cold, instinctively pulled away. Ever so slowly she looked at the one who had woken her. Blinking, she tried to focus, coughed and wiped her nose with the coat sleeve.

Sayuri was about to say something when, staring into the face, she gasped and said, "Kumi-san! What are you doing out here? You are freezing!" Helping the woman stand she said, "You must come in. Come, come."

With the steps of someone three times her age, Kumi allowed herself to be led into the shop. Once in, she sank to the floor, head drooping onto her chest. Sayuri snatched up the blanket and draped it around her friend, then with a towel wiped her face. She poured still-warm *ocha* into a cup and encouraged Kumi to drink.

For several minutes Sayuri said nothing. The warmth of the green tea began to revive her friend, who began to weep and quake. Sayuri wrapped her in her arms until the shaking subsided. Kumi sucked in a deep breath, coughed, then slumped.

"I'm sorry, so sorry," she said, her half-frozen lips mumbling the words.

"You have nothing to be sorry for," said Sayuri, brushing wet, tangled hair from Kumi's face. "It is I who owes you an apology, Kumi-san. You are guiltless. I drove you away with my foolishness. But now you are back."

Kumi closed her eyes, and Sayuri thought that she had fallen asleep, but then Kumi said, "He is gone. My husband is gone. I will never see him again."

"Husband? Gone? What are you talking about?" Sayuri said, with utter surprise, taking her friend's hands.

"Takagi-san. We married just before he went back to sea. We had but two nights together. He said that he would be back in a week or two. I waited at the gate of the navy base every day. I waited for weeks. Then I heard."

Sayuri felt like a pall had descended. There were the whispers, the terrible rumors that no one wanted to believe.

"He was on the battleship *Musashi* when it was sunk. And he died. Sayuri-san, my husband is dead, and now I am a widow. I had nowhere to go. If you are willing to let me, I want to come back."

"I pray that you stay, Kumi-san. Yes, you must stay. We will all be together. I will heat some water and bring you a towel, and you can wash. I will heat enough to fill the *ofuru* so you can bathe; it will take less than an hour. And my futon may still be warm. You should get some sleep."

She coaxed Kumi onto the futon, then set about to fill the round wooden tub, the type found in virtually every house. Within seconds her friend was asleep.

Sayuri felt tears run down her cheeks. Kumi-san had come back; but if it hadn't been for tragedy, would they ever have seen each other again? She pushed the question out of her mind. That Kumi was here was all that mattered.

Takagi-san, Sayuri thought. The man she had turned away, the man who had lost face but retired with his honor intact. Kumi-san had said that if she married, it would be to a man of honor, a samurai who fights for Japan. But now he was gone.

Once the bath was ready, Sayuri gently woke her friend. After the luxuriating warmth of the *ofuru*, Kumi donned a faded and worn *mompe* and knelt across from Sayuri. A low table held cooked radishes and a cup of rice: the only fare Sayuri had to offer.

Kumi ate slowly, savoring each morsel. Finally, she placed the two bamboo *hashi* delicately over the rice bowl and said, "I fell asleep before I could ask; you said, 'We will all be together.' Is there someone else living here? A refugee?"

"Not a refugee, and maybe no one at all, Kumi-san." Sayuri placed her own *hashi* over her bowl. "A few days ago there was another bombing, some distance from here. I thought of what you had said about my love for Tad-ishi. I thought about how far away he is, if he is even alive. And that he is an enemy of Japan. And I considered how alone I am, especially after you left. I feared that I would never see you again, and I began to think of how badly I treated both Takagi and Koizumi. And after a while I made a decision; perhaps one I should have made long ago."

"A decision?" said Kumi, a questioning look on her face.

Sayuri took a sip of tea and said, "I went to Koizumi—that is, I tried to. I took the train to the navy base where he works."

Kumi stared at Sayuri and said, "What were you going to tell him?"

"That I would marry him. If he still wanted me."

Kumi put her hands to her face in disbelief. In a half whisper she said, "But you don't love him. I don't even know if you like him, Sayuri-san."

"I don't dislike him. I think he would be kind to me if I acted kindly to him."

"I think he would appreciate those sentiments. What did he say?"

"He wasn't there. I was not able to say anything to him. I was met by a soldier who told me that Koizumi is on a mission and would not be back for a long time. I asked when he would return, but he wouldn't tell me. Then I asked where he is, but the soldier said that he wouldn't tell me even if he knew. He said that such information is confidential and that civilians, especially women, should not ask such things."

"So, Koizumi-san doesn't know you went to see him?"

"I gave the soldier my name, but I doubt anybody told Koizumi that I was there."

"All this is such a surprise," said Kumi. "But I must ask you, have you forgotten Tadishi-san?"

Sayuri sighed and said, "He is gone, like your husband. I will never see him again, and I must be realistic. I am exhausted, I am always hungry, and until you returned, I was alone, terribly alone. Who else could I turn to, Kumi-san? Perhaps he would have me as his wife. I honestly don't know;

but he once said that he was in love with me. And I thought I might be able to revive his affection."

"So you will visit the navy base again when he comes back?"

"It's what I must do."

"Would you like me to go with you?"

"That is very kind, but it might appear that I dared not face him alone, that I was not be certain of my commitment."

"And you are, Sayuri-san?"

"I think so. I mean, I'm sure I am."

Kumi took another sip of tea and gave her friend a long sympathetic stare. Then she said, "Oh, Sayuri-san, I wonder if you really are."

* * *

Lieutenant Commander Karamatsu, come into my office," said Admiral Karamatsu to his aide.

Dutifully, the senior pilot followed his uncle and stood while the admiral glanced at papers on his desk. Looking up he said, "You will go to Yontan Airfield and see if any transports from Tokyo have recently arrived. Don't be conspicuous and don't talk to anyone unless absolutely necessary. An aircraft may have come in without my awareness."

"Is there a problem with its occupants?" asked Koizumi.

"It's something I can't discuss now. But this assignment is of utmost importance."

"*Hai*," said Koizumi, saluting the admiral. He was about to leave when Karamatsu said, "Drive there yourself, check the logs and hurry back. If any questions are asked, say that you are following Admiral Uta's orders."

Six fighter aircraft were parked near a large hanger. Koizumi peered in and saw mechanics working on a Zero.

One of the mechanics saw him, saluted, then returned to his work. Koizumi said nothing, walked around the hanger and spied a twin-engine transport with its propellers turning. Its door was open and a naval officer peered out. Beside the aircraft was an ambulance, and a pilot was being placed inside. A moment later the emergency vehicle sped away.

Koizumi, having seen what he wanted, began to turn away. Just then, Admiral Abe descended the aircraft's ladder.

"Lieutenant Commander, come back," barked the admiral. With an abrupt halt, Koizumi turned and saluted. The salute returned, Abe peered at the insignia on Koizumi's uniform. Pointing with his thumb he said, "I require a pilot. Can you fly that plane?"

Koizumi glanced at the aircraft and said, "Sir, I can fly anything, but I am on assignment and have to return to my commanding officer."

"I am now your commanding officer, and you will fly my plane. I am an admiral in the Japanese Imperial Navy and I'm giving you a direct order. Do you understand?"

"*Hai!*" said Koizumi with a quick bow. In a last attempt he said, "Sir, I am an aide to—"

"Get in the plane!" said Abe with a cold glare.

Shinroki Hitanka emerged from the plane holding a pistol and joined Abe just as a soldier peered out from the control tower thirty yards away. The observer cocked his head and watched before reentering. Another soldier appeared with binoculars and quickly retreated inside. Glancing toward the tower, the admiral said, "Put that away, Hitanka. This fine officer will fly the plane."

With trepidation, Koizumi ascended the stairs and saw three other men, all in civilian clothes. No one said a word as they took seats in the Nakajima L2D, a Japanese version of the American DC 3.

"Is there no copilot?" asked Koizumi as he settled into the pilot's seat.

"No, and you saw the ambulance? That's the former pilot. He is very ill. You said you can fly anything. This should be easier than a fighter. I will sit in the copilot's seat," said Abe.

"Sir, may I ask where we are to fly? I mean, have we enough fuel and do we need a fighter escort?"

"We have enough fuel and no escort is required. Now get us in the air. I will tell you the coordinates when we reach three thousand feet. Then we will fly very low."

Admiral Karamatsu glanced at his watch when a phone rang in an adjoining room. A corporal answered it then briskly approached the admiral, saluted and said, "Sir, there is a phone call for you in the major's office. The caller said it is important."

Karamatsu snatched up the phone and said, "Who is this?"

"Admiral, this is Captain Ito Higachi. I'm in charge of security here at Yontan Field," said a concerned voice. "We've had a strange incident in the last fifteen minutes and I thought you should be aware of it. A transport aircraft took off without contacting the tower, requesting clearance or giving any information regarding its flight plan. And there seemed to be some disagreement between an admiral who was on the aircraft and a lieutenant commander."

"What lieutenant commander, what admiral?" Karamatsu demanded. He felt a mounting sense of dread.

"I have no idea of who they were, sir. But it was observed by two flight operations personnel in the tower. One had binoculars and could see what happened. It appeared the pilot was ordered to fly the aircraft against his will. A civilian with the admiral was holding a pistol."

"Does anybody at Yontan know the name of the admiral?"

"No, sir. The plane came in late last night and according to my security police there were a number of men on board."

"How many?"

"At least four, perhaps five. My men were denied entry. They were told that there was secret material aboard. The men said they had to remain with it at all times and nothing can be revealed about the flight."

"So they didn't go to morning mess or use the *benjo*?"

"No, sir. The only people who deplaned were the admiral and that armed civilian. There was a pilot on the aircraft, but when the plane landed he was taken away in an ambulance."

"Do you know where they took him?"

"I will find out and report back."

"Do it right away," said Karamatsu. After a brief pause he said, "Captain, how many fighter aircraft do you have fueled and available right now?"

"Six Zeros are on the field and the pilots are on standby. Two others are in the air and we have a search plane one hundred miles out. We have two Mitsubishi seaplanes here as well. There was a report of an American carrier in the area."

"Tell the air operations officer to have pilots man their planes and await further orders. Find out if the pilot of the transport is still alive and what he knows. One more thing. Did the lieutenant commander arrive in a staff car? Was he alone?"

"Yes, that's what the men in the tower reported."

"I see. Phone me back as soon as you learn of the condition of the pilot."

Karamatsu turned to a corporal and said, "Ask Admiral Uta to come to my office as soon as possible. Tell him it is most important."

A call came ten minutes later. A sergeant was about to answer it when Karamatsu grabbed the phone, ordered the noncom out and said, "What did you learn about the pilot, the one taken to the hospital?"

"He is dead, sir. I spoke to the doctor. The pilot was shot."

"Do they know who he was?"

"No, sir. His identification papers are missing, and we don't know where the flight originated. We were not informed of any incoming aircraft. It just arrived without communications."

"And what of the car?"

"It is from your complex. We checked with one of your sentries and he saw it depart earlier today. So the pilot had to be from headquarters. Have you any orders that I should pass on to Major Igumi, the flight operations officer?"

"Tell him to be ready for my call. Have him put the search plane up and tell the pilots for the Zeros to man their planes."

Admiral Uta entered the office wearing a simple navy officer's tunic. With a concerned look he said, "Is it about Admiral Abe and the others in the Kempeitai's note?"

"I'm sure it is. Nothing else would have been so secret. Senior personnel always report here, if only out of courtesy to see you. These men refused to leave the plane and they filed no flight plan."

"So we have no idea of where they are going. Did the tower try to contact them?" asked Uta, lifting the phone from its cradle.

"Unfortunately, no. But we have fighters on stand by and a search plane just took off," said Admiral Karamatsu.

"I want the Zeros in the air," said Uta. He was about to leave when he turned to Karamatsu and said, "The pilot ordered to fly the transport. Do you know who he is?"

"Lieutenant Commander Koizumi Karamatsu. He is my aide. My nephew."

Uta stood silently, looked long at the Vice Admiral, nodded, then left the room.

Karamatsu lit a cigarette and blew a long trail of smoke into the stale air.

Chapter 22
Western Pacific
Late December, 1944

The Aichi E16A Navy reconnaissance plane flew at ten thousand feet over an ocean that seemed to go on for ever. It had a range of seven hundred thirty miles and a ceiling of thirty-three thousand feet, but that would take them above the clouds and impair the pilot's and observer's visibility. Two hundred miles from the Yontan Field, the observer tapped the pilot's shoulder and pointed to a low, distant object skimming across the waves at six hundred feet. Pushing the stick forward, the pilot dropped down to four thousand, trailing the transport but keeping several miles behind.

"Don't spook him," the observer reminded the pilot.

"He doesn't see us. Just call it in and we'll follow him."

Fifteen minutes later a corporal handed Vice Admiral Karamatsu a message from the seaplane. "He is certain about the coordinates?" asked the admiral.

"*Hai.* He repeated it three times and sounded quite certain. The Nakajima transport is heading southwest at one hundred and thirty knots."

Karamatsu considered this, picked up the phone and said, "Connect me to flight operations at Yontan Field."

Seconds passed until a voice came on the phone. The admiral issued his orders. Five minutes later, six Zeros were headed toward the Nakajima transport and the admiral stepped into his superior's cramped office to report.

"It won't take long for the Zeros to catch up," he told Admiral Uta.

"Very well. Now we wait."

Admiral Uta filled two glasses with Suntory Red whiskey and offered a glass to Karamatsu.

"I have been in contact with the Supreme War Council and they approve of our actions. But they were quite surprised that Hitanka and Vice Admiral Abe were in on it."

"And I'm surprised that the war minister was not advised by the Kempeitai," said Karamatsu.

"I suspect that they didn't want anybody in government to alert Abe or the others. The Kempeitai would have wanted to snuff the whole thing out. Alerting the plotters would have delayed them, but they might have tried again and in a more ingenious way," said Uta.

He raised his glass and Karamatsu, though conflicted, did the same. Uta saw the distress in his assistant's eyes and said, "We have no choice; we must do this for the Emperor."

"I understand," said Karamatsu.

"I know our generals, admirals, and leading statesmen, but rarely do I meet the lower-ranking men. I mean the ones who actually give their lives for Japan. I would like to hear about your nephew."

Karamatsu took a sip of whiskey and said, "He is my sister's son, but I raised him. He is a brave pilot and a true patriot." Karamatsu felt as if he were delivering a funeral speech. He would never see his nephew again, the man who was a son to him. There would never be a grave to be tended;

there was never any burial for pilots shot down over the water. He told Uta about his nephew's training and war experience, but little about his parents and nothing about his brother. That secret would die with Koizumi.

* * *

"Why the hell can't the army take care of this?" Jack complained they left the ready room. Usually he was as excited as Tad at any opportunity to fly, but this morning's call to the ready room had interrupted his breakfast, and he was grumpy.

"Because the land-based planes don't have the range or the time on station. Tad sounded cheerful. "The carrier is only a hundred miles away, so we get to babysit and fly cover. It shouldn't take long. Come on!" Tad had outpaced his friend and paused to let Jack to catch up.

"Do you know what this is about? What's so riveting about a stretch of water with nothing in it but atolls?"

"No idea. Far above our pay grade."

"Isn't it always. Your plane fixed up?" Jack asked. He wiped dust from his goggles.

"Chief said that the leak was taken care of."

"Yeah, well, we've got some kids on board just out of school. No experience. Keep an eye on your gauges and head back if you have a problem."

"They do look young, don't they?" Tad grinned.

"Yeah, and they keep dropping screwdrivers and wrenches. I mean it, be careful."

By way of answer, Tad pulled on his own goggles.

The Hellcats flew at twelve thousand feet, escorting the "Gooney Bird," a C-47, the military version of the DC-3. It hummed along at nine thousand until it began its descent toward the atoll, a coral outcrop with a postage-stamp-size airfield and a dilapidated hangar. Ten years earlier it had been a refueling station for Japanese aircraft, but it had been abandoned and time had taken its toll. Weeds grew high on both sides of the runway, and lush, tropical vegetation nearly hid the building.

It was noon when the wheels of the transport touched the cracked tarmac, taxied, and stopped before the corrugated hangar. Five men deplaned and quickly entered. The pilot and copilot remained on board.

Flying cover, Tad heard Jack say, "You're leaking. Either fuel or oil, I can't be sure. I suggest you head back."

Jack was right. Perhaps the maintenance chief thought the new mech knew what he was doing, but the gauges didn't lie and hydraulic fuel was flowing like beer on a hot summer day.

"I'm losing it too fast. I'll land beside the Gooney Bird and see what I can do about it."

"I don't think you can do anything about the leak, Tad. Might as well leave it on the ground and get on the Forty-Seven. The Army can send some techs to fix it. Of course, you *could* stay on the atoll all by your lonesome like Robinson Caruso. I can have the Navy drop a load of cheese and pick you up in twenty years."

"You have a big heart, Jack. I'll go with the Gooney Bird and the Navy can decide what it wants to do with the Hellcat."

Jack peeled off from the flight and followed Tad down to five hundred feet, then watched as Tad's plane approached the field. Rejoining the flight, Jack keyed his mike and said, "There's another plane down there, sort of hidden with netting. It looks like another C-47."

"I'm taxiing up to it and will take a look." A minute later he said, "I don't think it's a C-47."

"Why not?"

"It's got a red meatball on the fuselage. I'll tell you more when I get back."

"Oh, this is going to be interesting."

Tad opened the cockpit and felt a blast of hot, humid air. He waved to the American pilots in the Gooney Bird and wondered why they chose to stay in the plane rather than the shade of palms growing only yards from the flight line. He swung onto the wing of the Hellcat, then dropped to the ground. Removing his leather flight cap, he squinted in the harsh light and looked about.

"What's going on?" he asked the pilot as he sauntered to the transport.

The pilot leaned out the window and said, "A meeting of some sort. Some high and mighty folks with scrambled egg on their hats and a few civilians. They didn't share anything with us, and we were told to keep out. And there are about five Japs in there too. Maybe some sort of parley. But I wouldn't go in there if I were you."

The pilot wiped sweat from his face, then said, "We saw you come in. Hydraulics, huh? I think the brass will let you on board, but I wouldn't ask them any questions." The pilot grinned, then pointed toward the other parked aircraft and said, "I doubt that you want to fly with that guy over there. He doesn't look too friendly, hand near his holster like some sort of Jap John Wayne. But I've got a forty-five if things get sticky."

"Just don't put a hole in your Gooney Bird," said Tad, glancing toward the pilot of the Nakajima.

"You think he knows what's going on?" said the pilot.

"I don't know, but I'll go talk to him," Tad said. "Maybe he knows something we don't."

"Be damn careful. You speak Jap?"

"Japanese? A few words," said Tad, and he walked away from the transport.

He was curious. Just what would this guy say, if anything at all? Then Tad wondered if the pilot had ever spoken to an American, let alone a pilot in the United States Navy.

The Nakajima pilot stiffened as Tad approached.

Tad stopped short. He tilted his head and said, "Koizumi? Koizumi-san?"

Koizumi's head snapped up. He opened his mouth but nothing came out.

"My God, you're actually alive! What the hell are you doing here?" blurted Tad.

His brother stayed perfectly straight and said, "And you're still alive too."

They stood there staring at one another. Tad considered shaking Koizumi's hand, but with the Goony Bird pilots watching, he decided not to.

"Is our mother well?" Koizumi finally asked.

"She was the last time I saw her, about six months ago. She's still a nurse. Pretty busy I guess."

"And Father? You told me he went back to Russia, but that was years ago."

"Still there, as far as I know. The Soviets made him fight the Nazis and he was wounded. We don't know if he's ever getting out of Russia."

Koizumi took out a pack of cigarettes and offered one to Tad. Standing away from the aircraft, they lit up and Tad said, "May I ask you a question? Have you any news of Sayuri? Is she okay?"

"She may still be alive. I haven't seen her in a long while, and Tokyo has been bombed. Of course, you know that. A lot of people, innocent people, have been killed by your B-29s."

"I know, but for what it's worth, I think you've heard of Nanking, the Philippines, China, and a few dozen other places raped by the honorable soldiers of the Japanese Empire. So much for honor."

"Some over-zealous soldiers, perhaps, but you're bombing children, civilians. How dare you talk about honor!"

"Maybe we don't have anything more to discuss," said Tad angrily.

He crushed the cigarette under his foot and was about to turn away when Koizumi said, "Wait. Wait, Tadishi-san. I have something to tell you."

"Like when Japan is going to call it quits? What do we have to do, bomb you into the Neolithic Age?"

"We do not quit. We fight like samurai."

"Is that so? What the hell do you suppose is going on here? High Japanese officers and officials meeting with Allied leaders? They're not drinking *ocha* and betting on sumo wrestlers. We sure didn't request the meeting. Your people did, and I'll give you five seconds to guess why. Do you have something to do with this?"

Koizumi stared at his brother, then the Hellcat with six Zeros painted behind the prop. Slowly he shook his head and said, "No, I have nothing to do with it. I was forced to fly this plane. I am an aide to our uncle, Admiral Karamatsu. What you suggest cannot be happening. That would be treason."

"Yeah, well, treason or not, some people close to the Emperor are looking for a way out. A very secret way. Hence this atoll. Maybe they're signing some papers that go back to Hirohito and Roosevelt. Maybe you are doing Japan a favor and will be famous some day. We'll be together in the *Tokyo Shimbun* paper: 'Brothers on opposite sides pose for peace.'"

Koizumi quietly said, "I don't think so. I will be accused of treason and shot as soon as I return."

"I doubt it. You said that you were forced to fly the plane. Your Kempeitai will know that, and our uncle will vouch for you."

In a softer tone Tad said, "This is a terrible war. It should never have happened and I think a lot of people in Japan understand that. You and I are both fighter pilots, warriors, and we have both killed many good men. You are still my brother, our mother's son, and always will be. I know that she wonders if either of us is still alive. I do hope you live through this war. Perhaps we can be together as true brothers someday. But I caution you, do not engage American pilots. Your machines are obsolete. Keep your head down and live out the war. Mother hopes to see you someday."

There was nothing more to say. They gave each other a stiff, curt bow and Tad returned to his plane. He turned and watched as the Japanese delegation, heads down, faces taut, hurried back to their Nakajima, its twin engines already turning. As it began to roll down the tarmac, Tad glanced at Koizumi in the pilot's seat. He thought that his brother gave a brief wave but he couldn't be sure. The plane lifted off the hot tarmac and disappeared into a mirage. Then it was gone.

Moments later, five Americans and an Australian colonel stepped out of the hangar and walked swiftly to the transport.

One, an American colonel, glanced at the Hellcat and said, "Lieutenant, what's wrong with your plane? There's oil all over it."

"Yes, sir. Hydraulic oil; can't fly it back. I have to wait for someone to get me."

"Well, that's a pile of horse pucky. The Navy can get it in their own sweet time. You get in the goony and fly with us." The colonel shook his head and added, "Navy. I don't know what's wrong with them, letting a man fly with a bummed-up plane."

Once the C-47 was off the ground, the colonel turned toward Tad and said, "Now listen, mister, anything you may hear is way beyond top secret. This mission, as far as you are concerned, never happened, and you didn't see any Japanese or speak with any of us. Understood?"

"Yes, sir. See no evil, hear no evil, speak no evil."

"Goddamn right. But they really fucked up when they hit Pearl."

* * *

Admiral Abe sat beside Koizumi and saw that his hands were shaking. "Are you alarmed, Lieutenant? You have done nothing wrong. You followed orders."

Koizumi's lips were tight and he did not look at the admiral. He wanted to shout, to scream that they had committed treason and would be executed upon their return. Instead, he concentrated on the instruments and glanced at the water below.

He wondered if he should avoid torture and humiliation by simply putting the plane into a dive and ending it all. The men in the seats behind appeared nervous, their talk low and worried. Faces were tight. Hitanka came forward and spoke to the admiral over the sound of the engines. All Koizumi could hear were the words, "Not Japan, someplace else." Evidently, Koizumi wasn't the only one with misgivings about their reception.

The admiral curtly shook his head, dismissed the man's concern and looked straight ahead.

* * *

The crew of the American C-47 alerted the carrier that the lieutenant was with them, then joined up with their escorts at ten thousand feet. Jack looked down as five Zeros passed several thousand feet below on an opposite course. They appeared to have no desire to engage and kept their formation tight.

Escorting the Allied officers was the mission, and command now resided with Vestergaard.

"Hey, Lieutenant, you see what I see?" called out one of the pilots. "Can we go after them?"

"That's a negative, boyo. Not our job."

"They seem to be in a big hurry, sir."

"Yep. I suspect they have a turkey in their sights. We let them go."

"Yes, sir, but I bet there's a story to tell."

"I reckon there is."

* * *

The Zeros first appeared as specks in the afternoon sun. They were flying higher than the Nakajima and coming in from three o'clock. One dropped out of formation and sped a hundred feet over the slow transport. Koizumi could see the face of the pilot, who stared at him for a split second before peeling away.

A feeling of dread pervaded Koizumi, and the admiral, startled by the interception, leaned forward, his eyes following the fighter as it climbed. The four other men stared out the windows and stirred nervously as four Zeros winged over and began their gun runs.

Koizumi heard the sounds of terrified voices behind him as he considered what evasive action he could possibly take. The admiral, stoic since leaving the clandestine meeting, was now gesturing, giving him orders to turn, dive, and weave to avoid rounds already ripping into the fuselage. The fighters came out of the sun one by one, their machine guns winking as bullets raked the lumbering transport.

Windows shattered, and Koizumi heard shouts and an agonized cry of pain from one of the conspirators. Altitude, he thought, and pulled back on the wheel. If only it were his fighter! He would launch into an Immelmann roll, turn the

Zero onto its back then dive and roll again before slipping into a cloud. But a Zero could speed a hundred miles an hour faster than the Nakajima, and Koizumi knew there was no escape.

In the distance was a scattering of islands, none of which he had paid much attention to minutes before. They were dense and tropical, some harboring mountains thousands of feet high. A few appeared to have black, sandy beaches, the result of wave action on volcanic shore. But the short, uneven beaches were heaped with tangled tree stumps and rock formations.

Frantically, Admiral Abe stabbed his finger toward the islands, just before his head exploded. Blood splattered the cockpit. Koizumi pushed the nose of the aircraft, over aiming for the surf of a lagoon.

Hitanka, ejected from his seat by the near vertical dive, fell forward, clutching at seats as cannon fire raked the wings. The port engine erupted in flame and the rudder, to Koizumi's alarm, responded sluggishly. Rounds from a third Zero, passing within one hundred feet, riddled the cabin and Hitanka fell dead, wedged between the pilot's and copilot's seats.

The starboard engine faltered, then burst into flame. Thick black smoke streamed in a dark trail. Koizumi eased back on the yoke, leveling out. The burning wreck skipped across the water like a stone as it headed toward a dense mangrove swamp.

The port wing sheared off and the remains of the tail caught a submerged log, bringing the smoldering plane to an abrupt halt. Another Zero made a last pass, strafing the shattered fuselage before forming up with the remainder of the flight.

* * *

The phone on Admiral Uta's desk jangled. He picked up the receiver, listened, then put it back in its cradle. Admiral Karamatsu, well into his third glass of whiskey, heard as if from a distance his commander say, "It's over. The Nakajima was shot down and crashed into an atoll. There are no survivors. I am sorry for Lieutenant Commander Karamatsu. He was a brave pilot, and I will make sure he is honored."

Admiral Karamatsu nodded, put down the glass and said, "I sent him to his death. I will pray for his soul at the shrine."

* * *

From their perch on the mountain, Jeremy, Maria and Hanabe watched the one-sided aerial attack. It was difficult to tell whether the fighter aircraft were American or Japanese until a Zero banked hard and the red ball shone in the afternoon sun. The larger, burning plane made a futile attempt to evade, doing nearly impossible maneuvers for a transport, until its engines caught fire and the aircraft, its flaps lowered, ripped into the swamp three miles away.

A languid trail of smoke hung in the air as they made their way toward the wreck. The Zeros were long gone, their mission completed. The three of them saw the remains of the aircraft half submerged in the swamp, its nose up at a forty-five-degree angle. It was perforated by bullets and cannon fire.

Jeremy waded into the water for a closer look. There were two bodies in the cockpit, one of them nearly headless and wearing a uniform with blood-stained gold braid. Moving closer, he made out the riddled red ball painted on the fuselage.

"Japanese," he said, turning back to Maria and Hanabe.

"That doesn't make sense," said Maria. "Why would they shoot down their own plane?"

"Are they all dead?" asked Hanabe, venturing into the swamp.

"It appears so," replied Jeremy. Then he saw a bloody hand move in the cockpit and the pilot's eyes met his, soundless words on his lips.

Chapter 23
Iriomote Island
Late December, 1944

Koizumi didn't know if his head would ever stop spinning. Blood in dark brown streaks was caked on his face and uniform. Was it his blood, he wondered? He heard flies, then the screech of birds as they pecked at the detritus, viscous and blackening in the sultry air. *Alive*, he thought. *Why am I still alive?* Slowly his eyes focused. As the blur resolved, he saw that strings and blotches of grey cranial matter hung from the shattered windscreen and covered the cockpit instruments. He turned his head and gazed at his left arm. *Broken*, he thought. And the blood staining the sleeve was his.

The pain, mercifully absent when he'd been unconscious, now coursed through his body as if it had been waiting for the right moment. He nearly wretched from the pain of moving the fingers of his left hand. His watch was dead, but by the position of the sun he calculated that the crash had taken place an hour earlier. He tried to stand, but the cockpit was at a fifty-degree angle and he fell back into the seat. When he tried again he realized that something was wrong with his right foot. Was it broken or just badly sprained, he wondered. He tried to put pressure on it, but the pain was nearly unbearable.

He turned his head to the right and saw Admiral Abe's corpse, the remains of its head thrown back and held to the torso by the bones of his neck. There was only one eye and a mouth, open as if in disbelief.

Behind him and rolled into a ball was Hitanka, his body punctured like an airplane skin ready for rivets. His blood, now dried, had streamed behind him, running down the ripped fuselage and spreading into the waters of the mangrove swamp.

The last thing Koizumi remembered was fire and jolting motions followed by a jarring stop. Then blackness. His head ached, and he surmised that the impact had thrown him forward into the aluminum frame of the windscreen. He lay back in the seat, thinking of what he had experienced, the ripping of metal, the raking of bullets, the screams of others. This, he considered, was exactly what he had meted out to a dozen other pilots.

Other sounds, human sounds, came to his ears, and he froze. A voice was saying something in English. A response, also in English, was followed by one in Japanese. He frowned, trying to make sense of it. Where had he crashed? Was he in Japan-held territory or...?

There was a pistol on board, he remembered. Was it Abe's? No, Hitanka's. He shifted to look behind his seat, but it must have fallen from Hitanka's holster and clattered away. He was defenseless, injured, and people were out there. He had moved his hand and they must have seen it. They would be coming, he knew, and there was nothing he could do about it.

He decided that he would speak only in Japanese. Perhaps the Japanese he heard was from a prisoner, since two of the voices spoke English. But one was that of a woman. Strange, he thought. What would a woman be doing here? Perhaps he was near an American base. The woman might be a nurse.

They were closer now, waist deep in the dark water. A man who looked Japanese was beside the ruptured fuselage staring up at the craft. Another man, also Asian, wore simple worker's clothes but looked warily about, as would a soldier on patrol.

"Can you hear me? Are you hurt?" asked the closer man, speaking Japanese.

Koizumi made no reply.

"I'm not a soldier; I can help you. It's too dangerous to stay in the plane. We can get you out of the swamp," said Jeremy.

"I don't think I can stand," Koizumi finally said, realizing that continued silence would be pointless.

"Hanabe," the man called, "come here; we have to help him get out."

Jeremy crawled into the fuselage. He was appalled by the carnage. Two men in civilian clothes lay crumpled and bloody in their seats. Their heads lolled back and the hands of one still clutched the arms of the chair. Another hand was attached only by cartilage, bullets having nearly severed the wrist.

Pulling himself up the angled fuselage, Jeremy dislodged a crumpled body and watched as it tumbled into the water. Squeezing into the cockpit, Jeremy pushed the nearly headless body aside and knelt down next to the pilot, who turned his head and peered into Jeremy's eyes.

"You are Japanese. Who are you?" the pilot said, his throat constricted.

"My name is Jeremy, and I am not Japanese, I'm American. I'll have to drag you out, and my friend will keep you from falling. We'll carry you out of the swamp but we must hurry."

Hurry, thought Koizumi. They must be hiding, especially if the man is not Japanese. But who was there to hide from?

It took nearly twenty minutes to extricate Koizumi from the plane and carry him to solid land at the edge of the swamp. For the first time he saw the woman, who, holding a spear, stood immobile. She stared at him, a look of contempt on her face.

Laboring under the intense heat, the two men sat him against an ancient palm. "Your arm is broken," said Jeremy. "I can put a splint on it later. And I will find a branch to help you walk. We have a long way to go."

"Go? Where are you taking me?" asked Koizumi, his head still spinning.

Then there was an angry shout from the woman.

Koizumi's eyes followed Jeremy as he joined her. They walked several paces but not far enough to be out of hearing.

Hanabe watched Maria and Jeremy; then, turning to Koizumi, he said, "Do you speak English?"

Koizumi evaluated the young man, barely out of his teens, then stared at the sky and made no reply.

"Just what the hell are you doing?" hissed Maria.

"What do you mean?"

"That man, the pilot, are you really thinking of giving him aid, bringing him to our compound? Think about it! He is a Japanese soldier. What reason would he possibly have for not wanting to kill us? You already told him that you are an American; I heard you. Why would we trust him? You can't bring that man up the mountain. You just can't."

It had been a long time since he had seen her so angry. Jeremy turned and looked at Koizumi, who stared back at him. Turning back to Maria he said, "So what should we do?

I'm not going to kill him. That would be murder. Are you going to kill him?"

She screwed up her face and gave him a hard stare but said nothing.

"No? Well in that case, we had better get out of here. You know the reconnaissance plane comes this time every day. And scouts on that island out there probably saw the transport on fire and going down. That will really pique their interest. So we better get a move on. The man is injured. I have a pistol and you have your spear. I think the odds are in our favor."

It took a while for Jeremy to find a branch that would serve as a crutch, and they had only gone a quarter mile when a Zero flew overhead. Jeremy pushed Koizumi into a copse of trees and they froze as the plane flew out to sea, banked, and circled back again. Perhaps the pilot spied a piece of metal glinting in the sun. It was even possible that he had seen the fuselage or bodies near it. Dipping his left wing, he came back around at a much lower altitude.

Koizumi saw the pilot crane his neck, then lift a radio mike as the aircraft sped toward the sea. Concentrating on the scene below, the pilot failed to notice three Hellcats dropping down from seven thousand feet. Finally realizing the danger, he pulled up as a fourth Hellcat stitched rounds into the underside of the aircraft. With no self-sealing gas tanks, the Zero became a flaming mass, cartwheeling into the sea. The Hellcats reformed and disappeared as fast as they had come.

It was the first time they had seen American aircraft fly over the island. They stared, awestruck by the speed and the finality of what had just happened.

"They have come back!" Maria exclaimed, her eyes wide, trying to see if the fighters would return.

"I think it's just a patrol," said Jeremy, but earlier that day he had seen pillars of smoke rising from Ishigaki Island.

He turned to Koizumi, who showed no expression. Jeremy stared toward the sea. Koizumi saw the glee on Maria's face and, to Jeremy, said, "I think that woman intends to kill me. There is no reason for me to go with you. If she is going to kill me she should do it now."

"If you don't try to kill us she won't kill you," Jeremy replied. "But we won't let you remain here to signal Japanese planes. Too many of our friends have been murdered."

"I have no desire to alert Japanese planes. I will not go back to Japan under any circumstances."

"Then you'd better come with us."

When Koizumi hesitated, Maria said, "Give me your gun. He's too dangerous. It won't bother me to shoot him right here and now."

"Don't fool with her," Jeremy said quietly. "I won't give her the pistol, but she's deadly with that spear. And you can't run away."

Despondent and bitter, Koizumi picked up the branch, put it under his armpit and said, "How far is it? I can't go fast."

"We'll go slow. Follow Maria and Hanabe, and I will follow you."

Maria insisted that the pilot sleep outside the encampment at night, and argued against him having a fire.

"There are animals about," countered Jeremy, and allowed him to have a banked fire in a pit.

"As far as I am concerned, he is one of them," she'd said angrily, closing the spiked gate behind her.

As darkness descended, Jeremy brought Koizumi a blanket, water and a bowl of rice. Koizumi, slumped at the base of a tree, said, "*Arigato.*"

"*Kinishinaide*," replied Jeremy, using the Japanese word for "never mind," taking a seat on a branch ten feet beyond. Then in English he said, "So why the hell did the Zeros shoot you down?"

Koizumi stared at him, not saying a word.

"You understood everything Maria and I said. I can tell. So speak English. What's the story? And what is your name?"

"Koizumi Karamatsu. I am a lieutenant commander in the Japanese Imperial Navy. Why I was shot down is none of your business."

"Okay, a big secret, huh? Something fishy. Well, just to make things crystal clear, Maria is from the Philippines. She has reasons to hate Japanese."

"You are Japanese."

"I told you, I am American. I was a slave laborer for the Japanese military until the ship I was on was torpedoed. I am no fan of the Japanese military."

Koizumi said nothing, then sighed deeply.

"I was in Hawaii once, before the war," Koizumi began laboriously. "It was very pleasant, very indolent. I even met an American family and they treated me well. It was strange... one of them was a pilot, a fighter pilot in the United States Navy."

"Is that so?" replied Jeremy, relieved Koizumi seemed willing to talk. "I was a graduate student in Tokyo until the war began, but before that I was also in Hawaii. Honolulu, in fact," Jeremy said to keep the conversation going.

Again there was silence. "I saw Pearl Harbor," Koizumi finally said.

"Saw it, or bombed it?" Probably not the best way to learn more about this man, Jeremy thought.

Koizumi said nothing. Then Jeremy ventured, "I also knew an American fighter pilot. We became friends. I hope he is still alive." With a grin he said, "He spoke fluent

Japanese. His mother was from Japan. Damnedest thing; his father was from Russia. Can you beat that?"

"What?" Koizumi said, sitting up with a start. "This American pilot, what's his name?"

"Tad Kuchenkov. Sounds like something right out of Tolstoy or Dostoyevsky, doesn't it?"

Koizumi stared at Jeremy in the glow of the fire.

"And he was nuts over a Japanese girl. I think he wanted to marry her. She went back to Japan, and I visited her there when I was at the university. I don't imagine he ever saw her again." He then took a long look at Koizumi and said slowly, "I know you. You were in Oahu with Tad. My God, you are his brother!"

The silence was interminable, then Koizumi said, "I recognized you too. In fact, I did after you got me out of the plane."

"But you didn't say anything?"

"What should I have said? Hi, Jeremy, I'm Tad's brother, Japanese Imperial Navy. I just got flamed by a bunch of Zeros. So what's for lunch?"

"Okay, I get it. Do you think he's still alive?"

"I know he is. I saw him on an atoll this morning. He was flying cover for some Americans, had a hydraulic problem and had to land. We talked a bit. It didn't go too well."

"I can just imagine. Does he know you were shot down with some high-ranking Japanese aboard?"

"I don't think so."

"And the Americans? What were they doing on that atoll?"

Koizumi sighed and said, "It's of no importance. The Japanese they met with are all dead."

"And the Zero the Americans shot down, did that pilot know your mission?"

"I doubt it. The whole mission was secret. I had nothing to do with it except to fly the plane. And I'd rather not talk about it."

"Uh-huh. But that's why you can't go back to Japan."

When Koizumi didn't reply, Jeremy said, "That girl, the one that Tad is in love with, did you ever see her once the war began?"

"A number of times."

"Do you know where she is now? Is she still alive?"

"Perhaps. But I have no idea where she is."

Jeremy stood and said, "You'll be okay out here tonight. I'll fill Maria in on who you are and she might let you sleep in the compound."

"You take orders from her?" Koizumi said, picking the last grains of rice from his bowl.

Jeremy stopped and stared coldly at Koizumi. "Don't fuck with me, mister. We're not exactly friends. Maria and I work together to survive, and I like her. Mutual attraction has some nice benefits. But as for you, I would not cross her. As I said, she has reasons to hate Japanese."

"What about the Japanese kid in your little compound? Why is he so privileged?"

"Because he is a kid, not a soldier. He's on the right side of history. Maybe you should consider that."

Jeremy took a few steps toward the compound, turned and said, "Tomorrow we go back to your wrecked plane. I don't want another Zero pilot to see it, and we have to get rid of the bodies."

"I don't want to go," said Koizumi.

"That we met each other four years ago is of no consequence. Neither is the fact that you are Tad's brother. Until Maria and I say different, consider yourself a prisoner. So where we go, you go. We leave when the sun comes up."

Tired as he was, Koizumi could not sleep. From time to time he put a stick in the fire, listening to the sounds of the jungle below. It all seemed bizarre, surreal. Yesterday he was an aide to an admiral, respected and dutiful, an honored fighter pilot in the Imperial Japanese Navy. Now, his clothes tattered and blood-stained, he lay against a log, hoping that ants would not have him for a late night snack.

And what might his uncle be thinking this night? Perhaps the order to shoot down the plane had come from Tokyo, but it would be his uncle who had sent the fighters aloft. Would his uncle realize that he'd been coerced to fly the plane? Or would he revile him as complicit, too weak-minded to sabotage traitors?

The word "traitor" rankled in his mind. He was hardly a traitor, he told himself. He had not known the purpose of the five men; he had been given an order by a superior officer. But what was he now? A prisoner, Jeremy had said. It would not be difficult to disappear into the jungle, he reasoned. But how would he live and defend himself? He sighed again and resolved to make the best of it. He would not stoop to befriend Maria, but he might make things easier by getting along with Jeremy. And he would be compliant unless things became intolerable. And then who knows what he might have to do? Conversely, once he recovered his strength, other options might present themselves.

Before sleep overtook him, he remembered an envelope forwarded to Okinawa by a colleague in Naval Intelligence. It had been handed to him just before he left for Yontan field. The chaos of the morning and all that followed had prevented him from reading it. Now, reaching into a pocket he extracted its single sheet of paper and examined it in the fire light. He read the plaintive words and felt very sad.

The letter lay beside him when the sun rose. "It's time to go," said Jeremy as he, Maria and Hanabe emerged from the compound.

"Yes," said Koizumi, rising and starting down the trail without another word. *I will survive this war*, he vowed. And perhaps he would again see the lady who had apologized as a deferential woman should.

They were in a clearing near the base of the mountain when they came to an abrupt halt. In shallow water just beyond the lagoon lay a Japanese destroyer, its boats already ferrying more soldiers to the site of the wreck. The men were carefully examining the aircraft and carrying the corpses to the beach. There was quiet conversation between officers, wondering how Americans had found it and shot it down. It was a mystery—until a private found shell casings inside the aircraft. Once those were examined, the men fell silent. But the why hung in the air.

Then officers saw soldiers excitedly pointing toward Ishigaki Island, where great plumes of black smoke rose into the sky. Suddenly an American Hellcat flew over them and disappeared. Moments later, the shapes of four-engine bombers appeared. And with them were ten fighters, all bearing down on Iriomote Island.

Chapter 24
Iriomote Island
Late December, 1944

Jeremy, Maria, Hanabe and Koizumi watched the Japanese troops swarm over the crash site. If they were scouts enough to read the signs, they'd quickly realize that a survivor had left the plane. The inevitable search would be impossible to elude for long, Jeremy knew, and he gazed at Maria, seeing the same terrible realization in her eyes. Before, they had been ghosts; now they would be quarry. They turned their attention to the sound of approaching planes. Jeremy closely watched Koizumi, wondering if he would reveal their positions, but the pilot was as still as Hanabe. With a wave of her hand, Maria motioned for them to retreat to the safety of a hillock behind them.

"Get down," Jeremy hissed. Once they were under cover, they peered through the mangrove trees and high grasses. Two of the four bombers headed for the Japanese destroyer, which was had already retreated to open water and was attempting to turn and increase speed. Its anti-aircraft guns began spitting out hundreds of rounds, but they seemed to have little effect on the four-engine "Flying Fortresses," each carrying up to ten thousand pounds of bombs. At two-hundred miles per hour, the Flying Fortresses with their seventy-four-foot wingspans were much slower than the escorting fighters, but they bristled with fifty-caliber machine guns.

"Stay down!" repeated Jeremy, but Maria rose to her knees, staring at three small craft two miles off shore. They were in a loose formation but coming on very fast. She pointed excitedly. Jeremy pulled her down as two bombers peeled away to roar over the island, their shadows momentarily blocking out the sun.

"So big," she said, but the noise of their engines erased her words. Japanese soldiers watched with a mixture of curiosity and fear as the planes did a reconnaissance run over the site, then, gaining altitude, came back around.

The soldiers abandoned the wrecked Nakajima and sprinted for the shallow craft pulled up on the beach. The tide, high when they'd first arrived, had turned and now the boats rested nearly twenty feet from the water's edge. A number of soldiers began pushing boats toward the outgoing tide, but they scattered when five-hundred-pound bombs began detonating around them.

Burying their heads in the crooks of their arms, Jeremy, Maria, Koizumi and Hanabe felt the air sucked away as ground and swamp were blasted aloft and shrapnel whistled through the palms.

The screams and shouts of dozens of men, terrified and running, reminded Jeremy of an ant hill upon which heavy boots have trampled. He raised his head only to see bodies flung a hundred feet into the air, the fuselage of the Nakajima blasted into silvery fragments.

Smoke billowed and bits of debris cascaded down. Ten or fifteen of the survivors, many wounded, attempted to rise, only to see the Hellcats coming toward them at treetop level.

Their machine guns raked the sand and swamp: relentless doom for the fleeing men.

The planes departed. There were no longer screams, not even a plaintive moan; nothing remained of the Japanese platoon.

The four witnesses stood and looked toward the sea. Great geysers of foam bracketed the destroyer as it corkscrewed though the sea. The ship's guns were firing high at the bombers as torpedo boats approached at forty knots.

Finally, and all too late, the main batteries of the destroyer aimed salvo after salvo at the patrol torpedo boats. From their hillock, Jeremy saw two eruptions rack the destroyer. One set off a magazine, and the resulting series of explosions tore the ship apart. When the water subsided, there was nothing but debris in the water. The patrol boats slowed to a crawl and criss-crossed the area, searching for bodies to pull from the water.

Much later, the four of them mutely gazed at the blue expanse, once again placid, as if a sea monster, having devoured its prey, glided serenely on as if nothing of import had disturbed its day.

"All gone. They're all gone," Jeremy murmured.

The land between them and the shore was a landscape out of hell. Great swatches of ground had been burned and smoke still rose from scorched brush and ragged craters in the ground. It reminded Jeremy of pictures he had seen of No Man's Land at Verdun during the First World War.

"I have never seen such enormous planes," remarked Maria.

"Those are not very big," said Koizumi, looking past her to some far distant place. "Those are B-17s, smaller and slower than the planes bombing my country. You see the carnage here?" he said, turning to Maria. "The B-29s, nearly twice their size, have brought death and unbelievable pain to hundreds of thousands. This is nothing. Nothing!" he said, glaring at her bitterly. He turned away, then in a subdued voice, said, "We did what we thought was good for Japan. We were told that our efforts were good for all Asia. I took part in making that happen. Right or wrong, I cannot say, but now this is what we reap," he said, waving his hand toward the cratered landscape. "This is the stuff of nightmares."

Then, his eyes raking his audience, he said, "And it will go on until all my people are all dead. Until Japan is dead!"

He dropped to his knees and in a whisper said, "The Japanese military will probably not return. They have lost too much and the Americans are too near. Leave me to my thoughts. I will do no harm. I promise."

It was Maria who surprised him. She laid down her spear, rose and put a hand on his shoulder. "I cannot and will not forgive Japan, but there is nothing you should fear from me."

Koizumi looked at her and said, "That is a kindness I did not expect. *Domo arigato.*"

Jeremy said, "It's time we went down there. I want to gather any weapons that were not destroyed. We may have need for them, and I would not want them to fall into enemy hands."

"Is that really necessary?" asked Hanabe. "As he said, the Japanese army will not be coming back any time soon, and any weapons will be rusted and useless in a few weeks."

"I agree that it is necessary," said Koizumi, "but we must be careful. There could be unexploded ordnance. In Tokyo many people have been killed or maimed by munitions that exploded days later."

It was a grisly and laborious process, for they had to pick their way among the corpses. Most of the rifles were splintered, their barrels bent as if struck by lightning. But some were still serviceable, as was the ammunition scattered about the ravaged landscape. For nearly an hour they scoured the site.

Hanabe, with three rifles slung over one shoulder and a pocketful of grenades, approached a shiny object protruding from the swamp's muck. Curious, he walked toward it, the slime of the shallow water's edge making his footsteps uncertain. A conical nose stood six inches above the mud.

"Something here," he said, turning toward Jeremy, a hundred feet away. "I... I think it's a bomb."

"Get away from it!" shouted Koizumi.

As Hanabe turned, a scant foot from the metallic canister, his feet sank into the viscous mud. Working energetically, he freed one foot and strained to extract the other. Suddenly the ooze gave way and he pitched backward, the rifles falling from his arms.

The explosion was immense. Jeremy was hurled backwards into the swamp; Koizumi and Maria were knocked off their feet.

A stunned silence followed in which they rubbed their eyes and opened their mouths so that ear drums could once again register sound. Slowly they rose and looked to where Hanabe had been. He had vanished. Tentatively, Jeremy approached the spot, unable to believe that anything could be so thoroughly destructive. Not a fragment of the youth remained. It was as if he had never existed.

Maria put her hand to her mouth. "Oh my God. Oh my God."

Koizumi simply stared at the gaping hole in the ground. Then he said, "There could be more bombs. Some could be at the bottom of the swamp. I think we should leave. I am sorry for him. He was right, the weapons would have been rusted and useless in a few weeks."

Hours later, the three sat silent inside the low wall of the encampment. The sense of desolation, of the fragility of their lives and others, left them drained and empty.

"Do you believe in the spirits?" Koizumi finally asked.

"Ghosts, the Holy Spirit?" asked Maria. "I was instructed in catechism, but I am not much of a believer. But I once saw a ghost, a little girl. She stared at me and smiled. And then she vanished. I dream of her and sometimes ask her to return. She seemed very sweet. I think she was my sister."

When Jeremy said nothing, Koizumi said, "We Japanese believe in spirits. They are all around us. Our ancestors, the great warriors, everyone who ever was. I think that Hanabe is now a spirit. The soul, I believe, cannot be extinguished. He may be here right now with you, his friends. We should leave an offering tonight. Yes, here by this fire so that he knows he is cherished and not forgotten."

With that, he placed his partially eaten bowl of rice by the embers, put his hands together and whispered soft words.

The bowl was still there in the morning, but the rice was gone.

Chapter 25
Tokyo, Japan
Early March, 1945

Every day Sayuri and Kumi watched as hundreds of schoolchildren, mothers, and elderly men walked or boarded crowded trains to leave the city. Neighborhood associations attempted to find trucks to deliver people to the railroad stations or villages in the mountains.

One day Mrs. Onagi, an elderly member of the council, knocked on the door of the ikebana shop and was invited in by Sayuri. The woman bowed and looked about in dismay. "I used to come here before the war," she said, shaking her head. The woman's pantaloons were ill-fitting, but she held herself erect. Kumi offered her a cup of rationed tea. "Yes," she said, thankful for the warmth of the cup, the winter's cold not having yet passed. "I was a student of Sensei's when I was young. This little shop was a magical place. I loved its quiet serenity. It reminded me of old Japan, the pre-Meiji days my mother would tell me about."

She sighed deeply and said, "I would like to help make this shop be beautiful again once the war is over. But no one will ever take the place of Sensei."

Sayuri and Kumi nodded and Sayuri said, "We miss her very much. We pray for her spirit and like to think that it guides us."

"Time doesn't lessen our love for our teachers or our children." Then Mrs. Onagi said, "And that brings me to the reason I came today. The association has appealed to the government to help with the evacuations. A little money has come in, not nearly enough, of course. But there has been a lull in the bombing and I am told that much of the railroad track has been repaired. I thought of you this morning and hoped that you might accompany some of the orphans to a safe place. Many of them are young and terribly afraid. Your companionship and supervision would be very welcome."

"Kumi-san and I have considered going to the mountains, but there is something I must do first," said Sayuri. "We will likely be available in one or two weeks. I will be pleased to inform you as soon as I can."

Mrs. Onagi departed, saying that they should not delay too long; the American bombers could come back any day and the railroad was vulnerable.

It had snowed again; a soft powder covered much of the city's destruction. Sayuri took the train to the same military complex that she had visited months before. She had received no reply to the message she had left for Koizumi. She wondered if it had even been delivered. She remembered the disdain on the guard's face and how he had rebuked her for not wearing the requisite pantaloons. Angered by her lack of patriotism, he'd probably thrown the note into the first waste bin he encountered.

She had no idea of how long Koizumi would be away on his mission, but weeks had gone by and it was time to return, to try again. This was not what she wished for, but an honorable marriage would be a protection she could also extend to Kumi.

In quiet moments, Sayuri dreamed of the days before the war, those wondrous, distant days in Oahu. But that was all in the unreachable past. It would not do to put off any longer the decision she had made, and so again she approached the gate, this time wearing the *mompe* to avoid the disapproving glare.

She bowed twice before the same soldier. Brusquely he said, "You are back."

"*Hai,* honored soldier. I do not wish to intrude upon you, but I'm wondering if this letter and little gift might be given to Lieutenant Commander Koizumi Karamatsu. I do believe that he expects it. The officer did a favor for me," she quickly added, "and I must show my appreciation."

The guard noted that this time she wore the required pantaloons, and a hooded jacket as protection against flying splinters. Imperious but less disdainful, he turned his head a few degrees and called for a second guard.

Sayuri held the letter and gift out with two hands as was proper, the package wrapped in faded green silk cut from a kimono, one not worn since the start of the war.

"Open it," said the second guard.

"Of course," she said, bowing, "but you can see it weighs practically nothing. It's only poems I have written, though they are imperfect." The guard shook the small box then tugged on the ribbon. The silk blew away on a gust of wind as he opened the lid. Sayuri bolted for the scrap, snatching as it tumbled across the snow. She returned and offered it to the soldier. He inexpertly fitted it around the box, and Sayuri quickly retied the bow. Then she bowed again saying, "*Domo arigato.*"

The guard nodded, then carried the gifts into the building of Naval Intelligence.

He returned minutes later and said, "Wait here. Someone will see you."

"Who?" she asked, but he had turned away and resumed his post beside the secured door.

Snow began again and a sudden flurry caused her to look away. When she looked back she was surprised to see a high-ranking officer emerge from the building. The guards saluted smartly and she took several steps away, expecting the officer to summon a car and speed through the gate.

But there was no car, and the officer walked toward her. She bowed and was surprised when he did the same.

The first guard looked on, curious that an admiral would bow to the girl. Perhaps, he thought, he should have been more respectful towards her.

"You are Saito Sayuri, aren't you?" Admiral Karamatsu said formally, with a grandfatherly smile.

"*Hai*, Admiral. It is most gracious of you to see me. I did not wish to take you from your work and I certainly did not expect that..."

"This is not a good place to discuss matters of import. I know of a tea shop, probably the only one around for miles. Let us talk there. It isn't far."

He walked briskly despite the snow, holding his sheathed sword to his side. Had she been wearing a kimono she could never have kept up, but the *mompe* offered no hinderance.

He glanced over at her, smiled rather sadly and said, "It's just down this street, not far."

Soon they were seated at a small table in a dim alcove. With alacrity rarely seen in Tokyo, tea and four crackers were quickly placed on a low table. The waiter poured the hot green *ocha*, crisply bowed to the admiral, then disappeared.

Karamatsu indicated that she should indulge, then sipped from his cup and spoke.

"Lieutenant Karamatsu, my nephew, told me about your serenity, your aura of *shibumi*. He admired you. I should say, he loved you."

She leaned forward, hearing the words spoken in past tense. Her mind went numb. He must have sensed this, for in a very un-Japanese manner he took her hand and said, "I am sorry to tell you this. My nephew perished defending his country. He died fighting in the Pacific like a samurai and went down with his plane. I myself just got back from Okinawa. I shall go to the shrine and pray for his soul. You may accompany me, if you wish. He would be thankful for that."

Sayuri bowed her head and said, "Koizumi Karamatsu was a fine man and a great soldier, and his death truly saddens me. I shall deeply mourn his loss." She stared down at her hands. "I'm sure the Emperor is proud to have such fearless and dedicated warriors willing to give their lives for Japan. Yes, Excellency, I would be honored to accompany you to the shrine."

The admiral said, "I was hoping you would say that. And I should mention that he had received a letter before going on his last mission. I suspected that it was from you but, of course, I would not pry."

"Do you think he read it?" asked Sayuri, still reeling from the news of Koizumi's death.

"I honestly don't know. But if he did I'm sure it gave him solace and hope during his last hours."

A customer entered and the admiral withdrew his hand and sat straight. He tapped a finger on the table and said, "This is a sad time for so many of us. I greatly admired my nephew, having raised him since he was a very young child. I considered him more my son than my nephew."

They were both silent. Then the admiral tilted his head and in a very low voice said, "Sayuri-san, I know that there is, or at least was, another man in your life. Koizumi-san told me that you are in love with him. That man, as you well know, is an enemy of Japan, and it has been a long war. He may have died long ago fighting for his country, as Koizumi died for his. What I do know is that, had you married Koizumi-san, he would have been extremely proud. And he would want you to go on with your life and try to find happiness. Wherever that would take you."

The last sentence hung in the air, and Sayuri had no idea of how to reply.

"And he would council that you go somewhere safe," the admiral continued. "I regret that it is not safe here, and conditions will only get worse."

In a near whisper she said, "Admiral, will it be that bad?"

"I am in Naval Intelligence. All I can tell you is that the enemy has amassed great air and naval forces, and our defenses are extremely limited. If they choose to invade, they will suffer terrible casualties. We will fight to the very end, but many of us will perish. I implore you, go to the mountains."

That evening, Sayuri forced herself to confide in her friend. "I waited too long to tell him, Kumi-san," Sayuri said softly. "You were right all along."

"So in a sense, we are both widows," said Kumi.

Sayuri sat immobile, wondering why she felt as if a burden had been lifted from her.

In the following days, she contemplated what marriage to Koizumi might have been like. She would have done all she could to make him happy, and he would have reciprocated in the way expected of a person of a military mind. But it would, she knew, have been a labored existence. Each day, and each night, he would wonder with whom her real devotion lay. How often would she have had to lie when

Koizumi, her brave, noble husband, looked into her eyes? And how often would he wonder when, if ever, she would cease doing so?

She attended the shrine with Admiral Karamatsu, bowing deeply and offering her prayers. For those reverent, sacred minutes she gave homage to the man with whom her life had been so entwined, and so overshadowed. After the service she said goodbye to the admiral and thanked him for the courtesy he had shown her. She returned to the ikebana shop and, exhausted, fell asleep.

In the morning, she and Kumi began a trek to find food.

Peering into an unlit shop window, Kumi-san said, "Did I ever tell you that when you are disturbed, you talk in your sleep? Sometimes it's only a word or a phrase, but you repeat it over and over again."

"You should wake me if I disturb you," replied Sayuri, knitting her brows.

"Oh no, that must not be done. What one says in sleep is a window into the soul. It's what we cannot say or must not say in the light of day."

"Did I talk in my sleep last night?" asked Sayuri, worried that she had disturbed her friend, and worried more that her soul had spoken unmentionable things.

"You did, and it made me cry for you."

"What did I say?"

"You said, 'Where are you? Where are you?' And then you said his name." She paused.

"It was not Koizumi. It was the American."

Chapter 26
Tokyo, Japan
November 26, 1944

Two days before, twenty-four B-29s had destroyed the Nakajima aircraft company near Tokyo. The destruction was complete and there was great loss of life.

Several miles away, Sayuri and Kumi scraped dirt and dug shallow depressions that were supposed to provide refuge from flying debris. But the six-foot slots appeared like receptacles for coffins; tiring, they sat with their feet resting in a trench as they observed smoke rise from what had been one of the most important factories in Tokyo.

Without a word Sayuri rose, leaving her shovel where it lay, and took Kumi's hand, then walked to the low, blue-roofed building of the neighborhood association. They bowed to Mrs. Onagi, who bowed in turn.

"We are ready to go," said Kumi. She noted the little boxes of food, blankets and clothing to be given to children fleeing the city.

"And are you willing to assist the little children?" asked Mrs. Onagi.

"Yes, we will be happy to," replied Sayuri.

"That is very kind of you. I will have all the children assembled here in one hour. Twenty will be going today. There is one special child I will bring here myself. He lives a short distance away but doesn't fit in well with the other children."

The woman thought for a moment, then said, "If you have blankets I suggest you bring them. We only have enough for the children. The trains are full, so you will go by truck."

"Where will it take us?" asked Kumi-san.

"There is a village in Nagano Prefecture called Achi. It's in a mountain valley about half way between Tokyo and Kyoto. We've been told that the farmers will take the children in. They probably need the additional labor, since so many sons are away and there are refugees to feed. It will take most of the day to get there, so there is little time to lose."

Less than an hour later, twelve girls and seven boys dutifully stood in two lines, each carrying a blanket and a cardboard box of food. They all bowed to Sayuri and Kumi, who returned the courtesy.

"Miss Sayuri-san and Miss Kumi-san will accompany you to the village," said Mrs. Onagi. "They are very nice ladies, and I want you to obey them as you would your teachers. Is that understood?"

"*Hai,* Sensei," the children responded very seriously.

Sayuri smiled and one little girl giggled. An older boy gave her a stern look and she immediately looked down, a sad look on her face.

Sayuri's heart went out to the child, and she knelt to address them without seeming to tower over them. "On the way we will sing many songs. We will go into the mountains. You may even see deer and other animals, just like there used to be in the Tokyo zoo."

"Why aren't there any more bears or lions in the zoo?" asked a five-year-old boy.

Sayuri looked to Kumi, then to Mrs. Onagi.

The woman pursed her lips, about to rebuke the child for asking such a question, but Kumi replied, "The zoo keepers were afraid that some of the animals might be dangerous if they got out of the cages. So they were taken to a nice, safe place. They will come back a little later and you will see them again."

"Yes," said Sayuri, looking at Mrs. Onagi, who nodded, grateful that the answer pleased the child. It need not be mentioned that most of the large animals had been shot, in part because there had been nothing left to feed the carnivores, in part because keepers feared that falling bombs might release wild animals upon the city.

Mrs. Onagi was called from an adjoining room, and she motioned to Sayuri to join her. "I would like to speak with you without the other children hearing. Please wait here, I'll be right back."

She returned holding the hand of a six-year-old boy with curly blond hair and blue eyes. "This is Chad-ishi. He is the child I mentioned." Then, in a soft voice she said, "This lady is Miss Sayuri-san and she will take you to the village in the mountains. She will find a nice home for you, and there will be children to play with."

Sayuri stared at the little boy, then bowed. The boy also bowed, but lower, as he had been taught. Then Mrs. Onagi said, "Chad-ishi, please join the other children. Miss Sayuri-san will be with you very soon."

"You see why I said that he doesn't fit in. His mother was English and his father Japanese. He is Japanese in every way except for his gaijin appearance. It's for that reason the other children shun him."

"Are both his parents dead?" asked Sayuri.

"I'm afraid so. The boy had gone into a candy store without his mother when the American bombers came. His mother was looking for him when she was killed. I think he saw his mother in the street after she died. His father died on Guadalcanal. The child has nightmares and rarely speaks. He cries at night, and I'm worried that it might be difficult to find a home for him. He does look like our enemy, you know."

"I will care for him," said Sayuri. "He will remain with me as long as there is a war."

"You will?" said Mrs. Onagi, very surprised.

"Yes. I once knew a gaijin who, as a child, probably looked like Chad-ishi. I will be honored to care for him."

Chad-ishi sat beside Sayuri and Kumi as the ancient truck coughed and bounced over the potholed road. As promised, the two women led the children in songs, some patriotic, some very silly, until fatigue overcame them. The children had been told to eat only a portion of the rice, crackers and pumpkins in their food box, but some, after being hungry for weeks, ate every last grain of rice.

There seemed an interminable line of trucks, cars, bicycles and pedicabs on the road, all carrying evacuees. Wealthier people piled their precious belongings on the tops of cars; others, who trod along the road, carried suitcases or pushed carts. Still others, many of them leading small children, had nothing but the clothes they wore.

Kumi-san noticed how tightly Chad-ishi held onto Sayuri's hand. He did not look at the other children, nor did he take part in any of the singing. He seemed small for his age, but Sayuri thought that might be due to lack of food and exercise. He said not a single word on the entire trip, nor did he seem at all interested in the villages they passed, not even the sight of Mount Fuji far in the distance.

From time to time both Kumi and Sayuri asked him if he was thirsty or hungry, but he only gazed at them with his deep blue eyes and slowly shook his head. None of the other children attempted to speak or even look at him. It was as if he wasn't there.

It was quite late in the day when the truck rolled into the village of Achi in Nagano Prefecture of central Honshu. For centuries it had been a favorite stopping place for weary travelers, situated near Mount Kazakoshi.

Sayuri was amazed at how many refugees had crowded into the village. Children seemed to be everywhere, many carrying hoes and other farming implements. Very few had school books, and all seemed tired from long days in the fields.

A few elderly villagers helped the children alight from the truck. Several farmers examined the children and took thirteen of the healthiest. Sayuri glanced at a sheet of paper given to her by Mrs. Onagi, then led the remaining children two blocks to another group of houses. There, three families took in all the remaining children except Chad-ishi.

"What's this?" exclaimed the wife of a farmer as she bent her frail body and stared at the child. "He's not Japanese."

"He is, but his mother was British. I am taking care of him; he will not be a bother," replied Sayuri.

"No, he will not be a bother because I will not have a gaijin in my house," hissed the woman.

Holding his hands, Sayuri and Kumi stood in the unpaved road as the other children were led into their respective homes. Some people returning from the fields stopped and pointed at Chad-ishi, and a few made unpleasant comments.

"What should we do? We have visited the only people contacted by Mrs. Onagi," said Kumi.

"I don't know. I don't want to go back. There is nothing for us in Tokyo, but the truck isn't going any further."

"Where do you want to go?" asked a distinguished looking man, who stopped in front of the women.

"Someplace where we can survive," replied Sayuri. Then nodding toward Chad-ishi, she said, "Nobody will take us in."

The man, who wore heavy glasses, peered at the boy, then said, "My name is Mr. Temuchi. I have lived in this area for many years. Many people in these villages have had enough of refugees; others are either superstitious or unlearned. And many have lost sons and fathers in the war. This child seems like a nice boy. I have lost children of my own. But what I am about to suggest will not be a picnic. Are you willing to work?"

"Of course," replied Kumi. "We were digging safety trenches in Tokyo before we volunteered to bring children here. We can work in the fields for food and shelter."

The man nodded, then said, "I own land and house in Nagiso not far from here. It's not very big, but I will allow you to stay there if you tend my fields. I grow pumpkin, artichoke and squash. You will also take care of the house. My mother and her sister live there, but they are quite elderly. I am a plant supervisor in Nagoya and must hurry back. My neighbor has a truck and he's driving to Nagiso. He will show you the house. Government trucks come by to pick up the harvest. You must be ready for them. But there will be enough left over for the three of you."

The little boy cried during most of the night. "*Okasan, okasan,*" he repeated, but his mother would not come. Sayuri held him close and spoke soft words in his ears until he fell asleep. In the morning Kumi woke and tiptoed to the *irori,* the open hearth, where two women squatted in front of the fire. Mrs. Temuchi laboriously rose and bowed, saying that her elderly sister would have done so had she not been so weak. Kumi-san bowed to both and said, "We are grateful to be in your home and we will help in any way we can."

"Hayumi-san and I are pleased that you have come," said Mrs. Temuchi. She offered Kumi and Sayuri tea, then said, "How is the child? I heard him crying last night."

"He is very sad," said Sayuri. "I don't know if he will ever recover." She sipped her tea, then said, "It is gracious of you to allow him to stay here. He is not gaijin, but he has been rejected by almost everyone."

"A child is a child and is not responsible for his parentage. I see great sensitivity and love in the little boy. And I do believe that he will be happy one day."

"My sister is a seer," said Hayumi, speaking for the first time. "What she says is true." She gazed at Sayuri and said, "You are his new mother, even though he does not yet know it."

Mrs. Temuchi showed Sayuri and Kumi the rakes, shovels and hoes and where the furrows were to be dug for spring planting. Chad-ishi stood beside Sayuri, watching her scrape the hard soil. He picked up a hoe and tried to do the same. But he tired quickly and squatted down without saying a word. Sayuri smiled at him and said, "*Domo*, Chad-ishi, thank you for helping me. I found an artichoke and will cook it tonight. I think you will like it."

The boy gazed at her, but still no words came.

"It is peaceful here," said Kumi-san, resting on her rake. She raised her eyes and saw the gleam of three dozen bombers high above, their contrails leaving white scratches across the sky. A look of sadness came to her and she said, "I woke very early this morning and thought something was very strange. It took me a long time to understand what that was."

"And what was it?" asked Sayuri.

"It was the silence. No sirens, no bombs, nothing. It was unnerving. How could that be?"

"That is the sound of peace," said Sayuri, wondering whose last moments it would be when the bombers finished their day's work.

It was late in the afternoon, two weeks later, when Sayuri noticed Chad-ishi struggling to free a sweet potato from the ground. Turning to Sayuri he said, *"Okasan,* can you help me. I can't get it out."

"Let me help you," Sayuri replied, tousling the child's unruly hair.

"He called you 'mother'," whispered Kumi-san when the boy presented the sweet potato to Mrs. Temuchi.

"Yes," replied Sayuri, "as far as the world is concerned, he is my son."

Mrs. Temuchi, overhearing the exchange, looked at Sayuri and a smile came to her lips.

Nagiso
March 8, 1945

At Kumi's urging, Sayuri agreed to travel back to the city in honor of Armed Forces Day. Kumi hoped to see friends again, and as a war widow she was expected to honor the memory of her husband and his heroic sacrifice for Japan. Sayuri guessed that her friend was also eager to get away from the muddy village, the grueling farm work, and the care of orphans, if only for two days, and remember what life in the city had been before the war came home to them.

Chad-ishi clung to her, silent but terrified, and all her assurances that they would be back by the 3rd sunrise, with presents for all the children, failed to console him. Mrs.

Onagi had to gently pry Chad-ishi's fingers from Sayuri's *mompe* before she could follow Kumi-san.

Tokyo

March 9, 1945

The sound of drums and bugles announced the procession of regiments, all carrying rifles with fixed bayonets. Most onlookers remained silent, having witnessed countless parades for soldiers, most of whom never came home. There were a few who waved at the passing troops, but others stood with dull, tired looks on their faces. The war had drained the populace of enthusiasm for almost anything except food.

"Do you really want to stay here and watch this?" asked Sayuri.

"No, I think we should take the next train to the docks near the Sumida River. I know it's cold, but we might buy some fish, and there are vegetable vendors. What we buy will stay fresh for days, and the trains run past dark. When we return to Achi, we shall have a feast!"

The Sumida River flows through low-lying working class areas of Eastern Tokyo. There were numerous bars, but most were shuttered by government order. Intoxication was not prudent when long hours and commitment to production was mandatory. The train trundled past hundreds of workshops, all turning out materials essential for the war effort. Interspersed were tiny markets with poorly stocked shelves.

Kumi said wistfully, "They say that bombs never drop in the same place. Do you think that is so?"

"We know that is not true, Kumi-san. We remember what bombs did to Tokyo, and Mr. Temuchi told us that just two weeks ago many buildings were destroyed in another attack.

He said our valiant pilots saved the lives of many, for the bomber did not dare fly low enough to be engaged by our air defense. But bombs, just like snowflakes, fall where they fall."

It was twilight when they approached the docks. Dozens of small boats plied the river. Workmen in short baggy pants and wearing white bandanas scurried about packing fish or attending to stalls. Women carried loads suspended from poles balanced on their shoulders, as women had done for hundreds of years. Sayuri and Kumi stopped at a fishmonger's table. An ancient woman with teeth still blackened from pre-Meiji days took Sayuri's coins and wrapped three fish in newspaper. She put the coins in her stained apron, then lit a cigarette stub. A low, throbbing noise came from over the sea.

As the sound came closer, market-goers squinted in the gathering dusk, desperately hoping to see a flight of Zeros or Japanese bombers, perhaps a patriotic showing for Armed Forces Day. But the parade in Tokyo had ended hours earlier. Then the ground began to shake, and American B-29s appeared over the city. A deep, thunderous sound caused people to stop and stare upward. For a long moment nobody spoke. People looked at one another in fear.

A feeling of dread and helplessness coursed through Sayuri. She and Yumi stared as the last flickers of sunlight reflected off the fuselages of dozens, then scores, of B-29s, larger and sleeker than anything in the arsenal of the Rising Sun. They came in low, the blue stars on their wings and black numbers on their stabilizers dimly visible. The roar of their four engines shook the ground, and windows cracked. Dogs that would normally bark at strange objects slithered under anything they could.

Frantic shouts began to sweep through the crowds. "Run, run, run!" People began to dash about, visitors seeking shelter.

Among the American military it had been determined that napalm, a jellied petroleum, would be the most lethal agent against wooden buildings. The conflagration would be impossible to extinguish, and virtually all houses and shops in the districts of Koto and Chuo in the Sumida River region were constructed of wood. The other weapon chosen was white phosphorus, which burned with unimaginable intensity.

While some ran, others were paralyzed and simply stared at the enormous craft as strings of bombs rained down. Gradually, ignited buildings began to explode, like a terrible concert, while fireballs ripped through the air.

There had been a high wind all afternoon, and a conflagration of one block ignited a second. Entire communities vanished in flame. Wave after wave of bombers delivered terror as white phosphorus and napalm turned the sky into a cauldron of orange and red.

Metallic wails like thousands of banshees keened over the city. Terrified survivors ran; many caught fire, writhing as they fell. Others ran past them, disappearing down narrow streets and alleys in an effort to evade the maelstrom.

There were few anti-aircraft guns in the low-lying districts, and those that were manned fired high, a calculation General Curtis LeMay had taken into consideration during the planning of the raid. But some effects had not been foreseen or calculated. Turbulence from the explosions and superheated air rocked the bombers, propelling many of them hundreds of feet above the formations. But still they came on, almost three hundred in all.

Thousands, then hundreds of thousands of panicked citizens ran for the river as a cyclone of fire swirled ever higher. Roofs, people and animals were ripped up by swirling winds and fed the raging conflagration. Suffocating as the oxygen was burned away, thousands gasped and fell.

Swept up with the panicked, hysterical mob, Sayuri and Kumi were pushed toward the turbulent river, now glowing red with the reflection of fires. But the sanctuary of the river was illusory. People clawed over one another in their frenzy to escape the inferno bearing down upon them. Pleas and screams of men, women and children went unheeded; scorched and terrified people were pushed and shoved beneath the surface. Gasping for air, flailing about, some floated downstream while others, unable to swim, sank to the bottom.

Blackened corpses littered the river and terror continued to rain down from the darkening sky. A dozen Zeros rose to attack, but nearly all were shot down. The few B-29s that were fatally damaged added to the carnage as they fell, their bombs exploding upon impact.

It was with extreme difficulty that Sayuri and Kumi broke away from the multitude. Over the din of screams Kumi yelled, "We're not going into the water?"

"No, we must follow the river to the higher districts. Crowds are too dangerous! People in the river will be drowning."

Holding hands, they broke through stampeding crowds, finding shelter in alcoves yet unreached by the advancing flames. Darting from one alley to the next, they kept the river in sight, glistening red from blood and the fire's reflection.

Fifteen blocks further on the crowds began to lessen. A platoon of soldiers carrying medical supplies rushed past, and Sayuri wondered how so few could possibly help the thousands of people fleeing the flames, but it was wonderful and brave of them. Exhausted but too fearful to stop, the women watched wave after wave of bombers drop incendiaries only two miles away.

Sirens wailed. Blackened, unidentifiable bodies and parts of bodies floated down river or beached themselves wherever the eddies carried them.

A convoy of army trucks snaked down the narrow road, horns blaring, pushing people out of the way as they headed toward the immolated wards. A single truck carrying wounded up the hill stopped to let the others by, and Sayuri and Kumi were allowed to climb on board. After the convoy passed, the overladen vehicle continued on, depositing their burden at the first aid station they came to.

An unlit train was waiting at a railroad siding, the engineers anxious to be on their way. "It's going toward downtown Tokyo," said Kumi. She and Sayuri were pushed on board by the frantic mass behind them. Filled beyond capacity, the train lumbered down the tracks. Except for crying children, the passengers were silent. Thankful that they had escaped death, families held onto one another, praying that the train would not be the next target. Covered in ash and seared by embers, they exited the train as it pulled into the Tokyo station.

It took two more hours for Sayuri and Kumi to transfer to another train that eventually brought them within blocks of the ikebana shop. Exhausted, they collapsed on futons and tried to ignore the wailing of sirens that continued long after the bombers had flown back over the sea.

But Sayuri could not sleep. She was surrounded by the ghosts of the newly dead; dozens, hundreds, they swarmed about her, women, old men, children, piteously crying for help. She did not know how Kumi could sleep through the maelstrom of sundered spirits. "I will go to temple, I will say prayers for you, I shall make offerings," she promised over and over and over, her bowed head pressed to the floor. "I will offer prayers for you, I will offer prayers for you," she whispered through dry lips.

Gradually the moans and wails around her faded. She did not know if the ghosts had departed, or if she'd simply become too exhausted to hear them. In the silence, perhaps she could rest a while, before she and Kumi-san began the arduous journey back to Nagiso. Would the trains even be running? Suddenly she sat bolt upright. "The packages! I dropped our packages. We will be empty-handed when we return, and I promised gifts."

It was too much. Sayuri burst into tears. She wailed like a child, like a little girl standing beside a ruined building, her parents buried under the rubble.

Earlier that evening, a staff car had moved slowly through the streets of Tokyo after a meeting near the Sumida River where Admiral Uta, along with Itomo Karamatsu, had congratulated the captains of two submarines for sinking an American supply ship off Okinawa.

The Sumida River flowed through the low-lying working-class areas of Eastern Tokyo, not a particularly grand location for accolades, but the admiral had also wanted to inspect a local facility manufacturing a new naval gun.

Haggard workers made way for the car, and soldiers stiffly came to attention and saluted. Ota and Karamatsu returned the salutes.

Then, though the open windows of the slow moving car, they heard a low, throbbing sound in the west, from the direction of the sea.

A cold chill swept through Ota and Karamatsu, a feeling of sudden helplessness. The driver, a corporal, turned to Ota, his eyes wide with fright.

"Drive! Don't stop for anything, just drive," shouted the admiral, and slammed his hand onto the car's horn.

People bolted out of the way, but nearly a dozen were knocked down as the car accelerated. They were already far away before the crowd began to panic, before the bombs fell.

The fires continued to burn for days, and acrid smoke hung low over the city. Trapped by flame and smoke, over one hundred thousand died, bodies piled one atop another three and four feet high. Block after block had been turned into ash. Those who survived ventured back to where their homes and businesses had been, only to find charred debris. Old residents said that it reminded them of the earthquake and fire of 1923, when thousands died. But that had been a natural disaster, with no one to blame. This was man-made and might have been defended against. It had become evident that there was no defense. The city and likely the nation lay helpless. No one knew when another attack would come, but that attacks would come was certain.

In a room cut into solid rock deep beneath Mount Fuji, the Office of Naval Intelligence, as well as many other government and military sections, had been relocated in the wake of the renewed bombing. Many miles of caves had been hewn out, some for treasures captured by Japanese troops in areas of conquest, others for construction of advanced aircraft based on German design.

Both Admirals Uta and Karamatsu had been apprised of the Me 262, a two-engine jet that the Nazis had already sent to Japan. It flew one hundred miles an hour faster that any of the Allies' piston-driven fighters used in the Pacific. The Japanese military believed that, as kamikazes flown against American carriers, the amazing aircraft would prove invaluable, altering most favorably the course of the war.

Only the hum of a generator in an adjacent cubicle disturbed the silence as Uta poured drinks. He and Karamatsu, faces drawn and lined with fatigue, peered at a map. Uta drew a line from Pacific islands to Japan, then said, "Our men are still fighting on Iwo Jima. The Americans are being bloodied, but if they take it, Okinawa is next."

"I think both Iwo Jima and Okinawa will stiffen our resolve," said Karamatsu. "The inhabitants of Okinawa are Japanese."

"True," said Uta, "especially since they will want to prove their loyalty. They will sacrifice themselves to convince us that they're not second-class citizens. Regretfully, they have always been considered so."

"Will sentiments alone motivate them to die for Japan?"

"That and what the Kempeitai have told them to expect from the American Marines."

"And they believe it?" asked Karamatsu, lighting a cigarette.

"Why not? They are very frightened. They've been told that enemy soldiers eat babies and will rape every woman. Even suicide is nobler than surrender."

Karamatsu looked away and said, "Who wrote 'Truth is the first casualty of war'?"

"I don't know. But we are long past academic arguments of what is truth and what is not. I'll tell them that they'll dine with the Emperor if they fight for Japan."

Wisps of cigarette smoke hung ghostly around the bare electric bulbs.

"The new prime minister has silenced any talk of negotiating with the Allies," Uta said, finishing a third cup of saki.

"But I heard that the Vatican has been approached again," said Karamatsu.

Uta shook his head and said, "The Holy See can't do anything. They say that our demands and those of the Americans are too far apart, especially with the Allies' insistence on unconditional surrender."

"So, the attempt at negotiations by Prince Noributsu and the others would have ended in failure, regardless," said Karamatsu.

"It would have gone nowhere," replied Uta, refilling their saki cups.

Karamatsu pondered that a bit, then said, "What do you think would have happened if we had allowed that plane to return to Japan?"

"You are having a problem of conscience?" said Uta, lighting another cigarette.

"Perhaps we acted hastily. At the time it seemed quite urgent, since it appeared that the cabal might initiate something the government could not allow."

"There was that risk. We don't know what they might have proposed or how the Americans responded. Itomo-san, war is about death, sacrifice and mistakes. Was it a mistake? I don't think so. It's unfortunate that your nephew had to die, but how much longer do you think you or I will survive? A month? Three? A samurai went to sleep each night thinking of how he should die. I have been thinking about that, and maybe you should too."

That night, in one of the caves set aside for high-ranking officials, Admiral Itomo Karamatsu lay on his hard bunk and wondered if he should have misdirected the interceptors, or if he might have dissuaded Uta from his fateful decision. It would have only taken minutes to contact the Kempeitai and exonerate Koizumi. He might have tried to convince Uta that the cabal be interrogated. If nothing else, they would have known the American position. And Koizumi-san would have lived, perhaps even married the girl he had adored since childhood.

He sighed deeply and wondered what his sister, Kimi-san, would say if he could speak with her.

Much later that night, the specter of Koizumi began to haunt him. He could see the pilot staring into his eyes, his head slightly tilted as if asking a question. A question that Karamatsu knew he could never truthfully answer.

Chapter 27
The Northern Pacific
Mid-April, 1945

"It was your fault, and you should admit it," Jack Vestergaard was saying to Tad when Lee-Beauregard Smythe joined them at the railing to watch signals flash from ship to ship.

"The hell it was! I told you that you were doing it all wrong, but you were stubborn," said Tad with exasperation.

"What did you do? Is this worth listening to?" asked Smythe.

"Only if you want to hear how stupid Jack was," said Tad.

"I can't wait. The suspense is worse than the Hindenburg. And that blew up."

"So did Molly," said Jack.

"What! A woman blew up?"

"Not a woman. A cow," explained Tad.

"Oh. Then tell me more. I love explosions," said Lee-Beauregard.

"Go ahead, tell him," said Jack. "Personally, I get sick just thinking of poor Molly."

"Um," said Tad, suddenly feeling idiotic, two senior pilots recounting an event from twenty years ago. "Well, Jack and I were in a chemistry class at UCLA, and we accepted a challenge from the prof to find a new and natural energy source. We would get an 'A' if we could come up with one that was commercially viable. Since the alternatives were getting bad grades or studying hard for the final exam, we hit upon methane and looked about for a plentiful source."

"I got it already," said Smythe. "This is not going to be pretty."

"Not pretty," echoed Jack. "So Tad remembers that my pop has a cow with a severe gas problem. Major eruptions. People fled when Molly let loose."

"You exaggerate wildly," said Tad. "But I thought that if we could connect pipes and a storage container to hundreds of cows, well...."

"So our brilliant chemist here decides to put Miss Molly in my pop's barn and wait for the emission. To test the theory of combustibility, he places a candle to the rear of said source," iterated Jack.

"Uh-huh," said Smythe.

"Well, we went to the house to get a camera to document the results. When we got back—"

"I *told* you to prop the door open!" Tad interrupted.

"How was I supposed got know the wind would kick up and blow the door shut! Anyway, just as we got back with the camera, the barn blew up. Boom! The roof went to pieces, and so did Miss Molly. It was a real shame," said Jack.

"But the concept was sound," argued Tad. "Maybe we'll go into the methane business after the war. I know where we can get lots of cows."

"Idiots! I'm flying with idiots who want to blow up cows!" said Smythe. He was about to leave in disgust when he turned back and said, "The Marines are shit deep in unhappiness and we're flying ground support tomorrow. You better be bright-eyed and bushy-tailed, or I'm signing on to Andy's squadron. His bombs are not for cows."

The invasion of Okinawa, code named Operation Iceberg, had begun on April first. The island in the Ryuku Archipelago is sixty miles long and eight wide, and it lies between Taiwan and Japan's most southern island, Kyushu. Okinawa's capital, Naha, had been almost entirely obliterated before the invasion by American bombers. It was estimated that the island was defended by more than one hundred thousand Japanese troops and over fifteen thousand Okinawan volunteers.

An enormous armada of U.S., British, Australian, Canadian and New Zealand warships assembled to push the Pacific war further west.

The Allies were surprised that the landing went unopposed. Coming ashore, the American soldiers and Marines swept forward so quickly that their artillery and supplies had difficulty keeping up.

The island's two airfields, Yontan and Kadena, were quickly wrested from the Japanese. Marine fighters, gull-winged Chance Vought Corsairs as well as heavy bombers, had use of them as soon as the Army Engineers repaired bomb holes in the runways. Only days later, those same bombers were unloading their destructive power on Japanese cities in Kyushu, the first of the four Japanese home islands planned to be invaded after the fall of Okinawa.

At first, the resistance the Americans encountered consisted of poorly trained support personnel. From captured prisoners, interrogators learned that veteran Japanese troops were dug in on high ground near the town of Shuri. The Japanese had spent years digging multilevel interconnecting caves and tunnels through which they could move troops from one threatened location to another.

Within weeks the Americans had incarcerated thousands of civilian inhabitants, all loyal to the Emperor. But thousands of others still roamed the countryside, informing the Japanese military of the location of American troops.

The rapid, almost painless American advance came to an abrupt halt at General Ushijima's Shuri Line. Within days American casualties skyrocketed. Entire divisions were reduced to regiments and many of those cut down to battalions. The Americans repeatedly attacked the line only to be repelled with horrific casualties.

Japanese losses exceeded those of the Americans, but the attempt to take Okinawa resulted in some of the heaviest fighting of the Pacific war. Reinforcements were ordered in and slowly, inexorably, ground was taken, but always at a terrible cost. Corpses lying in pathways were trod upon until they became part of the mud. Men who slipped and slid down hillsides found themselves knee-deep in maggot-filled bodies, the stench making them vomit.

Marine and Navy fighters and bombers dropped their munitions on enemy positions, but while those in exposed positions fell to concentrated fire from artillery and naval batteries, the troops deep underground were unscathed.

It was a grim assembly of pilots the next morning. A commander, using a pointer, indicated the coordinates for what would be the day's most intense efforts. "We will provide suppressive fire," the officer told the fifty men of the first sortie. "Naval gunfire will be redirected while you are over the target areas, but Japanese anti-aircraft batteries have been beefed up, and you are vulnerable at low level. Fly in pairs, keep your eyes open and no unnecessary chatter. Army units are taking one hell of a shellacking, so be ready when they call for help. Questions?"

"What about kamikazes? asked Jack. "I've heard that they are going after troops as well as ships."

"That's right," said the commander. "We would like to think that the Japanese airfields in Kyushu have been rendered unusable and the aircraft destroyed, but they're pretty good about patching up the fields and hiding the Zeros. Two squadrons have been assigned to go after kamikazes. Your job is ground support. Look for large concentrations of enemy troops. Put your ordnance on the targets given to you by the forward air controllers. The Army needs all the help they can get."

As Tad's squadron approached the Shuri line, he could see Army shell fire and counter fire going off like a fireworks below, on the mountain slopes and in the valleys between. Great explosions from Army batteries slammed into Japanese bunkers and redoubts, while troops wielding flamethrowers inched their way up slopes, incinerating and asphyxiating the determined defenders.

The first sortie came in from the east with the morning sun. Helldiver bombers swooped down, wing over, towards a Japanese gun emplacement. Their bombs destroyed the position and set off its store of ammunition, which created a series of secondary explosions.

The flight reformed and tore over fields, shredding palm groves with the wind of their passage. The radios transmitted appeals from Army regiments making perilous but steady progress against the Shuri line.

An enormous explosion flared on Tad's port side and the concussion rocked his Hellcat. Two American tanks and a troop-carrying truck had been obliterated by a single shot, and Japanese troops were rolling a large-caliber Japanese gun back into a cave for reloading. By the size of the blast, Tad figured it for an eight-inch naval gun. The Japanese

Navy had been all but wiped out, so their heavy guns had been reassigned to ground defense, he realized.

Whether they received the order to or not, that gun had to be taken out. *Too bad we already expended our bombs and rockets. Fifty-calibers won't do the job,* he thought.

On their third pass Jack broke radio silence. "I see dozens of civilians and a squad of Japanese troops heading for the cliffs."

"I see them," said Smythe, as women carrying children ran toward a precipice a hundred feet above the sea.

"Let's see what's going on," said Tad.

"There's an anti-aircraft battery down there, too. Permission to take it out," said Jack, already turning his fighter.

"They're jumping! Some are being pushed by troops!" exclaimed Smythe, watching in horror as women, many of them with babies in their arms, hurled themselves off cliffs to the rocks below.

"No!" yelled Jack. "The kids are being thrown off! I'm going in!"

"Wait!" ordered Tad. "Well go in together. Just hold on."

"I see the bastards pushing the women. I'm going in."

As Tad peeled around, rifle fire peppered the Hellcats. Tad saw Jack's fifty-calibers rip through the Japanese squad and the gun crew, just as an anti-aircraft round tore into his fuselage. A thick plume of smoke gushed from the plane as it slewed toward the sea.

"I'm hit, I'm hit," said Jack, attempting to gain altitude. But the aircraft stalled at three hundred feet.

"Jump, goddamn it! Jump!" shouted Tad.

"No good, pal. I'm all shot up. Heading down."

"Jack, get out when you hit the water," Smythe yelled.

The Hellcat bellied into the water and flipped on its nose when it hit a wave. With its back broken, the Hellcat broke in two pieces, and the heavier nose section and the cockpit disappeared beneath the waves.

"I want this plane rearmed and refueled immediately!" Tad shouted to the chief of the deck crew.

"Sorry, sir, but this plane ain't going up. Your rudder and flaps look like Swiss cheese. You're lucky you made it back. I won't bet a wooden nickel you get off the deck with this. You got some righteous damage, mister."

Not waiting for another word, Tad ran down the deck to where Lee-Beauregard stood, watching the placement of a five hundred-pound bomb beneath the fuselage of his Hellcat.

"I'm going back up," said Tad.

"Your plane's being taken below. You just going to flap your arms and clear the deck? We're not scheduled to go up for twenty minutes. Squadron seven goes next."

"Fuck that," said Tad. He scanned the deck. Hellcats, Helldivers and Avengers were being pushed to the aft end of the deck; the fighters would take off first, then the dive bombers, and then the bigger, heavier Avengers, which would be carrying two thousand pounds of bombs instead of a torpedo.

A lieutenant junior grade was climbing onto the wing of a Hellcat when Tad grabbed him by the leg. "Get down! I'm taking your plane."

"Sir, you can't do that. I'm on the next launch."

I'm bumping you back a cycle. You fly when I get back, Lieutenant. That's an order."

"The skipper's not going to like this," muttered Smythe, but his own face was grim. Losing Jack felt like he'd just lost his own right arm. He climbed into the cockpit of the readied Hellcat. He and Tad started their engines, then waited for the taxi directors to motion them forward.

Suddenly, a voice came from the tower: "Kuchenko and Smythe, hold you position."

Too late. The deck officer had already touched the deck and thrust his arm toward the bow of the carrier, Tad's Hellcat was already airborne. Seconds later, Smyth's Hellcat lifted.

"If those two idiots make it back, I want them in my quarters under guard!" barked the squadron's commanding officer to a lieutenant. "You hear me?"

"I do, sir. They will be under guard."

"Remember where it was?" asked Smythe over the com.

"Near the Ishimmi Ridge. Just watch for one hell of an explosion; that will be the gun."

"You realize we'll be busted when this is over, don't you? Probably court-martialed," remarked Smythe. "That's if we survive."

"I really don't give a shit. They killed Jack, and they pushed women and children off cliffs. They're going to pay. And unless somebody takes out that gun, this entire mission goes FUBAR."

So here comes retribution, Smythe said to himself, *and we'll pay our own price.*

From four thousand feet the scene below was one of utter devastation. American tanks lay like broken and discarded toys, dozens of soldiers in contorted positions lying beside them. As they gazed down, a three-hundred-pound high explosive shell slammed into the reinforcements. Another tank exploded in flames. Dropping down, Tad could see parts of bodies flying through the air and broken bodies lying on the ground.

The Japanese gunners were rolling the naval piece into its cave as Tad leveled out. A fusillade of protective anti-aircraft gunfire flashed in his eyes as he sighted on the gun, now almost hidden from view.

"I've got a bomb; let me get the gun. You've got rockets, so take out the anti-aircraft gun," said Smythe.

Even through the fog of rage, Tad realized Smythe was right. The bomb stood a better chance of destroying the big gun, or at least burying it in a rockslide. And if he cleared out the anti-aircraft guns, fewer of his fellow pilots would end up like Jack.

"O.K., rolling in."

Forty minutes later, reeking of smoke, sweat, oil and aviation gas, the two of them stood stiffly at attention before their squadron CO. Two extremely sturdy armed Marine guards, their "escort", stood behind them. The CO's face was as red as the meatball on a Japanese Zero. Tad sensed he was not pleased.

"I don't give a good goddamn if you were going after Tojo himself! You two are grounded. You defied a *direct* order. Just who the hell do you think you are? Grounded? I should have you in irons, stripped down to J.G.s!"

Apoplectic, he glared at the two pilots, neither of whom looked particularly remorseful, nor intimidated.

"Told ya," muttered Smythe out of the side of his mouth.

"What? Told him what?" demanded the CO.

"Nothing, sir," said Lee-Beauregard Smythe, wondering how hard he should punch Tad when they were busted to junior grade lieutenants.

There was a knock on the door, and an enlisted man stuck his head in. "A message from fleet, sir. The admiral thought you should see it."

Scarcely acknowledging the sailor, their CO grabbed the clipboard and skimmed the page. Then he glanced up at the two men before him, re-read the message, slowly this time. He cleared his throat.

"I'm hard pissed; you've got to know that. You idiots pulled something not even an ensign would do. What you did compromised squadron discipline. It was unwarranted. Disgraceful. Understand?"

"Yes, sir. Unwarranted. Disgraceful, sir," said Smythe.

"Don't you dare mock me. I'll read this, but I'm still pissed, you got that?"

"We understand," said Tad, "You're pissed."

"Fleet forwarded this from the Army. Now I have to read this goddamn thing. 'I wish to commend the two carrier pilots for eliminating an enemy naval gun that had been terribly effective in its concentrated fire, resulting in the death of dozens of brave soldiers. Well done, Navy. Major General Andrew D. Bruce, US Army.'"

A long moment of silence followed, while the CO stared at the two pilots.

"We're going back to Pearl," he finally said, anger only partially dissipated. "This morning we had to shut down five of our eight boilers due to steam leaks and a fire. We're turning a one-eighty with our escorts, as soon as squadron seven lands. You two cool your heels. That is all I have to say. You are dismissed."

Subdued, the two pilots strode down the corridor, ignoring the stares of other pilots and support crew.

"I think the old man's still pissed," said Smythe.

"So am I." said Tad, darkly. "More pissed than you can ever imagine."

Chapter 28
Pearl Harbor, Hawaii
Mid-April, 1945

Lee-Beauregard Smythe and Tad found a vacant table in the back of the Officers' Club, a gaggle of newly minted ensigns having taken up space in front of the bar. They were too loud, too damn egotistical and too un-blooded, thought Smythe. Give them thirty minutes in the air against veteran pilots, or on a ship being targeted by an insane kamikaze, and they wouldn't be quite so ebullient.

"Full of themselves, aren't they?" remarked Tad, downing his second Scotch.

"Yeah, but we were too, when we got commissioned. At least we had time to learn how to fly. Some of those kids won't be coming back."

"A lot of it is luck," said Tad. "Fate. Nothing you can do about it. It's got your number or it doesn't. Sometimes it just doesn't matter how damn good you are."

The thought hung in the air like a lowering cloud.

"Jack flew directly into a firestorm. You told him to wait, but he wouldn't listen. Not that he was cocky, not like those kids over there. He saw something bad happening to people and it got to him. He tried to stop it. He was that way, Tad.

Heart of gold. But like you said: sometimes it just doesn't matter how good you are."

"That doesn't mean I'm ever forgiving the bastards who killed him. I never thought I would come to this, Smythe, but I hate them. I hate them and I just want to kill them all. And I'm pretty damn good at it."

"I think you are forgetting a few details, Tad-*ishi-san*."

"Stow that, Smythe."

Four army nurses entered and put coins in the jukebox. A Sinatra ballad came on and two of the ensigns, dressed in their immaculate whites, sauntered over to the women and turned on the charm. Amused, Smythe watched as the act played out. Deflated, the ensigns returned to the bar, hoping that no one senior had noticed.

Smythe chuckled and said, "Well, they tried. Took some guts, considering that brunette is a major and probably has a full colonel or a brigadier for a boyfriend." When Tad refused to acknowledge Smythe said, "You know, Tad, this may seem a bit out of place considering the fact that we're going to invade Japan, but wars do come to an end. Maybe the animosity lasts a long time, but sooner or later the fighting stops and enemies are no longer enemies."

"Tell that to the Russians. They've probably already lost fifteen million to the Germans. I seriously doubt they're ready to kiss and make up."

"Two, three generations from now, that will be ancient history and they'll probably be allies. People make up or forget. That's just the way it is. Now look at us. There was a time you were going to shoot me down; now we're friends, comrades in arms."

Tad muttered something inaudible.

"Right. And look at the Brits and Frenchies, Tad. At war since 1066 when William put an arrow through Harold's eye. Battle of Hastings, as I recall. But in '40 the Brits saved fifty thousand Frogs off the beach at Dunkirk. Just as a sign of sweetness and goodwill."

"You're on a roll, aren't you?" said Tad, looking away.

"And what about our own war of northern aggression?"

"You're referring to the Civil War?"

"That's the one. Yes. Very uncivil war, actually. Daaayyyuummmyaaaankees," he said, slurring the words together, "burned my grandpappy's barn, house, and stole his mules."

"'Damn Yankees' is two words."

"Is that so? The point I'm making is that Confederate General George Pickett of Gettysburg fame, his son wound up in the United States Army. Died fighting the Huks in the Philippines. General Joseph Wheeler fought for the South; then, at sixty-one, he rejoined the U.S. Army and fought alongside Teddy Roosevelt." Smythe chuckled and said, "Did you ever hear the story?"

"I have a feeling you're going to tell me."

"Sure am. He was given a regiment of Pennsylvania boys. Charging up San Juan Hill he said, 'Let's go, boys; we've got the Yankees on the run again.' Some lieutenant turned to him and said, 'But General, we *are* the Yankees!' So you see, we all sort of made up."

"And you think we're going to be eating sushi and drinking saki when this is over?" said Tad.

"Stranger things have been known to happen, boyo."

They stirred their drinks and tried to ignore the raucous ensigns, three weeks out of flight school.

Two of them, braver than the rest, left the bar and walked to Tad and Smythe's table. "Sirs," said a sandy-haired youth in starched whites, "I imagine you have seen a lot of this war. We've seen newsreels, sure, about how the Japs are yellow and running scared. But you have been there, and—"

"The word is 'Japanese' said Smythe. "Or Nipponese. They don't run and they're not scared. Tell your buddies to knock off the bravado; it just makes you look like idiots. But I'll tell you, son, the war you are going into is screaming, fucking terror. It's planes going down in flames and heads blown off, not to mention the bloody mush that was your best friend's face. There's nothing fun or glorious about it, Ensign. You get damn serious about what you're doing out there, or else write that 'goodbye' letter right now. So good luck. Now, having expressed my personal opinion, is there anything else you care to know?"

Ashen-faced, the two ensigns saluted and walked back to the bar. Five minutes later and far more subdued, they nodded silently to Smythe and Tad and walked quickly to the door.

Tad said nothing as Smythe downed his drink. "Think I was too hard on the kids?" asked Lee-Beauregard.

"Besides making them wish they never signed up, no. But you can't blame them. All they've seen or heard is propaganda. They'll be scared enough pretty soon."

"That makes me wonder, Tad. Something strange. I've never seen you scared. Do you ever get scared?"

"When flying? I don't have time to get scared. Do you?"

"More than I care to admit. Sure. A Zero on your six that you didn't even see, a friend burning up in his cockpit, screaming, unable to get out. That terrifies me. Gives me the willies. But don't you dare tell anybody."

"I won't. It's not uncommon."

"Maybe I shouldn't say this, but someday something is going to scare you, scare you shitless. I hope it doesn't happen but I suspect it will. Something so terrifying that you will scream in the night, just like I do. If that happens, remember I told you, and remember, you're not alone. When that happens, call me. Any time, any where. As long as I'm breathing, I've got your six."

A few days later, Kimi was tending her garden in the golden afternoon sunlight. Tad came out of the house, bringing his mother a glass of iced tea, and stopped to admire the calla lilies and the bright amaryllis blossoms, like red trumpets. She smiled and accepted the glass. Thirsty, she drank nearly all of it before telling Tad her news.

"Lee-Beauregard came by earlier when you were sleeping. It looks like he got a jeep from the motor pool. He said there's a dance at the USO club tonight, and a lot of nurses have been invited," said Kimi. "He said that he would be back for you around eight tonight."

"I hope you told him that I'm in no mood for a dance," said Tad, looking from the flowers to his mother. She seemed to have aged years in the last few months, he realized.

"I thought you might want to get out of the house. You've been cooped up here for almost a week. I think it would be good for you. Some nice girls are going. A few of them who work for me even asked about you."

"I'm not interested in any of the girls, Mom. You know that."

Kimi pruned weeds from the flower bed before answering. When she spoke, her voice was low. "Tad, I haven't seen what you have seen, but some of the men in the hospital talk about it. Not to me, of course; they don't want to alarm me, but I overhear them. I hear about the ceaseless killing, the tough Marines who cry when their buddies are killed. I hear about the slaughter and the drenching rain, the heat and the terror in the jungles and onboard the ships when the kamikaze come at them. We nurses try to comfort the dying and give strength to the boys who will never be whole again. Many of the men want to go back, want to kill to avenge the loss of their buddies. I know that it is hard, but it's important not to crawl into that dark hole of loathing. Talking to the girls, socializing, that might take your mind off it all."

"You know the only girl I care to be with. And it would not be fair to make friends or romance one of the nurses only to tell her that I will never see her again."

"This is wartime, Tad. They know you might never see them again. God forbid, I may never see you again, but this funk is no good. Go out, enjoy yourself."

She stopped and looked toward the harbor. "So much has happened since December forty-one. The whole world has changed, and so have we all. I have not seen Alexei in almost five years. I don't even know if he is still alive. I just pray that he is. I miss him so badly."

"And I miss Sayuri. But even if I could find her, I don't know if...."

His voice trailed off and Kimi said, "If you can keep from hating? If you can have compassion? I can't answer that for you, Tad. I hope you can someday, and I do hope that Sayuri is still there for you when this is all over. But I've seen the newsreels, the firestorms over Tokyo. And we all know the military is planning a full scale invasion of Japan soon."

"She might live through it," said Tad, without much conviction.

"Perhaps, but I want you to go with Lee-Beauregard tonight. I will be working late, and I don't think you should be alone. And there's a very pretty nurse who really wants to meet you."

* * *

The blaring music of the swing band made it nearly impossible to talk. Sailors, soldiers, officers and enlisted men swung ladies around, or held them tight in the densely crowded hall. Walking past the bar, Smythe craned his neck, looking for the nurse he'd met the day before.

"There she is," he said to Tad, who was wishing he were anywhere but here.

"I'm going to ask her to dance. She said that she has a friend, a girl who works with your mom."

"I really don't want to meet her, Lee. Just go dance; I'll be at the bar."

"Suit yourself," said Smythe. He found the nurse, and a few seconds later was doing the jitterbug with her.

Tad ordered a drink and turned away from the swirl of closely packed dancers. Three more dances followed; men and their girlfriends sallied in and out of the club. He felt a tap on the shoulder, and turned to see an attractive blonde standing beside Lee-Beauregard.

"This is Caroline; she's the nurse who works with your mom, Tad. And this other beauty, who is all mine, is Sandy."

Caroline held her hand out and Tad shook it briefly, a fleeting smile on his lips. The lady, some ten years younger than Tad, looked at him and said, "I know that look. I think you need some company and a little fun. Do you dance?"

"No; I mean, I'm honored that you would want to meet me, but I'm not good company. I don't want to disappoint."

"Hey, Commander," said Sandy, "she's not asking you to marry her. At least not right away."

The girls laughed.

"Okay," said Smythe, "Let's all take a walk. It's too hard to talk in here."

Sandy put her arm through Smythe's, and they headed for the door. Tad followed, but did not offer his arm to Caroline.

Lee-Beauregard started up a conversation about how great it was to be back at Pearl after nearly two years, and to be able to speak with a woman again.

"So, Tad," said Caroline, tilting her head, "your mom, who I think is the best nurse in the entire hospital, sings your praises. But she alluded to the fact that you might have a girlfriend. Do you?"

"Sort of. I mean, yes, I do."

"That's a bit vague. I don't take you as a vague person. Fighter pilots are usually very specific, focused."

"You have to forgive me. I'm a little..."

"Conflicted," said Smythe. "But I think he'll get over it. Right, Tad?"

"So, about your 'sorta' girlfriend," persisted Caroline, now very curious, "is she here in Hawaii, on Oahu?"

"No, though I met her here in forty-one."

"And you haven't seen her since?"

"Unfortunately, no. She is not here."

"Stateside?"

Tad shook his head and said, "I really don't think you want to know, and again, forgive me. I don't want to upset you. I think you are a fine lady, but this just isn't going to work."

"How can you be so sure? Any girl who leaves a guy like you alone for four years obviously isn't very serious." Caroline had a half-teasing, half-hopeful look on her face, and she pressed herself against his arm.

"Okay, if you really want to know. She's in Japan. The last I heard, she still lives in Tokyo," said Tad.

"She is Japanese? You're a pilot in the United States Navy in love with a Japanese girl?" exclaimed Sandy with a horrified glare. "I can't believe it," she said, looking at Tad, then Caroline.

Then, turning to Lee-Beauregard, she shot, "And you, mister, you knew all about it and set Caroline up with a..." she stammered, hunting for the right word. "A traitor. That's what he is! A traitor! Does the Navy, the F.B.I. know about this?"

Taking Caroline's arm she said, "Oh no, that sailor is absolutely right, this isn't going to work. We're out of here!"

Caroline glanced back at Tad as Sandy tugged her toward the USO. Tad watched them go, turned and walked away.

Smythe, after calling to the girls and trying to make hasty amends, caught up to Tad, grabbed him by the arm and hauled him into an alley.

"What the hell! You completely fucked up the evening. You didn't have to tell her any of that. I'm surprised that you didn't throw in the fact that your brother is a fighter pilot in the Japanese Imperial Navy!"

When Tad didn't reply, Smythe went on glumly, "Those girls were hot. They were practically asking for it. I don't know about you, but I haven't gotten laid in two years. Now they're going back into the USO, and do you know what they're going to tell their friends? They'll say that the son of the head nurse has a girlfriend in Japan and I'm in his squadron. I can't go back in there, and neither can you."

"I have no intention of going in there."

"Well, that's just ducky. I'm not sure what I'm going to do now, but whatever it is, it won't be with you. There's a cab; I suggest you take it and think really hard about your screwed up life. And one more thing, boyo, if I think you're a liability to me, yourself or the squadron, I'm thinking of going to the XO and have you grounded for the rest of this goddamn war! Now go home where you won't do any more damage."

Tad did just that. Once inside, he turned off the living room light and sank into the worn, padded chair that faced the radio, a four-foot piece of mahogany furniture his mother prized. A music station was playing, but boogie-woogie was the last thing he cared to hear. Tad rose and turned it off, then rotated the chair so it faced the wall. His depression grew deeper. Perhaps it was the drinks, the built-up fatigue of years, of hearing the klaxon blare and "Pilots to the ready room. Operations commence at 0500 hours," but despair settled upon him like a smothering pall.

He had told Lee-Beauregard the truth; he didn't have nightmares, but now he plunged into a waking dream of sucking horror. He was a lone pilot, staring down as great black wings fluttered, rose, and fell about him. His gargantuan, demonic plane ripped through roiling clouds with a sound of shrieking metal.

He was the bringer of death. He would rage and consume the enemy in a savage gluttony of killing. He felt a mindless glee at the prospect as he armed the bombs. Now he was laughing hysterically as his hands frantically worked the huge levers. He peered down into terrified, pleading faces that stared up at the thing that screamed downward, announcing the end of their world. Hate and vengeance seared his soul, his very being. His hands pushed a lever and the bomb bay doors opened. He shoved another lever forward, and the cylinders of apocalypse plummeted into the night.

Jack's face was suddenly before him, imploring him to stop, his ghostly hands frantically trying to intercept the bombs, his arms spreading out in a vain effort to shield the populace, but Tad would not hear, dared not hear.

The face of his friend vanished; another morphed into view, serene, beautiful beyond all measure. A smiling girl, long black hair floating about her face. A calm tenderness surrounded her, a sense of acceptance for what could not be changed. Raising her hands, she called his name and slowly shook her head. Tears came to her eyes and the words, "No, please no," issued from her lips.

Terrified at what he had done, he pulled back the levers with all his might, but it was far, far too late. The immolation consumed her and all those about her. The pleading face turned into a charred skull as the world became a maelstrom of fire.

"Sayuri! Sayuri!" Tad shouted, waking from his nightmare. Shaking, drenched in sweat and oblivious of his surroundings, he bolted upright from the chair—and slammed headfirst into the wall.

A cool compress was on his forehead, and his head throbbed. He squinted in the morning light and realized he was lying on the chaise lounge in the backyard of his mother's house amid birds of paradise and a coconut palm.

"I want to see your forehead again," said Kimi, removing the compress to examine the reddish-purple lump. "You might have a concussion; I think you should see the doctor."

Tad tried shaking his head, but that increased the pain. "I'll be okay. It's just a swelling. It'll be down by tomorrow."

His mother looked at him compassionately and said, "What happened, Tad? I found you in the recliner when I came home this morning. You were asleep, but blood was clotted on your head, and there is a hole in the wall."

He was silent for a moment, then said, "I had a bad dream. I guess I forgot where I was and tried to run."

"Run? From what? Or... who, Tad?"

"From..." Again he stopped, and took hold of her hand. "I was trying to run. I was running from myself. I saw her, Mother; I saw Sayuri. She was beautiful, and I am so ashamed. I dropped a bomb and..."

"It was just a nightmare, Tad. We all get them. I do every time I think of what might be happening to Alexei. But somehow, I think Sayuri-san will live. I really do."

"I doubt it. Tokyo is a smoldering ruin. Hundreds of thousands have died. Whatever, whoever was there, is gone."

Tad's despair rendered Kimi silent. She sighed and began to walk away, then said, "Caroline saw me before I left the hospital this morning. She was really embarrassed. She said she had no right to condemn you, that people can't help who they fall in love with. And she said that she and Sandy both want to come by to apologize for what they said last night."

"They don't owe me an apology, and I'd rather they not come by. Please tell them that I have no enmity toward them. It's I who should apologize. I was very angry and my world was very dark."

"And now?"

"I don't know, Mother. I really don't know."

* * *

"Is this idiot really asleep, or doesn't he want to talk to me?" a familiar voice drawled.

"You are addressing your squadron leader, I'll have you know," said Tad, opening one eye.

"That seriously depends on your state of mind. And the state of your head, which looks like it might be scrambled, if the inside matches the outside. What *is* your state of mind, if I might ask?" said Smythe, adjusting his sunglasses.

"Fine; just fine."

"So you say. I guess you're going to tell me that you fell down the stairs and propelled your head right through the wall. But this house has no second floor, boyo. Were you trying to commit suicide or room alteration?"

"Neither. I had a bad dream."

"Scared shitless, I would say. I vaguely remember something I said about that. Maybe it's a catharsis. Happens to a lot of people when they see what my grandpappy saw during the war of northern aggression. He called it the elephant. Something about Hannibal and the Romans. Yep, I think you saw the elephant."

Tad looked away and remained silent for an interminable moment. Then he said, "Well, did you get laid last night?"

"No, I didn't, thank you. I did go back in there, but the feeling was gone. Besides, the girls all ignored me, just scuttled away as if I carried the plague. I found a bar, had a few drinks and drove back to the BOQ."

"I'm sorry," said Tad. "I screwed up."

"No shit. Well, I pulled out my little black book, made a few calls, and I have a date tonight. And no, you won't be within five miles of me."

"That's not a problem. I'm thinking of going back to the ship."

"Why? We're not heading out for another three days. Relax, walk on the beach, have a few beers. And besides, you want that swelling to go down. I don't want to have to explain that I pushed you down the stairs of a one-story house."

Tad grinned, then said, "The beers do sound good. And I hope you have better luck tonight."

"All the signs look promising. A hero's welcome, a hero's send off." Smythe's grin faded. "This is going to be the big one. Kyushu, Japan. There is a betting pool in the mess for how the operation will be named, with suggestions like Operation Retribution and Operation Eclipse — because the Nips call their country 'The Land of the Rising Sun', see? Another idea is Operation Downfall." His lips twisted. "That one sounds as if someone consulted a Greek oracle. *If you attack, a great nation will fall.*' Yeah, a lot of people on both sides are going to die."

"I think a lot of people are scared."

"Maybe it's good to be scared. It means we're human."

"But are we?" asked Tad reflecting on the past night. "I am scared. More scared than ever before."

"So am I, boyo. It's going to be hell. We'll have to take Japan inch by bloody inch, and it won't just be Japanese blood soaking into the ground and turning the tide red."

"No," said Tad, thinking, *But once it's shed, there's no way to tell the difference.*

Chapter 29
Germany, West of Oder River
Mid-April, 1945

The shrapnel wounds had healed sufficiently for Alexei to rejoin the infantry under the command of Marshall Ivan Konev, already engaged in the battle for Berlin. The field hospital was ten miles from the city, and with no organized transportation available, he began walking. Hundreds of vehicles passed him, sending up plumes of dust and noxious fumes, some of them carrying men and munitions to the front, others transporting wounded soldiers to the tents he'd left behind. Tiring, he finally flagged down a small American Ford truck. After a few pointed questions, he was hauled aboard. Two swarthy soldiers, one with missing teeth and the other with a broken nose, occupied the cab, while three others sat sullenly in the open bed, their unsmiling eyes on Alexei and the medals he wore on his chest. Half hidden by a tarpaulin were a number of heavy sacks. The soldiers eyed them, then gave Alexei a dangerous look.

"It is good to have a medaled soldier with us, very convincing," said the man next to the driver, then added something else. He spoke Mongolian, of which Alexei understood very little.

The truck joined a column of vehicles snaking its way toward Berlin. Except for the wounded, most Soviets on the road appeared jovial, triumphant and vengeful. After the loss of over twenty million Soviet soldiers and civilians, their final objective was in sight. But the men on the truck did not smile, nor did they seem excited about the conquest of German's capital. Their few sentences, and the looks they exchanged, seemed conspiratorial.

Alexei was amazed that he still lived. He had hoped, after being wounded and receiving the vaunted Order of Glory and the Order of Bogdan Khmelnitsky First Class, that he would be transferred back to Leningrad, liberated in January of 1944, and allowed at last to return home. But he had been ordered back to the front.

"You are an officer and a veteran. We need that, an inspiration for the young men. And you will be able to say, as an old man, 'I helped defeat the Fascists and conquer Berlin," said the colonel.

"Yes sir, but I am already an old man," replied Alexei.

"True, but you have not yet conquered Berlin."

Fearing horrific retribution for their atrocities in Russia, three hundred thousand German troops, all those available for the city's defense, fully intended to repel the Soviet hordes facing them. Hitler had ordered his Ninth and Twelfth armies, along with aging citizens and Nazi youth brigades, to defend the city to the last man. To strengthen the defenders' resolve, evacuation of civilians was denied; instead, they helplessly awaited their fate at the hands of two and a half million Soviet veterans, six thousand tanks, forty thousand artillery pieces and seven thousand aircraft. The Germans had only twelve hundred aircraft, and far fewer tanks.

By mid-April, two Russian army groups encircled the city, cutting off all escape. On Hitler's birthday, April twentieth, Marshal Georgy Zhukov aimed his artillery at the center of Berlin with devastating effect.

Heavy projectiles along with shrieking Katyusha rockets fell among the terrified populace. The war that Hitler had unleashed upon Europe had returned home.

It was dusk when the truck driver turned off the autobahn onto a two-lane road that skirted a forest and deserted houses. He increased the speed, rounding one curve after another. Alarmed, Alexei gripped one of the truck's sacks, while the soldiers beat on the rear window of the Ford.

The driver ignored the protestations and tore around a blind curve. A half-dozen men stood in the roadway beside a military truck. The driver slammed on the brakes, but the distance was too short and he plowed into the troops and the lorry. The collision threw the driver and his shotgun passenger headfirst against the windshield, and launched Alexei and the others into the trees lining the road.

Screams and appeals for help came from the stricken military vehicle, and five soldiers lay dead or dying on the dirt road. One of the men from the Ford, only slightly dazed, rose and started to run into the forest, but three rounds from an enraged lieutenant left him crumpled before he had gone five yards.

Alexei and the other two survivors lay stunned, surrounded by a dozen soldiers, submachine guns pointed at them. At a barked order all three were dragged into a shell-pocked building and thrown against a wall. As Alexei's head cleared, he heard an argument in an adjoining room, but his attention focused on the soldier next to him.

His shirt and jacket had been ripped open, revealing a tattoo emblazoned on his chest. The soldier, a private, attempted to cover it, but a sergeant saw it and tore the shirt away.

"What's this?" scowled the sergeant. He peered at the ink work: a menacing eagle with sharp talons.

"Tattoos?" asked the lieutenant as he entered, holstering his sidearm.

"This marks him as a member of the St. Petersburg gang, *Vory v Zakone*, all criminals. The tattoo shows allegiance to the thieves' code. Special language, bribes, murder. I wonder where they were going in such a hurry," said the sergeant.

"Check the other one," said the lieutenant.

"I am a loyal Soviet soldier," protested the corporal, but he unbuttoned his tunic, exposing tattooed stars on his shoulders, signifying exalted standing in the *Bratva,* the extensive underworld of thugs.

"I want to see your knees," barked the sergeant. Dutifully, the man lifted his trousers, and stars were displayed.

"A criminal gang sign, it means that he won't kneel before anyone," the sergeant said.

"Is that so?" said the lieutenant. "We shall see."

The corporal clenched his fist and said, "The *Bratva* has always defied authority, but we volunteered to fight in this war, Comrade Lieutenant. We didn't have to, we could have stayed in the shadows as we always have. But we didn't. We have fought the Nazi bastards since forty-one. We should be honored for our patriotism."

"Everybody is required to defeat the Fascists. I think you took that road to avoid our patrols. In fact, I think you were going someplace other than the front," said the lieutenant. "Those sacks in the truck are filled with jewelry, silver plate and gold candlesticks. Black market contraband, all stolen. You were heading west, toward the American lines. In other words, you were deserting. We shoot deserters."

The private stared at the lieutenant and said, "You are NKVD, aren't you, Excellency?"

"Yes, everyone here is state security. How fortunate you found us, Comrade. And 'Excellency' won't do you any good. My father was a landless peasant, not some fucking aristocrat."

The sergeant then stared down at Alexei, still slumped against the wall. "And just who are you?" he asked, peering at the medals on Alexei's jacket. Like all Soviet troops, he was ordered to wear his medals when not in combat.

"Lieutenant Alexei Kuchenkov. I was released from the hospital and needed a ride. Unfortunately, I got on the wrong truck. I am assigned to the Eighth Guards Army under Marshall Zhukov on the southern front. I have orders, Sergeant."

The sergeant stuck out his hand and Alexei pulled the document from an inside pocket. The noncom looked them over, then handed them to the lieutenant. "Lieutenant Rishka, I think he's telling the truth," said the sergeant.

"Help him up and let him sit in the chair. We'll get him on his way," said the lieutenant.

The voices from the adjoining room got suddenly louder, and everyone stopped to listen. A voice of authority shouted, "That is none of your concern, Major. The whole war has been an atrocity and a thousand or ten thousand more will not matter. It will not even make the history books."

"But they are soldiers of the Directorate. They are your men. I was there; I saw it happen with my own eyes. Surely you will hold them to account. It is a crime, Comrade Colonel," responded a woman's tense voice.

"And you want me to do what? Go to the front and lecture the men? So they raped the women. They are German, Nazi women. They knew what their men were doing to our people in Russia, and do you think they protested? Did they say that it would be a blemish on the honor of the Third Reich? No, they deserve whatever they get. Even Comrade Stalin said that the men should have some fun with them. Yes, Comrade Stalin's exact words. Do you know how many Russian women were raped by the Nazi bastards? My sister in the Ukraine was. So her daughter, and she was only twelve. She died giving birth! Don't get sentimental about this, Comrade. We have a job to do, a very important job, and you know exactly what that is. Now you leave my office and get to Berlin."

The major left the cramped office and the colonel leaned out and said, "Do what I ordered and report back with all the materials. And do it quickly. I must inform Comrade Stalin personally."

Then seeing the men lying against the wall and the one in the chair, the colonel said, "What's going on?"

"A bad accident, sir. Some of our men are dead. Those two, the ones sitting down, should be executed but I will await your order. This lieutenant is a true soldier. He has orders to the front. I suggest that we allow him to leave.

"I am going to Berlin; the lieutenant could drive me there if he is able," said the major, glancing at Alexei.

"I'll allow it," replied the colonel.

"Sir, I need my weapon," said Alexei, coming to his feet.

"Corporal, get a papasha to the lieutenant. Make sure it's in working condition."

The corporal went outside and the colonel said, "Major, I'll send Lieutenant Rishka and a squad to accompany you in a truck. I order you not to engage in the fighting. Your mission is too important."

"Can you drive?" asked the woman as they approached a jeep.

"Certainly, Comrade Major." Alexei had to force his voice to stay calm.

"Good. We will talk later, away from here." The corporal returned and silently handed Alexei a PPsh-41 submachine gun.

Alexei started the jeep. They entered the roadway and followed a convoy of trucks, all towing heavy artillery.

Six miles outside the city the convoy was halted to allow the crossing of several tank brigades. At least a half dozen infantry troops hitched a ride on each T-34 tank as the vehicles clattered over the road before churning up fields beyond.

"You recognized me, didn't you?" Alexei asked quietly, as they waited for the tank columns to pass.

"Of course, I did, but I dared not show that I knew you. They would ask questions, and there would be complications. The NKVD lives on suspicion," said Major Tatiana Shushkin.

"And I have learned not to claim acquaintance with anyone who does not acknowledge me first. I did not think it would be a good idea to say, 'The Major can vouch for me. We were revolutionaries together before the Glorious Revolution started. She saved my life four years ago, when your Comrades wanted to execute me for desertion.' The colonel had already decided not to kill me; why give him any reason to reconsider?"

Alexei looked at the woman he had first seen so many years ago in St. Petersburg, half-dozen years before the 1904 war with Japan. She had been slender, pretty, and terribly intense, with eyes impatient for revolution. Now she was drawn and wary. She wore her military tunic with its major's NKVD badge and a red star on her cap and shoulder boards, an assertion of her authority in a male-dominated force. And, thought Alexei, her face had become lined from having seen too much terror, perhaps some of her own causing.

"Are you worried about your mission in Berlin?" Alexei asked, as the interminable line of tanks finally disappeared into the gloom.

"No, I'm worried about Rishka, the one behind us, and Sheplov, the colonel."

"The one you were arguing with?"

Tatiana nodded and said, "I was stupid, protesting the rape of German girls. He would not care, would rape them himself if he could. That's not to mean that I don't despise the Nazis. I have seen what they have done. I want every one of them butchered. But little girls, innocent girls..."

She shook her head and said, "This is not the way it should be. I spent my whole life believing in something different, Alexei. A worker's paradise. But I have seen the purges, the assassinations in Lubyanka and other prisons. I have seen the massacres in the Ukraine. And I have seen the rapes of young girls, by our own men. That is anathema. We must win this war, but there is a stain, a terrible stain."

Then she looked away and said, "I have seen too many die. And yes, to answer the question you have not yet asked, I sent men to their death, as a good soldier of Comrade Stalin. And now people are plotting against me. I know that; I can sense it. Now I am the one who must look over my shoulder and keep my pistol cocked at night."

"I heard part of your argument with the colonel," said Alexei. "Is he the one you fear?"

"The man hates me, despises me, as he does most women. He has been looking for a chance to accuse me of disloyalty, anti-socialism. I would be in the Gulag if it was up to him. And the lieutenant, the one who shoots everyone, is no better."

"Maybe you can transfer to another unit after the war," said Alexei.

"After the war is what I worry about. Scores will be settled in the Soviet Union when the Nazis are finished. The façade will be stripped away. The knives will come out and no one, not even those in the NKVD, will be safe."

The columns of tanks passed and the artillery convoy started again.

"We go this way," said Tatiana, using a flashlight to examine a map. "A command post has already been established. You stay in our building tonight; tomorrow you can join your unit."

They turned off the main boulevard onto a shell-pocked road that led into the *Treptow-Kopenick* suburbs in southeast Berlin. "What are they asking you to do?" said Alexei as he maneuvered the jeep past burned-out vehicles and bodies of German soldiers lying in the road.

"I cannot say; it's secret," replied Tatiana, staring at the skeletal four- and five-story apartments, many of them lacking roofs, doors or entire floors. The few trees that remained stood like scarecrows, splintered branches and scorched leaves, or no leaves at all. A few houses had white bed sheets hanging from windows, a sign of surrender, but that did not guarantee respite from invasion.

Alexei slowed to a crawl as they approached a Mongolian infantry company supported by two medium tanks and an artillery piece. The gun thundered away at the base of an apartment, joined by shells from the T-34s. The building erupted in flame and collapsed in a pile of stone, brick and splintered beams. Dust and debris clouded the square in front of the ruin. Remarkably, as the dust settled, two civilians and three German soldiers stumbled out with arms high above their heads. Despite their frantic attempts to surrender, they were machine-gunned.

Russian troops rushed into an adjoining building where a sniper had been picking off soldiers exposed by the light of fires. Machine gun fire rattled in the structure and there was a series of blasts as walls were blown in, allowing Soviet troops to gain entrance to adjoining rooms.

From the first floor of the building the bulbous head of a *panzerfaust* stuck out, the favorite weapon of the Hitler Youth, feared for the devastating power of its warhead. Attached to a long pipe, the rocket-propelled charge was fired at the lead tank, which exploded, incinerating its crew.

The second tank rotated its turret and fired. The youths and their *panzerfaust* disintegrated, and the walls of the first two floors were reduced to rubble. Broken and charred furniture fell from the building and littered the street.

A squad of Soviet troops carrying stormed the building. Shots rang out, followed by the screams of women. Springing from the truck behind Tatiana, Lieutenant Rishka rushed toward the building, ahead of four NKVD soldiers.

"We have a mission; you must not enter that building!" shouted Tatiana over the sound of tank and artillery fire concentrating on nearby structures.

Rishka turned his head and said something unintelligible as his men joined the Mongolians. Tatiana got out of the jeep and Alexei, clutching his automatic weapon, joined her. More shooting tore through the apartment, and a civilian male, bleeding profusely, was tossed from the fourth floor. Moments later two women emerged and were dragged into an alleyway. One, a girl of about twelve, was carried by two of the NKVD who'd accompanied by Rishka, while an older woman was manhandled by three of the Mongolian troops.

"Stop!" shouted Tatiana as she took a half-dozen steps forward. The enlisted NKVD soldiers, their pants down and weapons laid aside, had already ripped off the girl's dress while the woman, perhaps her mother, was thrown onto a ripped sofa.

Gleeful with their find, the soldiers ignored the mother's pleas as they raped the girl, whose screams could be heard between the firing of artillery. One of the privates laughed and, seeing Tatiana's rage, shouted words of contempt as he shoved his member into the girl.

White-faced and livid, Tatiana drew her pistol and fired a round in the air, but the men ignored her. She then leveled the revolver and fired three more, each round hitting its mark. An NKVD corporal reached for his weapon, but his head exploded from the impact of two more shells.

The remaining soldiers dived for cover, but Rishka, pistol in hand, rushed Tatiana. He was screaming and pulling up his pants as he aimed his weapon. He didn't see Alexei, but a half-dozen rounds from Alexei's PPsh-41 stitched across his torso.

"Get in!" Alexei shouted, and Tatiana threw herself into the jeep. Shoving the stick into drive and ramming the pedal, Alexei spun the jeep and tore over debris as NKVD troops ran to their truck. Wildly twisting and turning past flaming buildings and through narrow alleyways, he tore past startled infantry, leaving the Directorate's truck far behind.

"There!" said Tatiana, pointing to a narrow road past a battery of truck-mounted rockets. Once past the Katyushas, Alexei drove until they were beyond the final wave of troops.

Nine miles beyond the city he spotted a farmhouse. Its front door was splintered and bullet holes pock-marked the front of the building. A stone and timber barn stood behind the house. Alexei parked beside it and said, "Wait here, I'm going to scout." Minutes later he returned and said, "Three bodies in the house, but no one alive. We can stay here and think of what to do."

"We must leave before dawn," said Tatiana, as they entered the house.

Furnishings were strewn about and drawers had been ransacked. Anything of value was long gone. The bloated bodies of two males and a female lay in a pile beside a back door. One man wore the uniform of a German sergeant. The other, much younger, appeared to be his son. A pre-war photo of both standing before the Chancellery in Berlin lay on the floor, its glass and frame shattered.

Alexei dragged the corpses behind the house and threw a blanket over them. It was the best he could do.

Tatiana drew chairs to the window and closed the heavy drapes, allowing only a sliver of moonlight to penetrate the room. Alexei sat beside her, his submachine gun at his feet. It was eerily silent and he felt as if the ghosts of its previous occupants were stealthily walking about, distrustful of the intruders who sat where they had lived their once sedate lives.

"It's all over for me," said Tatiana wearily. "The NKVD troops, the witnesses, will report the killings to Sheplov. He will want to execute me himself, a bullet through the back of the head. That's how the NKVD does it. That way they don't have to see the faces."

"I know; I have seen executions in the Gulag and at the front. But if the solution is not to get caught, the question is, where do we go?" said Alexei.

"We certainly can't rejoin Soviet forces, and we don't want to run into the Nazis," said Tatiana.

"Almost all of them are defending Berlin. Once Zhukov finishes them off, he won't halt until he encounters the western allies. And on the central front, nothing is going to stop Zhukov's armies."

"So we will be trapped behind Soviet lines," said Tatiana.

"Unless..."

"Unless what?"

"The Americans," said Alexei, his mind churning. "But I do not know where they are. I heard that the west forfeited Berlin, let Stalin have it."

"True. The British and Americans pushed across Germany. Sheplov said that the American Ninth Army has crossed the Elbe, has already taken Leipzig and perhaps Magdeburg." said Tatiana.

"How far is that?"

"From Berlin, Magdeburg is about one hundred and fifty kilometers, two hours driving time."

"In peace time. We can try to get to their lines, but we'd have to take back roads and be cautious," said Alexei. "We'll continue as Soviet scouts for fifty or sixty kilometers."

"And then?"

"Then we become like the rest of Europe, Tatiana."

"Refugees."

"Yes, refugees. We will have to look like German refugees fleeing the Soviets. Thousands of civilians are on the roads. I speak German; I learned it as an engineer and at the front. Do you?"

"Oh yes. We interrogated many Germans before they were sent to Siberia or their executions," said Tatiana.

"So that's what we do. I am an American and I want to go home."

"And what about me? Where do I go, Alexei?"

"West. We keep going all the way to France. There, you blend in as an emigrée, a lady who fled the Bolsheviks. There are thousands in France, entire Russian communities of aristocratic women living with their memories of life before the revolution. No one will know who you really are, who you worked for."

She slowly nodded, and a rare smile came to her lips. "How ironic, Alexei. I am to pretend to be an aging Romanov aristocrat, one of the people I spent my youth attempting to eradicate. I knew all about them: their trysts, their wealth, their useless lives. Oh yes, I would know how to play that role." Her expression became an alarming mixture of feral and fey.

"Madness, Alexei. We are all insane."

Chapter 30
Germany, On the Road to Magdeburg
Mid-April, 1945

Alexei drove slowly over fields illuminated by moonlight. He stopped when they heard German voices and vehicles on the main road.

"Military," whispered Alexei, as three trucks passed in the opposite direction, their fog lights dimmed with newspaper and rags. Once they were out of sight and hearing, Alexei started the jeep once again.

"It wouldn't be a good idea to arrive in a contested area at night," he remarked. "It's a good thing I know the area. As an engineer, I visited Leipzig long before the war and spent a day in a town named Genthin beside the Elbe-Havel Canal. It's about thirty miles northeast of Magdeburg. We might find a place to rest near that town."

"Will it be safe? I heard that Magdeburg was bombed by the Americans," said Tatiana.

"There won't be any more bombing if they've occupied it."

They pressed on another four miles. A dim light appeared in a house separated from others by a copse of trees. Beside the house were the remains of a garden. A shovel and rake glinted in the moonlight. A figure on the second floor stopped by a window, then moved away.

"How many do you think are in the house?" asked Tatiana.

"There can't be too many; there are no cars or trucks, only a wagon. I see a few horses in a corral."

"Much of the German army moves by horse-drawn wagon," remarked Tatiana.

"I don't think that's a military wagon; they would've confiscated anything they wanted."

Alexei drove the jeep beside a stout tree out of view of the house. "We don't want to do any shooting unless absolutely necessary," he said. "But unholster your pistol, just in case."

The ghostly spire of the Trinity Church could be seen through the trees, their spring leaves glistening in the moonlight. They peered into windows of the first floor and saw no one. The house was silent. Not wanting to alarm the occupants, Alexei knocked softly on the front door. He heard footsteps on creaky stairs, and a light came on.

"Ja? Who is it?" came a man's voice, wary of a knock in the morning darkness.

"Hans. I need help," said Alexei in German.

"Hans? From church?" the man replied anxiously.

"Ja, from church. Hurry, it's important," said Alexei.

"Yes, please," added Tatiana, knowing that a woman's voice would add urgency.

A bolt was released and the door opened a crack. Instantly Alexei threw it open and pushed the man back, who grunted and fell back against a woman wearing bathrobe. She screamed, seeing Alexei and Tatiana in Soviet uniforms. The man glanced at Alexei's submachine gun and, shielding his wife, instantly threw up his hands.

"Don't shoot, *bitte*, don't shoot. We are not Nazis, just farmers. Take anything you want," said the man.

"Sit!" ordered Alexei, nodding at a sofa a few feet away.

"Ja, ja," said the man, tugging his wife onto the couch. Dutifully, she too raised her hands.

"Watch them, Tatiana," said Alexei as he hurried upstairs, weapon trained as he opened doors.

Moments later, he returned and stood before the terrified couple. "Silver plates, jewelry, gold bracelet," the man said, gesturing with his head, his hands still held high. "Take. Take all you want."

"Yes," echoed the woman, her face drawn. Dropping one arm she pointed to the slender necklace she wore. She gave her husband a worried look when Alexei and Tatiana ignored her offer.

"They're harmless, and there's nobody else here. I checked for weapons in closets and drawers, and didn't find any. There are suitcases under the beds, but they held only clothes and the like," Alexei said to Tatiana in Russian.

"We need to put the jeep in their barn," said Tatiana. "We can't let anybody see it."

"Blankets, we need two or three blankets. Get them," Alexei said to the woman in German.

Surprised, she hurried upstairs, followed by Tatiana.

Alexei, still holding his weapon, pointed to a telephone and said, "Is there another?"

"No, only one in this house."

Alexei yanked the cord from the wall, then said, "Put your hands down. Cooperate and you won't be harmed."

Cautiously the man obeyed as Alexei lowered the gun.

"What do you want from us?" the man asked, his voice uncertain.

"Food, something to drink, and some rest."

Tatiana and the man's wife came downstairs. She held three blankets, and Tatiana carried an armload of clothes.

"We can change into these, farmer's clothes and old hats. I will put the jeep in the barn and cover it up. I'm hungry, Alexei; have her cook something."

Alexei slung his submachine gun and stood by the kitchen door as the woman prepared eggs, cabbage, and several slices of ham. Hands shaking, she glanced furtively at Alexei, but said nothing as she placed dishes and cutlery on a table.

"*Schnaps?*" asked the man, ducking his head.

"Thank you, but no," said Alexei. "Water is fine."

"*Ja, wasser*, Hilde, *wasser* for our… guests," he said with a tremulous smile.

Tatiana returned and said, "I didn't smell it before, but there is an odor out there. An odor of death, like burning flesh." She peered at the farmer and said, "Was it from a bombing, a fire?"

The man shook his head. "We are not Nazis, detest Nazis," he repeated. "But they have perpetrated a crime, a terrible crime. There is…" He stopped and glanced at his wife, a worried expression on her face. She nodded her head, then went back to her cooking.

"The smell, it comes at night from beyond the town; the wind carries it. Two years ago, a prison was built, a camp for women and foreign workers, slave workers for the Reich."

"A prison camp, a death camp?" asked Alexei.

"*Ja,* for Jews I think. I saw dogs, SS and women. Children too. No one is supposed to know anything about it. But I know that it's an offshoot of the Ravensbrück camp. I don't know if they actually burn bodies in Genthin, but it's possible. The smell. It's a terrible thing," he said, shaking his head vigorously.

"What is your name?" asked Alexei, as he indicated that the man and his wife should sit at the dining room table.

"Gunther Kautzman," replied the man, surprised that a Russian soldier would be at all interested.

The four sat at the table on which Hilde had placed the meagre dishes, and Kautzman said, "We are a religious family and we pray. If that is alright with you."

"It is fine with us, Herr Kautzman," replied Alexei, ignoring Tatiana's look of distain. "My name is Alexei and my friend is Tatiana."

"And I am pleased to meet you," the farmer said, noting that he had been addressed as "Mister." Solemnly, he prayed for an end to the war, then said, "I thank you for your kindness toward us. I like to think that many Russians are still religious, even though they are ordered not to believe in God. You allowed me to pray; might I assume that you are Christian?" he asked, his eyes going from Tatiana to Alexei and the medals he wore.

"I am not a believer," said Tatiana. "I think that if God existed he would not have allowed the Nazis and others to commit such atrocities."

Gunther said nothing, wondering if "others" included Soviets as well. Then he gained the courage to look directly at Alexei. "And you feel the same?" His wife looked surprised that he was asking such a direct question of armed invaders.

Alexei looked back at him for an extended moment, then said, "Herr Kautzman, I am a Jew."

Hilda put her hand to her mouth and gasped.

"Does that shock or offend you?" asked Alexei.

"*Nein, nein,* not at all," replied Gunther hurriedly. "We have... I mean, perhaps, being Jewish, you might..." He broke off when his wife gave him a cautionary glance.

"Might what, Herr Kautzman?" responded Alexei.

"Let me say this, if I may. You would be surprised at how many Germans loathed the Reich and still do. And some of us have tried to help certain people, those in serious danger," he said, glancing at his wife. Continuing, he said, "You have arrived at a very difficult time for us, but perhaps an opportune one. Lieutenant, you desired civilian clothes, work clothes. I can only guess why."

"And you have packed suitcases. Herr Kautzman, we might be able to help each other. I think I can trust you. Can I?"

His eyes focused on Alexei, he said, "*Ja,* and I think I can trust you."

"We intend to proceed west to the American lines, whether that be Magdeburg or Leipzig," confided Alexei. "Neither of us can remain in Soviet-controlled territory. We have our reasons."

"You saw what we keep ready under the bed. We were hoping to leave in a few days, perhaps a week, going west."

"You don't have a week, and neither do we. Soviet forces may arrive here any day."

"That soon?" asked Hilde with a surprised look.

"Nazi resistance is crumbling like a house of cards. And terrible things are happening in Berlin," said Tatiana.

"We have a complication," said Gunther, putting down his knife and fork. "As I implied, some of us have tried to help people, Jewish people."

"You have Jews here? You are hiding them from the Nazis?" Alexei asked.

Slowly, cautiously, Kautzman nodded. "For two years. It has been dangerous for us. If it was found out we would be shot. Instantly," he said.

"A mother and her daughter; they escaped during a train wreck. There have been wrecks here before. In December of 39 there was an accident, and hundreds of travelers died or were injured. Two years ago a train derailed, and some, and these were Jews, attempted to escape. It was night, the time when prisoner trains come through. Most who escaped were shot, but this woman and her daughter ran across our field and hid in the barn. They expected to be turned over to the SS when I found them in the morning."

"But you didn't turn them in," said Tatiana.

"I am a Christian; I do not send women and children to their death," Gunther said vehemently.

There was a moment of silence, then Alexei said, "Then they will come with us, all of us."

"We would not leave without them."

"We have a few hours before dawn," said Tatiana, finishing her breakfast. "It will be best to leave then."

"Hilde," said Kautzman, "I will ask you to hitch the horses. I will put our luggage and some furniture in the wagon. And a few bales of hay." Then to Alexei he said, "I think you will change out of your uniforms."

"Of course," said Alexei, then adding, "Tatiana and I will stay down here. I suggest that you and Frau Kautzman get some rest before we start. It will be a very long day."

He noticed that Hilde cleaned all the dishes and put them away before going upstairs.

Alexei and Tatiana reclined on the couch. The house became silent. "I have questions, if you don't mind talking," said Alexei.

"I might not have the answers, but ask if you wish," replied Tatiana.

"Colonel Sheplov said that you had a special mission, and I guess that if... things had been different yesterday you would have carried it out."

"Yes, and I would have been promoted for it, in spite of Sheplov. The entire matter is very secret, but I have contacts. I always have. So I know that the Soviet Union is very far behind the West and Germany in its development of atomic weapons, and that's what Stalin wants. There is something called Operation Borodino, named after the great victory against Napoleon. This Operation Borodino is intended to get uranium oxide in Berlin from the Kaiser-Wilhelm Institute for Physics. We are also required to capture German scientists, as well as research, from the University of Berlin."

"So now somebody else will have to complete the mission," said Alexei. "But maybe the Nazis will destroy their work before it falls into enemy hands."

They were contemplative for a long moment, then Tatiana said, "I've always wondered, Alexei. Did Sergei die at Tsushima?" Despite her access to secret political information, she never learned what had happened to her first lover, confidant, and fellow revolutionary.

No," replied Alexei, sorrowfully. "He was executed along with other saboteurs before our fleet was sunk off Korea. He was on the cruiser *Mikhail III* with me and tried to destroy the ship. There were revolutionaries in the fleet, and many sailors knew that the Japanese navy was far superior, that we were sailing to our deaths. They thought that a mutiny would be safer. Some of them wanted to take over the ship and return home, maybe join in the riots against the Tzar."

"And was he one of the leaders?" asked Tatiana. It warmed he heart to learn that Sergei had died true to their convictions.

"He believed that sinking the ship was a way of striking back at the Romanovs, I spoke to him before he was shot. He said he would miss you, but you were wed to the revolution even more than he. Yet he died for it."

"He was right; I lived for the revolution. For a while I thought you did, too."

"No. I sympathized with the movement and detested conditions in Russia, but I wanted to be a naval officer. Then I fell in love with Kimi-san; and after Tsushima I had no reason to stay in Russia."

"You must miss her."

"The image of her is in my mind day and night. I miss her more than you can even imagine. I had no idea in 1940 that I might never see her again. My son warned me the situation in Europe was dangerous, but my father was dying in Leningrad and I wanted to see him. Then the invasion, the blitzkrieg, came so quickly. I got swept up, like so many others who had lives they just wanted to return to."

"I am sorry that I was unable to do more for you, when I saw you that day in Moscow. I hoped that you would get out of Russia, but you wound up in the Gulag."

Alexei fell silent, remembering his time in prison, and the cruelties he had witnessed since. Then he said, "You shot those men. I can understand that, but you must have known it would jeopardize your mission."

"You wonder why I was so enraged that I chose to kill them when it jeopardized not only the mission but my life? I would have shot them all if I could. I too was raped, Alexei. I was destroyed for years, just as that girl will be. That is if she lives, if she does not commit suicide... like so many others."

Tatiana seemed to shrink within herself. "It was in Kiev just after the revolution, a meeting of Bolsheviks. It was night and I was walking to my flat. There were three men, Alexei; I could not fight them off. A Bolshevik, a man I admired and eventually married, came to my aid, but it was already too late. I was pregnant."

"So you have a child?"

Tatiana was silent for a long moment before she replied.

"A daughter. But she died during the famine, along with so many others. The American grain your President sent over came too late. Only the most senior officials did not go hungry in those years; the rest of us suffered. The man I married became a commissar, but he was executed when Stalin came to power. By then I had joined the NKVD; it was the safest thing, to be a member of the most feared organization in Russia. That's where I met Sheplov. Even then he outranked me."

"Were you his lover?" asked Alexei.

"No, I did not want to be anybody's lover. When I refused his advances he turned against me. He even accused me of treason, but I had friends. Now you know why he hates me. And why I hate him."

"But you were always loyal to the regime and everything it required," said Alexei.

She looked at him sharply. "You want to know if I sent people to the Gulag? If I killed people? That's what we were expected to do. Yes, I did turn people in for what was deemed treason. And on occasion it was. If I did not report them others would have, and for not reporting them I, too, would have been shot. Did I regret it? Did I have nightmares? Yes, but I believed in the system, in the U.S.S.R. It had to be better than what we took down."

"And now?"

"I'm tired. I'm old and simply want to live. I don't need ideology. I just want a world without ceaseless fear."

"I truly hope you find that. Rest now, and dream of living in such a world. I will keep watch."

It was still dark when Gunther came downstairs and began carrying furniture to the wagon. At first light, he and Hilde crept downstairs, suitcases in hand. Together, the four of them walked towards the barn. Hilde went to feed and harness the horses, and Tatiana followed.

"Please understand," Gunther explained to Alexei, "they haven't seen anybody except me and Hilde for two years, and I don't want them to be scared by seeing a stranger. I must tell them what we are going to do, then I will introduce you and Frau Tatiana. Come."

The two men entered the barn. Kautzman pushed aside floor boards, revealing a stairway of weathered stones descending steeply. "Hilde and I come here once or twice a day to bring food and water, under cover of caring for the animals."

"A basement?" said Alexei.

"*Nein,* a sanctuary, built during the Thirty Years War when Protestants and Catholics were slaughtering each other. I found it by accident when I was building the barn. No one else knows about it. I keep it very secret. Wait here."

Gunther carefully picked his way down. Minutes later he reappeared, helping a woman and child ascend the stairs. They blinked in the daylight that shone through the open door. The wagon, loaded with hay, luggage, furnishings and farm implements, was backed against the door. The horses pawed the ground impatiently.

"This is Herr Alexei and Frau Tatiana, and this lady is Sarah and her daughter is Leah," said Kautzman, making the introductions. "Our new friends will be coming with us."

The woman and child, wraithlike after their virtual incarceration, stared at the strangers, then back at Hilda and her husband.

"They are good people and can be trusted," said Gunther, laying his hand gently on the child's head.

Alexei smiled and Hilde said, "Sarah, you and Leah will be hidden in the wagon. No one will see you under the blankets and hay. We will all be sitting around you, but make no sounds. There is still great danger and we have many miles to go."

"Are there still Nazis about?" asked Sarah worriedly.

"There will be some, but they will have thrown away their uniforms and will be trying to blend in with refugees," said Gunther. "I doubt that they will be any problem. Besides, they won't see you."

"And I will protect you," said Alexei firmly.

Hearing the strange accent, Sarah glanced at Hilde.

"I am not German and I am not Russian," said Alexei. "But I was a soldier."

By midday the road was a sea of refugees. Most walked, carrying suitcases or bags filled with clothes and food. A few cars, filled with the wealthy, honked and skirted pedestrians and wagons. The occupants had likely been government officials, Nazis, or owners of businesses friendly to the regime. Some Wehrmacht soldiers tramped along the road, but few carried weapons. Others wore their overcoat or cap but had changed into civilian clothes.

The procession of thousands stopped and started countless times as horses fell from exhaustion or wagon wheels broke on the bomb-cratered road. Exhausted children, thirsty and glassy-eyed, held parents' hands. There was little talking, and heads turned nervously when distant artillery was heard. The frightening sound caused some to hurry forward, but most trudged on, having heard explosions for many weeks.

There was little rancor on the road. Strangers helped one another, especially if children were involved. The hope of reaching American lines ahead of disaster was a common denominator.

Alexei rode beside Herr Kautzman while Tatiana sat with Hilde at the rear of the wagon among the odd assemblage of belongings. Every once and while they would feel movement beneath the blanket or hear a moan as the wagon went over a shell hole with a jarring thump.

Tatiana had put on extra clothes to make herself look stouter and had employed Hilde's make-up to increase the lines in her face. What she hadn't mentioned was the pistol she carried, nor had Alexei mentioned the submachine gun hidden in a blanket beside him.

Even though almost no one spoke, there were the noises of a thousand plodding feet, the creaking of wagons, and the snorts of horses and oxen. And so, almost no one heard a sound from far away and very high. There were no contrails streaming dazzling white in the mottled sky. But Alexei had heard the sound before; tapping Kautzman on the shoulder, he pointed upward.

The farmer shielded his eyes. "A Messerschmitt ME 109, and two others, maybe British Spitfires."

The Messerschmitt turned and dove, followed by two Allied planes. Flashes spewed from the wings of the pursuing aircraft, then a black plume erupted from the German fighter. It pulled up sharply just as cannon fire ripped into a wing. The plane rolled over on its back before it dove toward the road. It leveled off at about one hundred feet off above. By now, it was a flying torch.

Hundreds of people, suddenly aware of the approaching cataclysm, rushed from the roadway into fields or cowered behind abandoned vehicles. Tatiana jumped off the wagon, pulled the girl from beneath the covers and, with Sarah only steps behind, started for the field. A dozen frantic people cut in front of her.

The horses, wild with fright, reared up, skewing the wagon, and tried to bolt into the crowd. Alexei and Kautzman were thrown onto the road.

Alexei saw Tatiana, trapped by the press, push the girl to the ground and protectively cover her.

"Go, go!" Tatiana screamed at Sarah, just as the plane struck the ground and exploded. Fire engulfed a dozen people, shards tore into others. The conflagration left people writhing on the ground, many of them on fire. The plane's propeller broke off and cartwheeled down the runway, slashing refugees.

Two sleek aircraft with blue stars on the wings roared over the confusion. Alexei glanced upward, his eyes following the fighters, never having seen such aircraft before. "P-51, American," he heard a voice say.

As survivors pulled wounded people to the side of the road, Alexei was able to push his way past the struggling mass to Tatiana.

Leah, sobbing hysterically, had squirmed out from under Tatiana. Sarah wrapped her arms about her daughter while Hilde and Herr Kautzman gathered close. Alexei dropped to his knees. A jagged piece of aluminum protruded from Tatiana's side. He attempted to staunch the wound, but he knew it was useless; he had seen wounds like this before: arteries severed, internal bleeding impossible to stop.

She must have known too. One hand clasped his, and she gasped, "So close, Alexei, I was so close. A pity."

"You did a noble thing, Tatiana," he murmured. "A sacrifice."

"Yes," said Sarah, "a mitzvah for my daughter. Bless you, in the name of the Lord. We will remember you and light candles for you as long as we live."

Tatiana smiled, then grimaced as her vision dulled. "Not a sacrifice." Her voice was little more than a breath. "Penitence. For all of them."

She went still for a moment, then seemed to rally. "You are a good man, Alexei. Go home to your wife. Go, Alexei. You are done here."

He picked up the body and laid her beneath a tree, remaining there with her for a number of minutes. On an impulse, he used his knife to sever a lock of Tatiana's hair, and placed it in his breast pocket. All around people reformed in family groups and, with reverence, walked around him and the woman. Some who had seen the sacrifice made the sign of the cross.

"My wife and our friends cannot stay, Herr Alexei. I know you do not want to leave your friend, but there is nothing more you can do. There is no time to bury her. Stay if you wish, but we must go," said Gunther.

"I understand," said Alexei, rising and taking one last look at Tatiana. He wished her well on whatever journey lay before her.

"I don't think it is too much further. People seem to be moving faster," said Hilde.

"We will have to walk now," said Gunther. "One of the horses is dead and the other is crippled. Could you shoot him? End his pain?"

"Shooting will only frighten people. I have a knife. I will do it."

The trek continued. A mile on there was a commotion, but not one of fear. Men in unfamiliar uniforms and dozens of armored vehicles crowded the town square. Alexei saw a tank with a very long barrel and words painted on its turret.

"Americans, Americans!" he shouted, grabbing Leah's hand. She and her mother struggled to keep up with him as he raced toward the soldiers. Suddenly Alexei tripped and fell, sprawling in front of a pair of boots and bloused leggings.

He looked up, saw a lanky infantryman and said, "I'm an American, Corporal. I am a citizen of the United States."

"Is that so?" replied the soldier around a wad of gum in his cheek, peering down. "Then I reckon yuh should stand up if y're fixin' to go home. Americans stand up," he said, extending his arm.

"Thank you, I'm fixin' to. I just want to go home," said Alexei with a grin.

"That sounds 'bout right. We all want to go home, but we're fixin' to kick some Kraut butt first."

"It might be hard to find them," said Alexei. "The Soviets are a just down the road, and they are being unruly."

The corporal pointed to the long-barreled tank with the writing, "Sam Houston's Big Gun!"

"That's Texas, mister. They best not mess with Texas."

"I reckon not," said Alexei.

The corporal gestured down the road, "Home is that way, mister. But it's a hell of a long walk."

"I've come a long way, soldier. That's not so far."

Chapter 31
Nagiso, Japan
August, 1945

In early August, Mr. Temuchi returned to his house in Nagiso and brought with him an assistant, a soldier wounded on Guadalcanal three years before. This new addition to the household required Sayuri, Kumi and Chad-ishi to occupy a tiny room attached to the house. The walls were decorated with the ubiquitous print of the Emperor on horseback and a hand colored photo of the Meiji Shrine. It was cramped and quite warm during the day, but temperate in the August nights.

Mr. Temuchi and his friend, Major Hiro Kanabe, often talked late into the night over cups of saki.

"You heard about Toyama," said Temuchi, "a night bombing. The city has been obliterated. The Americans strike at will." He sighed. "Fortunately, our village is insignificant."

"Just so," said Kanabe. "With Hitler dead and Germany defeated, I suspect that most of the Allied troops in Europe will be readying for the invasion of Japan."

"There will be millions sent over," said Temuchi. "And we have no idea which island they will invade first."

"Some say that the government is trying to have the Soviets intercede, perhaps arrange a truce, keep the Emperor on the throne," said Kanabe.

"And what would the Soviets demand in exchange for brokering a truce? I fear the Russians more than Americans. They are brutal people, beasts," said Temuchi, pouring himself and Kanabe more saki.

"How can we possibly defend ourselves when our army and navy have been defeated?" asked Temuchi, his voice just above a whisper.

"I don't know. Perhaps fate will favor us, a divine wind, a true kamikaze like the one that destroyed the Mongols, all seventy thousand of them. Beyond that, I have no idea."

The evacuation of major cities continued apace. Many hundreds found refuge in mountain villages like Nagiso and Achi in Nagano Prefecture. Food had never been plentiful, but now the fields were stripped bare. Everyone in the Temuchi household scoured the fields in search of a sweet potato or edible bulb hidden deep in the soil.

Sayuri and Kumi sensed the concern of Mr. Temuchi and his mother with so many refugees crowding the house. So when Kumi received a letter, she announced she would be leaving to assist her ailing aunt.

"How did your aunt learn that we are here?" asked Sayuri as Kumi packed her few belongings.

"She wrote to Mrs. Onagi, our neighborhood association chairwoman, and learned that we are in Nagiso."

"The neighborhood association is still intact?" asked Sayuri.

"Some of the shops and government buildings were not too badly damaged," Kumi said, "and Mrs. Onagi is a force of nature; not even bombs deter her."

Sayuri hid a smile behind her hand, and Kumi continued. "Nagasaki, where my aunt lives, is a quiet town. You and Chad-ishi should come with me. Mr. Temuchi has been very gracious letting us stay, but we are becoming a burden. My aunt has a garden and grows sweet potatoes and cucumbers. She is very sweet and will make room for all of us."

"But will one small garden be enough for the four of us?" asked Sayuri.

"I'm sure it will, and she does need our help. I really don't want us to be separated, and it might be months before my aunt is well." Then as an afterthought she said, "Nagasaki is surrounded by beautiful hills. I know we will like it there. And it is a safe place to be."

"I promise to join you after Chad-ishi gets over his cold. He is feeling better, and trains run almost every day. But I will go to the station with you."

"That would be wonderful. Mr. Temuchi offered to take me to the train station in two days. It's a long drive, so it is very kind of him."

Sayuri took Chadi-ishi for a walk and to count the birds they saw, and Kumi, anxious for her aunt, kept to herself that evening, so neither were present that evening, August seventh, when a visitor stopped by. Colonel Sato, a long-time friend of Temuchi, came into Nagiso along with his aide. The officer rapped on Temuchi's door and was ushered into the house. A calm man of deliberate actions, he appeared shaken.

"What news?" asked Kanabe.

"The government isn't saying anything specific, but something terrible happened in Hiroshima yesterday. There is no communication from the city at all. I heard it from a friend; all lines are down, phone and telegraph. And no trains have left the city. He said that there were only a few American planes, B-29s, over the city before a huge flash and explosion. He said that there might have been only one bomb dropped, but the city is gone. Completely gone."

"Is that possible? Just one bomb?" Mr. Temuchi look bewildered.

"Let me tell you something," said the colonel. "When I was a student at the university, there was an accident once; several people sickened, and after a few weeks they lost all their hair. One, a professor, died. He had been experimenting with uranium. Uranium can be made into a bomb. If the Americans have done so...."

"And dropped it on us, on Hiroshima," said Major Kanabe, aghast. "What if they have more of these terrible weapons?"

"Will they drop them on other cities?" asked Mrs. Temuchi, her hand covering her face.

"They may," the officer somberly.

The elderly woman gasped on a sob and ran from the room.

August 9th, 1945

"Sir, Kokura is all clouded over and we've already made three passes. I have to have a clear visual and I don't think that's going to happen," said Commander Ashworth, U.S. Navy, responsible for accuracy and for timing the drop.

"Got it. We'll proceed to the secondary. We have enemy fighters coming up and the flak is getting a bit nasty," said Major Charles Sweeney, piloting *Bockscar*. "I'll tell the tech plane to alter course. We're running low on fuel so it's a one-shot deal, then we head back."

Eleven feet in length and five in width, "Fat Man," a plutonium bomb and the only one on *Bockscar,* was less prone to accidental firing, which gave the crew some comfort, since the mission had been plagued by pounding rain and lightning flashes since leaving the Marianas.

There had been no response from the Japanese government following the bombing of Hiroshima; therefore it was decided that a second nuclear detonation was necessary to end the war without a full-scale invasion. Unknown to the Allied governments, there was conflict at the highest levels in Japan regarding conditions of surrender. All agreed that a negotiated peace in which Japan would retain the Emperor was the primary concern, but there was much argument over issues of freedom from foreign occupation, the right to handle their own disarmament, and the right to try their own war criminals.

To further complicate the delicate situation, the Soviet Union declared war against Japan on August 8th, only a few hours before *Bockscar*'s wheels left the ground. Suddenly the Japanese offensive in China, already stalemated by the efforts of Mao Tse-Tung and Chiang Kai-shek, was confronted by over a million Russian troops.

There had been a brief air raid alert in Nagasaki earlier in the day, but most of the citizens disregarded air raid warnings as false alarms, even after an actual bombing raid on August 1st. That had led to the evacuation of most of the children, but a quarter of a million people still resided in the city. When two B-29 Super fortresses were spotted by Japanese observers, it was assumed that they were reconnaissance aircraft—after all, there were only two of them. Everyone knew that bombing raids were carried out by dozens of planes, fighters and bombers swarming in the sky.

No alarm sounded to warn the oblivious populace.

"Still cloudy," said Ashworth as *Bockscar* closed on the city.

"Can you see anything? I don't care to land with the bomb, nor do I want to drop it in the ocean if we can help it," replied the major.

"Wait, Major, the clouds are parting. I see the Mitsubishi Steel and Arms works, and over there to the south is the Mitsubishi-Urakami torpedo plant. We're on target."

The photo plane turned on its cameras and sensors, and two minutes later the atomic weapon plunged from the bomb bay doors toward the unsuspecting city of Nagasaki.

An intensely blinding flash was followed by an enormous column of black smoke streaked with red bursts of flame. *Bockscar* was bounced around by the concussive blast, then it leveled out, and the aircraft headed away from the devastation below.

* * *

Mr. Temuchi drove his truck up to the rural Chiyo station, a mere platform beside the Tenryu River. The line maintained a single track; a schedule was posted on a rough wooden board beside the rails. Black smoke from a train's smokestack rose in the distance, but the train was coming from the opposite direction.

Mr. Temuchi, Sayuri and Kumi walked to the signboard, where their attention was drawn to a handwritten message posted over the schedule. Putting on his reading glasses, Mr. Temuchi stared at the notice and read:

Due to unfortunate circumstances having occurred in Nagasaki, no trains will be allowed to proceed there until further notice. In addition, no civilians other than medical personnel will be allowed to travel within three miles of the city.

By order of the Military Authorities and the Director of the Lida Railroad Line.

"What unfortunate circumstances?" said Kumi, looking worriedly at Sayuri and Mr. Temuchi.

"I have heard nothing, but I didn't turn on my radio today."

"That train is coming from Nagasaki," said Sayuri, "It's supposed to stop here. Perhaps someone has information. I think we should wait."

A locomotive slowly sidled past the station platform and stopped with a hiss of steam and the sound of a bell. A half dozen passengers alighted, while others anxiously peered through windows.

"Is this train coming from Nagasaki?" asked Kumi, bowing to an army captain.

"It's from a station three miles from the city, or what used to be the city. Nagasaki is destroyed, just like Hiroshima. This train is carrying some of the survivors to army doctors in Tokyo," said the officer.

"Why all the way to Tokyo?" asked Mr. Temuchi, glancing at two men on stretchers, one with a bandage wrapped around his head so that only his mouth and nose were visible.

"Radiation poisoning. You would not want to go to Nagasaki even if you could," said the captain.

A man wearing a business suit and fedora said, "I was looking the other way when the flash went off, or I too, like the man on the stretcher there, would have been blinded. The sound of the explosion was like nothing I had ever heard before, and I lived through the Tokyo bombings. Terrible. There is nothing left in the center of the city."

Kumi put her hands to her face and said, "My aunt lives near the torpedo plant...."

Sayuri put her arms around her and said, "I am so sorry, Kumi-san. I am so sorry."

A BLOSSOM IN THE ASHES

With the shriek of a whistle, the rumble of wheels and clanking of overcrowded carriages, the train built up speed and disappeared down the single track. The burned victims were placed in a truck that drove off once the attendants were aboard. Other passengers picked up their luggage and began walking to the village of Chiyo a quarter mile away.

All was silent until Mr. Temuchi said, "We shall go back. There will be no more trains."

"But I will be a burden at your house, there is so little food," said Kumi.

"We will make do, Kumi-san. It's just the way it has to be."

* * *

No official pronouncements were made about the bombing of Nagasaki. American B-29s dropped conventional weapons on the populace of Japan while her military and statesmen debated terms of surrender. Life anxiously continued in Nagiso as the inhabitants contemplated the terrors of a probable invasion. An Imperial Army captain arrived and ordered the populace into a rough formation and reminded them of their duty to the Emperor. He told them there would be a preparedness drill on the fifteenth of August, during which spears would be allocated and defensive positions upgraded. Following the speech, all were dismissed and the captain was driven away.

"I will help train the women's spear brigade," said Major Hiro Kanabe that night.

"I am not a soldier and have never been one, Hiro-san," said Mr. Temuchi, "but I remember reading of the samurai revolt against the Meiji government some seventy years ago. The samurai were great warriors, yet even their final cavalry charge was of no use against artillery and rapid-firing weapons. What good would spears be against machine guns?

I worship the Emperor, but I suggest that our women hide and live. The battle for Nagiso will last not more than ten minutes, if that."

Kanabe stared into his tea and finally said, "Some would say your words are treasonous, but you are right. And yet, as a soldier, I will do my duty."

Mr. Temuchi turned on his radio at eleven in the morning of August 15th while members of the community were still scouring the fields or assembling for the spear drill to be conducted at noon. The radio, a large upright in an elegant pre-war cabinet, was the only one in the village. Mr. Temuchi listened carefully to the government announcement with some trepidation. Sayuri, Kumi and Chad-ishi entered the room upon the conclusion of the announcement. Mr. Temuchi, quite excitedly, said, "You must all come with me into the fields and to all the houses. We must spread the word."

"What is happening?" asked Kumi, they hurried after Mr. Temuchi.

"There will be an important announcement from the Emperor himself. It will be at twelve o'clock, and everyone will want to hear it."

"No one outside the palace has ever heard the Emperor," said Sayuri, awed. "Did the announcer say what it will be about?"

"No. Perhaps the Americans have invaded. This is very serious. Everybody must come to my house to hear it," said Temuchi. They relayed the message to men with hoes and rakes.

The radio was carried to the front steps of the house, and villagers crowded about, voices muted and worried. The army captain, along with a squad carrying spears, also arrived, ready to take immediate command if the invasion was underway. He worked his way to the front and stared at the crowd, hand on his sheathed sword.

Mr. Temuchi turned up the volume, giving an anxious glance to Kanabe. There was a moment of static, then an announcer said, "Please stand by for an address by His Majesty the Emperor."

The assemblage listened with rapt attention as Hirohito began in a high, strained voice. The reception quality was imperfect, and for most, the formal Classical Japanese was difficult to understand, but the essence of the speech was clear.

"To Our good and loyal subjects," he began. "After pondering deeply the general trends of the world and the actual conditions obtaining in Our Empire today, We have decided to effect a settlement of the present situation by resorting to an extraordinary measure."

Mr. Temuchi glanced at the captain, who stiffened, for this opening statement hardly sounded like a call to arms.

"We have ordered Our Government to communicate to the Governments of the United States, Great Britain, China and the Soviet Union that Our Empire accepts the provisions of their Joint Declaration. To strive for the common prosperity and happiness of all nations, as well as the security and well-being of Our subjects, is the solemn obligation which has been handed down by Our Imperial Ancestors and which lies close to Our heart."

Eyes in the crowd stared at the radio, hanging onto every word. The captain clenched his jaw, his hand gripping tightly the gleaming scabbard of his sword. People leaned forward to hear better.

"We declared war on America and Britain out of Our sincere desire to insure Japan's self-preservation and the stabilization of East Asia, it being far from Our thought either to infringe upon the sovereignty of other nations or to embark upon territorial aggrandizement. But now the war has lasted for nearly four years. Despite the best that has been done by everyone—the gallant fighting of the military and naval forces, the diligence and assiduity of Our servants of the State, and the devoted service of Our one hundred million people—the war situation has developed not necessarily to Japan's advantage, while the general trends of the world have all turned against her interest."

There was a shuffling of feet as people glanced at one another, uncertain.

"Moreover," the thin voice continued, "the enemy has begun to employ a new and most cruel bomb, the power of which to do damage is, indeed, incalculable, taking the toll of many innocent lives. Should we continue to fight, not only would it result in an ultimate collapse and obliteration of the Japanese nation, but also it would lead to the total extinction of human civilization. Such being the case, how are We to save the millions of Our subjects, or to atone Ourselves before the hallowed spirits of Our Imperial Ancestors? This is the reason why We have ordered the acceptance of the provisions of the Joint Declaration of the powers ....

"The thought of those officers and men as well as others who have fallen in the fields of battle, those who died at their posts of duty, or those who met with untimely death and all their bereaved families, pains our heart night and day. The welfare of the wounded and the war-sufferers, and of those who have lost their homes and livelihood, are the objects of our profound solicitude.

"The hardships and sufferings to which our nation is to be subjected hereafter will be certainly great. We are keenly aware of the inmost feelings of all of you, our subjects. However, it is according to the dictates of time and fate that We have resolved to pave the way for a grand peace for all the generations to come by enduring the unendurable and suffering what is unsufferable ....

"Beware most strictly of any outbursts of emotion which may engender needless complications, or any fraternal contention and strife which may create confusion, lead you astray and cause you to lose the confidence of the world.

"Let the entire nation continue as one family from generation to generation, ever firm in its faith in the imperishability of its sacred land, and mindful of its heavy burden of responsibility, and of the long road before it."

Sayuri thought she could sense a lessening of tension in the assemblage. She saw tears welling up in eyes and streaking down cheeks. The high voice was still speaking.

"Unite your total strength to be devoted to construction for the future. Cultivate the ways of rectitude, foster nobility of spirit, and work with resolution so that you may enhance the innate glory of the Imperial State and keep pace with the progress of the world."

"That concludes the address to the people of Japan," said the announcer.

It was as if the moment was frozen. People stood dumbly staring at one another. Then many dropped to their knees, head touching the ground. The captain put his hands to his face and said, "I am so sorry for having failed you, my Emperor. I am so sorry."

"We did our best; you heard the Emperor," said Major Kanabe to the crowd. "We have suffered greatly and we could have done nothing more. It is over. It is our duty now to obey the Emperor and, as he said, suffer the unsufferable."

As the people disbursed, Mr. Temuchi said, "Perhaps they will treat us humanely. We can only pray."

That night Sayuri said, "Kumi-san, I think it's time for us to go home."

"Is there a home to go back to?"

"There is always a home. Yes, we will go home."

Chapter 32
Tokyo, Japan
September, 1945

"That's all of them," said Lee-Beauregard Smythe as the last of the Hellcats touched down on the deck of the U.S.S. *Lexington,* the *Essex*-class carrier named for its predecessor.

"It's hard to believe it's over, that the they actually surrendered," said Tad.

"If it wasn't for the two bombs, we would be flying ground support now. As Wellington said at Waterloo, 'It was a near run thing.' We would be seeing salvos from battleships and thousands of troops going ashore."

"And a lot of dead people," added Tad.

"Ours and theirs. I sure would have enjoyed being aboard the *Missouri* this morning. I imagine it was one hell of a ceremony," said Lee. They headed to the officers' mess where a celebration was taking place.

"I bet it was something for the history books."

"Too bad that we and the other big carriers are a hundred miles out. But I heard we're going into Sagami Bay when Tokyo and the port is secured. Maybe we can go ashore in a week or two," said Smythe.

"All depends on whether the people obey the Emperor and put down their guns. If not, things will get ugly real fast," said Tad, descending the ladder.

* * *

Three days after the arrival of Admiral Halsey's Third Fleet into Sagami Bay, landing forces began the occupation of Tokyo under the protective guns of American battleships.

On August 28th, over four dozen C-47 aircraft landed with occupation forces at Atsugi airbase thirty miles from Tokyo; large-scale landings of the Sixth Marine Division began two days later.

Two weeks of anxiety passed as the Japanese awaited the next major event. Meanwhile, aircraft from the U.S.S. *Bon Homme Richard* flew low over Honshu, looking for prisoner-of-war camps and certifying that no hostile activity was being prepared. To the relief of the Army and Marine divisions still on shipboard, no violations occurred.

On the morning of September 2nd, the destroyer *Landsdowne* transported the Japanese delegation to the battleship *Missouri.* General MacArthur, along with admirals and representatives of all the Allied powers, quietly observed the signing. Leaning over superstructure railing, thousands of sailors watched as Japanese Foreign Minister Shigemitsu and General Umezu, Chief of the Army General Staff, put their signatures to the document.

Within view of the *Missouri* were eleven Allied battleships, including the U.S.S. *West Virginia,* a survivor of Pearl Harbor four years before.

Secured to the *Missouri's* superstructure was the American flag flown by Commodore Matthew Perry on his frigate when, in July of 1853, he forced the Japanese to end their isolation and open their ports to world commerce. Now the same flag was prominently displayed so as to be seen by the Japanese delegation, a symbol of strength and historical importance.

General MacArthur gave a speech, then he uttered his final statement, "These proceedings are closed." The years of hostilities had come to an end.

With a thunderous roar, aircraft of the Third Fleet flew over the three hundred ships of the U.S. and British navies moored in Tokyo Bay.

Admiral Halsey signaled the fleet with the time-honored message, "Well done," as transports disembarked troops to establish control over hundreds of Japanese military facilities.

Once the signing was completed, the Japanese were piped off the *Missouri* and saluted by American officers. That was considered proper, for Japan was now at peace with the United States.

* * *

On September 5th, Admirals Uta and Karamatsu, no longer having a naval function and wearing civilian clothes, walked through the streets of Tokyo toward the docks where Americans were debarking with all the supplies required for an occupying force in a devastated land. They were surprised to see former Japanese soldiers and even civilians saluting the Americans, who usually returned the salutes. Standing at attention on roadways, hundreds of Japanese troops faced throngs of citizens, their purpose to deter anyone considering a hostile act.

"I am actually relieved," said Uta as they gazed at the sullen crowds observing the arrival of those they'd fought against so desperately.

"I suppose I should feel the same," said Itomo Karamatsu. "Japan still has two and a half million soldiers in the home islands, but who knows how many more atomic bombs the Americans have."

"And they would have used them, along with poison gas," said Uta, observing wary American infantry boarding trucks.

"But not a single shot has been fired," said Karamatsu. "Not a single death on either side since the surrender. When in history has that ever been the case? Certainly not during the time of Rome or Genghis Khan. Quite remarkable, but of course it's still early."

The two men boarded a tram and got off at the municipal office in Yokusuka. There they were to meet the mayor. They found him flanked by officials, some in formal dress, observing the arrival and unloading of American trucks.

"That's eleven more since this morning," said Mayor Akagi.

"Eleven trucks? What are they unloading?"

"Supplies, Admiral. Supplies for the people. There were twenty trucks yesterday. Do you see what they're doing?"

Karamatsu stared as an American lieutenant called out, "Chief Sweeney, get some of these local men to help; I don't have all day. We have another load waiting."

"Yes, sir," replied the petty officer. He began waving his arm and directing a dozen Japanese men to the trucks. Standing to the side and watching the activity was a woman and her young son. The boy, curious about the tall Americans in their navy whites, left his terrified mother and approached the petty officer. The boy stared at the man, who after a moment grinned, tousled the child's hair and said, "Okay, kid."

He reached into the truck, extracted a small box marked "canned food" and put it in the child's hands. "Give this to your mom. Courtesy of the United States Navy."

Wide-eyed, the boy bowed, as did his mother. The sailor nodded and turned his attention to the sacks and boxes being piled up in front of the municipal building.

"Bags of rice and flour are still coming in; today they're unloading medical supplies," said the mayor.

"Why?" asked Uta, as more helpers lined up at the rear of the trucks.

The mayor shook his head and said, "I really don't know. They must surely hate us, as we hate them. They're very strange. I don't understand their generosity at all. I ask you, just who are these people?"

"So, what do you think?" said Uta as he and Karamatsu left the prefectural office.

"I think that people may learn from history," said Karamatsu. He watched a squad of U.S. Marines politely decline the offering of onions, fruit and meat from an old woman.

"We both studied what happened to Germany after the First World War, Ota-san. The war debts and reparations forced upon Germany. Their money was worthless. It took a whole wheelbarrow-full to buy a loaf of bread. They could never pay the debt to the Allies, and their despair and contempt led to the next war. I don't know what the Allies intend, but if this is their response to a war we began, well, perhaps there is a measure of hope."

* * *

It seemed to Sayuri that everyone was on the road. She and Kumi had said goodbye to their hosts, and along with Chad-ishi they had walked and taken any available conveyance toward the capital, but they had been on the road for many days before they alighted from an overpacked train into the ruins of downtown Tokyo.

"I don't know why we have come back," said Kumi, gazing upon the burned remains of shops and houses.

"Where else would we go?" said Sayuri, holding Chad-ishi's hand. The child stared around as the September winds churned dust and ash in eddies. The scent of burnt wood hung in the air. A procession of American jeeps and trucks rumbled past, and Chad-ishi pointed and said, "Are those the enemy?"

"Not anymore," said Sayuri. "The war is over. I don't think they will hurt us."

Carrying their worn suitcases, Sayuri and Kimi left the station and began walking past blackened structures and people listlessly picking through the remains of their homes. Here and there a street sign was still legible, though most metal poles had drooped in the fires.

A U.S. Army bulldozer scooped up debris clogging a street and rumbled to a deserted lot before dumping its load.

"Can we watch?" asked Chad-ishi, never having seen such a machine before.

"Not just now. I'm sure you will see many of them when we get home," said Sayuri.

"Where is home?" he asked, wiping dust from his face with a tattered sleeve.

"The ikebana shop where Kumi-san and I used to live."

"But how will you find it?" he asked.

"Because it has a cherry tree beside it."

"But everything is burned," he persisted.

"Chad-ishi is right," said Kumi. "What makes you think a single tree can possibly survive the firestorms? And surely the ikebana shop is nothing but ashes. Just look around, Sayuri-san. I think it will be very disappointing, even if we can find the street."

"Perhaps, but we can't leave Tokyo without seeing if Sensei's shop exists. I'm sure we can find the street if we look for it. There was a big concrete building beside it, remember? That would be a good landmark… if it's still there."

* * *

Only a few newspapers were still printing. One, the *Mainichi,* reported nine rapes by Americans in the first week of the occupation. Fearful, many women remained in what was left of their houses. But the great dread of mass rape subsided within the next few weeks as those responsible faced severe punishment. To further lessen the possibility of rape, the Japanese authorities were allowed to establish the "Recreation and Amusement Association," brothels that were frequented by long lines of American service men.

"The navy set up some PX Quonset huts and that's where I'm going. There's not much available in the ship's store. Are you coming?" Lee-Beauregard Smythe asked Tad.

"Just to get some foodstuffs. I might need to hand some out. Then I'm getting a jeep and looking around," said Tad.

"I don't think you're going to see much, and you'll be very disappointed if you're looking for something or someone in particular. You know what I mean. We leveled the place, pal. It looks like the surface of the moon. Of course, I haven't been to the moon, but…"

"I'll recommend you to some rocket people if you want to go,. I think you'll fit in nicely with the little green men."

"I bet I would. It's all about good looks, charm and personality. But as I said, don't be disappointed if you can't find what you're looking for. It's been a goddamn ugly war."

A late September chill had fallen upon Tokyo, and people bundled against the cold. Hundreds of young Japanese men still wore pieces of their uniform, unable to afford new clothes even if they had been available. Many stood sullenly, watching the American military fill in bomb craters and clear debris.

Tad glanced at the tiny scrap of paper he had secreted in his shipboard locker and studied the few street signs in the Tokyo Prefecture. He drove slowly past former soldiers camping out among the ruins. In most places there was not yet running water, and electricity was sporadic. Most appalling were the piles of bodies stacked beside roadsides, awaiting transport to burial pits. Most had been covered by tarpaulins, but gusts of wind revealed faces blackened by fire.

A rancid stench assaulted Tad as he passed sewage waste, for disposal trucks were not yet available. People lived "bamboo sprout fashion," selling off their remaining possessions piecemeal on street corners.

He drove past people lined up at the offices of the neighborhood associations for *zanpan shichu,* a "leftovers stew" concocted from the discarded food of the occupation forces, while hundreds of orphaned children, sick and hungry, roamed the ruins. Staring dismayed at the rubble were soldiers, some of the five million repatriated from Japanese-occupied Asia. Having heard little of the bombing, they were appalled at the enormity of the destruction.

It soon became apparent to Tad that he was completely lost. One block looked like the next as he drove past refugees, bombed-out vehicles and American troops operating bulldozers, cranes and dump trucks.

Stopping at a crossroads, Tad spotted a man wearing the tunic of a Japanese major. The man looked at Tad without expression. Idling the jeep, Tad motioned and, in Japanese, said, "Major, I'm looking for this address. Can you point the way?"

The man looked surprised, hearing an American officer speaking perfect Japanese. He looked hard at Tad, then said,

"I can help you, one officer to another, but my men and I have had little to eat." Pointing to sacks in the jeep he said, "Is any of that food?"

Tad pulled to the curb and handed a sack to a corporal, one of five men in the tattered remains of uniforms.

"Take it; I can get more," said Tad. The men bowed and saluted. Tad, after returning the salute, turned to the major and said, "Hop in." He drove past the soldiers, who bowed once again.

"It's Yuri Street," he said, noting the major's amusement to be riding in an American Jeep.

"Yes, what you would call Lily Street. I learned English at the university. I was a professor before the war."

"What did you teach?" asked Tad, as he turned where the major pointed.

"I taught Spanish at Hoksei University in Hokkaido. A girl's college."

"Well, amigo, I'm from California, and Spanish is pretty common there."

"But you also speak Japanese."

"That's right. My mother was born in Japan, so I spoke Japanese as a child."

The major stared at Tad but said nothing. At his silent directions, they turned down one shattered street after another.

"Were you in the Pacific during the war?" asked Tad.

"I was in China, then sent back here with my battalion. We were preparing for the invasion."

"Well, we invaded. But probably not like you expected."

The major looked bemused and said, "I expected worse. We are pleased that General MacArthur has treated the Emperor well. We are especially thankful that he kept out the Soviets."

"They would not have been very civil," said Tad, as they approached Lily Street.

A scattering of houses and shops remained. The owners who had survived were washing away ash and soot. Tad glanced at the piece of paper once again and drove the jeep toward a shop beside which leaned a withered tree. Not forty yards beyond stood a squad of American troops energetically waving people back. There was a sudden commotion, and civilians began to run. Alarmed, an American sergeant, holding up his hands, ran toward the jeep.

He glanced at the major, then at Tad, and said, "Sir, you can't go any further. Our unit disarms unexploded bombs and there are two inside that big building, or what's left of it. They are too dangerous to approach. And there's another bomb we're going to detonate two blocks from here. We have to pull back."

A tremor shook the ground and bricks fell from the building. A plume of smoke rose, and as more debris fell, the Explosive Ordinance Disposal team hastily retreated. A number of people, suddenly aware of the danger, emerged from their houses. A great plume of smoke rose as a wall splintered and collapsed. Debris rained down and people dropped to the ground, hands and arms held over their heads. Children screamed, and shards of brick and concrete splattered around them. Lengths of pipe and broken beams, ruptured by the blast, began to rain down in tangles of wood and steel.

Two women and a child stood, miraculously uninjured, fifty feet from the explosion. Panicked, they turned to run, but one of the women slipped and fell. She struggled to rise, but two large pipes rolled onto her. The other woman attempted vainly to move the pipes away. Terrified, she pleaded for help, but the detonation had revealed another bomb, and people backed further away. A pall of dense smoke rolled over the site as Tad got out of the jeep. He glanced toward a section of the building that swayed toward the women, then spied the bomb, tilted precariously on the remains of a steel desk.

He moved forward through the smoke and heard the sergeant say, "Sir, don't go there. It's gonna go off. You're going to get killed!"

"It's not safe!" shouted the Japanese major. He too had sprung from the jeep. Broken stone continued to plummet, pelting them with sharp, jagged fragments. The woman pushing on the pipe was on her knees, the child, a small boy, wailed helplessly, pulling on the arm of the trapped woman. Tad tripped, stood, and, the major by his side, scrambled toward them, wary of the second bomb.

Pushing away a pipe, Tad reached down and picked up the woman, flinging her over his shoulder. He grabbed the child and began to run. The major picked up the other woman and followed. The bomb exploded, knocking all five to the ground and covering them with a fall of debris. Four soldiers scrambled over and helped them to their feet.

Tad slowly stood. He was bruised, and his uniform was coated with dust, but nothing seemed broken. He rubbed his eyes. Behind him, the child clung desperately to the woman Tad had saved.

Shaken, he breathed deeply, wanting only to get away, to return to the safety of the ship. But the major was tugging on his sleeve, saying, "Commander, behind you."

"What? I just want to go; I'll drive you back."

"The woman, *tomodachi*, the woman."

The sound was faint and perhaps, he thought, someone else's name was being called.

It came again. "Tad, Tad-san. Is that you, Tad-san?"

He stopped. Tad-san? Who here would possibly know him? His eyes watered from the smoke. He wiped them with a soiled sleeve. The name came again. He slowly turned. People were watching, but he was oblivious to them. He saw only the woman, long black hair blowing. Her hand rose to her face. Tad stared at her. An apparition, he thought. He opened his mouth, but no sound came out. He took a step, staggered, then started to run, again hearing the words, "Tad-san, Tad-san!"

She was so light. He picked her up and spun her around and around as Kumi, the boy and one hundred people watched in amazement. His ears cleared and he heard a babble of voices.

"Sayuri, my God, it's really you!" he said, putting her down gently.

"Yes!" she replied, breathless with astonishment.

The boy stood shakily beside Kumi. He glanced up at her and she nudged him saying, "Go to your mother. Go to her."

The boy walked over and slipped his hand in Sayuri's. He stared up at the man, who gazed back at him.

"This is Chad-ishi. He is an orphan," said Sayuri.

Tad knelt and pulled the boy to him. He smiled and said, "He is no longer an orphan, Sayuri-san. He is our first son."

He rose, holding the boy's hand. She said, "My house, Sensei's house, is still here." She took Tad's hand. "Please come; I will make some *ocha*. Oh, Tad-san, it has been so very long."

A breeze swirled dust and leaves across the tiny porch. A fleck of pink caught Chad-ishi's eyes and he stooped down and picked it up. He gazed at the fragile, dry petal and offered it to Tad.

He leaned down and whispered, "Let's give it to your mother."

Sayuri smiled, looked into Tad's eyes and said, "A blossom from the ashes. A wondrous thing."

The boy pointed to the cherry tree and said, "It's from there. Will it grow again?"

"Yes," said Sayuri. "It will grow again. It will be fine."

And so will we, thought Tad.

Epilogue

Pearl Harbor, Hawaii,
1949

Itomo Karamatsu stood on a veranda overlooking the beach one hundred yards away sipping a mai tai. Alexei accepted a glass from Kimi and said, "I think the Admiral has developed a taste for my favorite drink. But if you offer the old man another he may fall asleep, and we're talking about writing a book."

"I'm only five years older than you, and the drink is very smooth. So, Kimi-san, another, if you please." Then turning to Alexei he said, "I do like the idea, Alexei-san. A collaboration, very novel."

Alexei watched Kimi re-enter the house and said, "Your sister is still a beautiful woman, Itomo-san. I can't tell you how much I missed her during those war years. Truly, I thought I would never see her again."

"And I never thought that I would see you again, or my sister. You and I are both fortunate to have survived the war. I am pleased that you invited me and Koizumi to visit you."

"We thought it was about time. None of us are getting any younger."

"So much has happened since we met in Tokyo, over a half century ago. There is so much to write about. You were fencing at the Russian consulate when I first saw you. I was intrigued with western-style fencing and you became my teacher."

"And you taught me karate. And then I met Kimi-san and you were displeased."

"Yes, she had been promised to another man. I was worried for her and for you. Then after the incident with your father and the geisha you went back to Russia and I thought it was all over. And then the war came. I was very proud of being a destroyer captain."

"And I was on the Russian cruiser at Tsushima where almost the entire fleet was sunk. If it hadn't been for you, I would have died that night."

"And I would have missed out on the mai tais."

Sayuri and Kimi joined the two men, and Alexei turned to Sayuri and said, "So how are your students doing? Are they still mischievous?"

"They're very sweet, especially the third graders, but everything is funny to them. They are totally undisciplined, but I love them. Once a week I bring Chad in. They think of him as their big brother, since he's ten now. He has become very academic, just like Koizumi-san."

"Ah, an academic," said Itomo. "Perhaps a future professor. What does he like to read?"

"Everything about rockets and space," replied Sayuri.

"I should put him in touch with Tad's old Navy buddy, Lee-Beauregard," said Alexei. "He's working on rockets and talks about going to the moon someday."

He sipped his drink, looked out on the broad Pacific and squeezed his wife's hand. Yes, he mused, he and Itomo-san would write that book.

A flight of pelicans swooped low over the sea. They all followed the graceful, effortless movements and Alexei smiled. It was good to be home.

A soft breeze blew the palms, and lazy waves caressed the beach as Tad and Koizumi watched Chad and his three-year-old brother construct a sand castle. Every time Chad built up the castle, Jeffrey knocked it down.

"You can't do that!" Chad howled with disgust.

"Can!" replied Jeffrey. "It's my castle, you said so."

"It sounds like the start of a war," said Koizumi.

"I think they'll negotiate. Chad has a big supply of candy, and that usually works, but the little one drives a hard deal."

The two men walked down the beach away from Tad's and Sayuri's new clapboard house.

"I never really learned how you got off that island," said Tad, picking up a coin half-buried in the sand.

"I became good friends with Jeremy and Maria, though Maria took a bit longer. We lost track of time, but it must have been around May or June of 1945 when all military activity around the islands ceased. We watched for planes and ships, but none came. Eventually we gained enough confidence to go down to the shore and fish. We were even thinking of repairing a beached boat and setting sail. But we were wary; coming ashore on a Japanese-occupied island would have been very dangerous. I thought that I would be considered a traitor and summarily shot."

Tad handed the coin to his brother, who said, "This is Japanese yen, very old. The Admiral collects coins, perhaps you should give it to him."

"I will," said Tad. They walked barefoot through the incoming tide.

"So we were on the beach one morning when a strange craft flew over. It was a helicopter, an American one, and none of us had ever seen one before. We then heard a loudspeaker announce that the war was over and Japan had surrendered. We were told that a boat would come for us in a day or two. It was quite a surprise. I had very mixed feelings about going back to Japan. In fact, I wondered if I should go there at all. You must understand that even though the war was over, I might still be tried as a traitor if a Japanese government was in place."

"But you did go back," said Tad.

"Yes, but not right away. We boarded an American Navy freighter that took us to Saipan. I thought that I might be interned or interrogated, but I was put aboard another ship that was taking Japanese casualties and former prisoners back to Japan. I said goodbye to Maria and Jeremy, and they boarded a ship going to the Philippines."

"Are they still there?"

"No, they were married, but Jeremy doesn't speak Tagalog, so they moved to California where his parents are. Jeremy wrote to me a few months ago and said that he completed a doctorate and is teaching at Stanford University. They invited me to visit. I might do that after the baby comes."

"And how is your wife?"

"She's doing very well for seven months pregnant. She was hoping to come, but an ocean voyage would be too hard on her. She wants to see Sayuri again, so maybe we'll stop here on the way to California."

A squadron of navy aircraft roared overhead and they looked up. "Jets," said Tad. "If I were still in the Navy I'd be flying one of those."

"Do you miss flying?" asked Koizumi, watching the aircraft head toward a distant carrier.

"As much as you do, but I don't miss war."

They walked silently for a time, then Koizumi said, "I did not know what to expect when I got back to Japan. The Japanese government and military were under the complete control of the United States. American soldiers were everywhere, especially in the big cities. Everything was changing very quickly."

"You mean the reconstruction?" asked Tad.

"Not just the rebuilding, which will take many years. I mean the entire nature of Japan. The mentality, the re-education, the constitution giving women the vote. The very outlook of the nation."

"Democracy. What do people think about it?"

"The women seem to like it, but a lot of the men are only lukewarm. We were taught that the Emperor was divine and that the Japanese were a race of superior beings. Now we are being told he is not divine and we're not superior to anyone."

"So what happened when you got back?" asked Tad.

"I wandered about for a few days, stunned at seeing so many Americans and the horrible condition of my people. I decided to see if our uncle still lived. His home was twenty miles outside Tokyo. I was pleased to see that his house hadn't been destroyed in the bombings. When I knocked on his door, he nearly fainted."

"Because he thought you were dead?"

"Yes. He did something very unusual for a Japanese man. He shouted and wrapped his arms around me before bowing very deeply. He was ecstatic beyond words. I was overwhelmed, but there was something I wasn't aware of, why in fact he was so happy to see me. General Ota, his drinking partner, joined us and we went to a reopened geisha house. I had never seen my uncle emotional before. At one point he actually broke down and said that he knew that I was not in on the conspiracy with the traitorous peace party, but it was he who ordered the plane shot down.

"But then General Ota said that my uncle was only following instructions and it was Ota who had ordered the execution of the admiral and the others. But that hardly consoled my uncle, because it was he who actually gave the order. I said that they were blameless, that it was war and the people I transported did not have the explicit permission of the Emperor."

"I imagine that the Admiral and Ota were amazed that you lived."

"That and the fact that I met you on that atoll. The three of us got quite drunk that night. I have no idea of how we ever got home."

"It's almost dinner time," said Tad. "I think we should head back."

They turned and began the long walk to the house. Tad grinned and said, "So now you are a happily married man."

"That is true. Quite astonishing, really. The Admiral happened to meet Kumi in Tokyo and told her that I was alive, and he asked her to come to his house. I was staying there, and I was astonished to see her again. We talked for hours. It was she who told me that you and Sayuri had married and moved to Hawaii. I was glad that Sayuri survived the war."

"But not pleased that she married me instead of you," hazarded Tad.

"This is not true. I admit that I once loved Sayuri-san. The thought of her kept me alive, but also brought me unfathomable pain."

He stopped and turned to Tad. "You may not believe this, but I was pleased when I learned that you married her. I love Kumi-san, and I have come to see you as my brother, my *tomodachi*, my friend."

Tad threw his arm around Koizumi and they walked back to the children still on the beach.

"Time for dinner," said Tad.

"But I'm rebuilding the castle," protested Jeffrey.

"Nope. Time to go. That's an order."

"Still a commander," said Koizumi.

"Damn straight!" said Tad with a big grin.

Two Navy jets flew overhead and the brothers watched them with unmistakable envy.

"I know where we can find an old biplane, a two-seater with dual controls. We can fly into the wild blue yonder," said Tad. "What do you say?"

"Of course," said Koizumi, "but I should pilot it."

"Like hell!"

"You forget Tad-ishi, I can see the stars in broad daylight."

They argued about it long into the night, but the next day Tad let Koizumi fly the plane first. He was quite content as they slipped through billowing clouds. They looked at verdant peaks below, turned and flew low over a clutch of houses. Children waved and Tad waved back. Koizumi pulled back on the stick and the biplane shot upwards.

"Your turn," signaled Koizumi, and Tad did a roll, then a long glide over the sea. The wind whipped through open cockpit. He glanced back at Koizumi. They were pilots again, but their world was at peace. And that was as it should be.

THE END

Author's Notes

With but two alterations, all historical events described are accurate as based on the author's research. The following is intended to add additional information regarding the war in the Pacific as well Russia's "Great Patriotic War."

Numerous people in the Japanese military realized that the inability to destroy American aircraft carriers at Pearl Harbor nullified any real success, since the carriers had been the main target. All the U.S. carriers were at sea during the attack. Fear that the Japanese armada would be discovered and placed in peril had motivated the high command to proceed with the attack. The failure to bomb the oil storage dumps and submarine pens contributed to Japan's defeat at Midway six months later.

To the best of my knowledge, the battles of the Coral Sea, Midway and the Mariana "Turkey Shoot" took place as described.

Following the Midway disaster, Japanese survivors were ordered to say nothing of the carrier's sinking, and since the government controlled the press none of the public was any the wiser. As a result, even two years after its destruction, footage of the fleet carrier *Hiryu* and its crew were still being shown as part of the propaganda campaign.

Hundreds of civilians did jump to their death in Okinawa, some being forced by Japanese troops.

The firebombing of Tokyo with its great destruction of life occurred as written.

American aid began to arrive in Tokyo within days of the surrender.

Ishigawa Island is in the Sea of Japan, 430 kilometers southwest of Okinawa. There was a Japanese military force on the island. Gold had been mined on Iriomote prior to the war, and coal can be found there. Both islands are tropical, with numerous caves and rushing rivers. The islands are further apart than indicated in the novel.

The Japanese delegation was piped off the battleship *Missouri* following the signing of the surrender documents and Commodore Perry's 1853 flag was displayed on the ship's superstructure.

American B-29s did continue the bombing of Honshu after Hiroshima and before the destruction of Nagasaki. When asked if another atom bomb should be dropped, President Truman said, "No, I don't want to kill any more kids."

The author did invent the meeting of Japanese officials with Americans on the remote Pacific atoll as well as the shooting down of the aircraft carrying the Japanese cabal. There was a peace faction in Japan late in the war but it gained little support, especially following the Allies' demand for unconditional surrender. However, the Japanese government, through its representative in the Vatican, did appeal to the Holy See to negotiate an end to the conflict. But due to the great divergence between the waring parties, nothing came to fruition.

The Soviet Union did declare war on Japan hours before the second atomic bomb was dropped, just in time to fulfill Stalin's promise at Yalta to do so within three months of Germany's defeat. A Russian delegation did arrive in Japan following its surrender, but General MacArthur promptly ordered it off the island.

A Blossom in the Ashes is the sequel to *A Cherry Blossom in Winter,* which takes place before and during the Russo-Japanese war of 1904-5.

Russia's penal battalions did exist and their troops were considered expendable. Large numbers of the soldiers had been accused of political crimes. Casualty rates were up to eighty percent and retreat in combat would by met with NKVD machine gun punishment. Release from a penal battalion could be earned by heroic action in combat.

Joseph Stalin did order the NKVD into Berlin in the last days of the war to obtain nuclear materials and scientific papers.

It has been ascertained that over one hundred thousand German women and girls in Berlin were raped by Soviet troops with the permission and encouragement of Stalin. Approximately ten percent of the women committed suicide.

Other historical novels by the author include *Villa of Deceit* and its sequel, *The Silk and the Sword*. The former is set in Rome during the first century B.C.E. and its sequel begins in Rome and continues across the Great Silk Road to the Great Wall of China after Rome's defeat at Carrhae in 53 B.C.E. All four novels are featured on Amazon and are published by Penmore Press.

ABOUT THE AUTHOR

RON SINGERTON

After graduating from California State University at Long Beach in 1965 Ron Singerton joined the U.S. Army Security Agency and spent his overseas time in Asia.

The subsequent twenty-five years were devoted to teaching history and art in Southern California High schools, where he developed a particular love for writing and historical research.

During the early 1980s, he authored a series, *Moments in History*, of some thirty mini books on famous people and events ranging from Columbus to the moon landing. The books were adopted as supplementary teaching material for the State of California and approved by the Los Angeles School board as a teaching aid. Published by Santillana Publishing Company, the original ones are considered collector's items.

An avid horseman and saber fencer with a special interest in the American Civil War, he "heard the bugle and the sound of the drums" and became a re-enactor, riding with the Union cavalry in dozens of engagements from California to Gettysburg, Pennsylvania.

Always interested in an exciting but obscure story, his historical research meandered from the nineteenth and twentieth centuries back to the ancient world. Singerton once said, "Technology of the past often appears elementary to us; the emotions do not." For a writer, the thoughts of peoples long past, as well as civilizations now little more than sand-pitted ruins, still evolve into a pageant of love, intrigue and dire conflict. "It is nothing less than a shadowed mirror of our own world."

Through the writings of Plutarch, Pliny and Julius Caesar he uncovered an epic event that would take him from Rome in the last days of Republic to the Great Wall of China. After years of research the tale became the gist of a two-volume novel: *The Villa of Deceit* and *The Silk and the Sword*.

In his third historical novel, *A Cherry Blossom in Winter*, Singerton turns to the tumultuous opening years of the Twentieth Century with a stirring novel of the Russo Japanese war of 1904.

Ron is also an award winning artist, with artwork in glass, stone, paint and bronze sold and displayed online, in galleries, and numerous art shows.

IF YOU ENJOYED THIS BOOK

Please write a review.
This is important to the author and helps to get the word out to
others
Visit

PENMORE PRESS
www.penmorepress.com

All Penmore Press books are available directly through our
website, amazon.com, Barnes and Noble and Nook, Sony Reader,
Apple iTunes, Kobo books and via leading bookshops across the
United States, Canada, the UK, Australia and Europe.

Villa of Deceit
BY

Ron Singerton

Action Adventure, Crime, Mystery,

Rome, 70 B.C.E.

A house in turmoil: a controlling father, an adulterous mother, and an angry son made reckless by a forbidden love. Young Gaius defies his father Toronius, fleeing with a slave girl whom he marries, only to see her die in childbirth. Disinherited and grieving, Gaius leaves his infant son Tacitus behind with a trusted aunt and devotes his life to the sword.

On the battle field Gaius is trained and tempered into a hardened veteran of war. His leadership and bravery in campaigns earn him respect and the rank of Senior Centurion. But his greatest challenge is returning home to face his son Tacitus, now grown to a wild, undisciplined youth. Gaius forces the errant boy against his wishes into the army that he may be molded into a man.

Like Gaius before him, Tacitus must fight to become his own man in defiance of his father. But together as Legionnaires, they must survive an invasion mired by betrayal and confront the fury of war.

PENMORE PRESS
www.penmorepress.com

Silk and The Sword
BY

Ron Singerton

Action Adventure, Crime, Mystery, Roman History

Young Tacitus, torn from the girl he loves and accused of defiling his late mother's temple, is dragooned into the Roman army by his father Gaius, a bitter and unbending Centurion. With his father and seven legions, he joins General Marcus Crassus in an ill-fated attack on the sprawling Parthian Empire. After the Roman forces are decimated at the Battle of Carrhae, Tacitus, Gaius, and four hundred survivors venture eastward on the fabled Silk Road to find a river beyond a wall that will lead them back to Rome.Tacitus becomes the soldier he never wanted to be while battling bandits, trekking through frozen mountain passes, and dealing with a formidable foe on the other side of the world. But his greatest challenge is a personal quandary: should he return to Rome for his long-lost love or seek the hand of a princess in the mysterious land beside the Great Wall?

"A tour de force of Roman military survival across a long and arduous trek through the Parthian empire, the silk road, and into the celestial kingdom

PENMORE PRESS
www.penmorepress.com

His Most Italian City

BY

Margaret Walker

WWII, Italian Fascists, Italian Resistance, Austrian submarines, sea stories , engagements at sea

Fascist Italy 1928.
Trieste, once the port of the Austrian Empire, has become Italian. As fascism strives violently to create a pure Italy along its streets, Matteo Brazzi is forced to choose his loyalties with care.
When his office is bombed, the police are baffled, but Brazzi knows who committed the crime, and he knows why.
Though he is no seaman, he can easily identify the dark shape that disappeared into the Gulf of Trieste that dramatic night and, as he escapes to Cittanova in Istria, the mysterious vessel follows him down the coast.
Brazzi has successfully exploited fascism to protect himself - many people would call him a traitor - but he's only ever had one real love. Now Nataša is dead and Brazzi owes his share of the blame.
Too soon he discovers that not even Mussolini can save him from an enemy who is bent on revenge.

PENMORE PRESS
www.penmorepress.com

Penmore Press

Challenging, Intriguing, Adventurous, Historical and Imaginative

www.penmorepress.com

www.ingramcontent.com/pod-product-compliance
Lightning Source LLC
Chambersburg PA
CBHW032157180726
48284CB00001B/75